About the Author

Bailey Vos was born and raised in Grand Rapids, Michigan. She attended the University of Michigan for her undergraduate degree and went on to become a lawyer. She opened a law firm in Austin, Texas, where she met her husband and had her daughter. Much like Mercer, the idea for Unblind came to Bailey in a dream.

Unblind

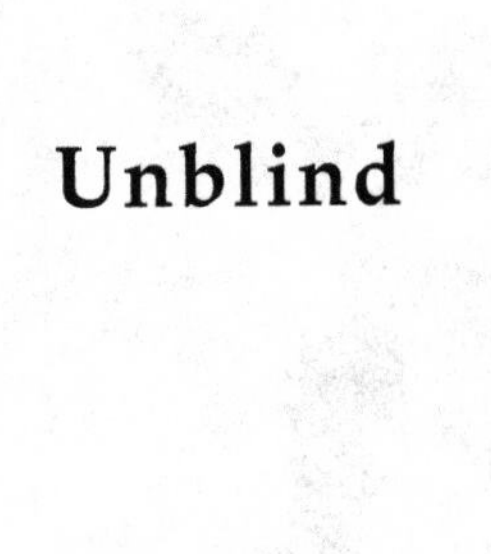

Bailey Vos

Unblind

Olympia Publishers
London

www.olympiapublishers.com
OLYMPIA PAPERBACK EDITION

A CIP catalogue record for this title is
available from the British Library.

ISBN: 978-1-80439-336-9

This is a work of fiction.
Names, characters, places and incidents originate from the writer's
imagination. Any resemblance to actual persons, living or dead, is
purely coincidental.

First Published in 2023

Olympia Publishers
Tallis House
2 Tallis Street
London
EC4Y 0AB

Printed in Great Britain

Dedication

Mom, thank you for supporting me no matter what crazy idea I follow. This book is dedicated to you.

Acknowledgements

Thank you to my loving and supportive husband, Torrey, daughter, Taytum, and business partner in everything, Jessica. Thank you to KK for believing in this vision before anyone else. A special thank you to my Mother, Amy, for proofreading. Without you, this book wouldn't have come to life.

Chapter One

"Kill them faster," Aunt Pam huffs.

Her bony fingers work a dull knife into an apple while she speaks back to the government-issued television screen. The morning sun streams through the sliding door of our kitchen, brightening the yellow walls of the too small space, as if the rays are trying to force early summertime happiness into us to compensate for my guardian's topic of conversation.

I lift my chin, focusing on Aunt Pam's perfectly manicured fingernails while she portions breakfast for the three of us waiting at the table. Try as I might to ignore her during meals, her comment brings me to awareness. There's only one group of people Aunt Pam would be referring to.

The short man on the television continues, "*For that reason, these new laws may impact us all far greater than anybody realizes.*"

Aunt Pam grunts her displeasure while music fills the room. My twin, Lizzy, sits across the table, blissfully unaware of the tension suffocating me.

The Eramica government symbol flashes across the screen to signal the next media break and I scowl at myself, frustrated that my inattention caused me to miss whatever was reported.

My shoulders are rigid and I fidget in the wooden seat while it creaks its response in protest. I'm certain Uncle Al's knowing eyes are watching closely, waiting for me to slip up. He and I both know who Aunt Pam would kill in this kitchen.

Thankfully, she approaches the table, silhouetted by the sunshine, sparing me the discomfort of a standoff with my uncle. The music fades in the background and static buzzes over the television.

Aunt Pam finishes handing out the portions of apple slices and toast, then quickly returns to the screen to adjust the antenna before joining us at the table.

I look down at the faint flowers painted along the edge of the porcelain dish in front of me. My knee bounces up and down beneath the table, rocking the poorly made thing with the movement. I can see curiosity wrinkle Lizzy's otherwise flawless skin across from me, so I stop before she can ask questions.

I shovel the meager breakfast into my mouth as the feelings of helplessness and anxiety continue to bubble up inside my chest. This pressure inside me isn't foreign, and it's only cured with space from these people.

After eating too quickly, the toast lodges in my dry throat, forcing an uncomfortable cough. All three of them stare at me with surprise and disgust, seemingly stunned by the speed at which I scarfed down my food. I should have slowed down, but I had already been on edge when Aunt Pam turned the conversation toward my least favorite subject.

"I'll see you after school," I mumble through tears that have appeared because of the toast mishap. My body rises at an awkward angle, trapped between my seat and the wall. There isn't enough space in this kitchen for four seats, but like everything else, they simply made it work after we moved in.

Before I can move, though, my uncle's thick hand wraps around my wrist, tugging me back into the wooden chair with a concealed forcefulness. His hand is warm and sweaty and leaves a disgusting clamminess after his fingers peel away.

"Mercer, you will slow down and eat with us," he says through a forced smile as his haunted eyes meet mine. He's an unattractive man with a commanding presence that makes his demands all the more menacing.

I take a calculated breath through my nose, earning a small nod from him in response. His request will appear like he simply wants to spend time with his niece, but he and I know the truth: he doesn't want me leaving for school so quickly until I can act normally again, lest Lizzy and Aunt Pam find out the topic of Unnaturals is what set me off and drove me away.

So, I sit.

"My goodness," Aunt Pam croaks while her dainty fingers reach up to touch the strand of fake pearls she always wears. For a moment I consider whether she's going to stand up to Uncle Al for me. I should know better. Her widened gaze stares at the television, which I now realize I have once again tuned out. Lizzy's head whips around to watch as well. Aunt Pam's voice is near hysteria as she continues, "Now they're not even going to tell us when they kill them?"

I silently chastise myself a second time this morning for not listening to the news program. Although calling the government propaganda 'news' is a stretch in my opinion.

"How are we to know when they make progress?" The sun continues to shine on Aunt Pam's face, illuminating the worry etched in her features. Her skin, like my sister's, is so pale it's nearly translucent. It would look alarming if it weren't so striking paired with hazel eyes and perfectly curled brown hair.

"They'll always be making progress, dear." Uncle Al's voice is one of reasoning and calmness. He's not wrong.

I don't remember life before the Censorship. I barely remember the time I had with my parents, let alone the population crisis or the political upheaval during their lives.

A longing tightens in my chest, and I breathe in the smell of burnt toast to ground myself. The feeling isn't because I wish for that lifetime; things weren't so great then either. But I desperately crave a reality different from my current one.

Eramica, our government, is always hunting… searching for the now-teenagers who have developed strange abilities. They're hard to find. I've only met one Unnatural in real life and thinking of him makes my knee bounce in nervousness to get out of this stuffy kitchen.

"I'm sure they're dealing with *them* the best they know how," my uncle placates her without so much as a twitch in my direction. Thick fingers wipe at his mustache, sprinkling toast crumbs on the table surface before he takes another bite.

"Actually," Lizzy says across from me. I release a huff of air at my twin's involvement. "I don't believe they're killing them at all anymore."

All three of us silently stare at her, Uncle Al's toast grotesquely visible in his mouth.

"I've been studying it," she continues with a slight shrug of her shoulders. The movement makes the curls of her long hair bob up and down. She looks at us, matching each gaze in turn, before continuing, "I think they're being collected."

My uncle breaks the silence with a harsh cough that seems to vibrate off the yellow walls.

"Collected," he grunts. "As if anyone would want to keep them."

I don't miss the pointed look he throws my way.

"Lizzy, dear," Aunt Pam coaxes as she places a hand on my sister's shoulder, "be mindful of how you speak, darling." Her voice shakes, betraying how deep her fear truly runs. Rightfully so. If the wrong people had just overheard her, Lizzy could be in a world of trouble.

My twin looks at me through her lashes, her head still bowed. Something flashes across her face before she composes herself and looks away. She picks at the toast in front of her, and I can feel my confusion etch in my features.

"Your aunt is right, of course," Uncle Al contributes with a lean toward Lizzy, his eyes fixed on my sister with more kindness than has ever been offered to me. "Though I'm sure you already know that."

I've often wondered what would've happened if I never learned the truth about my uncle all those years ago. The truth that I always try to forget. The truth that robbed me of any childhood I might have had, despite all the other obstacles. Would he praise my intellect and worry about my safety? Then again, if I never learned the truth, Lizzy and I wouldn't be here for me to find out.

"I know, Father." Lizzy blushes without looking up from her food.

I hate how she addresses our guardians. I hate how she jumped right into life with them. Shortly after our parents died, Lizzy even chose to take their last name; something I will never do.

Both Uncle Al and Aunt Pam seem satisfied with her response as they let out a collective breath. The voices on the television mix with chewing around the table.

"Pam, darling," Uncle Al says into the silence. I know he's been waiting a calculated amount of time before changing the subject, "did you say you needed a ride to the City Center tomorrow morning?"

The City Center is where everything is located: our doctor,

the grocery store, and anything else we could need, all run by the government so they can control every aspect of our lives. It's been like that since the Censorship.

I dare to stand again and mumble, "I need to get my bookbag from upstairs," before he can yank me back to my chair. His glare tells me that I haven't waited long enough despite the topic change, but he won't force the issue a second time.

I push my seat aside and shimmy around Aunt Pam's place at the table.

"Have a good day, dear," Aunt Pam practically sings to me, whether to keep up with the cheerful housewife image or because she's happy about my departure, I'm not sure.

As I walk the short hallway that connects the kitchen to the front of the house, my fingers absentmindedly trace the wall. The yellow of the kitchen is connected to a faded pale pink that feels like it's closing in on me. Aunt Pam painted everything the bright colors after our parents died in an attempt to make us happier. Several years later, the pink laughs at me.

Since I had already deposited my bookbag by the front door knowing I would want to leave quickly, I scoop it up and grab the textbook I was using this morning, too rushed to stuff it in my bag. My aunt and uncle's voices become louder, and it seems Aunt Pam brought the topic back around to Unnaturals.

Our government is scrambling to atone for creating Unnaturals, not that they would ever admit they caused the problem, but other countries aren't dealing with this.

The discovery of Unnaturals came at a time when the country couldn't handle any more damage. The population was reaching dire numbers, and then supernatural children came along. Some people even go so far as to blame those children with strange abilities for the population issues, as if that makes any sense.

America became Eramica: a new name for new and limited freedoms. They implemented strict rules for the upbringing of Generation Novus in an attempt to fix the population and start over. The era of the Censorship began, outlawing free speech because misinformation and conspiracy theories were deemed dangerous. Only a few citizens fought back. Those few died.

Thanks to Eramica's quick action, most citizens feel indebted to the country, including Aunt Pam. Now, everyone's greatest fear is only tamed by constant reassurances that the government is tracking, finding and killing Unnaturals.

It's no wonder why freedom seems so far out of my reach. Aunt Pam is in good company with the rest of the country: Unnaturals need to die.

The problem is… I am one.

Chapter Two

The bright grass holds dew from overnight, and I ignore the pathway to walk on the meticulously cut lawn. Every inch of the B Region looks like this, as if the yards are able to mask the dysfunction hidden beneath. The tension from the last hour still courses through me. Neither Lizzy nor Aunt Pam understand why Uncle Al and I loathe each other.

Unfortunately, I'll never be able to tell them either, since Uncle Al and I have been forced into this twisted secret truce with each other. My ability to dream the future is how I figured out what he planned to do. He knows I can never tell my aunt what happened without telling her about my ability. I know he can never tell her about my ability without explaining how he found out. We're bound by each other's life-ruining secrets.

The smell of freshly cut grass clears my head, allowing me to think for the first time today as the birds sing to the rhythm of my steps. It's a short walk; the sun hits my face, having risen just above the houses, but it's still cold and too early for the warmth to sink into my skin. I didn't bring a jacket, but that's fine. It will be too hot and stuffy in our classrooms by noon.

A familiar dark car with tinted windows drives by. There's a single, blacked-out eye on the side to signify its Eramica affiliation. I grind my teeth together and divert my gaze.

Eramica is everywhere. But at least I have my small haven amid the fear.

Breyson Jones is my best and only friend. He comes into

view at the halfway point between our homes, pacing back and forth, eyes focused on the path his feet have made in the grass. His cropped blond hair looks unnaturally disheveled compared to his usually perfect style. He still doesn't see me but runs a hand through the messed-up hair, making the short pieces stick out in strange directions. Even with his stressful movement, the knots in my stomach start to unwind at the sight of him.

I close the distance between us as the calming breeze whips my hair around my face, whispering a reminder of how near summer is. He stops midstep to look at me, his shoulders tensing. I crane my neck to meet his eyes as the sun shines down on my exposed face.

"What has you so worked up?" I ask, unable to help my small smile. His cool blue eyes hold mine longer than necessary. For a moment, I can see something in his expression that he doesn't want me to see, thanks to our years of friendship and ability to read each other so well, but it's gone before I can put words to it.

He doesn't answer but starts our short journey to the school, so I follow and allow him this silence.

Finally, he responds, "*Nothing. Your turn, what's wrong?*"

The words appear in my mind, spoken silently but clearly as he uses his Unnatural ability to communicate. Each Unnatural has one strange ability, and as far as I know, there's only one person to possess multiple abilities. Me.

When we met, Brey hadn't intended on telling me that he was an Unnatural, but he accidentally spoke to me without opening his mouth. He had been so worried about what I would do and whether I'd report him, that the only way to get him to calm down was by telling him about myself. Our shared secrets made us closer.

"Nothing," I respond to him out loud. It would be so much easier if his ability worked both ways.

"You're lying. Spill." He silently pushes without meeting my gaze. His hand returns to his hair.

"You know, you're going to show up to school with your hair all messed up if you keep doing that." I arch an eyebrow and glance up at him. His hand snaps down to his side as he scowls at me, one eyebrow raising at the sight of my appearance.

Without thinking, he reaches over and grabs the book I hadn't stuffed into my bag yet. I sigh at his obvious attempt to tell me to fix my own hair. I comb my fingers through the blonde mess a few times in an attempt to undo the craziness from the wind before tying it up in a bun. It's not pretty, but it's the best I can do. Unlike Lizzy, I put very little effort into my physical appearance. His silence throughout the ordeal doesn't go unnoticed.

"Ready to tell me what's wrong?" I ask him again.

"Are you?" He dodges my question, depositing the book in my bag instead of my outstretched arms. The worn leather straps press on my shoulders from the added weight.

"It's just Uncle Al." I give a small sigh and pull the straps tighter. Brey immediately tenses next to me, and I know if I were to look at him, I'd see a small twitch under his right eye.

"What happened?" he nearly growls, choosing to forgo his ability so that I can hear the anger in his voice.

"Nothing new." I sigh with a shrug of my shoulders. Brey is the only one who knows the truth about Uncle Al. Explaining small interactions like this morning's not only forces me relive uncomfortable moments, but it also means I have to talk Brey down from doing something stupid.

"Your turn," I say with more determination. "What is it?" We walk in silence while I let him consider what to tell me.

We don't keep secrets, so it's just a matter of when he's ready to explain.

"My mom's being weird," he finally says with a sigh. His shoulders continue to tense, and I have a sneaking suspicion that he's still holding something back. "Have you had any dreams about her?"

My dreams often haunt me. One of my abilities is that every dream I have is of the future, and unless I do something to change what I see, my dream will come true.

Brey calls upon my rare ability often. He thinks it's a gift to dream about the future and says it's far more useful than what he can do. It's strange that all my dreams come true, because while most people probably strive to be able to say that, it's what I hate the most about myself. Maybe because when you know the future before it plays out, it's more like a nightmare.

"No." I draw out the word while thinking back.

We walk by a bush that's trying to pry off the winter months we're emerging from, and the smell of fresh soil hits my nose.

"My mom was talking about Nick Rickter this morning. How horrible it was for them to murder a baby," he thinks to me as if we were just talking about that. His tone is solemn, despite being silent.

While our government cares greatly for my generation, the generation that's meant to restart the population, their concern really only applies to those without supernatural abilities. Of course, the only Generation Novus children that the government *would* kill are the Unnaturals.

Nick Rickter was the first Unnatural ever caught. He was a fire-starter and nearly burned down his entire street. He's a household name because he represents the beginning of the fear and new rules. That was when America stopped trying to rebuild our broken world and Eramica started trying to control it instead. I don't blame his mom for getting emotional about our country's handling of Unnaturals, given she's raising one.

Brey's mom knows he's an Unnatural even though it's illegal to harbor one. The parents of babies born around the time Unnaturals were created are questioned annually in an effort to find, locate and kill us. Somehow, though, Mrs. Jones always passes her inspection.

Another black car drives past me, windows too dark to see through. Fury ignites inside of me and seems to flow through my veins at the injustice of what Eramica does. I jut my chin out and try to make eye contact with whatever government official sits behind the wheel.

Brey's fingers curl around my wrist, warm and familiar, but tight enough to send a warning. It hurts, pulling my attention from the car.

"What the hell are you doing?" His voice is silent as he yells at me.

"I'm just sick of it all." I don't bother to lower my voice. "Let them find out. Who cares?" My words don't hold the authority that the meaning demands.

He looks over my head and mutters a quiet curse before pulling me away from the sidewalk. It's all I can do not to topple over as he forces me to follow him.

"Where are we—" I start to protest. But his strength silences me as he simply grips tighter and forces me into a run to keep from falling down.

We're a few blocks from the school, surrounded by houses on every side. Our region is repetitive to a fault. Every house and yard look exactly the same, to the point that you could get lost if you didn't know where you were going or how to trace your steps. Brey reaches a tall, wooden fence that mirrors the fencing around both of our own houses. He turns back to look at the sidewalk we just vacated, fear clear in his eyes.

"Jump it," he demands silently, refusing to look at me. *"Now, Mercer."*

For the first time, I let myself consider that someone could have heard my foolish statement. It was reckless and not entirely truthful. I'm not ready to die, so I *do* care that they don't find me.

My fingertips reach for the top of the wooden planks, a splinter pushing itself into my right hand, but I ignore it. Sawed wood overpowers my senses as my body grates against the fence. I launch over the top and land on the grass beneath. The entire movement is familiar and comfortable since Brey and I used to jump the backyards of the B Region all the time. Seconds later, he lands with a soft thud next to me.

"Come on." He grabs my wrist again and doesn't explain as he drags me to the other side of the backyard, only briefly looking back at the house to see if anybody is watching from the kitchen. "Again," he instructs. I want to comment on his grumpiness, but something in the pit of my stomach is curled in fear that he's reached some conclusion I haven't yet. My heartbeat races with a surge in adrenaline as we run.

It isn't until the fourth fence that I see where he's leading me. As we emerge from another backyard, he walks me down the street.

I'm impressed with his sense of direction, as we're almost to the school. I once heard that there are fifty-seven schools in the B Region, but that's not information willingly shared with the citizens, so I have no idea if it's correct.

I glance to the right at the old parking lot. Cars are such a luxury that no students drive. The town is intentionally set up so that we all live within walking distance of the school. The parking lot is used for our athletics class instead. Our gym teacher is setting up dingy cones for his first period, and I'm already eager to be able to run in the fresh air later today.

Brey walks with radiating anger next to me, and I'm too much of a coward to try and confront his mood.

The air around us shifts as soon as we enter the school, buzzing with different conversations and lockers being slammed while my classmates rush to their first period. A clamminess takes over as the sweat from our brief run dries. I use the sleeve of my shirt to wipe my forehead and hope my face doesn't look too flushed.

I can't remember a time when my school didn't feel like a prison, teaching me to hate what I was born into. I inhale deeply, craving another burst of fresh May air. Instead, the faint smell of disinfectant hits me, a sign that this area has been sanitized per government regulations.

Teachers stand in the doorways to watch us, because Eramica is always watching. My eyes dart to the checkered floor, as if someone could learn what I'm hiding just from eye contact.

From what I've heard, school has changed drastically since the Censorship. My father was a history professor when he was alive. It's illegal to talk about what the government was like before the Censorship. I suppose the Eramica leaders are scared we might rebel and insist on returning to how things used to be if we know too much.

But even though he was forbidden from discussing it, my father couldn't change that he was a professor at heart. Perhaps when you find your calling, like he had with teaching, you aren't able to simply turn it off because you're told to. I don't remember much from when he was alive, but he left journals, books, and writings. I'm lucky to learn what I can from him and his memory.

The first bell rings, but instead of following the teachers into their various rooms, Brey turns, pushing my back into the lockers and leaning toward me so closely that I can smell mint in his breath. The movement is so quick and aggressive that it startles me, and I struggle to catch my breath. It's unlike him to be late to class, a sign that makes my insides squirm, knowing whatever he's about to say must trump his own moral code of school attendance.

"What was that?" he hisses. My first instinct is to play dumb, but we both know what he's talking about. The mint caresses my face while he speaks to me.

"I don't know," I mumble, admitting what I had already realized myself. "It was stupid."

"They noticed." His voice holds pain and urgency underneath the anger. "The car stopped."

"I said it was stupid." I try to push him away from me, but his hands hold my shoulders firmly in place against the locker, and I ache from the hard metal behind me. He doesn't respond, but just lets those icy blue eyes bore into my soul. His jaw doesn't relax while he takes controlled breaths through his nose. I could say something to calm him down, but I don't. His anger is justified.

The second bell sounds and he closes his eyes, his jaw still not having relaxed at all as he struggles to gain his composure.

"It's going to be worse if we don't go now," I say.

I hate how close to tears I am. The urge to cry pinches the back of my throat. I bite my lip to try and calm myself. He finally backs away from me and I immediately shift from the cold lockers.

Brey reluctantly follows me to the back of the classroom. Most of our peers ignore us, which is how I prefer things. Unfortunately, though, not everyone feels that we're best left alone.

A large, brown boot shoots into the aisle in my path, snagging my feet. JC has been tormenting me since I joined this school the year after my parents died. Normally, I would be more attentive to his antics, but my mind feels fuzzy from everything that's happened this morning.

Brey's strong hand reaches out and steadies me before I topple to the ground.

I don't bother to turn around and give JC the satisfaction. Although our teacher likely saw what happened, JC won't get in trouble, thanks to who he's friends with. Besides, I don't want him seeing the blush that I'm sure fills my cheeks.

"Want me to punch him?" Brey offers weakly after we take our seats, his attempt to try and regain normalcy after our talk. His kind blue eyes hold pity that makes me grind my teeth.

It's not that I don't appreciate his support, but JC nearly killed Breyson when we were younger. I have no desire to put Brey in his line of fire again.

"What's up with him..." Brey's thoughts fill my mind and I look up confused. JC's behavior isn't out of the ordinary, but Brey isn't looking at JC, so I follow his gaze to see Mr. Miller acting strangely, sulking behind his desk in the corner of the classroom.

As if in answer to Brey's question, the door opens, and several men in nice suits walk in. The suits all have a single eye stitched to the pocket. Government officials.

Brey doesn't have to speak silently for me to pick up on his immediate fear. It's as if he and I are holding a collective breath.

I don't risk a glance at him, and apparently, he doesn't think it's worth the risk to communicate silently to me.

Eramica officials only report to schools to capture Unnaturals.

Chapter Three

My throat, thick like sandpaper, struggles to swallow. I force myself to sit up straighter in my seat. Eramica officials are trained to notice the smallest of clues, which is why my behavior earlier was stupid. I raise my chin and look forward, not meeting any of their eyes.

"Class," Mr. Miller needlessly calls as everyone is watching the newcomers, "please welcome our guests."

Silence coats us like a thick blanket. Nobody has as much to lose as Brey and I, but these men can threaten anybody's reputation. I wait for the older men to talk, but then, something I would have never expected happens.

A boy, maybe just a few years older than we are, steps through the wall of Eramica men. He has flaming red hair and a face full of freckles. My jaw opens. I want to ask Brey what he's thinking but can't risk looking over to him.

"I'm Tanner," the boy says with a pudgy grin. "For those who don't know yet, Eramica has employed a few Generation Novus individuals so we can help set curriculum and practices for your continued growth." His smile doesn't meet his eyes.

Tanner continues his speech while walking up and down the aisles, his crisp, black, dress shoes providing a squeak of rubber on linoleum every few steps.

"We carry a burden to change the state of the nation. This isn't something we can take lightly, as all future generations depend on us."

He grips JC's shoulder and the bully flinches underneath the touch.

"We need to embrace the role that life has thrust upon us."

Every few steps, he touches a student on the shoulder or elbow. By the time he reaches me, I can't help but coil away as his palm is hot even through my shirt. It rests there longer than the other students and Brey shifts in his seat next to me.

"I hope you'll embrace this effort with me. So in the following years, we can look back at our progress and be proud."

He finds his spot with the Eramica men and one of his fingers flicks an orange curl from his forehead. None of the men seem surprised by his speech, the weird way he put a hand on all of us, or the fact that he took control of this brief visit, despite being half their age.

"Thank you," Tanner says with a last smile. He pauses and it's obvious that he's thinking more than he's saying. He glances around us, seeming to focus on a few key individuals. His eyes linger on me before he finally strides out of the room.

I don't understand what we were supposed to get from that speech, and evidently I'm not alone in that line of thinking.

The Eramica men follow him from the room, leaving a vacant hole in their wake with our confusion. I have no idea what role this boy was put in, or by whom.

"That was..." Brey starts to say, but I cut him off.

"Weird." The relief between us is mutual. Nobody hears us since the entire class seems to have erupted in conversation about the strange visit. "What is it?" I ask Brey when he still refuses to look at me.

"I think I want to talk to him," he finally says silently. I hadn't seen him touch his hair again, but it's even more messed up now.

"Why?" I demand, knocking my notebook to the floor with a soft thud.

Brey reaches down to get it, and I know that he can sense my disapproval. The government doesn't care about us. Sure, we're Generation Novus, but unlike our classmates, Brey and I are also Unnaturals. Between protecting us because we're Generation Novus and killing us because we're Unnaturals, he and I both know which they would choose.

"It doesn't matter," he thinks back as Mr. Miller succeeds in calming the class down.

I can't fight the anger that begins to boil inside me. Brey hasn't adopted the same hatred for our government that I have, even though they would hunt him down. He's always been too desperate to please authority figures. I wouldn't be surprised if he wanted to be part of the Generation Novus students working for Eramica. I slouch lower in my seat and cross my arms over my chest. He must pick up on my sour mood because he doesn't offer any other explanation.

On the chalkboard in bold letters is *Processed Food.* We've spent three weeks talking about the additives our ancestors used in their food before consumption. I can't imagine how we haven't exhausted the subject. I let out a deep breath of frustration and sit as low in my seat as possible. The air feels like it's suffocating, and despite the promise of a beautiful day, the windows are closed.

"Can anybody tell me why the current regulation is called 'Two Steps Are Best?'" Mr. Miller's usual bounce is back now that the visitors are gone. He's a short man and often walks in front of his podium since he can't see over it.

Brey's hand unsurprisingly shoots up next to me, earning a smirk between JC and Varick Dolion. Brey either doesn't notice the interaction between our class bullies, or he doesn't care.

"Mr. Jones," our teacher prompts.

Varick's head flicks toward Brey and I clench my hands into fists. I can't fight the overprotective anger that boils inside me whenever Varick mocks my best friend, even if said friend is pissing me off at the moment.

"The 'Two Steps Are Best' process started after the Censorship." Brey's answer sounds straight out of a textbook. "Natural foods are not to go through more than two steps of processing before consumption." Brey's intellect used to annoy me. Now, I find it funny and sometimes useful.

"Very good, Mr. Jones," Mr. Miller praises. "As we were forced to learn, there's a severe price to pay in consuming foods that are overprocessed. Who can tell me what came out of the use of overprocessed food?"

I fiddle with a wooden pencil, passing it over my fingers and back. Jefferson raises his hand from the front row. He's been Brey's intellectual rival for as long as I can remember.

Mr. Miller nods at Jefferson, who then responds in a voice that holds too much disdain, "Unnaturals, those who walk among us with dangerous powers… that's what comes from overprocessed food."

Jefferson may be right. That's the narrative Eramica is teaching us: that the Unnaturals came about as a body's defense mechanism to the poison humans constantly fed it. But they don't know if that's true. Nobody knows what really started this.

Only a brief moment of silence fills the room while our teacher implores all of us to take the threat of Unnaturals seriously.

"Dangerous... right," Brey thinks to me silently. His jaw is so tight, I worry about what someone might think if they were to

look his way.

I give a weak smile in response. We both know the propaganda they teach in this class isn't worth our time. For that reason, it's one of the few classes Brey will feed me test answers telepathically. It's infuriating how moral he can be in our other classes, the ones he deems essential for my future.

Instead of continuing to listen to Mr. Miller drone on about how dangerous I am as an Unnatural, I look outside, toward the green wall of trees that edge the school property and let my mind wander.

The day doesn't improve from there. Something has been nagging at me since I woke up. It isn't until my last class that I realize it's my mom's birthday. I can't believe neither Aunt Pam nor Lizzy mentioned it this morning.

I spend most evenings at Breyson's house. But not tonight. Instead, I walk around our old neighborhood, the one I lived at until I was six. I plant my feet on the sidewalk and watch the lights turn on in an upstairs window. It's a larger build than what Aunt Pam and Uncle Al have. That's because both my parents had such good jobs after the Censorship; she was a police officer and he was a teacher. I've heard that those were some of the lowest paid employees before everything changed. I can't imagine that kind of reality.

I was only six when I had to leave this home. One of the worst parts of life is that the memories and feelings from the people most important to you grow dim with time, stolen every second that passes, every day that you get older. My parents made me feel safe in a world out to get me. That's the feeling that I try to focus on, despite how quickly it fades.

Once, in one of the notebooks my dad left, I found a single, ripped page with his cursive writing that said, *"When in doubt, the truth should win out!"* It's impossible that he was talking to me, but sometimes I like to imagine it was a direct message from him. It's almost as if he didn't want me living a life of secrecy despite my status as an Unnatural.

I have no idea how long I've been standing here in front of our old house as I run the back of my hand under my nose. I'm sure my eyes are puffy, so I can only hope everyone is already asleep at home. I don't want more uncomfortable conversations today. I shuffle my feet back, wishing I had brought a coat. The nights are even chillier than the mornings.

I don't know when sleep finds me. For a brief moment, I question if it ever does. Eventually, I find myself in Mr. Miller's class. As I walk to my desk, surprise catches me off guard and I nearly stumble backward. There's already a body sitting in my desk. Well, not just any body. *I'm* already sitting there. I sigh loudly, but nobody turns to the noise because I'm not really here.

This is a dream.

Dream-Mercer looks tired, even more than usual. Her hair is disheveled, with some up and some down, like she just rolled out of bed. Her hands are fixing the buttons on a dark blue top, buttons that she must have fastened incorrectly in her tardiness.

I can't help the annoyance that makes me grind my teeth. It's bad enough I have to live through school once when I'm awake…

Brey looks over at dream-Mercer and the movement catches my attention. He must say something silently to her because she lifts her head and meets his gaze before nodding. A half-smile fills his face, and she rolls her eyes in response. I've seen similar interactions in other dreams, our silent conversations that nobody seems to care about or notice.

The door opens and Mr. Miller walks through. I wish I could just slip into a peaceful sleep. Unfortunately, my only option is to sit back and listen to the same information that I'll hear again sometime in the future.

Mr. Miller walks to his podium carrying a single sheet of paper, which he places carefully. His glasses drop down his nose and he makes no effort to stand on his toes to see us, letting the wooden podium act as a barrier.

"Mr. Craw, Mr. Jones, Ms. Lewis, you're needed in the office," he reads.

I have no idea what this is for and based on a glance between Breyson and dream-Mercer, neither do they. I see my dream-self look hesitantly at Brey, and he meets her gaze with concern but stands. After all, Brey would never disobey a direct instruction.

Dream-Mercer stands, as well. She glances down at her shirt and I shake my head as I watch her eyes widen. Even though she tried to fix the buttons, she still didn't do it right.

I follow the unlikely group, not sure I have much choice. My dreams tend to force me to watch my own point of view. We walk the short hallway of our school, passing lockers and closed classroom doors, the only sound filling the empty halls is their footsteps. Mercer and Brey are in front. JC, also known as Jack Craw, follows them closely. The latter watches the back of dream-Mercer's head, his arm flexing menacingly.

Finally, we arrive at the office. It's unusually empty, with a fan whirring in the corner. Even Ms. Jenkins' desk is vacant, which never happens.

"Where is everyone?" dream-Mercer asks in a low voice.

Evidently, she's had the same question I did. You would think we would share the same ideas more often, but I'm usually surprised by my dream-self's choices.

A door to the right opens and the principal comes out. I've had many visits to his office. None of them have been because of my stellar grades.

The group follows the principal into his already crammed room. JC has to push himself into a corner to fit since his body takes up more space than the rest of us.

There are two girls, the Nguyen sisters, already here in the red chairs that sit across from the main desk, making the entire scenario that much more confusing. Like Lizzy and me, they don't look anything alike for being related. Lottie, the younger of the two, is tall with long hair and Jaylee is short. I watch Breyson nod to Jaylee, his lab partner in a class that I'm not smart enough to be in, and she gives him a meaningful look.

The clock on the wall ticks, providing the only noise in the room, while the anxiety surrounding us seems to grow with each of the loudly marked seconds.

"You're probably wondering why I've asked you to come to my office today," Principal Frank mumbles without his usual authority. He tries to maneuver around the group, grunting with the exertion. Once he's sitting, I can just barely see his pudgy hands fidget in his lap. He refuses to look at the group of students in front of him as he continues, "The thing is, your teachers have recommended that you might benefit from a summer program."

"You mean like summer school?" dream-Mercer asks, her voice harsh and demanding.

I glance around the room, sharing her confusion. It isn't like me to speak up, but the injustice of Breyson in summer school must have us both defensive on his behalf.

Brey's eyebrows pull together and his forehead creases while he runs a hand through his hair. Summer school wouldn't make sense for him. He works too hard to achieve great grades. I have a feeling he's been like that since his dad died before I met him, embracing the burden that he'll have to support his mom someday, or perhaps it's his way to prove his worth to a country that wants him dead. Either way, this must not be right.

"Well," the principal continues, realizing he's quickly losing control of the situation, "it would be a summer program, more than just school. Your guardians have all been informed and you'll be leaving immediately."

The room erupts in response. The sisters are now standing, demanding answers. JC's voice is louder than anyone else's while he screams about his summer plans, spraying the principal with spit as he voices his frustration. The door opens but thanks to the volume in the room, nobody else notices, not even dream-Mercer or Brey.

Three men in suits walk in. They stand tall, with an authority that resonates even though it's unspoken. They seem unbothered by the commotion. One approaches JC from behind, takes out a metal syringe and stabs him in the neck without a hint of remorse.

I gasp audibly as my heart jumps to my throat. I reach out to grab Brey's shirt but my hand doesn't make contact because I'm not actually here.

JC's large body sags, hitting the wall and then breaking a chair before coming to rest on the floor, his arm shoved at an awkward angle beneath his torso.

The scene seems like something from a nightmare. If I didn't know that my dreams come true, I would just assume this *was* a nightmare. One by one, the men in suits calmly stick a needle into each student, until the room is silent. Principal Frank surveys the fallen teenage bodies draped around his office with a look of reluctant remorse.

"I don't want to take the big one." One of the suits points to JC. "You take him."

He casually nods to one of his companions while throwing

Lottie's body over his shoulder as if he participates in kidnappings regularly.

"Let's just get the others out. We can come back for him." The man grabs Jaylee.

Principal Frank, while clearly stunned, doesn't bother to say anything to the men working.

When one of them grabs dream-Mercer, I have no choice but to float beside him, out of the building and into a black van that's parked nearby. Nausea that's been building threatens to choke me now and I wonder what would happen if I threw up while dreaming.

"Mercer," Brey thinks to me. I look around for him as I register what hearing his voice means, but his body is lifeless in front of me. *"You're so late. I don't know if you're hearing this, but I gotta go. Meet me there..."*

My body feels heavy. The light behind my closed lids is too bright. Without giving myself time, I snap up, wrenching my eyes open. The ceiling light is off, but the sun streams through our window. I look out over the roof to see the green, manicured lawn.

A cold sweat covers my forehead. For someone who can see the future, I sure don't have my life together.

I throw myself out of bed, not bothering to shower, and grab the first outfit I can find. I have to get to school and tell Brey about my dream. Could what I saw possibly happen today? Surely, we have more time. In fact, maybe that wasn't even a real premonition dream at all. Maybe I'm starting to have real nightmares.

There aren't any voices in the house.

"Aunt Pam?" I call. There's no answer. The house is small enough that she would hear me. I rush out the door, not bothering to turn around and lock it. Nobody commits crimes anymore because the punishment is too severe, so we never lock the door.

My pace picks up to a light jog, but I don't break a sweat. The movement helps me focus on my thoughts, although that focus is singular at the moment: I have to get to Brey.

The school comes into view and as I'm about to run up the steps, my hand grabs the railing. I stop in my tracks, my instincts ahead of my rational thinking. My grip tightens on the cool, metal railing, pulling me back.

What now? I still don't know if the dream happens today or not.

I need to make a decision, or someone will see me soon and wonder what I'm doing.

My hands are sweaty and I wipe them on my shirt. The blue cotton beneath my palms soothes me, but I get distracted at the sight of the buttons that aren't fastened right. I start to fix them, even though that's hardly a priority.

Somehow, the easy task settles me. As I get to the top button, I take a deep breath, satisfied that I could at least do this one thing right, unlike dream-Mercer. She wasn't able to fix the buttons, even after multiple attempts.

My breath catches and gets stuck somewhere in my throat.

Either my dream is coming true today, or I wear this shirt too often.

Chapter Four

It's as if I'm not really in my body anymore. My feet are frozen on the sidewalk. I mentally berate myself for not moving, but my body refuses to follow orders. It knows that once I take a step, I'm making a decision that's bigger than I'm willing to make.

Skipping our required learning is not a luxury that Generation Novus students are allowed. I've suffered their so-called consequences before, and it's nothing I want to repeat.

But what if the dream *does* happen today? Fear of exposure has always trumped any punishment I may face. I might lose the only upper hand that I have if I walk into the school.

A metallic taste washes over my tongue and I realize I must have been biting my lower lip, a habit picked up a few years ago when I struggled with keeping my thoughts to myself. A deep breath rattles my chest. I shake my head to try and clear the fuzziness. I continue gnawing on my lip, ignoring the blood that covers my tongue. Pain increases in my abdomen, as if my gut is trying to literally speak to me.

I know that I'm not making things up. In a way, it feels like I've been waiting for this my entire life. I knew they'd find me. The last sixteen years were only a strange limbo of fear and unease.

My heart rate feels like it's beginning to calm now that I'm starting to have an idea of my direction. I cannot go into the school, that much is obvious. But where do I go? Do I simply return home and wait until school lets out? Then what?

"Ugh." I curse under my breath and kick the side of the building with the toe of my shoe. A few pieces of stone crumble to the ground from the brick.

My hand fidgets to my face, tracing my bloodied lip. The wind picks up, whipping strands of my blonde hair around me and my eyes start to water. It's not ideal conditions considering what I have to do: I have to run.

I need to stop at home and get as much as I can. It'd be nice if I had a car to take, but that makes things difficult. I don't know how to drive, though I'm sure I could learn. I could steal Uncle Al's car, but it would be years before he could save enough to buy a new one. I wouldn't care, except that would impact Aunt Pam and Lizzy, too. Brey's mom has a car, but I doubt Brey would be willing to take hers, since we'll be abandoning her and that wound alone will be difficult to heal from.

Breyson. In the urgency of everything, I had forgotten about my best friend.

If my dream comes true today, and my timing is accurate, then he must already be in the principal's office. My mouth dries as I picture the scene… the fear and panic spread throughout the tiny office.

I have a plan, and now that I've decided, it seems so obvious and I silently reprimand myself for not considering it sooner.

Of course, Breyson is my single focus. I can't run away without him. I head toward the side of the school that has the closest entrance to the office. Just as I'm about to turn the corner, laughter and deep voices stop me. I have to hold the orange brick wall in front of me to steady my dizziness.

I peer my head around the corner, and immediately wish I hadn't because now I can't pretend otherwise. An unmarked black van sits close to the school door. The two back doors are open wide. One of the men sits on the back bumper and the other is pacing, checking his wristwatch every few seconds. They're both dressed far too professionally to be driving that type of vehicle. The one sitting down laughs again, throwing his head back.

"Stop worrying, nobody is going to see us," he barks through the laughter.

The pacing man stops his movement like he's about to respond, but he must change his mind because after clenching his jaw, he returns to his steps.

The door to the school opens loudly, thanks to the old hinges. I pull my head back quickly so that I'm completely concealed, although from how close I stand, it seems impossible that they can't hear my heart as it thrums inside my chest.

"We're ready for you, but we're missing one," a raspy voice says.

I recognize it as the man who claimed he didn't want to carry JC. It takes too long to realize they're talking about me and that I'm the missing one.

The pounding in my head threatens to take away my consciousness. It was a mistake to be here. I thought I needed to get to Brey, but I was already too late.

I curse under my breath. Why haven't I practiced my abilities more? Not that they would be much use to me. Desperation makes my arms shake, so I cross them to try to gain some control. How worthless am I? I'm the only Unnatural with multiple abilities, yet none of them can help me because I don't know how to use them.

I have three abilities. The dreams obviously won't do anything more than they already have.

The first ability to manifest in my life was the compulsion, my ability to force someone to do something just by demanding it. I used it on my parents before they died, and that's how they found out about me. They immediately created a homeschool curriculum, sending Lizzy off and keeping me behind for my own safety. But my compulsion ability is unpracticed. I haven't learned how to do it on command. In fact, I've only ever done it accidentally. And I've never used it on more than one person at a time. Trying it on these men would be suicide.

I'm not even really sure if my third ability is real, but Brey thinks it is. He calls it my disarming ability. Sometimes I can prevent him from using his telepathy ability. He thinks I can stop another Unnatural. But we've never tested it on any other Unnatural and it's really just a suspicion right now. Not to mention, these men look too old to be one of us, so it's also useless right now.

For being the only known Unnatural with more than one ability, I've never felt so powerless.

A sob chokes out of me as an obvious solution becomes a consideration. They have Brey, but they don't have me yet. I need to get away from here if I'm going to have any chance of getting him out, too. We don't know how long Eramica takes to kill an Unnatural, only that death is imminent. My sobs feel like they're being pushed back as soon as my feet begin running. I have to leave him behind.

Understanding what I have to do, fear chokes me. As much as I hate my life at home, I'm not ready to leave yet. The hostile dynamic with Uncle Al is only a fraction of my home life. There's still Lizzy and Aunt Pam. I feel robbed of my chance to mend relationships and say goodbyes. What will Lizzy wonder when I don't return home? And what kind of impact will my running away have on my family? Will they suffer because it might look like they were trying to protect me? No, not Lizzy and Aunt Pam. I've been so careful to never let them know anything for this very reason. Their innocence will be obvious if Eramica starts questioning them. As for Uncle Al, well, I hope they find out he knew, and I hope they kill him for it. I don't let myself mourn Brey. I'm going to get him. Somehow. I have to.

I tear open the front door of our small house, grateful that it's never locked, and slam it shut so hard that the photographs along the walls shudder.

"Aunt Pam?" The silence is deafening. I suppose I should be relieved, but a piece of me is sad that she can't offer support or beg me to stay.

I race up the carpeted stairs to our bedroom, grabbing the first bag I can find and stuffing clothes inside. My mind feels sharp while I make quick decisions and fly through the movements, but I can sense the fuzziness of grief threatening to take over. My jaw clenches as I focus on what I need to accomplish in order to keep the cobwebs of doubt away.

Breathing heavily, I race down the upstairs hall. I just need a few things from the kitchen and then I'll go. I know adrenaline is pushing my steps further, but there's a shakiness in my hands through my movements, threatening to overcome at any second.

Go where? The thought stops me. I've never been outside this city before, let alone the B Region. I'm not even sure if I know what exists outside of the B Region. Do the rest of the cities look like ours? Act like ours? What will I do when I get there?

Wherever I go, I just need to move now.

I rush down the stairs, my hand on the wooden railing as I propel forward so fast that I'm surprised I haven't tripped and fallen yet. The doorknob rattles as someone tests whether it's locked. I'm about to take the final two steps with a single jump when my hand tightens around the railing and pulls me back. My feet slip on the carpeting, and I fall back, a sharpness shooting up through my behind.

Of course they came to look for me. I scramble to run back up the stairs. My shoulder catches one of the photos hung on the wall, the sound of shattering glass echoes in the space.

"Upstairs," one of them growls. I don't turn around, knowing that it won't do me any good. There's no lock on the bedroom door. I run to the other side and wrench open the window that faces our backyard. The smell of fresh grass mixed with the promise of rain surrounds me, beckoning me onward.

My movements are being propelled by my desire to survive, as if they aren't mine at all, but a moment's hesitation stops me before I climb outside. What if I die from a fall like this? I suppose I'd rather die trying to get away from them than die however they intend to kill me. I climb out on the shingles and shimmy to the edge. A few gray pieces of the roof tear away under my movement, taking far longer than I would like to fall to the green grass beneath.

I take calculated, small steps to the edge, then turn my body around and lower myself so I'm hanging by my fingers. The shingles are rough but provide the grip that I need. The sweat beneath the pads of my fingertips threatens to make me slip off before I'm ready. I take a breath, gathering courage before falling.

I'm about to let go, I really am. I just need a few more moments.

A scream escapes me as a rough hand closes around my right wrist. I'm too late. A strong hold starts to pull me back onto the roof, inch by inch. The pressure of his fingers is so tight that it burns.

He pulls me higher and higher. My body thrashes violently against his hold, my legs jerking at odd angles while he increases the pressure in response. It's as if I'm as light as a feather for how much my struggle affects him.

I shake my head to myself. My throat feels swollen with emotion. This can't be the end. I'm not sure how I find my voice, when everything inside of me feels shaky.

"Let me go!" I say while my fingertips start strangely tingling.

Tears spring to my eyes and I'm about to give up when I feel his hand suddenly release me. My hair whips around my face as I fall through the air, seemingly taking too long and also no time at all.

And then, it's over. A sharp pain shoots through my right foot as I make contact with the springy grass beneath me. My fingers weave into the green blades while I shake my head and try to gain composure.

Compulsion. My ability is what forced him to let go. My body always tingles when I'm using my compulsion.

My lungs haven't started working yet, but thanks to my compulsion ability, I've been given another chance and I won't waste it. I have to get up and move. I stand before my lungs fill, resulting in a disturbing dizziness and black spots in my vision.

Although I've jumped the fences hundreds of times in my childhood, I've never done it with an injured foot or a dizzy head. The black spots get larger and my foot protests, but I start a limping run toward the back fence.

I'm vaguely aware of the men arguing about who let go of my arms and why. It occurs to me that they don't know about my ability. Maybe they aren't chasing me because I'm an Unnatural. How would they know? But then again, why else would they be here? All these thoughts feel jumbled as the adrenaline threatens to wane.

"Stop yelling at each other. I got her," a man calls.

Despite my best judgement, I turn around to put a face to the voice. My heart jumps up to my throat at his proximity; he's so much closer than I had thought, close enough to reach out and touch me.

“Hurry,” another voice yells out with a slight edge of panic. “They’re here.”

I wonder if they’re talking about my guardians, and what would happen if Uncle Al saw this scene.

Strong arms in a black suit jacket enclose around my body and the foreign smell of cigarette smoke is so thick that it suffocates me, which is strange since cigarettes are illegal. I’ve only smelled it one other time and it was so vile that I gagged. The arms circle me in a bear hug, restricting my upper body completely. I kick my legs out, pushing my back into his chest as I let my legs fly. I scream as loudly as I can muster, hoping someone will hear.

“Keep her quiet!”

The pressure holding my arms loosens, only to be replaced with a sweaty hand slapped over my mouth. The saltiness from it covers my tongue but I don’t think as I bite down hard.

The voice holding me grunts in pain and then tightens his hold around my arms to the point of it hurting.

“Who has it?” His low voice vibrates my back when he speaks.

“It’s here.”

The idea that these will be my last few moments makes the tears come faster.

The men are now talking over each other. There are so many of them. I feel a prick in my neck and my feeble attempts to get free suddenly seem unimportant. Everything gets foggy and I can feel my body start to sag in the man’s arms. I try to make myself stand, but the ground feels funny beneath me, and no matter what I do, my eyes don’t seem to be working.

Everything turns black.

Chapter Five

My body, sore from exertion, protests the light streaming through my eyelids. It can't be morning already. Something nags at me and a heat claws at my chest like it's trying to get me to understand.

With a groan, I finally let my eyelids flutter and my mouth opens with an audible pop. I'm not in my bedroom. In fact, I have no idea where I am. The anxiety that starts welling up inside me reaches my throat until I feel like I'm choking.

I'm in a small room, but it's not anywhere I've been before. The walls are a boring gray with no windows and only a single, metal door. There are desks, but not like the old wooden ones we use in school. Instead, they're shiny and new. A table is pushed into a corner opposite the door. Considering there's no other option, I start to walk to the exit when it suddenly opens with force, slamming against the wall with a loud thud, clearly heavier than a normal wooden door.

A short girl storms in, her cropped, blonde hair whipping wildly around her head, startling me, and I back up a few steps so she won't knock me over. She's about my height, but that's not what stands out. My eyes bulge a little and I can't seem to look away from the muscles in her arms. I'm still gawking, but I force myself to break my gaze when I see another, much taller, person follow her into the room.

"Sorry, I was just—" My apology stops short as I glance up to the joiner. His shaggy blond hair is longer than I've ever seen but I could never miss those deep blue eyes, even though they're different somehow. What could have happened to him? The perfect blue now holds a kind of pain I've never seen.

"Brey?" I ask him. My voice shakes, but I don't care. I don't even try to clear my throat.

He doesn't answer me. He doesn't even acknowledge my presence. As I get closer, I notice the deep bruises beneath his eyes. Whether he was in a fight or hasn't slept in weeks, I can't tell.

"Brey." This time it doesn't sound like a question as my fists clench tightly into balls at my sides.

He still hasn't looked up to acknowledge either myself or this other girl. His hand runs through his long hair while he continues to look at the ground. It's strange to see his hair as anything but the short style I've grown used to. The pieces flop back into place after he messes with them, instead of holding their shape and sticking out in all directions. He presses his lips together and shakes his head in an almost unnoticeable way.

"Mercer, you know I have to do this." He finally acknowledges me, flicking the long strands of blond from his eyes. I've never seen him do that before.

It distracts me from the fact that his words don't make sense.

"What?" I stutter out in question.

"I know." The other girl talks over me. She looks up at him and her hands fidget in front of her body.

Her interference is frustrating, as he was clearly talking to me. I clench my jaw and move a step toward Breyson in an effort to keep the girl excluded from our conversation. Then the memory of her bulging muscles makes me wince. Perhaps I shouldn't have my back to her.

Brey finally lifts his head and his eyes look right through me.

He takes a few calculated steps in my direction, his quick breathing audible in the otherwise silent room. Shock catches like a bubble in my throat as Brey's body passes right through mine.

This is a dream.

But then how did he know I was here?

I turn around to face him and this other girl. He grabs her hands, which seem to be covered in scars and scabs, and holds them in his own. His light blue eyes focus on hers with a ferocity that I've never seen. A knot forms in my stomach, but I don't know why. I look to the girl, the one who seems to have stolen my best friend. Her blue eyes, which are not nearly as pretty as his, look back in earnest.

"No," I murmur as I float backward, a movement that would have been a stumble if my body were really here.

The girl is me.

Her obvious strength is so foreign. I've never looked like that. I didn't even know it was possible to look like that. Her hair is short and mine is long, but it's her face that really confuses me. It's as if I'm looking at myself in ten years. But how can that be? I've never had a dream that far out before.

"It didn't end with him," Brey says to dream-Mercer, pulling me out of my speculation.

Dream-Mercer bows her head, so her forehead leans against Brey's chest. The movement highlights her jawline. How is it possible that even her jaw is sculpted like that? Her shoulders hitch suddenly as she takes a quick breath. Perhaps she'd have an easier time hiding her tears if not for the complete silence surrounding them in this cold, metal room.

"Hey," Brey says in a gentle tone, "don't cry. I'll be back." He caresses the side of her face, resting his pointer finger under her chin and then lifting it so that her tear-stained eyes are forced to meet his own. “Besides, you need to be here. You’re the only one who can change his mind. He won’t listen to anyone else.”

“You don’t know that.” But even I can hear the defeat in her voice. I desperately want to know what they’re talking about, but I also feel the urge to turn my back so they can be alone. I’ve never witnessed anything so intimate.

Brey smiles like he wants to say something else but isn’t sure whether it’s appropriate. He takes a deep breath and continues holding her face.

“What I do know,” he says with too much gentleness in his voice, “is how I feel about you, which you seem to want to avoid all the time.” A half-smile tugs at his lips.

“Brey…” dream-Mercer protests while pushing her hands against his chest in a weak effort to force him away. He doesn’t allow it, tightening their embrace and grunting an almost amused laugh at her efforts. My mind is spinning with this turn of events. I feel unprepared to process what’s happening and frustrated that my subconscious is springing this on me out of nowhere.

“It’s never a good time, Mercer.” There’s a bite to his response with a pain that’s tangible. It seems that they’ve had this conversation before.

She chews on her lower lip and Brey seems to have noticed because he watches her closely until she stops.

Something feels almost alive between them as their heads move together with a magnetic pull.

My chest warms and I have to look away. Although I’m watching my future, it feels oddly inappropriate for me to witness this. I can hear them as their mouths meet and I make a face that nobody can see. When it stops, I open my eyes slowly.

Except, we’re not in the room anymore. I’m in the back of a van, but the seats are all pulled out and instead, benches line the wall around a table that's placed in the middle. Grids and diagrams are scattered around the table, and despite how much space there is, the air feels tight.

"Congratulations on your graduation," a man says. He's sitting near the front divider that separates us from the driver. "After your success, you'll have independence and freedom. The Domain thanks you for your service."

His words make no sense and as I replay them, I get more confused.

Dream-Mercer stands, along with the only other passenger in the back. The van shifts under his movement and a gasp escapes me at the shock of realizing it's JC. He's five times bigger than what I know him to be.

Dream-Mercer follows JC out the side door of the van and I have no choice but to trail them. The air is crisp and a chill runs through me. I'm sure if I were really here, I'd be able to see my breath in the air. The first snow must be quickly approaching based on how bare the trees are.

The man who spoke stays back in the van while dream-Mercer and JC walk through the dark. We're in a nondescript neighborhood, although the homes don't look anything like what I'm used to.

"No funny business, Lewis," JC says quietly. It seems like most of the houses are fast asleep.

"You know what they say… third time's the charm," my dream-self replies. I can't help but think she should have a touch more fear in her voice given the mass of a human who she's talking to.

I have no idea what her words mean.

JC seems to be overcome with fury and he turns to her before gripping both of her shoulders tightly.

"I'm not kidding," he says. Spit flies from his mouth as he tries to speak through a clenched jaw. "None of that projecting stuff. No warning them. They both die. You have to pull the trigger. We're graduating today. End of story."

His words have a far greater impact on me than they do on my dream-self. I have no idea what he means by projecting, but the last part of his demand still rings in my ear. Why would I ever agree to end a life? With JC of all people?

I'm forced to follow both of them as they close in on one of the houses. I would have no way of knowing which house they were going to approach, and frankly, I'm not sure how they can even be certain that they've chosen the right one; the homes all look so similar.

JC's hand closes around the doorknob to the front and he turns it violently. It seemingly opens without issue, and I have no idea why these people wouldn't lock their door at night, although we never lock our door either.

JC looks to dream-Mercer and points to himself, then the room on the left. He then points to her and the hallway. She nods and I follow her through the hall, once more letting my confusion ring loudly in my ears.

The house is nicely decorated, with items that are much more modern than what Aunt Pam has. I join dream-Mercer through the long hall, and we come to the kitchen, which seems to join the room JC had gone in because he meets us there.

"Clear," he says.

"Clear," she says back.

I rub the back at my neck and consider what I'm seeing. My questions outnumber answers at this point, but I don't have any other choice than to continue following along.

JC takes the lead as we walk back down the hall and he

approaches the stairs. He takes them so quietly that I have to wonder how someone so big can sound so small.

On the second level, there are several doors. JC and dream-Mercer approach one after another, opening them to find empty rooms beyond.

Finally, they reach the last closed door.

My gut churns at the knowledge that whoever is behind it is who dream-Mercer is after.

JC stands to the side and motions a count to three before shoving it open with his foot.

Just as I suspected, the entire house is asleep. Upon hearing the alarming noise of JC's foot to the door, a woman with dark brown hair sits up in her bed. She's clearly disoriented having just woken up, but her eyes are on us as she tries to become more alert. A mound next to her starts to stir under the blankets as JC raises the gun he's been holding in front of him and fires it at the woman without a second thought.

A scream escapes me and I clap a hand over my mouth. It happened so fast that I hardly understand what I'm watching. I've never seen someone die before and terror claws at my chest while reasoning yells at me to find a way to explain that I'm not actually seeing this.

The woman slumps over, crimson flowing out of the spot on her forehead that JC hit, as if to force me to acknowledge that this is actually happening.

"Your turn," JC says to dream-Mercer as she holds her gun pointed at the bed. She doesn't seem to have the same determination that he did.

"He's just a boy," she says back to JC.

My head whips toward the bed, confused. I had thought the mound of moving blankets was the woman's husband, but dream-

Mercer is right. A little boy, no older than five, starts crying as the blood from his mother stains the white sheets.

"Mommy," he cries out and my heart twists into a vice at the noise.

I want to go to him and tell him that it'll be okay, and frustration burns in me that dream-Mercer isn't doing just that.

"Do it, Lewis," JC says again.

I glare at him, urging her to turn the weapon on him instead.

The boy cries over their argument, calling out, "Mommy, Mommy," as if he could wake her up somehow through his pleas.

"No," dream-Mercer says, finally agreeing with me. "What's he going to do, kill me?"

I tilt my head at her question, wondering how she could question if a child would kill her.

Except JC almost seems to relish that response. His answering smile gives me chills as he says, "How stupid are you to think it'd be your death. We both know that's not who he'll kill."

"Mommy," the boy cries again, this time letting out a choked noise that makes it sound like his broken heart is going to suffocate him.

JC's words make no sense to me. This entire situation makes no sense to me. I want to wake up. I want to leave here.

But instead, I watch as my dream-self focuses on the gun, tightening her grip. It's not aimed at JC, but at the small boy who's still crying in the bed. My heart shatters at the image of myself doing something so utterly despicable and I shut my eyes to keep the image away. I plug my ears and wait for the shot to fire.

A voice becomes clearer, and I realize that it must be someone awake, trying to pull me to consciousness. I want to ignore her so that I can mourn this boy in peace, but I can't.

Finally, as if my body were trying to protect me from my own memories for as long as possible, the events leading up to now surge back like a floodgate being ripped open. My memories burn with the smell of smoke and a feeling of helplessness sinks in.

My eyes flutter at the same time that I jerk upright. My head spins from the sudden movement, but I try to ignore the discomfort and focus.

I can still see that little boy from my dream, crying over his mother. It feels like every time I blink, I can picture my future-self holding up the gun, pointing it at an innocent child.

"Oh!" The owner of the shrill voice moves from where she stands near me to sit on the end of the bed I'm in. She's small but squat, with eyes that appear to be as wide as her face, lined with ringlets of dark brown hair, so I focus on her and this room.

As I look around, I notice that I'm in the nicest bed I've ever seen. It's plush and seems to melt around my body, supplying a strong feeling of comfort. I'm surrounded by white pillows, and I'm covered with a down comforter, keeping the warmth around my body. Heat rises through me, and the blanket suddenly feels like a prison. It's too hot. I need to get out.

"Hi." When she talks, her hair has a way of bouncing up and down. "I would have woken you up soon. You looked like you were having a nightmare." Her voice is high, like she's singing when she speaks, making it difficult to take her seriously.

I look at her wide eyes but don't respond. I've never seen this room before and I have more important things to figure out.

My nice bed isn't the only one. There are six in here, all of them either occupied or recently slept in, by the looks of it. The walls are a sickening shade of pink, not like the pink at home, but brighter, newer. The focal point is a massive, crystal chandelier on the high ceiling.

"Do you know where we are?" My voice is broken from sleep.

"No, but I expect we'll find out soon," she informs me. "There are clothes in your armoire for you to change into."

I follow her gaze to the side of my bed. Sure enough, a tall, oak closet is next to it. There's one next to every bed.

The girl stands, pulling my attention back, and does a small twirl. She wears simple gray pants and a long-sleeved gray shirt with a single pocket on the front. The outfit is familiar.

"Gray hasn't ever been my color, but I don't think these are too bad," she chirps, seemingly determined to be helpful, maybe too helpful.

These clothes were in my first dream. When I—I have to stop myself from remembering the kiss with Brey. My cheeks grow warm, and I pray that this girl won't be able to notice.

I look down at what I'm wearing. I still have on jeans and the blue shirt with buttons that started this nightmare. I'm covered in grass stains and dirt, making me look wildly out of place in the otherwise pristine bed. The memory makes me flex my right foot and pain surges up my leg. I wince and the girl flutters to my side.

"It's okay! The clothes aren't that bad, and yours are gross anyway. Can I help you change?" She extends her arms in my direction.

"No thanks." I grit my teeth. There's no way I'm putting on their clothes.

I rip the comforter off, prepared to storm out, if only my foot would allow it. The plush carpet swallows my toes, offering spongy softness. Gingerly, I test the pain with a few steps.

"The bathroom is over there." She points to a side of the room. Definitely overly helpful.

"What's that door to?" I nod in the other direction to the only other door.

"I don't know, it's locked." She smiles at this information.

I can see the occupants of two of the beds now. Jaylee and Lottie, the sisters, are stirring in their sleep but haven't woken up yet. My stomach drops at the sight of them. I don't know them very well, but this can't all be a coincidence.

"Do you know why we're here?" I ask the girl on my bed.

"The summer program." Her hands fidget in her lap and she seems to slump over ever so slightly, refusing to look at me. I want to know what she could be hiding, but it seems too argumentative to ask outright.

"What's the last thing you remember?" I push for anything useful.

"I was brought into the school office, and they told me about the program. They needed to do a blood test to make sure that I was up to date…" She speaks too fast. "That's the last thing I remember." She meets my eyes and smiles; her hands have relaxed in her lap.

Was the scene at my school different than what I saw in my dream since I wasn't there to ask about summer school? Did Brey simply cooperate because I wasn't there to feed into his suspicions?

"Anyway," the girl says, "I'm Trinka." She smiles widely. Even when she smiles, her eyes are the most prominent part of her face.

"Mercer." I acknowledge with a nod. She opens her mouth to say something else but is interrupted by the bathroom door opening.

Two girls walk out, giggling. They look like the exact same person, both with red hair and a face of freckles. They must be twins, but unlike Lizzy and me, they're identical.

The girls notice that I'm awake and size me up in a way that is familiar, given my high school experiences. I decide that now's as good a time as any to attempt walking on my injured foot. Crossing the dormitory is excruciating. To my dismay, Trinka follows me.

"Sorry," she whispers as we enter the large dorm-style bathroom with just as much girly décor as the bedroom. "Ginger one and two scare me and I don't like being alone with them." I can't help my smirk at her nickname for the girls. At least she has the courtesy of knowing it's weird that she won't leave me alone.

I let my mind wander. I need to get to Brey and tell him what happened, but if that other door is locked, then I don't see how I'm going to do that. I guess I'll just play along until I can make a move. The good news about those strange dreams is that they must not have plans to kill us if I'm seeing the future that far out.

In the privacy of the bathroom stall, I examine the extent of damage on my foot. It seems like it might be my ankle and not the foot itself, which could be a good thing, but I have zero medical background to confirm that.

When we enter the dorm again, Lottie and Jaylee are awake and freshly dressed. Lottie's long hair looks smooth and perfect, but Jaylee's cropped style is completely messed up. They're talking to each other and it's apparent that they aren't afraid either, which doesn't make sense if they were taken in the same way I thought they were. Everyone is in the sickening gray clothes they've been given.

The sisters look to me, and their eyes widen.

"What are you doing here?" Jaylee demands. Her mouth

pulls down at the corners and her voice is accusatory, far more than is warranted in this situation. Her question has silenced the room and the two redheads are now paying attention.

"Same thing as you, I suppose." I try to hide the pain in each step as I cross the space. At least the shag carpet provides some relief as it softens the steps and weaves between my toes.

I don't want to change clothing but fighting their rules might be more dangerous than simply trying to fit in at this point. Although I cannot follow all their rules. I won't let that dream of the boy and his mother become my reality.

Reluctantly, I cross to my armoire and open the heavy wooden doors. Trinka was right. Everything is a shade of gray.

My fingers brush over the options and I carelessly select a pair of pants and short-sleeved shirt. They're exactly my size. I fight the nausea that wells inside me at how creepy that is. I put the clothes on, frustrated at how much it hurts my foot to thread it through the pant leg.

A clicking noise pulls my attention to the door that was previously locked.

It opens and a tall, dark-skinned girl walks in. She's strikingly beautiful, and everything about her is intimidating. I try to make a mental note of her movements.

"Oh good," she says to the group, although her eyes linger on me before looking away. "You're up, that'll make things easy."

Nobody moves.

"My name is Cynthia Livingston and I'll be showing you around. I'm a student here as well, I started a year ago. If everyone's ready, we can get going." Her hair is fluffed out on top of her head and she pulls at a strand as she waits for us.

The other girls scramble to finish what they were doing

before closing in around Cynthia. Trinka moves to follow, but glances back at me, then stays by my side. Evidently, she's determined to make us companions here.

"This is your dormitory," Cynthia says. "I see you've found your things. If you would, please follow me."

Trinka and I are the last to exit. I wish I could say it's because I'm not interested in following this girl around, but really, it's because my foot is throbbing and I feel that walking on it is going to do further damage.

We enter a long, narrow hallway filled with other doors but no windows or indications of where we are. Cynthia swings her arms as she leads the group.

"This is the girl wing," Cynthia explains. "All these doors are dorms."

Her statement begs the question of how many of us are in here. Were we all kidnapped?

We follow her down the hallway to a large set of metal doors.

She pushes them open and I hear gasps from the other girls as my breath catches in my throat.

The room is a big recreational room, painted a dark, metallic gray. Couches and armchairs are grouped together in different sections. There are dartboards, ping-pong tables, board games and more.

It's unlike anything I knew existed in this world; nothing that any of us have ever seen before.

"Is that a television?" One of the gingers pushes forward while asking. Of course, nobody is used to watching anything but the small, government-issued, black and white televisions at home. This one is large and playing something colorful and animated.

Cynthia turns to face us, evidently familiar with this

reaction. She raises her arms and gestures around her at the room.

"Welcome to the Domain."

Chapter Six

The hair stands up on my arms, as if it can feel the electricity running through the group. I swallow to try and push down the curiosity that I can feel bubbling inside me at the sound of laughter.

The walls give the gray, metal space an enclosed feeling, despite how very large it is. If I yelled, I doubt someone on the other end would hear me, that's how far away they are.

"This is where you'll spend most of your time," Cynthia continues. "It's called the Eye. We're all in the same boat, so we're expected to self-regulate. If you know your peer is acting out, you should report it. This room is the Eye because hopefully, someone will always be watching for signs of insubordination, to keep us all at our best."

I flex my jaw, making an audible snap when my teeth clench. I take a controlled breath through my nose to calm down my racing heart and try to focus on the fact that at least it doesn't look like they'll be killing us any time soon.

I make eye contact with the two redheads. One of them gives me a satisfied smirk. It doesn't take a genius to figure out they're giddy with anticipation to find a reason to "self-regulate" my behavior.

I stay rooted to my spot, letting the other girls move forward so there's a decent amount of room between Cynthia and me.

Only when I'm in the very back, do I shuffle my feet to follow.

Cynthia's pace is slow and intentional. She wants us to take in our surroundings and it's obvious why. This room would entice anybody to want to stay. Anybody but me, that is. I suppose the effect isn't as strong after seeing what I saw, after learning of what they'll make me do in the future.

I glance to my left, keeping my head down in the process. A green beanbag is large enough that three kids are comfortably in the middle of it. There's a chess board on the table nearby and two people are moving pieces while the three in the beanbag laugh.

To my right, two students bend over a table that has poles sticking out of it. They grasp the poles to make little men move on the table. One of them must score because he jumps up and down while the other boy scowls.

"Oh, sorry," I mutter after I bump into a man in a suit.

My body is pushed back from the force, while the bulky man hardly moves. He reaches his arm out to steady me, before dropping it and moving on without a second glance. Looking around, there are several men in suits walking around the room without a purpose. Some of them are older, but all have a stitched eye on their jacket. They seem to be patrolling in pairs; side by side, regulating the self-regulating.

It's hard to make out the murmurs in our group, but the excitement doesn't seem to need verbal communication. Judging by our ages, everybody was born around the time I was, which means we've only known society after the changes of the Censorship. We only know a little of how things were prior to the Censorship thanks to whispered conversations, but it's hard to imagine a place where teachers aren't making the highest salary, televisions exist in every room of the house and food isn't made up of vegetables.

As one of the guards passes me, I can't help but wonder… does he know he's an accomplice in these kidnappings? Does he know what we're going to be made to do? My mind jumps to the dream I saw and how we broke down the bedroom door. My stomach turns as I think about what happened next. I squeeze my eyes tight to try and block the image, but the crying boy seems to appear immediately. A clamminess breaks out over my neck and arms, threatening to make me sick on the floor.

I'm missing a huge piece of information. I want to ignore the ending of my dream as much as possible. There's no way that will be my future. I won't let it happen. But, even that aside, there's more. JC said something about projection, and dream-Mercer didn't seem confused. But I've never done that before.

I grind my teeth at the obvious answer: I'm going to develop another ability.

I pick up my pace, opening my eyes and breathing through my nose slowly to calm myself. It's not safe to think about this right now or right here.

Several kids directly to my right are laughing and it pulls me back. I try to focus on their conversation as my heart rate slows.

"You did not do that. Connor already ratted you out," a pale boy announces with humor in his tone.

Everyone is in gray, except the guards, who wear black. It gives a militant feeling, despite the laughter.

"There are two sets of stairs and two sets of elevators." Cynthia's voice drowns out the conversation and points to the far ends of the Eye.

I turn around and notice a door near where our dormitory hall is.

None of the kids seem bothered by the fact that they're in this room. Surely, that must mean they're here by choice. I swallow and the movement is thick, like my body is trying to get me to realize something that I don't want to acknowledge.

"Please head up the stairs to floor four." Cynthia opens a metal door and stands to the side. I pretend not to notice the way her dark eyes look down to my toes and then back to my face when I pass her.

There are several floors above us, but only one below. If Cynthia weren't directly behind me, I'd take my chances and race down to the lower level to find the exit.

She lets out a frustrated cough, so I jog up the rest of the stairs before her annoyance turns into something more, regretting the movement as my foot protests.

The cold metal railing seems to freeze into my hand, giving me a chill. I wish I had grabbed one of the gray long-sleeved shirts instead of leaving my arms exposed.

The smell of disinfectant and cleaner fills the air, making me feel a little dizzy as we enter the hall.

The hallway is short and industrial. The image makes my chest constrict and it takes several moments for me to realize it's because it's making me feel claustrophobic.

Surely, they intentionally chose to build this place without windows, which begs the questions: why are they trying to keep us from seeing the outside and from finding out where we are?

I follow the girls who have already started venturing down the hall. We walk by the other closed doors with our destination clearly marked. The door at the very end of the hall stands open and voices bleed into where we are.

"What's through these?" I ask Cynthia, gesturing to the doors on both sides of the hall. A few of the girls closest to us, including Trinka, turn to hear the answer.

"Everything you need to know will be told to you. No point

asking now." Cynthia tries to keep her voice low, but her anger is making it louder than she wants.

I narrow my eyes in return.

"Is it normal for someone to be kidnapped and *not* ask questions?" I'm loud, getting the attention of the rest of the girls who hadn't been listening. I realize my hands are clenched too tight at my sides. I try to release them to alleviate the pain from my fingernails digging into my palms.

"Kidnapped?" Trinka stammers.

I don't look away from Cynthia, but I can imagine Trinka's round eyes bulging out of her head.

The moment seems to suspend in mid-air while nobody says anything. Someone comes up and grabs my hand. Their fingers soothingly close around my own, trying to get me to break the eye contact that seems to be turning into a deadly game of chicken.

"Mercer, we weren't kidnapped. You'll see!" Trinka's voice shakes with a weariness that she shouldn't carry on my behalf, considering I just met her.

I concede and turn my head to look at her. It's enough of a pause to let Cynthia get out of the situation.

"This is where I leave you," Cynthia says through clenched teeth when we reach the open door.

I bring up the rear and as I move to pass her, she grabs my arm.

"Questions will have you making enemies very quickly." Her jaw barely moves. "You'd be surprised what we already know about you. You might want to just close your mouth and try to behave."

I narrow my eyes at her and I swear my chest is radiating heat. I consider some witty response, but when I open my mouth to deliver it, she releases my arm and walks away from me so quickly that I'm left standing at the door's entrance with my mouth still hanging open.

I take a deep breath and try once more to unclench my fists. My palms are an angry pink and her words make my mind spiral. What could they know? And who told them? What does that mean for my future?

The room is long and lit with artificial lighting, likely to make up for the lack of windows. The chill from the stairwell permeates the air, even though the room is full of people. The smell of cleaner is even stronger in here. Rows of wooden benches face the front, all full of kids my age. The girls from my dorm are seated in one of the back rows, but Trinka waited for me by the door. We take our seats by the gingers.

At the front of the room, a group of adults stand and watch us. Several of them are in black suits. A handful are in normal clothing. One of them is in a sweater vest. His deep wrinkles and gray hair suggest that he's easily the oldest in the group and his eyes peer out at me over square glasses. Even after I make eye contact and raise an eyebrow, he takes far too long to look away. A chill runs down my spine, the hair rising on my arms, and I'm not sure if it's from the temperature.

"Hey." Brey's voice interrupts my analysis, making my heart jump out of my chest in the process. *"I'm a few rows in front of you. Saw you walk in."*

My cheeks burn, so I clench my jaw and I drop my chin. Embarrassment grips my stomach. I don't know how I can look him in the eye after everything. After all, I wasn't fast enough to save him. I had decided to run, knowing they had him.

"You weren't at our meeting place or at school," he thinks to me. There's a note of sadness in his tone. Or maybe that's my

own imagination and guilt.

"What are you doing?" Trinka asks in an urgent whisper. Her sweaty hand is on mine again as she tries to pull me down. I can tell she's using all the strength she can muster, but I could fight her if I wanted to. In my distraction, I had started lifting myself up in the seat to find Breyson. I'm nearly standing now, and the movement has gained the attention of a lot of my peers. A girl near me narrows her eyes before turning back to the front of the room.

"Nothing." I sink back down to the smooth, wooden bench, shaking my head. But my eyes give away the lie as they continue to scan the backs of the heads in front of us. Where is that blond hair that sticks up in strange directions after he messes with it? Nobody is turning around anymore, and Brey's voice doesn't come again, adding to my suspicion that he's mad.

"I think you should try to follow their rules," Trinka continues. I break my search to look at her. She lets her eyes dart between the adults in the front and me.

The older man has stopped staring at me, allowing me to look closer at the group. Everyone has a single eye stitched to their jacket.

"Did you know they were government?" I ask Trinka.

"What?" she whispers back without fully giving me her attention.

I nod my head to the front of the room. "The Eramica symbol."

"Makes sense, doesn't it?" she says like it's obvious. "Schools are regulated by Eramica."

I don't have the heart to tell her this isn't a school. Whatever it is, clearly it's regulated by our overcontrolling government, the same government we thought wanted us dead.

Before we can continue the conversation, a tall man with jet-black hair walks into the room with calculated steps, his shoes greeting the floor with a slow staccato that echoes his authority. The smell of aftershave follows him, drifting into the rows on either side. Although nobody has signaled that we were waiting for him, the voices around us quiet down.

"Welcome!" he yells as he gets to the front, turning to face us with an award-winning smile. "My name is Stealth and I'm the director of the Domain." His voice is silky and sure, and I wonder how he's able to speak while also maintaining the obviously artificial smile. "Thank you so much for your cooperation in traveling here. We have to keep our location a secret, for your own protection, and most of you played your parts fantastically, which leads me to believe you'll be a good fit here."

It seems silly to think his words are directed at me, but when his eyes pass over mine, his smile falters for the briefest of moments. I'm assuming it wasn't their plan to have to chase me to my home, off a roof and across my yard.

"Now, you were brought here under the pretense of summer school, but I'm here to tell you that's not the case." My eyebrows pull together. "We know that you're Unnaturals."

I can feel the collective breath that's being held. Despite the nervous energy making my skin prickle, Trinka seems to be calm next to me. A satisfied grin is plastered across her face and her eyes shine with the same sparkle that's occupied them since we met.

"You've been taught to fear who you really are, but that has changed!" Stealth's voice booms through the silence with a practiced authority. "We know that you didn't *ask* for this!"

Trinka sits up straighter next to me.

"We have, with the backing of Eramica, created this place to give you freedom and to help you learn how to control your real self. You'll continue your education, but you'll also learn how to use your ability. You can be who you truly are here."

Applause and cheering have made it impossible to hear him, so he stops for a moment and gives us the big smile again. I can't help but feel a little bitter that our lives were safe this entire time and they didn't tell us. How differently would I have lived if the threat of death wasn't dictating my every move?

Trinka is clapping wildly next to me, her arms flailing with little control.

Eramica, the government we've been taught to fear our entire lives, is the one responsible for this. Nobody is going to look for the kidnapped victims when the only remaining force of power is the one to have locked us away.

"A few rules and guidelines for your safety, and then I'll let you get to dinner, as I'm sure you're famished."

The room quiets after a few more hoots while I consider if I was taken today, just hours ago, or if they forced us to sleep for the last day and a half. My stomach grumbles as if to answer. Trinka is at the edge of her seat again, and I wonder how that can be comfortable with the sharp edge of the wooden bench.

"Depending on your success, your teachers," he motions to the people wearing normal clothing, "and I will graduate you from the program, at which time you can choose to live in the Domain as a guard, or you can continue your life in the real world."

Suddenly, I can't see past my dream. His announcement of graduation brings me right back as if I'm walking across that yard, about to embark on the worst thing I could ever do in life. JC's words were so clear when he growled, "*They both die. You*

have to pull the trigger. We're graduating today. End of story."
Was that my graduation? If so, I already know that I want no part of it. Based on Stealth's explanation, that might mean I'm stuck here.

Stealth continues, despite my private breakdown. "We're going to train you so you can serve your country. There are threats all around us. Specific groups exist just to take us down. With your help, we can create a better tomorrow."

I shift in my seat as the static starts to burn in my chest. My body aches from sitting on the bench this long, or maybe it's just my anxiety making me feel like I need to get up.

"This place operates because its residents *want* to be here and *want* it to be successful. After living your lives in hiding, you can finally be free. In order for that to work, you must treat this as your home. You must take action if somebody threatens the lifestyle of your home, and you must protect your home at all costs."

My throat dries and I try to swallow. Based on Cynthia's reaction, I have a feeling that they already view me as a threat to this "home".

They're not wrong.

After a few more instructions, he dismisses us but I'm not listening. We rise to leave, and I try to wait for Brey, to find him or at least meet his gaze. But the crowd forces me to shuffle out.

The narrow hallway doesn't provide more room to find him, but I step out of the way, so everyone can file past me. My back pushes against one of the metal doors, making me shiver from the cool touch against my thin shirt. I fight the urge to twist the handle and see what's on the other side.

"Now what are you doing?" Trinka whines. I look behind me to see that she's stepped to the side, too.

"I think I saw my friend." I can hear the annoyance in my tone at her inability to leave me alone.

"Oh! Cool!" she chirps.

"You should go on to dinner. I'll meet you there."

Silence greets me and I turn to see if she's left; instead, I find tears forming in her eyes.

"Or you can stay," I offer quickly, unsure why this girl's feelings have an impact on me. She smiles immediately in response to my suggestion and the whites of her eyes show.

"What does she look like?" Trinka asks. "I'll help look."

"He," I correct her.

I'm about to tell her about Brey when his eyes find mine. His face breaks into a half-smile, but it isn't as deep as I'm used to. Either way, I'm so grateful to see it again.

"Hey," he thinks to me.

I smile, catching the attention of the people nearest us, but I don't care.

Brey closes the final few steps and embraces me tightly. He also chose a t-shirt instead of the longer-sleeved options, but I'm grateful as our naked arms touch and the heat from his body warms me for what feels like the first time since I woke up. I breathe in the scent of him, wrinkling my nose at the missing familiarity of his mom's detergent. These clothes smell too much like florals and sweat.

"I didn't know what to do," I tell him urgently without waiting for a more appropriate time. "I tried to get there and when I didn't… I was going to come back for you. I—" A sob cuts me off but I'm glad.

"It's okay." His eyes soften, and his hands continue to hold me by both arms, burning the feeling of his touch onto my skin.

"I have so much to tell you, they—" I try to think of a way

to tell him that this place is going to end up making me murder a kid, but that just doesn't seem like something you casually blurt out.

I meet his eyes. The way he looks at me makes my stomach turn. Last time I saw our faces this close... I have to stop myself from thinking about the future kiss I saw as my cheeks blush and I look at my shoes to hide my reaction.

Not that my vision will come true any time soon. My hair was short, and those muscles were so defined that I didn't even recognize myself.

"Hi!" a high-pitched voice interrupts. "I'm Trinka."

She looks at me, her eyes widening as I brush away the tear that has fallen down. Unbeknownst to him, she grabs my hand and gives it a light squeeze. I don't know why, but I'm starting to feel like her presence is comforting, despite how annoyed I was with her initially.

We begin our walk to wherever the food is, my stomach grumbling along the way.

"So, how do we get out of here?" I say to the both of them. Brey's head whips in my direction and confusion breaks across his face before morphing into anger.

"Why would we ever want to leave?" he asks me with too much hostility.

Chapter Seven

It takes the rest of the walk down the hall to fix my composure after his words. I don't offer any other attempts to resolve the tension between us, so he drags me along in silence.

I favor my injured foot, trying to keep it in a certain position and only putting weight on it when I have to. A creative shuffle keeps the pain at bay despite the hurried bodies around us, but things get worse on the stairs. I slow down and grab the cold, metal railing for support. My hand is clammy from the sweaty nervousness of seconds ago, making my grip slick.

"What?" Brey turns around. The anger from his earlier statement ebbs in his reaction. "What is it?" His hand flutters with a moment's hesitation before he grabs my waist.

Trinka moves aside to let the flow of those descending the stairs pass while she stands right next to Brey. She frowns at the interaction.

"I hurt my foot," I say to him.

Trinka's eyes narrow but she doesn't speak.

"What happened?" Brey asks out loud. I'm grateful he isn't using his ability in front of Trinka. I want her to feel included, though I'm not sure why.

"There was… an incident." He studies my face while I look at the people passing us.

Brey nods and Trinka seems to accept his movement. They both guide me down the rest of the stairs without another word.

We don't walk back to the main level, or 'Eye,' as Cynthia

called it. Instead, we follow everyone to another floor, one just above the Eye, that leads to a single long hallway with no doorways. The hallway isn't in the same direction as the one we were just in, which is odd, considering this building just has pieces jutting out every which way.

I'm relieved that this floor doesn't smell like cleaning products but instead a thousand delicious and flavorful scents. My mouth begins to water as my stomach audibly grumbles its agreement to where we are heading. I'm famished, and I wonder again how long it's been since we were taken and since I last ate.

"This place seems like a maze, doesn't it?" I ask Brey and Trinka. I'm trying to create a map in my head, but it's proving more difficult than I thought. It doesn't help that all the halls have the same steel, monochrome look.

"This place is amazing," Trinka answers, like she's trying to correct my thoughts. Her eyes widen as she looks around the gray hallway that we're in.

I take a deep breath and try to meet Brey's eyes, but he doesn't notice, too busy taking in our surroundings.

"What if they're not telling us everything?" I offer.

"Do you know something?" Brey asks me silently, finally giving me his attention.

Trinka, who is unaware of the interaction Brey and I just had, grabs my hand while we walk.

"I think maybe you're looking for a reason to not like it here, but you should really just..." She pauses and takes a breath, shifting her eyes around the floor while she searches for words. "They're not against us. I can tell you more later, but just trust me." She lowers her chin and looks at me through her eyelashes.

We're unable to answer her anyway because at that same moment, we walk into an open space filled with sleek, black tables. It's a tall room and chandeliers hang from the ceiling above every table. There aren't any windows, and their absence is even more pronounced given the tall walls. It's impossible to make out any specific conversation, since all the tables are filled with students engaged in different topics.

"This doesn't make sense," I mumble. "Why aren't there windows. Why are they hiding our location from us?"

"That's quite the leap," Brey says in a tone too quiet for Trinka to hear. "Maybe we're just in the middle of whatever building we're in."

There's a shred of warning in his voice, but when I don't agree with him, he sighs and gives me a sympathetic look.

I walk with them across the space, thinking about what dinner might be, what aromas could be surrounding us in such an inviting way, until I stop suddenly.

There, sitting at a table not far from us, is Varick Dolion with JC.

When Eramica started learning of the existence of Unnaturals, they found a pattern. Mothers who were exposed to excessive chemicals were usually the ones who gave birth to an Unnatural.

Eventually, Eramica went after any children born to cancer patients.

JC's mother had cancer before he was born. She recovered eventually, although she still died a few years later, but I remember when Eramica took JC for several weeks to interrogate him. It was a big deal at the time as everyone considered whether or not an Unnatural existed in our sliver of the B Region. Eramica had cleared JC after a few weeks.

They were wrong, since he's sitting in front of me, although his presence isn't that surprising, given the dream of our graduation together, but Varick Dolion…

Brey must not have seen them because his front slams into my back, making me take a painful step forward to catch myself.

"What—" he starts to ask, but his voice cuts off when he sees them, too.

"Did you know?" I ask. He knows who I'm talking about. He and Varick were best friends before my parents died and my aunt and uncle sent me to the school.

"No." His voice is threatening. "But he knew about me."

I tug his arm away at the same time JC and Varick seem to notice us.

Off the dining room, a smaller serving area sits with buffet tables and food already plated. The room is shaped in a circle so you can walk around while looking at all the options. Workers stand behind the counter with a smile and a little, singular eye stitched into their chef jackets.

"Wow," Brey mutters as the scents hit us.

I take a deep breath, inhaling everything, like it might somehow get snatched away from me. Back home, unless you were from a privileged family, food consisted of the cheapest vegetables and grains. There was no variation, which meant there was never any flavor.

The serving stations have menu cards in front of them, showing the ingredients and nutritional data. I walk up to the first window and read *Bi Bim Bop*. I've never heard of it, but I recognize some of the ingredients, so I grab a bowl. It's warm in my hands, having remained heated by the lamps.

This serving is more than enough to fill me. I'm unfortunately accustomed to never eating enough food, so my stomach won't demand much. That's what happens when there simply isn't enough money for your family. But I follow Brey anyway and look at the other offerings. Brey grabs a cauliflower pizza, which sounds fake. I've never had pizza, but I've read about it, and nobody ever mentions cauliflower. Trinka takes a chicken dish that doesn't have many vegetables.

We walk back to the dining room and our eyes scan for a table. I follow Brey without question, as he leads us to a spot in the far corner.

It's frustrating that the food is the best I've ever tasted. My mouth seems to explode in happiness as it's introduced to flavors. I wonder if this follows the 'Two Steps Are Best' process, like they preach it should, or if the Domain is simply above the Eramica rules. We scarf down our meals in silence until Brey and Trinka go get seconds.

I push my chair back and look around, once more feeling confused by where we could be and how I can get out. My fingers rise to my temple, and I start rubbing away a headache.

Brey's empty chair pulls out from the table and Valor, Varick's younger and much more likeable brother, takes a seat without invitation.

"Hey stranger," he greets me.

Valor and I have never been particularly close, but I have always liked him. Valor is one of the few people who can stand up to JC and survive to talk about it. Everyone has a soft spot for Valor.

"Hi Valor," I say, and despite hating this place, I smile because of my full belly.

Valor is shorter than his brother, but not by much. They're both well over six feet. Unlike Varick, Valor keeps his hair cut at a more reasonable length. They both share the same tanned skin, defined jaw, and deep brown eyes that can either seem kind and warm, or dark and dangerous.

"So, you too, huh?" He leans toward me, eyebrows raised. A

slow smile builds across his face, revealing dimples deeply set into his cheeks. His fingers drum on the table in front of me, the noise of the soft thumps pulls my attention.

"Varick wasn't in the office and neither were you. How are you here?" I expect to see panic cross his features, but his calm expression never waivers. In fact, he smiles at my words.

"What, do you think we had to be chased off a roof too?" The smile turns into a smirk, but his eyes continue to hold the sparkle of curiosity.

"How do you—" I start to ask, panic slowly creeping up inside me.

He cuts me off. "So many Unnaturals at one school. None of us ever knew about each other." His eyes wander around the cafeteria.

I follow his gaze to his brother, who sits with JC. Varick's head is distinctly leaning in our direction, but his eyes are fixed on a girl across from him.

I bite my lower lip. Valor's right. There were so many of us from home and we all lived our lives in fear, desperate to be free but forced to live trapped. What would have happened if we had known about each other?

"I don't suppose you wanna tell me what your ability is?" He interrupts my thoughts. I can't hide the shock that flashes across my face at the sudden change of topic.

I clench my jaw.

"Yeah, that's what I figured." He releases a long, low sigh. Then his eyes meet mine again and he smirks. "Wanna know mine?"

"You'd just tell me?" I challenge, trying to hold the same bravado in my voice that he does. I clear my throat and my fingers fiddle with the hem of my gray shirt.

"My ability is so worthless. In a world of superheroes, what a gift it is to be averagely gifted," he complains.

It's wild that he can make jokes about something like our abilities, as if we hadn't lived our entire lives in fear of talking about such a thing.

I can't help the snort of laughter that escapes me. The familiarity of Valor's joking provides a semblance of comfort and home. I let that feeling permeate my chest.

"All right, what can you do?" I ask, resting my chin on my laced fingers.

He raises his hand, so it's draped over the chair next to him, then he tilts his head.

"I can *sense* danger." He sighs. "I mean, what a waste."

I can't help but laugh again. The sound is deep and genuine as it rumbles my stomach.

"What does that even mean?" Not that I don't appreciate the melodramatic assessment of himself…

"Sense it but can't do shit about it." He rolls his eyes, and raises an eyebrow, ignoring my laughter. Then he leans forward and tilts his head in my direction. "Which brings me back to you." He narrows his gaze.

I let my laughter die down. I can feel my heartbeat in my temples again, so I lift my hand to start rubbing the pain away. Suddenly, the conversations in the cafeteria seem extraordinarily loud and interfering.

"What about me?" I counter, leaning back in my seat to look beyond Valor for where Brey is.

"You're dangerous." He pauses, and his eyes watch my every movement. We wait several seconds. I don't know if he wants me to say something, but I can't think of any words that make sense in this situation. Finally, he winks. "Good for you."

I don't know what it means to be dangerous according to Valor, but in a place like this, it can't be good.

"Did you tell them that?" I ask him in a clipped voice with a nod to his brother's table.

"Nah," he responds quickly, shaking his head. His hand runs through his hair in a way that I've seen Varick do, though Valor doesn't need to with how short his is. "My brother may have bought into the Domain, but I haven't. I don't want to be here any more than I imagine you do." He pauses and looks around for something.

My eyes narrow again. Is he insinuating he had a choice in the matter? Or that he knew about it prior?

Brey and Trinka reach us before I can ask Valor anything else. Valor winks at me, then stands from the table, allowing Brey to take the same seat that he just stood from.

"Sorry bro," Valor says to Brey, patting him on the shoulder. "I was just leaving."

"Who was he?" Trinka asks in a low voice while watching Valor walk away.

I open my mouth to answer, but Brey cuts me off.

"What did he want?" Brey's voice is colder than I've recently heard, which is strange since he also likes Valor.

"I'm not sure," I answer honestly.

My mind reels from the information that I've just been given. I desperately want to talk to Brey about it so we can dissect it together. Instead, I stay quiet as they eat.

"I can't walk this fast," I protest as Brey drags me down the stairs after dinner.

"Sorry," he mumbles.

He guides me back down to the Eye, this time much slower. My winces only come every few steps, but toward the end of the stairwell, he's nearly lifting me entirely.

Not far from the door, he pulls me to an area that has two armchairs and a loveseat, all a deep purple. A small glass table sits in the middle. There aren't any games or activities in this section, which is probably why it's vacant. Breyson and I both walk to the small loveseat. Once seated, I turn to face him and let my fingers draw patterns into the velvet texture.

"Tell me what's going on with you," he says.

I glance over to Trinka, who's watching with wide eyes, then back to Brey. He doesn't comment on her presence, but it seems foolish to just start talking about my dreams that come true in front of a stranger.

"I just had some bad dreams, and they left me feeling weird about this place," I tell Brey with a pointed look.

"*You might have misinterpreted something,*" he thinks to me without even knowing what I dreamt of. "*Basing your entire opinion of this place on a dream is a bit dramatic.*"

"There's no way—" I start to defend myself, but he cuts me off by responding out loud.

"The Domain is doing the one thing that you've wanted your entire life. They're trying to give us freedom." His hand waves around while he urges me to understand.

"At what cost!" My voice hitches and frustrated tears pool in my eyes with the memory of the boy that's so clear in my mind. Brey's eyes narrow and he releases a frustrated sigh. He knows I'm not telling him everything, but a quick glance to Trinka tells me that he also knows I can't right now.

"They've given us no reason to doubt them," Trinka chimes in. "In fact," she hesitates and looks over her shoulder, "I actually knew about this place before coming here."

"What do you mean?" Brey asks her, almost annoyed that she's interjecting herself into this conversation.

"My mother is friends with a teacher here," she stutters, seeming to hesitate to finish the sentence. "This place is legitimate." Her wide eyes sparkle.

I clench my teeth tighter. Tears are threatening to emerge at the memory of my graduation. The back of my throat tightens, and I focus again on the deep purple velvet under my fingers.

It just feels so unfair to have to justify my hatred for this place when I witnessed what I did.

A guard with a bright silver gun holstered to his belt approaches us, interrupting the heated moment. I blanch at the sight of the weapon and what I know it can do, what I saw it do.

"Ms. Lewis," he says when he reaches us, "please come with me."

I look at Brey fearfully. I don't realize that I'm hoping for him to give me some kind of answer of what I should do. He doesn't meet my gaze. Instead, he stands and places himself between the guard and me, his eyes never leaving the man.

The guard puts a hand on his gun but doesn't remove it from its holster, the act intimidating enough. I can feel Brey's indecision next to me. I can also imagine what these guards are capable of if they don't get their way, based on what they'll send me to do in the future.

"It's fine," I tell Brey, despite my racing heart begging me to do anything else. "I'll be right back."

"If you're not, I'm coming to look for you."

Chapter Eight

The sudden attention from everyone in the vicinity makes my spine tingle. I've never particularly appreciated notice or recognition and having everyone stare is making my insides tighten. Varick's glower from an oversized armchair is the last thing I see before I follow the guard into an elevator.

The man leading me is tall and doesn't acknowledge me while we walk. He offers a single grunt, telling me to move away from the keypad before pressing the button for the top floor. Enclosed in this small space, the smell of cigarettes billows around us. They must have access to the cancerous products even though the rest of the world outlawed them.

"What's on these floors?" I motion to the other numbers. He gives me a look and subtly raises one eyebrow but doesn't say anything.

I can't help my fidgeting hands as the silence presses around us. The guard, however, remains calm with his eyes focused on the doors.

When we finally reach our destination, I huff in frustration. This new area doesn't do anything for the mental map I've been creating. It looks like all the other floors I've seen. We walk the length of the gray hall until he comes to a stop. He knocks once.

"Come in." The sound comes from the other side.

The room is very large for an office, but that's clearly what it is. A single, wooden desk sits near the far end. On it is a computer, something I've never seen in person. Piles of documents are placed in neat piles. Two leather chairs face the desk.

"Ms. Lewis," Stealth says, gesturing to one of the seats in front of him. I guess I shouldn't be surprised he knows who I am, but it's still unnerving. "That will be all, Keelan. Thank you," he addresses the guard who came and got me. The entire room smells like the aftershave that followed Stealth down the aisle earlier.

Up close, Stealth emanates power and control, even more than I had thought. Every movement seems calculated and determined. I watch as he puts his pen on his desk, opens a drawer, places a paper inside and then closes it. I want to know what's on that page to warrant it being hidden from me when the rest are on display.

The entire time he's silent and seemingly trying to unnerve me. It's working.

"I've been eager to meet you, Ms. Lewis." He folds his hands to a steeple on the desk. He seems to be waiting for a response from me, but I don't give one. "How have you been liking the Domain so far?"

"I'd like to go home," I reply quickly and set my jaw so he can't see it quiver.

He smiles again.

"And I would love for you to graduate and get there." Something flashes across his face that he quickly hides.

"What do I have to do to graduate?" I don't miss a beat.

He smiles. Somehow, despite clearly being older, he doesn't have any wrinkles. Maybe it's because his expressions never fully reach his eyes.

"Do well here and succeed," he says simply. He tilts his head to the side.

"And what does graduation entail?" I press with slow words while my eyes never leave his. The image of the boy crying over his mother's blood is fresh in my mind. That was my graduation, my ticket out of here. But I can't ever accept that. Stealth's smile falters for the briefest moment before he recovers.

"What makes you ask?" His eyes narrow a fraction. I lift my chin and when it becomes obvious that I don't plan on answering, he says, "It varies from person to person." He gives a small smile, urging me to accept this answer.

I make the mistake of breaking our gaze to look at my hands in my lap, knowing he'll interpret the sign as submission but feeling too angry to care.

"My men said that you were able to *make* them drop you from your roof. Is that your ability?" His hand strokes his clean-shaven chin.

I clear my throat to buy time. On the one hand, I don't want to admit anything. Keeping secrets seems like my only defense against these people. But alternatively, I'm here, which means he knows I have an ability, although I have no idea how he found out. It's safer to tell him this single thing, instead of him finding out I have multiple abilities.

"Yes," I finally reply.

"What would you call that?" he asks.

Again, I don't answer right away, wondering if it's smarter to keep the information to myself. But if I'm here, then it's because he knows I'm an Unnatural, and refusing to cooperate could be what leads me to the graduation dream I had in the first place.

"Compulsion," I say quietly.

"I understand your hesitation. You've had to deny who you are for a very long time," he tries to console me. "But you don't have to hide yourself here. That's a new ability, and we'd like to help you practice it. Is that something you could use on anybody? Say, for instance, on me?" His voice is calm, but a hint of worry is present.

"No, I don't know how to use it on command." I bite my lower lip at the admission. I shouldn't have any desire to prove myself to this man, but the truth in my statement is embarrassing.

He meets my eyes and studies my reaction without responding. It occurs to me that a man like him doesn't get into a position of power without being able to read every detail of someone's body language. I sit up straighter in the leather seat at the thought.

"Why did you miss school today?" The random line of questioning makes my head spin and from his reaction, he can see it on my face.

"I didn't feel well." I bite my lip so he won't see through the lie.

"There weren't any records of your aunt calling in to report your absence. Did she know you were ill?"

My eyes widen before I can control my reaction. He knows far more than I thought he did.

"I'm not sure, I was asleep." I let the words tumble out without any real conviction.

He watches me carefully and the seconds feel like hours.

"So, did your ability allow you to know what was going to happen at the school?" He rubs the back of his neck, and upon seeing my inspection of the movement, lowers his hand immediately. "Did you compel someone to tell you something that allowed you to know of the events that would unfold?"

"No, I was sick," I repeat with emphasis, hoping the anger that's making my fists shake isn't heard in my voice. My throat is dry, but I don't cough to clear it.

He sighs, without even bothering to hide his frustration as he responds, "Very well. I look forward to our relationship, Ms. Lewis. You're dismissed, but please know that I'll be watching."

He doesn't believe me. While we're done for now, he knows I'm still hiding something.

Rising slowly from my seat, I turn to the door. The same guard is standing right outside, ready to escort me back to the Eye. I'm not sure why I thought maybe they'd leave me alone up here, but I grind my teeth at the appearance of the babysitter. He pushes the call button for the elevator.

"Actually," I say to him as casually as I can muster, "I'm going to take the stairs."

I leave his side before he can object, reaching the stairwell with several glances backward to make sure he isn't following me.

While I watch the guard get onto the elevator, my body bumps into something.

"Oh!" I exclaim. Startled and favoring my injured foot, I fall backward from the surprise. "Sorry."

"It's fine," a deep voice murmurs as the smell of wood and moss becomes overpowering. I look up and find Varick's brown eyes. His long hair is pulled back into a headband.

"I didn't realize it was you," I mumble for no real reason. My cheeks grow warm.

He looks at me like he's trying to solve a difficult problem, then eventually holds his hand out in my direction. I take it reluctantly.

"Thanks," I say quietly.

"Whatever," he responds quickly and with anger dripping in his tone. I pull my arm away from him and his hostility. I want to ask what he's doing up here, but he continues climbing the stairs before I work up the courage.

For years, I had felt really bad for Varick. He and Valor were raised by a nanny. Unlike our peers who grew up without parents because they had died, Varick's parents *chose* not to be around. They're some high-up government figures who helped create Eramica, and apparently that means they can't be bothered by their children, even if their children are Generation Novus.

I grit my teeth as I make my way down far too many flights of stairs because I couldn't just take the elevator like a normal person. I count them as I go. Ten levels above the Eye, with one underneath it. Twelve places for Stealth to hide his secrets.

It's not difficult to find Brey and Trinka since they haven't moved, although Brey is now at the edge of his seat as one of his knees bounces up and down.

"Hey," I approach them. His knee stops shaking and relief is visible in his face.

"What did he want?" Breyson demands, standing at the sight of me.

"Just to meet." I try to keep my voice light in response. The velvet cushion is far more comfortable than the chair in Stealth's office.

He nods a single time, but it's clear that neither of them believe me.

"Here's your schedule." Brey hands me a piece of paper. I look at him and raise my eyebrows.

"They came around while you were gone!" Trinka exclaims. The whites in her eyes are showing again.

I look at the paper.

"These don't even look like real subjects." My eyebrows push together.

"It's just a little different." Brey's mouth presses into a thin line.

I can't tell if he's trying to convince me or himself at this point as I analyze my schedule closer.

Mercer Lewis- Ability Not Confirmed
8 a.m. – 11 a.m. | Agility Skills Rm P
1 p.m. – 2:30 p.m. | Ethics Rm 301
2:30 p.m. – 4 p.m. | History Rm 306

"Exciting, isn't it?" Trinka contributes. "They're probably teaching us what we need to know as Unnaturals!" Her fingertips gingerly clutch the paper to her own chest, as if someone removing it would take away her right to participate here.

Brey doesn't answer. Instead, his attention shifts to something on the other side of the room and I follow his gaze to see Lottie and Jaylee walking by with Cynthia.

"Did you know she was one of us?" I ask him.

At my words, Trinka turns around. Brey's mouth falls open. *"Jaylee?"* But we both know that's who I was referring to, so I don't answer. *"Yeah, I guess, I think I saw her use her ability. Never confirmed it, though."* I follow his gaze to the girl. She's looking at him as well, but when she realizes we're all watching, she looks down to avoid our attention. *"We should go to bed,"* Brey thinks to me.

I narrow my eyes at the obvious subject change. Whatever my best friend is thinking regarding Jaylee, he's decided he's not ready to share it.

My eyelids feel heavy and my temples are pounding. I've had vivid dreams the last few nights, which means I haven't really slept in a while. As much as I don't want to admit it, the plush bed is calling my name even though we haven't been awake that long. So, after a few more topics of conversation, Trinka and I say goodnight to Brey and make our way to the dorm.

Lottie is in the bathroom upon our return, something that shouldn't seem out of the ordinary, but the way she eyes me warily sets me on edge.

"Hey," I greet her with a friendly voice.

Her eyes widen and she takes a step backward. Frustration courses through me. The door opens and Lottie's eyes lock on our joiner with relief.

"Cynthia told us you're trouble," Jaylee marches to her younger sister. Though Jaylee is shorter, she's still clearly in charge of Lottie.

"Why?" I clench my fists at my sides while heat radiates through my chest.

"Just leave her alone, Mercer," Jaylee lashes back. "Come on, Lots, let's go." Jaylee steers her out of the bathroom.

"I just—" I start to defend myself. But Jaylee cuts me off.

"We've been warned about you. Just respect our space."

Jaylee's harsh words somehow make my nostrils flare as I clench my jaw to keep from saying something that will make it worse.

They leave the bathroom together and I let out an audible groan. How do I already have more enemies here than I did at home?

Chapter Nine

Something in my gut churns so strongly in the early hours of the morning that it wakes me up and no matter what I try, sleep doesn't find me again. My brain cycles through important things that I need to think about but refuses to give me relief despite how much time I spend considering any certain thing. As a result, I'm stuck trying to wade through the nervous energy in my chest that wants to claw its way out.

The strange conversation with Stealth seems even more menacing now that time has passed. There are only two things that I know for certain when it comes to him. First, he has been, and will continue to, watch me. And second, he knows I'm lying to him. Neither of those ideas are comforting.

Lying awake in my plush bed, the sound of soft snores and deep breathing brings a void. I try to stop the overwhelming and crushing feeling of being trapped. Nothing helps. I could get out of bed, sure. But could I leave the room? Thinking that the door may be locked, keeping us in here, makes my fists shake with rage while I start sweating under the covers.

Even the white comforter around me feels like a prison, the blankets getting too warm and tangled around my limbs. I let the hours tick by while my frustration makes my heart beat faster than is healthy. Finally, Trinka stirs next to me, and I feel relief as the big, brown eyes open.

Today is the day we start our new classes. I wasn't a good student at home, and always resented the monotonous routine.

I'm certain it won't be any different here.

I thought yesterday was the worst of my foot, but I was wrong. The swelling seems to have doubled overnight. Trinka winces as she helps me tie my shoe against the puffiness. She doesn't ask me about it further.

Jaylee and Lottie ignore me. I try not to care, but it isn't until after they leave the dorm that I feel like I can finally breathe.

I'm not too proud to admit that Trinka's presence is comforting. Her naivete and endless optimism is like sunshine in this otherwise windowless space.

"I'm starving," she says after donning a gray jacket over her gray shirt. "Aren't you? You hardly ate anything last night."

"Yeah, let's go," I agree. But it has nothing to do with my stomach and more to do with the fact that the ginger twins woke up and I'd prefer not to overhear their snarky comments.

We walk through the Eye, heading to the door that Brey indicated held his dorm, and I give myself permission to feel impressed now that Cynthia isn't next to me. One of the televisions in the corner by our dorm has bright colors on the screen. Two boys are engrossed in a game of animals driving cars, the animation unlike anything I've seen before, and the sound is inviting.

"What are you thinking about?" Trinka's inquisitive and knowing eyes watch me closely. Her brown curls bounce up and down along with the question.

"Nothing specific," I mumble in a low voice. My eyes have shifted to Valor, who's playing a game at the pool table with Jaylee.

The room is buzzing with fresh faces while we walk down the center aisle that runs from one end of the Eye to the other.

Varick and JC are ahead of us, walking in our direction,

though they haven't seen us yet. They seem to be engaged in a conversation, one that JC laughs deeply about. I've never intentionally run away from JC, but back home I always had Brey with me, giving me silent strength. Something about seeing JC this close makes the dream I had of my graduation feel even more real, and I can't confront those thoughts right now.

"Let's go." I grab Trinka's wrist to try and turn her around, but she fights against me.

"What about Brey?" She pulls her wrist back, the slick pieces of her gray jacket slipping through my fingers.

"He can meet us upstairs." My jaw hardly moves as I whisper the words. My eyes keep darting back to Varick and JC, who are fast approaching. She must sense the apprehension coursing through me, because she turns on her heal and skips ahead of me to the other set of stairs.

As soon as the stairwell door opens to the floor above the Eye, the smell of breakfast makes me realize how hungry I actually am. Once we find a table, her bubbly personality returns in full force.

"How are you feeling about everything today?" She's casual but watching me closely.

"I still don't want to be here," I tell her, guessing what she really wants to know. "I don't trust them."

Her mouth presses into a thin line and she uses her fork to rearrange the food on her plate.

"How great would it be," she finally says after looking at me, "if you were wrong?" I have to give her credit for being brave enough to push the conversation, when it's clear she'd rather speak about anything else.

"Uh." I bite my lip while I search for words, ready to try and justify my feelings to her.

"Just hear me out," she says, saving me from my awkward explanation. There's much more urgency in her voice. "If this place is what they say it is, then we can be free here."

I tilt my head to the side and narrow my gaze as I consider her words. The picture she paints… it would make this place pretty great. If I never had that dream of graduation, would I forgive them for dropping me off the roof? Would I be happy to feel freedom?

"Yeah." I look back at her. "That'd be great." My tone implies everything I'm not saying.

I can appreciate her willingness to buy into the Domain, and even her determination to convince me to like the place. The problem is that every time I close my eyes, I picture the boy whose life shouldn't be worth a simple graduation. Perhaps I could tell her about that dream and see what she says, but do I trust Trinka enough to tell her about my dream ability? Especially if Stealth thinks my singular ability is compulsion? Is that a risk I can take with a girl I just met, regardless of how much I like her? No, no it's not.

The maple sausage melts around my taste buds, giving me something else to think about, so I try to focus on that instead. Will I ever get used to how delicious the food is? If I get too used to it, it's going to be a harsh transition after I get out of this place.

I've almost finished my plate by the time Brey finds us with food in his hands. He looks well rested. It shouldn't bother me, but it does, because it means that he didn't share the same impending anxiety that kept me up all night.

"How'd you sleep?" Trinka asks him. Now that he's closer, I can see his deep frown lines, despite how rested he appears.

"Fine," he answers simply but definitely angry. "*Varick is in my dorm,*" Brey thinks to me, more like it's a thought he's having instead of in response to anything I asked.

I'm not sure what he wants me to say to that, to those cold and distant eyes. We eat in silence instead.

Brey and I will be starting our day with Agility Skills while Trinka starts her classroom sessions. We all stand by the stairwell as Brey and I say goodbye to her. It's silly because I've just met her, but I'm worried to let her out of my sight. Maybe it's because I know what this place is capable of.

"We'll meet for lunch." I try to reassure myself. "In the Eye."

Brey tells me he knows where we're going, and while Trinka goes up the stairs from the cafeteria level, Brey ushers me down, past the Eye, to the bottom floor. The chill from yesterday is back, even though I had selected a long-sleeved, gray option. Maybe it has less to do with the temperature and more to do with what my gut is trying to tell me.

We're running late and my injury slows us down, so I decide that now's not the time to fill Brey in on the dream of my graduation.

"I've heard this class is basically just a way to practice our abilities." His voice is grim while he stares straight ahead. I look at him dumbfounded, with no idea where he got this information.

A small eagerness moves me forward as we descend the stairs. It's a part of the Domain that I haven't been to yet, and I'm excited to see if the exit is obvious. When we open the heavy door that says 'Pitch', my eyes are busy scanning for the exit before I take in any other part of the space.

There is no obvious exit, unfortunately. The upper level is a gym. Except, not like any kind of gym we've seen before. Our athletics class at home used equipment that was manufactured before the Censorship, since that was reportedly all that was available, but everything in here is shiny and new.

The most interesting part of the room is a carved-out middle that descends by stairs from every direction so that a circular lower level sits at the center. Rimming the circle, there are pieces of plastic jutted out slightly. It looks like they could be raised to enclose whoever stands on that lower level, trapping them in place.

As we move farther inside, the strong scent of sweat and something metallic surrounds us. I cringe at my first thought of what the metallic scent could be.

I look to Brey. His eyes have also found the enclosure, and his lips pull down to a frown. Before I can ask him what he thinks of this place now, Cynthia walks by us. Her eyes scan me from head to toe and she smirks before walking away.

"That was weird," Brey thinks to me, having also noticed.

"Yeah, she doesn't like me very much," I say without emotion.

Breyson sighs, and I don't need him to tell me what he's thinking. It's loud and clear: try harder to make friends here.

Everybody seems to be milling around, with some people chatting and others using the equipment in the room. Brey walks with me along the upper edge of the descending circle. We pass a group of treadmills, then machines that look like stairs, then stationary bikes. We continue walking by a large storage unit with hundreds of drawers on the outer wall. I can't tell what's inside, but there must be thousands of different pieces of equipment to use, with ways to train that I never would have imagined. Brey stops near a grouping of large, black punching bags that hang from the ceiling. He looks at them with a hint of envy and longing before continuing on.

Varick and JC are on the opposite side of the room, because of course they're in my classes here. Varick still has the stupid headband holding his long hair back. Someone should tell him that if he wants it out of his face, he should just cut it. He sits on the edge of a bench with his elbows casually on his knees as he leans over. He throws his head back and laughs. JC continues whatever story they all seem to find so funny.

Suddenly, Varick looks at me. Our eyes meet for the briefest moment, but I look away first. A heat takes over and I can feel it lifting to my cheeks. I fidget with my shirt, trying to seem as if I'm preoccupied with something.

After several minutes, the door opens, and a man walks in. Well, 'man' might be a generous term. This guy almost looks like he's our age. He's taller, and oddly familiar with scars up and down his arms. He gives a nod to JC and Varick's group as he descends the stairs to the bottom center.

A gasp only audible enough for Brey to hear escapes my lips as my chest constricts tightly, threatening to deny any air in. I've been replaying the dream of my graduation over and over, always seeing JC lift the gun and point it at the woman, focusing on how red the sheets got, and trying to blink away the image before remembering the crying boy or how I would hold my own gun up in his direction.

But this man in front of me is bringing back the other parts, the parts that I haven't thought about since having that dream. This man is the one who was in the back of the van, the one to congratulate me for graduating. He sends me to kill the boy.

Breyson either doesn't notice my reaction or doesn't ask me about it. While I work to get a grip on my racing heart, I consider for the first time not telling Brey about that dream. He might brush it off or tell me I'm overreacting, but more than that, he might not be able to look at me the same way if he finds out about the boy. I'm not sure I can risk that.

"This," the man says, "is Agility Skills." He doesn't use the same dramatic arm wave that Cynthia and Stealth did. His chest is puffed out and his arms swing with a strange confidence. He doesn't wear a suit, but there's an eye stitched into his athletic shirt, which is so thin that it reveals all the distinct muscles along his chest and arms.

"I'm Nick. I'll be your instructor in this course."

A few students whisper things, interrupting Nick's introduction.

"This class," Nick continues loudly, ignoring the comments, "will accomplish a few things. First, you'll learn how to use your ability, regardless of what your ability is. Second, you will be introduced to tactical training and weapons. While you may not think weapons are related to what you can do as an Unnatural, you need to know how to use them. The world is hunting you and you need to know how to fight back." He smiles to the room, but the action doesn't seem natural. "Third, you will get into peak physical shape. To be the best, you need to have superior health. We'll give you that. After you graduate, you'll be expected to go on missions for the Domain. That can only happen based on what you learn here."

I look at Brey and he meets my gaze. I'm not sure what 'missions' look like, but it sounds like we're being trained as soldiers, and that idea makes my stomach turn.

Nick continues, "We've found that the best way to develop what you can do is by practicing it. And the best way to practice it is to use it defensively, since your adrenaline while reacting should open you up in ways that you may never have experienced. You must take it seriously. Students have died in this class, although that shouldn't happen if you follow my direction." His face looks bored as he delivers the news.

It's clear who is new to the Domain based on who looks fearful at his words. I watch as Cynthia stares down at her foot, which she uses to trace circles on the floor. I wonder if she's known anyone to die here.

"We have to fight each other," I say under my breath to Brey, voicing the conclusion that I'd started forming since we got here. The chill comes back, making me clammy. My palms are sweaty, but something screams at me not to wipe them, afraid it'll look too much like a sign of weakness.

Brey doesn't answer but his mouth presses into a thin line. It seems strange that we're encouraged to use our abilities in this class where there aren't any guards, whereas they seem to swarm the other part of the Domain.

"When you aren't training in the Ring," Nick says, "you should be working on your physical fitness. I will call names, two at a time, otherwise you'll spend your class getting in shape."

My eyes flick up to JC as he flexes his biceps. I wonder if it's on purpose or a nervous tick.

Varick yawns next to him. I have no idea how he could be bored by this when my own adrenaline and fear pump through me so hard that I could run a marathon. His eyes glance in my direction. I look away before they can meet mine.

"There are new students, as well as old, in both the morning and afternoon Agility Skills class. This is intentional, so you always work against different abilities when new students join us. For those who just arrived, your class schedules will change twice a year and you will be placed in courses that your teachers believe will best help you on your path here. However, no matter which classes you're in, you will always have Agility Skills for half a day."

Half a year. Six months until we even switch classes. Every

hope I'd had for them letting us out of here vanishes as my throat tightens with emotion.

"I determine when the training sessions are finished, depending on whether or not you're still learning. When deciding how long you need to train, I will take it into consideration if you use your ability," Nick says.

"Sounds like he can base his decision to end a training session on whether or not he likes you, which could be a huge issue for you and your charming personality," Brey thinks to me.

Despite my private meltdown, I have to hold back a snort of laughter.

"Use your ability if you can. Some of you have what we call 'passive' abilities. Which means it might not be readily apparent to the room if you use it. But I will know, or at least, I should be able to tell if you do it right."

That's the first time I'd heard of the abilities classified like that. They have known about us and studied us for so long, it makes me realize my knowledge of Unnaturals barely skims the surface.

Brey doesn't say anything, but I assume he must be feeling the same.

Nick goes through a few more rules, although I'm not sure how you can really call them rules. One opponent per day. We'll rotate through match-ups. If we show that we've used our ability or that our ability is growing, he'll end our session. He reassures us that the intention of the class is not to get hurt, and he'll do everything he can to avoid injuries. What really stands out is his explanation of the gym in the upper area. This class is designed to get us in shape. An image of future-Mercer floods my brain as I realize that they clearly succeed. Why do they need us in such good condition? What do they plan on doing with us?

"Well, that's that," Nick concludes.

I look around. Several of us continue staring at him, confused. Varick and JC stand. Varick starts using a jump rope and JC grabs a very large, very intimidating, hand weight.

"Now what?" I ask Brey. His eyebrows are still pushed close together as he watches the other students.

"I guess we should go over here." He leads us across the room. Nobody chooses the treadmills in the corner, but I eye them enviously. My foot won't let me run, but it would feel so relieving to let go, even just for a couple of seconds. I glance back to Nick, who holds a list in one hand and a remote in the other.

"First up, Lewis and Craw. Into the Ring," Nick says.

The Ring. What a stupid name. My brain hasn't seemed to comprehend what's about to happen, or why Brey is staring at me. I try to focus on other trivial things to calm my pulse, like the fact that my foot doesn't hurt when I'm careful about the way it rotates on the pedals of the stationary bike.

"Mercer." Brey's hesitation makes me look at him. I press the button to stop the machine in response to the worried look he gives me. His eyebrows are pulled together, and he glances beyond me, to something on the other side of the room.

I turn back to see the source, only to feel my breath catch in my throat. That's when Nick's words register. He said Lewis and Craw. Across the Ring, JC walks down the stairs as well. JC. Jack Craw.

I get off my bike and let my feet carry me across the room and down the stairs. Everything slows down like my brain is trying to give me time to catch up.

Shortly after the Censorship, JC's parents tried selling a fake antidote to common illnesses. They were arrested by my mother, a police officer. But there weren't enough people to staff the prisons, so all criminals were put to death, including his parents.

I enter the ring. My jaw stiffens as JC's foot takes the last step.

JC has hated me ever since he learned that my last name is Lewis. He blames me. I'm just grateful that he doesn't realize Lizzy is my sister, likely because she changed her last name to Smith.

After I joined the public school, we had a class field trip to the local river. When the teacher wasn't looking, JC pushed me in after he found out I couldn't swim. Brey saved me and we've been best friends ever since.

JC smiles when his eyes meet mine, as if he can hear my thoughts and agrees with what I'm thinking. His life's mission is about to be completed.

What am I supposed to do now? My abilities might help me, if only I knew how to use them on command. Although even then, Stealth can't know that I have more than one ability. So, I need to use my compulsion against JC, which is easier said than done.

It's ironic how the universe works. Ever since JC tried to kill me, I've spent most of my life avoiding him.

An overwhelming, suffocating bubble forms inside me. I swallow to keep the nausea at bay. Time seems to slow down and speed up all at once.

I turn around and my frantic gaze finds Brey. His shoulders are tight, and his head shakes back and forth. I guess it's become his habit now to let the blond strands stick up in strange directions when he's stressed.

"You'll be okay," he thinks to me. His lips press together and he runs a hand through his short hair, confirming my suspicion. But despite his words, his clear blue eyes scream the worry I feel. *"I don't know what his ability is,"* Brey continues. He keeps a

one-sided conversation running to make me feel better. It's working.

Nick backs to the side of the steps so he's not in the middle area with us. He pushes a button on the remote.

Like I predicted, plastic walls rise, trapping us. Nobody reacts from the upper gallery, which leads me to believe this is normal. My body tenses as I face JC. His biceps flex and his lip curls.

"Begin," Nick calls.

My heartbeat gets louder in my ears. JC smiles and takes a step in my direction. I instinctively step back and pain shoots through my injured foot. JC continues chasing me until finally, he pushes me and I jolt as my back hits the side plastic. I stare at JC as anger and fear swirl inside of me. I know I need to move, but I feel rooted to this spot.

"Come on!" Nick complains. "It's been one minute, and nothing's happened. One of you *do* something."

As if on command, JC lunges at me. My injured foot makes me trip while trying to take a step around him. JC isn't fast but he is quick enough to grab my good ankle while I'm on the ground.

I try to pull my leg to break his grasp, but his thick, sweaty fingers are completely encircled around me.

My body slides along the ground as he pulls me toward him, the back of my shirt rising up my torso from the friction against the floor. It's obvious he isn't struggling from the effort. With a final jerk, he yanks my body. The wind leaves my lungs and I see black spots in front of my eyes from the movement while I hang upside down in front of him.

I can hear the class gasp as JC continues pulling my ankle. While holding me, he lifts my body higher in the air, making my head hang several feet above the ground.

"Strength," Brey thinks to me in a dull voice. *"His ability is strength."*

The spots in my vision get worse and my body sways left and right. My arms flail, trying to hit any part of him that I can reach, but it seems like my efforts aren't doing anything as JC continues to hold my body upside down by my ankle.

"Compulsion!" I hear Brey scream.

I close my eyes to center myself from the overpowering dizziness. When I open them, I focus on the space a few feet from us. It won't work. I can't do it. There's no way I can speak, let alone find the strength to engage an ability that I don't know how to use.

But I can't give up.

My options are so limited. I ball my fist in desperation and throw out my hand, aiming for the only thing that can hurt this man enough to drop me.

I can tell I've hit my mark immediately. I'm dropped with a painful thud, with most of the impact on my shoulder. Out of the blurry corner of my vision, I see JC hunched over with his hands on his groin. Pain sears through my body, but I crawl away as fast as I can.

Laughter erupts from the students, but my head is spinning far too much to look around. The black spots are gone but it's taking a while to feel normal again. The metallic smell that fills the room is stronger now, and I rub the back of my hand against my nose to reveal bright, crimson blood. I shake my head a few times to try and get my bearings, but it isn't working. My neck hurts from the fall and my hands hurt from clenching them so tightly. Something must have hit my lip on the way down, because that's throbbing as well.

"Mercer, get up!" Brey screams silently to me.

I listen without thinking twice. I try to stand, but the black spots worsen because my head isn't ready for the movement.

"Done!" Nick yells. "Excellent, excellent. You both did great. Lots of room to grow."

His reassurance doesn't make me feel better. I survived, but barely. After a few more seconds, the room comes back into focus while I keep pressure on my nose. There are several hurried steps behind me and a gasp. I whip around in time to see JC rushing toward me.

"You son of a—" JC says through clenched teeth. He walks in a strange way, with one hand still over the area just below his belt. As he talks, spit flies and hits the floor.

I smile at him, not a normal smile, but one that I hope conveys a sense of gloating that I hardly feel.

Brey's right arm wraps securely around my waist, making me jump at the contact. I hadn't seen the walls lowered, let alone Brey walk down the stairs. He contracts his grip on me and moves my body, though not as easily as JC had, so that he stands between JC and me.

"The fight is over," Brey says. His tone doesn't leave room for argument while he keeps one arm protectively around my waist.

"Fine." JC looks at Breyson, then over at Nick, who's distracted and has already called the next two students. "This isn't over for us though, Lewis."

Somehow, I know he's telling the truth, and I wish I had thought ahead and figured out another strategy. Brey keeps his arm wrapped around me for a few more moments.

"You survived. We'll figure out the rest," Brey whispers in my ear.

I turn to Brey so that only he can hear me. My voice is pinched as I answer, "Great, what a way to live. I'm happy you're happy."

Chapter Ten

As the adrenaline wanes, the only thing louder than the anxiety coursing through me is my anger. I can't help but wonder if death in Agility Skills is common. If it is, I'm certain I'll be the next victim. It's beginning to feel like there are more threats to my life here than there were at home, which is ironic given the fact that we're in a protected bubble.

Stealth believes my single ability is compulsion. His guards saw it. Which means I can't use any of my other abilities in front of anyone here. I need to get a handle on the compulsion since it's the only ability I can use in Agility Skills. My control over it is flimsy at best.

Years ago, after I had realized my ability could make people do things, I tried to get Uncle Al to admit his sins to Aunt Pam. I'll never forget the confidence I mustered before storming into the kitchen and demanding things of him while we were home alone.

He laughed in response. Not a laugh of humor, but one of evil judgment. He asked me what made me think I could demand something like that. He already knew about my dreams, so I couldn't insinuate another ability; I remained silent. He then hit me so hard that my head rang for a week.

We must have gotten out before the classroom students, because the Eye is empty when we arrive to wait for Trinka. Brey and I take our spots on the purple loveseat.

"I don't think we should tell anybody about the dreams or

disarming." I finally admit what's been on my mind since we got here. Not that I think Brey would reveal my secrets, but it's important that we're on the same page. I decide not to mention the projection, since my theory about it being an ability is hardly solid.

"Alright," he agrees, but there's a twitch under his eye and I'm certain he doesn't like what my secrets insinuate. "Why compulsion?"

I swallow through the memory as I answer, "I used it on a guard the day we were taken. He dropped me off my roof."

He looks to my foot and his jaw clenches as he says, "I see." I'm sure he's fighting both his disappointment that I had to be chased and his overprotective response to my injury.

"I had a dream of my graduation. I was with JC and we had to kill people. Innocent people." I look at my hands, unable to watch his reaction while I replay the dream over and over.

Before he can answer me, Trinka bops up to us. The Eye is now packed and I had completely missed it.

"How was class?" she asks cheerfully.

"Maybe they weren't as innocent as you thought." His voice is silent to me before he answers Trinka out loud. "It was interesting. It'll take some time to get comfortable, but I think it's going to be useful to work on what we can do."

I stare at him, mouth open.

"What?" Trinka asks me with a bit of aggression in her voice.

"Nothing," I say without breaking my glare at Brey. "I just didn't realize he enjoyed the class that much. Personally, I hated it." My tongue runs over my swollen lower lip.

Brey's mouth puckers into a frown. *"It's not that I liked what happened to you..."*

“Maybe you’ll like it better tomorrow,” Trinka unknowingly interrupts Brey. She gives me a placating smile as I cross my arms over my chest. Trinka picks up on my sulky silence and changes the subject.

In Agility Skills, Breyson had been matched against a mousy looking boy, who was easily half his size. The boy didn’t have an active ability, so they circled each other for a few minutes until Nick gave them both instructions on how to fight with passive abilities. I wonder why Nick didn’t ask if I had a passive ability, although Stealth likely told him about my compulsion. Frustration pulses inside me at the thought that Nick knew about my ability and witnessed my weakness in not using it.

After the fighting, we had been introduced to two different types of guns and taught how to load them. I fought the urge to throw the weapon every time the cool metal touched me.

Trinka begins a dissection of her day while we walk to the dining hall for lunch. “Ethics is probably my favorite of the two. It’s taught by Mr. Clayton.” She pauses and looks down, as if she told us something she shouldn’t. “Then there’s history.”

“What did you learn in history?” Breyson asks. “Is it the same curriculum as back home?” We had learned last night that Trinka is also from the B Region.

“No,” she responds, widening her eyes. “We actually learn about things before the Censorship.”

There’s a reverence in her voice and it piques my interest. I’ve always wanted to know what life was like before they changed everything.

I decide to try the cauliflower pizza and am not disappointed. I want to have the real thing, but the healthy substitute still does wonders for my taste buds. The melted cheese oozes over the sides and I pick at the dripping pieces, placing them back on the slice before taking another bite. Brey and Trinka had continued their conversation about history the entire time.

"Actually, most people didn't know about the Censorship until it was too late," Brey says with his mouth full of chicken. "They've rewritten how it played out to make it look consensual."

I nearly choke on my food as I wipe the back of my hand over my mouth.

"How would you even know that?" Trinka asks Brey with skepticism.

"Mercer's dad was a history teacher and his notes are still at her house," he says simply, like he didn't just admit to something that would get him killed in the outside world.

Trinka eyes him closely, evidently torn between how she wants to handle the situation, before finally shrugging and focusing on her food.

Of course I had gone through my dad's research with Brey, but I had no idea he remembered those details. How can he be so supportive of Eramica with everything my dad's journals told us?

I follow them as we dispose of our dirty trays at the revolving machine, the smell of dish soap coming out with each movement of the metal. A pair of guards pass us and one of them looks at me longer than normal. I try to brush it off, but something about my conversation with Stealth makes me believe it's not just a coincidence. When he said they'd be watching, could he have meant quite so literally?

Brey and I say goodbye to Trinka and walk to the education floor. I add it to the mental map I'm building, which is jumbled and confusing at the moment. It doesn't help that all the hallways look so similar, with industrial lighting and gray walls. The classroom corridor is no exception. That strong smell of bleach and cleaner fills the hall, and it just makes me wonder why they don't clean the Pitch this thoroughly.

Our teachers stand in the hallway to greet us. Unlike back home, a guard stands right next to them, menacing and threatening.

A greasy looking bald man sneers at us by a door at the end of the hall. It seems that his attention is solely on me. I look at the floor, scolding myself for being so self-involved. There's no way Stealth meant his comment this literally.

I groan to myself as Brey walks right by the greasy man and into his classroom. We take two seats near the front, which isn't my choice, but I follow Brey anyway.

The metal desk is so different from the wooden ones at home. The cold seeps through my gray, cargo pants, resulting in a noticeable shiver.

As the class gets seated, the greasy teacher holds my gaze. I expect him to look away, but he doesn't. I pinch my lips together instead of looking down. The grease on his face makes his glasses slide down his slim nose, but he doesn't adjust them.

Several people have now stopped talking, and it occurs to me that they've also noticed this strange attention I'm getting.

"Good afternoon," he says, finally breaking our standoff. "My name is Mr. Clayton." He turns and writes his name on the chalkboard behind him with the word *Ethics* underneath. He seems to appreciate the silence of chalk clicking on the board as he takes his time, brushing his hands together after. "Who can tell me what the study of ethics is?" His pointer finger finally pushes the glasses back to their proper place.

Nobody answers immediately. His eyes are so dark, they look like they're black. His expression hardens the second his gaze finds me.

"You," he says with a nod in my direction.

I narrow my eyes and bite my lip while my knee bounces up and down, giving my head a slight shake back and forth.

"Nothing?" he sneers. I regret not having forced Brey to sit in the back of the room.

I let the nails digging into my palms calm me down. If I open my mouth and answer right now, things will get worse.

"Very well," he says coolly. "Anybody?"

Breyson raises his hand. Of course, he knows. Varick, on my other side, tilts his head in Brey's direction.

"Yes, Mister...?" Mr. Clayton asks. If the teacher doesn't know our names, perhaps I'm being sensitive and paranoid to think that he's targeting me intentionally.

"Jones," Brey dutifully responds, "Breyson Jones."

"Mr. Jones," Mr. Clayton repeats. "And what are ethics?"

Brey clears his throat and looks around before answering, "Moral principles."

"Excellent." Mr. Clayton writes Brey's answer on the chalkboard. "It was once believed that ethics could be viewed as right versus wrong. But that has changed. Can anyone tell me why?"

Nobody raises a hand, although I suspect Brey knows the answer. I look around, but all I can see is gray. The gray-uniformed students sit inside the gray-lined walls with no natural light or color to break it up. It's depressing and monotonous.

"The Censorship," Mr. Clayton answers his own question.

He turns back to us and has to use his pointer finger to push the glasses back up again.

"What's considered moral has not always been what's ethical, and vice versa. However, the deterioration of humanity has forced us to analyze what we view as both ethical and moral.

Now, we are much more focused on the outcome of a specific choice when looking at whether it's moral or not, simply because we need to."

He turns back to the board and neatly scrawls out: *outcome of choice = moral* on the board.

"For example, say you have the option to save a train full of twenty people, but in order to do so, you have to sacrifice one loved one. Given the fact that our country is trying to rebuild our population, what choice is moral?" He turns to face the class.

His eyes find mine again, the hardness returning, as he flicks his hand toward me, signaling he wants me to answer. I know what he wants to hear, but I tighten my arms around my stomach and look down again.

"No?" he says through a condescending snort. "It's a simple question. You can either save the twenty or the one. Which would you choose?"

"Just answer him," Brey thinks to me, annoyed.

"The one," I announce to both Brey and the teacher. My teeth grind together. I can't help but think about if Lizzy were the one, and I know I'm certain in my answer.

Mr. Clayton pauses and presses his lips into a thin line. He takes a breath to gather himself. "And you believe this to be the ethical option, thus making it moral, Ms. Lewis?"

My eyebrows pull together, and I tilt my head to the side, distracted. "How do you know who I am, but you didn't know who Brey was?" The question escapes my lips before I can even help it.

Varick shifts in his seat to my right, but I don't remove my gaze from the teacher. After several awkward seconds, Mr. Clayton utters a forced laugh which I interrupt.

"But yes, that's my answer. You first asked me which was

moral, but then you asked me which one I would choose. It's not my fault the population is suffering. Moral or not, I'd save my loved one."

Mr. Clayton's face turns a shade of red that has me wondering if he should go to the infirmary. The guard takes a step in his direction, but Mr. Clayton holds up his hand to the guard and asks another question, directing it at JC instead.

A sigh of relief escapes me, and I hadn't realized I was holding my breath. So much for trying to stay under the radar. I need to learn how to keep my reactions to myself.

The class continues like this. We're asked a series of questions that I disagree with, and the students give the answers they think are right. His focus doesn't come near me again for the rest of the time.

Before we can leave, JC lets me pass him. He leans down and says in a menacing hiss that only a snake could achieve, "Nice lip."

I fight the urge to raise a hand to my face. My tongue runs against my lower lip, which is still puffy.

During our short walk from one classroom to the next, Brey nudges my side with his elbow.

"*You're quiet...*" he thinks to me with a hint of amusement.

I don't respond, giving him a shrug instead. A sad smile lifts on one side of his mouth.

"*You still think this place is terrible?*" he unnecessarily asks. I don't answer. What good is knowing the future if I can't convince Brey about what's to come?"

He takes a seat near the front of the room, but I don't want a repeat of the last class so I walk to the back before plopping down. Brey looks around and gives me a sad smile but I ignore him.

Our history teacher is the older man who wouldn't stop staring at me during orientation. Up close, I can see the wrinkles surrounding his puffy cheeks. His hazy, green eyes show knowledge, almost like he's wiser than he wants people to think. The room doesn't smell like bleach, a nice reprieve from the rest of the classroom corridor. Instead, notes of cinnamon and cloves embrace me.

There's a guard with an eye stitched into his lapel, standing by the door. I guess it doesn't bother anybody that we have guards for simple lessons.

Almost immediately, the teacher looks at me. I want to look away, but it doesn't feel as threatening as it did with Mr. Clayton.

JC must have said the punchline to one of his jokes because most of the room erupts into laughter. I look at the group of ignorant classmates and then back to the teacher. In the split second that nobody else is paying attention, I swear the old man smiles and winks at me.

But almost as suddenly, he isn't looking at me anymore. Instead, he's quieting the class down. I don't understand what just happened but if he does know who I am, which would seem apparent given that everyone else knows, then what does that wink mean?

"My name is Mr. Regis and I have the distinct pleasure of teaching you about the history that you never learned." His voice carries a bravado; it's comforting and kind.

"As you know, everything changed when it became apparent that chemicals and computers were slowly killing us. It was shortly after that realization that the birth of Unnaturals occurred, and we are still unsure if it was a coincidence or if you're all here with your special abilities because our ancestors didn't take better care of our planet.

"The government, America at the time, couldn't control the panic. More importantly, they couldn't control the narrative. As a result, the Censorship was enacted. Most professions were cancelled, and mine was one such career."

Listening better than I ever have in a classroom, I lean forward in my seat. I should've sat next to Brey.

"Not that I blame you, the Unnaturals." He winks at us, and light laughter fills the air. "Now, the general practice of Eramica is that our history is not a necessity for young minds, lest those very minds choose to return to how things were. However, you're not just any young minds, are you?" A glint of sparkle shines in his eyes as he tilts his head forward. "It makes sense, therefore, that we teach our brightest students, those who have the capability of restarting our world, exactly what kinds of mistakes ought not be repeated." He turns to face his blackboard. "With that, we shall start at the 1900's, specifically, with the advancement of technology."

In cursive, he scrawls a timeline on the board. I don't have to pretend to pay attention like I did in the last class. This is information I've been craving my entire life. This knowledge somehow feels like power.

Our ancestors had nearly everything at their fingertips, literally, through portable telephones that were capable of ordering food, buying clothes, sending messages and more. None of it seems realistic, and yet, it's not impossible. We have the knowledge still; it was just sworn to secrecy.

Despite my burning curiosity, an ache starts building in my chest. I recognize the longing for the yesterdays of the world. How could things have gotten so bad that the only solution was to start over? It hits me, at some point during the lecture, that this is the warmest space in the Domain. Perhaps it's the smell of cinnamon, or maybe it's simply that this room has better ventilation than anywhere else.

My head is in a fog with all I learned by the time our class is released.

"*I'm starving,*" Brey thinks to me. He's waiting by the front of the class for me to join him as the students file by.

The guard near the door is speaking to our teacher. The guard reaches out and touches Mr. Regis on the shoulder. I haven't seen any of the guards act friendly, but maybe our teacher just has a way to reveal that part of people. The guard turns to look at something through the door. I'm aware of Brey waiting for me as I drag my feet up the aisle.

Mr. Regis catches my eye during the brief moment the guard is distracted. The teacher nods his head slightly, angling himself in my direction and winks again. I'm certain of it this time. Before I can ask him about it or see if Brey notices, the guard turns back to continue their conversation and Mr. Regis acts like I'm not there.

Brey and I walk down the hallway together in silence. Now that the doors are all open, the smell of bleach isn't so strong. All the doors hold a different classroom, and there must be upwards of twenty. Given the fact that we only have two classes here right now, it begs the question of how long they plan to keep us. How many classes are we going to cycle through when we change our schedules in six months?

I follow Brey down the stairwell, happy that it's only a few flights to maneuver. My foot slows me down but not by much, thanks to Breyson's feather-light touch on my side as he guides me. The point where we connect burns into my skin through my shirt as my cheeks warm. The dream of our kiss seems to always be lurking in my memory.

We walk over to the chairs that we had occupied last night. I sag into the velvet purple and put my sore foot on the coffee table in front of me. I might be delirious because a chuckle escapes my lips.

"What is it?" he asks me.

"I'm just thinking about how ironic it is that I had to physically battle someone who wants me dead, and yet, the most exhausting part of the day was a history class." I let my body relax.

"Yeah, it's weird, isn't it?" He puts one of his arms on the back of the sofa, nearly touching my shoulders.

"Did you ever know about the technology from before?" Aunt Pam and Uncle Al were so guarded with the information, this was the first I'd heard of it.

"Not really," he thinks to me. *"But one time my mom was frustrated that she had to go to the City Center for groceries and said she missed the days of online shopping. I asked her what that meant... I thought she was messing with me. I guess she was telling the truth."* His eyes look out at nothing specific as he remembers.

"You think she's wondering where we are?" I ask, noting his sudden sadness.

"I'm sure she's fine." His jaw sets as he tries to stubbornly defend this place again. *"She's probably happy I'm not in danger of being killed anymore."*

"If she even knows that," I mumble. Brey turns to question me but I quickly defend myself. "We have no idea what they told our families. She might already think you're dead.

He doesn't answer, but the responding hunch of his shoulders signifies the defeat my words have on him.

"Where's Trinka?" I mutter, looking around. The Eye

emptied significantly with students going to dinner. It's much easier to distinguish conversations happening near us.

"She would have waited for us, right?" Brey muses out loud, relieved about the change in subject.

"I'm sure," I answer quickly. Thinking that she may have found other friends makes my stomach twist in knots. We watch a few people walk by and it would seem that my performance in Agility Skills and then the interaction with Mr. Clayton has become a topic of conversation. I suppose it's only a matter of time before the self-regulating starts.

Valor, who is in Trinka's Agility Skills class, walks down the main aisle of the Eye.

"Valor," I call out.

He looks over in my direction and smiles widely before jogging the short distance to us. "You rang?"

"Where's Trinka?" Brey demands. I want to nudge him because of his hostility. Valor's never done anything wrong to us.

"The girl we've been hanging around," I clarify. His eyes light up in recognition.

"No idea." Valor shrugs his shoulders. "I haven't seen her since Agility Skills."

The way his voice hitches at the end suggests we don't know the whole story.

"What happened in class?" I ask him.

His mouth presses into a thin line and his eyebrows push together. I notice that the movement makes dimples appear on his cheeks.

"Did somebody hurt her?" Brey stands.

"Not… exactly," Valor stammers, but he doesn't take a step back from Brey. Now that I know what Valor can do, I wonder if he doesn't sense danger from Brey's bravado, or if Valor's just being stubborn. "You should go talk to her, though."

"Well, we would," I say irritated, standing as well, "if we knew where she was."

"Don't know what to tell you. I can't sense her right now." He winks at me like we have some inside joke. Cynthia calls for Valor from across the room and he gives us a final, apologetic look before running off to meet her.

"*What does that mean? Sense her*?" Brey asks me.

"It's not important right now," I mutter through the panic that's beginning to rise in my chest.

"Let's check your dorm," Brey suggests, shuffling his feet in that direction before I can agree.

We walk the length of the Eye and I have to wipe my sweaty palms on the hem of my shirt a few times before we get to the door.

"Are you allowed down here?" I hesitate with my hand on the door.

"Guess we'll find out."

We walk through together and I lead him to our dorm. It feels strange to have Brey in the place that I sleep. He was never allowed in my bedroom at home, and I never went in his.

Silent laughter from Brey enters my mind as we walk through the door. *"Why is it so... pink?"* he thinks dumbfounded. *"It's like the opposite of your personality."*

I glare at him.

Quiet sobs come from a pile under Trinka's blankets, pulling our attention.

"Trinka?" I ask. It surprises me how much concern is in my voice. We walk to the mound on her bed and I slowly peel back a blanket. "Hey," I say.

She sits up and tears cascade into her folded hands. She

refuses to meet our eyes as her lips quiver. I try to give her space, choosing to sit on the edge of the bed. I take one of her hands and give it a squeeze like she had when she saw me upset.

"How are they okay with us hurting each other?" she finally mumbles.

"Did someone hurt you?" Brey approaches the bed but doesn't sit down.

She looks up at him through teary eyes. The seconds seem to tick by as we wait for her to answer, and I can feel Brey's radiating frustration the longer it takes to find out what's going on.

"No, I was the one who hurt someone," she finally whispers between sobs.

Brey tries to recover from his look of shock, but Trinka sees it. She puts her face in her hands and her shoulders slump over. I have to fight my own surprise.

"It's not your fault." I try to coax her to lift her face again. "They're making you do it."

"What can you—" Brey starts to ask, but I shoot him a warning look and he stops.

"I hurt people. That's what my ability is," she says, answering Brey's only partially-asked question.

"How?" He's unable to stop himself.

She huffs a few times and her fingers twist in the white comforter, before answering, "My touch… it can hurt people. It only happens when I'm scared, but it's pretty bad."

"It's really not your fault, Trinka," Brey says. He sits on my bed across from us. I try not to think about Brey sitting on my bed, or the kiss that I saw. I look down at my hands while my cheeks cool down.

"I know, but it's just…" Trinka takes a deep breath. "It's

been haunting me for a really long time. That's why I'm here. They're supposed to help me stop the accidents." Her eyes become distant before she finishes her thought. "I almost killed my mother. Now she wants nothing to do with me. She's the reason I'm here. She sent me here."

"I'm so sorry," I say to her as I put my hand over hers.

"They're supposed to teach me how to control it. I can go home after they do." She looks up, finally meeting my eyes.

Part of me knows that I should console her and tell her what she wants to hear but there's another part of me, one that can't forget what my father wrote on that piece of paper.

"What if they don't want to teach you how to control it as much as they want to learn how to control you?" The words escape me before I mean to say them and it's Brey's turn to shoot me a pointed look. And perhaps it's not the right time, but the truth needs to be spoken eventually.

Chapter Eleven

The following day in Agility Skills, I get paired up with a girl who has a buzz cut. I don't know anything about her other than the fact that she hangs out with JC, which is enough to make me want to avoid her.

I try to muster my voice in a way that will bring the compulsion, but just like with JC, it doesn't work. I'm going to be covered in bruises here.

After that, Brey and I watch from the bikes as the hours pass until everyone is finished fighting. Most of our peers spend their time doing something obviously useful, whether it's weight training or practicing their specific abilities on the upper edge of the Pitch.

Brey seems content with joining me. I don't know if it's because he doesn't want to leave me alone, or if it's because he knows I wouldn't agree to do anything else. It vaguely occurs to me that it would be beneficial to train myself, even if it's just to become stronger. But to do that, I must seemingly cooperate with their agenda, and I can't bring myself to agree to that.

At the end of the class, Nick teaches us how to clear a room to ensure it's safe. The process is familiar and it hits me that it's because it's exactly what I saw myself doing in my dream. A determination sets in me as I learn from him. I won't let that happen to me in the future.

Finally, we get released for lunch. The ringing in my ear from being dropped by JC has stopped, so I suppose that's all I can really ask for.

The afternoon is the same as yesterday. Mr. Clayton seems to teach hypotheticals that we're not allowed to get wrong.

Today's question is whether killing is unethical, a controversial topic considering how many executions the government called for after the Censorship. Naturally, Mr. Clayton focuses on me as the example of what not to say. You'd think that a society with population issues wouldn't kill off its citizens left and right, but Eramica isn't known for being rational… something I was quite eager to point out to our teacher.

History with Mr. Regis is exhausting, but not for the same reasons as the other classes. My back aches by the end from sitting so far forward in my seat. It feels like it's too much power to know what went wrong, even if they believe we need the knowledge so we can keep history from repeating itself. We learn about the downfall of technology, including the removal of the internet and the negative medical effects caused by screens.

The rest of the week follows the same pattern. I spend my time focusing on my friends and survival. It's exhausting, and with how much mental energy is being used, I don't have time to practice my abilities.

The small amount of energy I do have is spent trying to find the exit. The way out must be a well-guarded secret. I've even started tapping on walls as I walk around rooms, just to see if they make a different noise. They never do.

Whispers follow me everywhere. After Cynthia's insinuation and JC's clear hatred, I have a feeling my peers view me as one of the threats Stealth warned them about. They likely started a campaign against me.

Brey and I sit on the purple velvet couch across from Trinka. It's the weekend again. Our third weekend here, if I'm counting correctly. I'm not sure how we're supposed to continue this monotonous routine week after week without getting bored, but since I can't find the way out, I don't have much of a choice.

The pads of my fingers draw small circles into the velvet while a guard walks by us, not even bothering to hide the long stare he gives me.

"Why are they still looking at you like that?" Brey thinks to me. His arm comes up along the back of the sofa, protectively circling around me as the warmth from him seeps into my chilled body. His clothes smell more like him now, though I'm not sure how that's possible since he doesn't use his old detergent here. But the mint and familiar smell of home encircles me with his arm. I shrug my shoulders.

"Guess Stealth wants to make sure I understand they're watching," I say through a clenched jaw. I'm sure my eyes reflect the tightness I feel in my chest.

Trinka turns around to see the retreating back of the guard. Her bright eyes find mine.

"They just want to make sure there's no trouble." She sits straighter in her chair. I scowl and cross my arms at the insinuation.

Of course, she's not necessarily wrong. I am the trouble they all need to look out for. The problem is that I have no idea how to tell my classmates about the future I know is going to happen when they think my singular ability is compulsion. Not to mention, nobody would believe me anyway since Stealth has created such loyalty here. As I swallow away the dryness in my throat, my dad's words come back to me again. *"When in doubt, the truth should win out."* I wonder if he would still say that if he knew my truth could get me killed.

I decide not to tell Breyson about my graduation, past what

I have already said. I don't trust him enough to hear his response right now.

Brey's eyes continue to follow the guard as he approaches Varick and JC. The guard leans down toward them and says something. Brey's eyes narrow at the interaction.

"It's too bad you don't have supersonic hearing," I mutter to Brey. His head snaps to me, warmth flooding his cheeks at getting caught watching so closely.

"We can't all have multiple abilities now, can we?" he says through his teeth, too quietly for Trinka to hear. I try to give him an accusatory glare, but he doesn't look back at me.

The weeks pass in a blur, so quickly that I have no idea what month it is. It feels like I'm just spinning my wheels trying to get through each day, and I can't ever remember a time that I was this thoroughly exhausted. That fact alone has me feeling panicked and anxious because of the looming pressure to find a way out of here. Easily the worst part of my day is Agility Skills.

I seem to have healed enough to run on my foot, though the pain still comes with each step. At this point, I've accepted that I might have caused permanent damage, but in a place like this, it's better to hide a weakness than get help for it.

My feet find a steady pace on the treadmill, and I fight to ignore the sting of pain, instead focusing on the thrill of the movement. The treadmill allows me to see down into the Ring so I can watch everybody else. Begrudgingly, I have to admit that the Domain has helped most of my peers grow their abilities. If my goal was to practice my abilities instead of finding an escape, this would be a good place to do it.

Not everyone's ability is obvious, even though it's been several weeks. Varick's, for example, isn't known by anyone. Although judging by his grace in the Ring, it must have something to do with combat.

Nick descends the stairs with a bounce in his step. He calls Cynthia and a boy named Larry.

Now that it's pretty well known what all our abilities are, nobody else in the class pays much attention to the training sessions. Cynthia, who can control water with her hands, holds a stream above her head. I don't think Larry has an active ability, but his footing mirrors hers while his fists are held protectively in front of his face.

Brey and I spend our time either on the bikes or treadmills, depending on how my foot is feeling.

"Lewis," Nick calls from the Ring when Cynthia's session ends.

I get off the bike and make the familiar walk to the edge of the Pitch. I've managed to limit the severity of my injuries, though I'm not sure how much longer I'll be able to keep it up.

"Dolion," he yells. The room isn't quiet, and nobody seems to stop what they're doing, but my vision becomes tunneled as I take each deliberate step.

On the other side of the Pitch, Varick's eyes refuse to meet mine. The dark brown seems hardened.

I'd been dreading this session. Varick doesn't take joy in hurting his opponents like JC does, but he also never loses, and his skills seem beyond what anyone our age should know.

I stand in the middle, waiting for him. My panic is the only thing keeping me company. Varick pulls off the headband from his wrist and ties his hair up.

Nick uncrosses his arms and pushes the button, locking me into the space with Varick. Somehow, it makes the scent of sweat even more potent, filling my nostrils, and threatening to make me gag.

A knot in the pit of my stomach tightens as Varick glances at me. The moment our eyes catch, I can feel a tug of certainty in my gut.

We begin. Our feet circle each other and I follow his slow and deliberate steps. My only goal is to not end up in the infirmary.

Across from me, Varick lunges. I back up in time, but I'm not sure how much longer I can simply spend my time in the Ring running away from my opponents.

Varick squats down low and does something strange with his legs, kicking mine out from under me. Before I realize what's happening, I'm on the floor, my back stinging from the sudden thud while I try to fill my lungs with air.

My brain tells me that in order to survive, I must get up. My legs feel weak, like even if I could stand, they wouldn't support me. I start to flail my limbs hysterically.

I can feel Varick shift me with his arm, keeping his body weight against mine. The touch seems to scald me through my clothing as Varick forces me into the ground with no place to go.

My limbs continue to reach out with no sense of direction. Varick's last movement shifted my body away from Nick's line of sight, so Varick can now do anything he wants and it won't be seen.

I try to look him in the eye, but he refuses to see me. Sweat beads along my forehead and my shirt sticks to me everywhere.

His left hand holds my shoulder in place with a firmness I can't fight. I take a deep breath and close my eyes to brace for impact as he cocks his right hand back. My breath stays hitched, waiting for the pain to come.

A thump next to my ear makes me wrench my eyes open. Varick's fist is on the mat next to my head. I try to sit up, but his other arm keeps me down, holding my shoulder firmly in place.

But he missed me. And I know he won't miss again; it's a miracle that I even got the few extra seconds of reprieve. I push harder against the arm that's holding me down.

He lowers his head. "Stay down," he whispers so close that it tickles. A shiver runs down my spine.

I know I should continue to fight, but my body feels like it's giving up and I freeze against his strength.

He lifts his right hand again and I still don't try to fight. I'm too tired to do anything but remain here. I close my eyes and scrunch my face up.

But once more, the sting never comes. A loud noise near my head makes me look around panicked to see his fist on the mat next to me.

"When you get up," he whispers, still tickling me, "hold the side of your face."

He releases his hold on my shoulder and I feel my hand lift to my face to follow his directions before I understand.

If he wants it to look like he hurt me, then he must have missed on purpose. And if he missed on purpose, then he wasn't threatening me; he was helping me.

And if Varick Dolion is helping me, then I was right.

Something is very wrong.

My feet find their way up the steps to Brey, who's hovering and waiting.

"Dolion, hallway, now," Nick calls. The tone in his voice makes me shudder and everyone starts to question what's happening. My heartbeat pulses in my ears through the now-silent room.

Varick holds his head high and follows our teacher, leaving murmurs and curiosity in their wake.

"Are you okay?" Brey's rushed thoughts become prominent. *"I'm going to kill him. Look at me, Mercer."* I realize that his voice was constant throughout the last few minutes, I just couldn't focus on it with everything else happening. He looks at my cheek.

I'm still holding my hand to my face, dutifully following the instructions Varick gave me.

I lower my hand, the feeling on my cheek still tingling with the ghost of the movement. Breyson's gaze doesn't break on my face as he analyzes what he thinks to be my injury.

"He didn't actually hit me," I mumble. I don't know if it's a secret.

"He what?" Brey's anger isn't allowing him to hear me clearly. His hand reaches up to my cheek, his fingertips lightly touching my face, sending a shiver down my spine.

I close my mouth but don't look away from the other side of the room. Varick and Nick walk back in, Varick looking grumpy and Nick seeming even angrier. My throat is thick and I can't swallow.

By the time we're dismissed, I'm convinced that Varick is intentionally avoiding my questioning looks and that makes me want answers even more.

I try to get his attention throughout ethics and history, but he refuses to look my way even once.

During history, a guard comes and pulls both Varick and JC from class and they don't return. Nobody seems to think much of it, but I can't help but feel like it's related to what happened in Agility Skills.

Dinner is a solemn occasion. I'm too perplexed to make small talk with my friends, and Brey keeps watching me too closely to allow much room for conversation, leaving Trinka confused. She keeps twirling her curls with her fingers and trying to spark something.

I don't know where Varick is. Maybe he's skipping dinner because of his regret. He had the opportunity to seriously hurt me, if not worse, and he didn't. Or maybe he's with JC, who's also missing, and they're planning their next move.

A part of me wonders if I'm being paranoid and irrational. Why would they care about me this much? Then again, if Stealth thinks I'm threatening the Domain, who knows what he would do? If my dream told me anything, it's that Stealth doesn't have limitations in how far he'll go.

Later, as insomnia keeps me awake, I decide that I'm going to confront Varick. I don't care if he's hoping I keep his help a secret or if he's plotting his next moves. I need to know what's going on.

By the time morning comes, I'm confident that at least today will be better than yesterday, because today I will get answers.

As I walk into the Pitch, the familiar adrenaline makes me flex my arms and fingers and the smell triggers my gag reflex. I should be used to it by now, but how can anybody be used to this?

Brey and I take the bikes and start peddling.

I watch Varick on the other side of the room, wondering when it's best to make my approach. Meanwhile, I can feel Brey eyeing me.

Nick coughs from the bottom of the Ring and my eyes shift to him, surprised to see that he's looking right at me. He's smirking; it's not his usual smile and it doesn't reach his eyes.

The class starts the same way it usually does. My chest tightens when Brey's name is called with Varick's. Varick is easily the best fighter in the class.

I watch them from my place on the top level while nobody

else seems to care. Varick and Brey circle each other. They appear to be more evenly matched than I was giving Brey credit for, although his anger toward Varick may be responsible. After a few more minutes, Nick ends things and gives them both suggestions on how to improve.

I decide that I'm going to corner Varick in the classroom hallway before ethics, which makes the time go even slower as I wait for us to get excused.

Brey comes back up from the Ring and joins me on the bikes. We keep this up while name after name is called.

"Last match of the day!" Nick finally calls and I dismount my bike, having not fought yet. It's been a pretty uneventful day, which means Nick's probably not satisfied. "Lewis!"

I start the dreaded descent as I listen for another name to come from his mouth. He waits until I'm all the way to the middle of the Ring, a smile pulling at his lips.

"Craw!" he yells eagerly.

My breath catches in my throat, and I can't swallow. My eyes scan the top of the Pitch for Breyson, but I can't find him fast enough. I look back to Nick to see genuine amusement in his eyes.

But it's too soon. I haven't fought everyone yet, and nobody else has been matched against the same person twice. This must be on purpose. This has to be planned.

"You don't have to do this," Brey thinks to me in an urgent voice.

My hands tremble at my sides. I try to clench them to stop the panic.

Brey stutters in his silent coaxing at the sight of Varick, who steps forward at the edge of the gallery and speaks loudly.

"I'll take Mercer's place." Varick's voice is determined and measured. His eyebrows are furrowed, jaw set in place.

My mouth opens with an audible pop. What could his motivation be? First yesterday, now this.

Varick's actions have momentarily stunned everyone else in the room. Silence seems to permeate everything.

"What the hell are you doing?" JC demands of his best friend.

Varick doesn't answer him but continues to stare at Nick, who simply shakes his head before responding.

"That's not how this works, Dolion." There's something in his voice that makes me cringe.

"Try to avoid him until the clock runs out," Brey strategizes, realizing the fight is inevitable. "*Maybe disable his ability.*" He's more urgent this time. "*He may not notice if you use something other than compulsion. Maybe nobody will notice. If they do, we can say that's your ability instead of the compulsion.*"

His rushed thoughts come out without making much sense and I don't have time to dissect them.

What would happen if they did notice me using another ability? No Unnatural has ever been known to have two, let alone four, as I suspect projection will soon be my fourth ability. What would Stealth do if he learned about my secret? Is that something I'm willing to risk to avoid getting hurt? Probably not. But is it something I'd risk to avoid death? Maybe, and as JC glares at me, I know death is on his mind.

Nick looks at his stopwatch as he calls, "Start."

Varick's presence is gone and Brey's voice is gone. I'm alone.

The room seems to move in slow motion. JC doesn't say anything even though he's spent the last few weeks taunting me. I make it a habit of not getting too close to him, so I'm surprised at how much… bigger… he's gotten. He was always shorter than his friends, but his bulk made up for it. Now, though, it's like he's doubled in size.

He sees my eyes examining him and flexes his bicep in response, making the tendons stick out.

I wipe my palms on my pants, but the friction from the material does little to cool the nerves inside me.

I'm still standing and that's an accomplishment. JC takes his time in his movements. He doesn't step toward me quickly, but instead uses slow and methodical strides. Fear grips my stomach and adrenaline makes my senses heighten as I watch him, eyes wide. He backs me into the edge of the Ring, and I sidestep to come back out into the opening.

A sadistic smile creeps up his face. "This is for my parents," he sneers.

His steps become different; faster and unreadable. It's not as easy to escape his reach when he begins to corner me. The movement is overwhelming and confirms that he must have gotten bigger. He did not have this kind of commanding presence weeks ago during our first match.

My chest heaves as the fear chokes my breath away. For the briefest moment, I want to stop moving and just give in. I can't believe the physical exertion this is taking. I refuse to look away from JC's relentless eyes unless I'm running away from him, for fear that I'll miss a decision he makes. His forehead wrinkles and he's sweating, showing that this is difficult for him, as well. He expected it to be easy.

He's trying to back me into one of the sides of the Ring again and it works as I feel my back push against the plastic wall. I wait a little longer, hoping that when he gets closer, I can rush past him and hurry to the other side. I'm faster than he is and that's the only thing saving me.

"*You're doing great!*" Brey's voice makes me jump.

I turn around to get the validation I crave but the sheer worry in Brey's features makes my heart jump to my throat as he looks at something behind me.

I turn around before he can issue a silent warning.

JC is too close to me and the grin on his face already reflects victory. I instinctively try to take a step back, but the wall greets me, pushing me into JC's arms. I start to lose my balance in my effort to avoid him.

JC's hand reaches out and wraps around my left bicep.

For a moment, I wonder if he's trying to help me, to keep me from falling down. My gratitude is short-lived as his fingers encircle my arm completely, continuing to tighten.

Something sickening crunches near me. It takes several moments to realize the noise came from my body.

My arm is on fire, burning from the inside out. I look down to see his hand, with giant sausage fingers, clenching tightly. My flesh squeezes out on both sides of his grip in a grotesque way.

Somebody is screaming and the sound won't stop. I wish I could ask them to stop; it's distracting when I need to focus on survival.

My eyes begin to close, and a fuzziness starts to surround me. His other hand reaches for my neck and I open my eyes to look at his face and beg for relief.

My throat feels raw, and I can't verbalize my request for him to stop.

As his hand tightens around my neck, the screaming stops. My eyes widen at the realization that the screaming was coming from me.

JC starts to close his other hand, the one around my throat

and black spots appear in my vision.

This is the end.

I think about Lizzy. The surprise of my thoughts turning to her are overshadowed by the regret that I'll never be able to explain why I've been distant our entire lives. I missed a chance at friendship with my twin.

It's with longing for Lizzy that a buzzing noise fills my ears. I can tell that JC's hold has lessened on both my neck and arm. I can't wade through the fuzziness enough to find out why or offer my appreciation. The floor greets me as my body slumps to the ground. The buzzing noise is still there, but so are other voices.

I try to open my eyes, but I can't. Instead, I see darkness.

Chapter Twelve

A fuzzy pounding radiates behind my temples; not terrible, but strong enough to be a nuisance. I open my eyes, which isn't as difficult as I expected, given the headache.

Sunshine streams through the curtains in Brey's living room, the warm rays touching my face and heating me. Breyson is nowhere to be found. I walk to the glass coffee table to pick up the old photo album that I've held dozens of times. It's the only place I've seen photos of Brey's father.

My hand moves right through both the album and the table. This must be another dream, which means my dream-self must be close by.

Someone rushes around the corner in answer to my thought. Dream-Mercer, with long hair and muscles that aren't as defined as the last dream, runs by me from the kitchen to the curtain by the window. A brush of air makes the hair on my arms stand as she passes.

"Okay!" she yells, her voice quivering and her nose slightly wrinkled. We're alone in the room, so I have no idea who she's talking to.

Outside, two men approach the house, clearly the source of her panic. They're nearly to the edge of the lawn, dressed in black, but before I can find out why they're causing dream-Mercer so much stress, I'm interrupted.

A steady beeping pulses in the back of my head, growing louder by the second. My eyelids try to flutter open, but something isn't right. Instead, I focus on the noise, wondering if it'll come closer to me.

Brey's living room disappears entirely.

My subconscious grants me the gift of not quite waking, while also not forcing me to watch more dreams. There's a vague awareness that I'm suppressing something, as if my body wants me to remember but my mind is allowing me a few more forgetful moments. So I let the rhythmic pulses lull me into a deep sleep.

The fuzziness seems to extend all the way down my arms and legs, like they haven't been used in days. Despite my body telling me that I've rested long enough, my head spins as the dizziness and nausea threaten to make me sick. The dream from Brey's house becomes distant, a memory not quite solidified, which is strange because I can usually remember my dreams vividly.

Those last few moments of what landed me here flood back and the memory of pain returns with a vengeance. I swallow and open my eyes to see my bandaged left bicep.

I can recall with complete clarity the last few minutes before I passed out.

Something nags at me. I don't want to jump to conclusions, but my gut is trying to tell me something.

The rational part of me doesn't think there's any way Stealth would target a 16-year-old like me. What kind of danger do I present to him? But as soon as I ask myself that question, I already know the answer. I threaten what he's built here because of my secrets. He might not know what my secrets are, but he knows I have them.

So what do I know? It wasn't my turn to go against JC again and nobody else has been partnered with the same opponent yet.

Varick seemed to know what his best friend was going to do; he even tried to stop it. We also know that students have died in Agility Skills.

I suspect that Nick was okay with letting the fight go longer. He saw JC's hand wrapped around my throat and he didn't interfere.

Based on the dream of my own graduation, I'd say it's safe to assume that Stealth doesn't have a problem ordering students of the Domain to kill other people, even children.

So, is it really that much of a stretch? My gut seems to settle into itself as my thoughts finally work to a conclusion and I know, although I'm not quite sure how I'm so certain, I know I'm right.

Stealth ordered my death.

Tears slip down my face and I don't bother to wipe them away. The only reason Stealth's plan didn't succeed is because he had no idea about my disarming power. That must have saved me. JC cut off my voice, effectively cutting off my compulsion. But something inside me snapped into place and my disarming ability took over, saving my life. JC wasn't strong enough to kill me without his strength, and I took his strength away when it mattered most.

So, what does this mean for me now? My heart sinks at the conclusion that not much has changed. I still need to get out. I still don't trust Stealth or this place. But then again, maybe something *has* changed. Brey wasn't fully on my side before. He had wanted to see the good in the Domain and that made him a difficult ally. Surely he can't see the good in this place now that they've tried to kill me. Maybe I can even talk Trinka into seeing things our way.

I look down at the bandage. Nothing can happen until I'm better anyway.

I flex my arm to test it, gritting my teeth immediately at my mistake. It hurts, but somehow it feels like it isn't as severe as it should be.

A pretty, dark-skinned woman steps into the room interrupting my analysis. Her hair is slicked into a neat bun at the nape of her neck, not a single brown hair out of place. She wasn't at the meeting from our first night here. She walks to me, although her movements make it look more like she's floating or dancing, given the elegance in each stride.

Her fingers work on the IV hooked to my hand. She touches the bandage on my bicep without meeting my tear-stained face. Her long fingers work with a delicate precision that calms me.

I'm in one of the six beds that occupy this room, which is otherwise empty. Medical equipment stands next to each spot. There was never a need to go to the doctor's office back home since monthly checkups were required at the school for Generation Novus students, so this equipment is all foreign to me.

"You'll have to wear a sling for a couple weeks," the woman says after clicking her tongue. "You can come see me every few days so we can check the progress of the healing. Thankfully, I had some help, so you're already further along than you'd be in the real world." Her hands fidget with something on the bag of liquid next to me. I wrinkle my nose at the sterile smell that I hadn't noticed until now. "Actually, not just in the real world, even only a few months ago here…" she rambles on. "Of course you are not to continue your Agility Skills until I clear you, but you're welcome to return to your other courses soon."

I can't help the sigh that escapes me. Agility Skills has tormented me since I got here and I can finally have a break from it, even if the circumstances are less than ideal. She notices my response and finally looks at me.

"I can release you in a few minutes, but you should tell your boyfriend that he doesn't need to sneak around here at night. He's always welcome to visit patients." The plump lips purse, and I get the feeling she doesn't like being deceived. I don't mention that Brey is only a friend because something about her is familiar and despite her involvement in the Domain, I like her, so what's the point?

"Okay," I assure her, my voice cracking. "What's your name? Where are you from? How long have you worked here?" My questions rush out of me now that I've spoken.

She smiles while removing the IV from my hand, then responds, "My name is Ms. Williams." She ignores the rest of the questions.

It only takes ten minutes before I'm placed in a sling and on my way out. My excitement to get to my friends seems like it's taking over my body and my feet trip over each other. If I'm not careful, I'm going to end up falling on my face and earning another trip back to Ms. Williams.

Despite being elated to move my stiff limbs, I also feel incredibly weak. I take the elevator instead of the stairs because of how little physical activity I've gotten in the last two weeks, which is the duration Ms. Williams said I was in the infirmary.

I still can't believe that's how long I was unconscious. So much could have happened in that time. I have to imagine that Brey's anger must have doubled every night I stayed in the hospital. The thought of my friends believing me along with my fast-paced walking is leaving me winded and I notice that my head is a little fuzzy from whatever medication is still in my system.

It's just after dinner and my feet bounce into the Eye before

I fully comprehend my position. If Stealth tried to kill me, should I really be showing my face? Then again, what other option do I have? My friends are right where I expect them to be, but instead of Trinka taking her usual spot on the armchair across from Brey, she sits next to him.

A few curious bystanders look my way as I take the first few steps in Brey's direction, but my feet seem to falter as I watch Brey and Trinka. Neither of them have noticed me yet, but Brey wraps his arm around the back of the couch. No, it's not on the back of the couch, it's around her shoulders. He leans forward and she seems to understand what he's doing and reciprocates the movement.

Their mouths lock together.

My brain seems to stop working and I stumble backward as they kiss.

They still haven't noticed me and I can't let them see me now. I'm not sure why I'm panicking so much, but I know I need to process this and to do that, I need to get out of here.

I open the stairwell door and let the slight temperature drop calm me. I can't risk someone seeing me like this, not until I pull myself together. I can't go up; there are too many people who might be coming from the cafeteria or even the classroom floor, which means my only other option is the Pitch.

My feet descend the stairs to the bottom level. As soon as I'm sure nobody will see me, I sink to the floor of the stairwell, letting the cold of the concrete seep through my pants.

Angry tears burn in my throat and I clench my jaw as an uncomfortable pressure hurts my chest. Here I thought that Brey would finally see things my way because of what Stealth did to me. I was wrong. Not only has he not come around, but apparently he's had time to do trivial things, like get a girlfriend.

I can't fathom spending my time doing something like that given the circumstances.

I let the fact sink in that Brey has spent the last two weeks kissing Trinka when I was in a hospital bed after someone tried to kill me.

He's not an ally. At least not right now. No amount of oxygen seems to be reaching my lungs despite my deep gasps. I've never felt truly alone because of Brey. He's helped me through my issues with Uncle Al and all the times I feared exposure with Eramica. While those were traumatic, he never left my side, but when my life was actually in danger…

I can't let Stealth win. He may have Brey's allegiance but I still know the truth. That little boy won't die during my graduation, and I won't let Stealth kill me.

So, here's the real question: how can I survive when I'm the only one who knows the truth?

Chapter Thirteen

Opening the heavy, metal door to the Pitch, the stench of sweat and blood brings back the memories as if it were happening again. I can hear my bone crack, the screams that took me a while to realize were coming from my own mouth, and my left bicep, neatly tucked in its sling by my ribcage, throbs at the memory. I grit my teeth and shake my head. I'm going to have to confront this room sooner or later, and if I'm being honest, I'd rather face this than the deep betrayal of what Brey really cares about.

The room is empty apart from the echo of pain that's inflicted within these walls. My feet continue around the upper area while I pass the equipment. I refuse to look to the Ring, as if I can spare myself the memories if I don't look directly at it. I've never been here when it's empty.

Frustration from the whiplash of the last hour buzzes through my arms, begging for a release.

I've spent months locked in this place, simply willing the time to pass quickly, thinking that freedom is closer with each passing day. In hindsight, it was foolish of me not to at least try to improve my strength or abilities. If I'm right and Stealth has targeted me, why wouldn't I do everything to try and survive?

My body settles in front of the punching bags. My shoulders tense with anticipation at the worn leather hanging in front of me. I've watched other people train here, but I've never felt skilled enough to do it myself. I visualize how my peers channel all their energy into the punches and excitement builds in my stomach; I crave that release.

My right fist flies forward before I can consider if I'm doing it right. It makes contact with the black leather, but I'm not prepared for what happens next. My hand doesn't even make a dent, but instead, the bag shifts the force back into my body, almost like it punched me back. I become unsteady and my good arm stretches out to try and regain my balance, fingers grasping for anything to help me.

It doesn't work. I fall backward as my back slams into the floor. The force of the landing racks through my body, pulsing my injury in excruciating beats. The only way to manage the pain is by breathing through my nose slowly until it passes.

Laughter echoes across the empty room.

Cold dread floods through me until it lands like a brick in my stomach and heat rises to my cheeks as my head snaps up to find the source; I was certain I was alone.

I can just make out a small, brown-haired bun on the other side of the space, partially concealed behind the lifting machines.

I try to stand as quickly as possible, but it's difficult with only one arm. I fall back down and the blinding pain courses through me once more, making me momentarily forget about the company I have. I grit my teeth and press my lips together. I can't believe this is happening. By the time the pain passes enough for me to open my eyes, the brightness from the florescent lights on the ceiling is blocked by Varick's looming body. I would do anything to make the red in my cheeks disappear.

"Here." He bends with an arm outstretched, and I flinch away. His mouth pulls down, but he doesn't comment as he helps me up.

When I'm finally upright, I can't help the involuntary few steps I take to put distance between us. I try to pull my arm away, but he holds my elbow firmly, following my retreat. My mind spins, screaming at me to run. After all, his best friend is the reason my arm is in a sling.

"I believe the words you're looking for are 'Thanks Varick,'" he says with a smirk. He flips his head to the side and the loosely bound bun flops with the movement. Sweat glistens along his brow, but he doesn't make a move to wipe it.

"What do you want?" I demand.

He finally releases his hold on me, allowing me to take another few steps away.

Varick's eyes seem to flash with a darkness, only for a second, before he looks back to my face.

"What do I want?" He repeats my question with far too much entertainment saturating his tone. He swallows and his jaw twitches. "I want to fix your form." My eyebrows draw close and my thoughts scramble as I replay his words. He continues before I can analyze fully, "If you fall over when delivering a punch, you're doing something wrong. You would think that'd be obvious, but I'm beginning to wonder if you understand the obvious."

"I'll keep that in mind," I say with a bite while turning around to end the conversation. Although I had wanted so badly to confront him about his strange behavior before my accident, my desire to be alone outweighs my curiosity.

I want to keep working with the punching bag, but I certainly won't do that until he walks away. With my back to him, I wait to hear his retreating footsteps, but nothing happens. Reluctantly, I turn my face to see if he's gone.

Not only has he not moved an inch, but he's smirking.

"Well..." he says, gesturing to the punching bag. "Be my guest." He raises a single eyebrow.

My nostrils flare. I turn my face away to hide the furious blush covering my cheeks.

"I'm not doing this for your entertainment," I mumble, wishing he would just leave me alone.

He simply chuckles to himself again, and I can't help but turn back to glare, regardless of how embarrassed I must look. He's biting his lip to contain a smile before sobering up. It's clear that his words are carefully selected before he says, "You need my help. We both know you need my help. Get over yourself and accept it." His jaw tightens and he clenches a fist at his side, making me take another step away from him.

I don't answer but hold his gaze as his hardened eyes study me.

"You're not doing well, and you don't seem to be improving," he explains. "Breyson isn't helping you, not in the way you need, and you're not going to survive if you don't get help."

I try to read his expression, but his jaw is set in a way I can't interpret.

"Well, thanks." My tone is flat. "But it isn't your problem." I turn so he's behind me, hopefully sending the message that this conversation is over.

Evidently, it's not. He steps around the punching bag, so I have no choice but to look at him. "Mercer," he says through a sigh as his eyes plead with mine, "you can trust me."

Except that's exactly what he would say if he wanted to trick me into trusting him. For all I know, he might be trying to lull me into a sense of security to finish what JC started. Maybe he was sent by Stealth.

"You're so skeptical." He rolls his eyes before I can even respond. "Just give me today and then you can decide on tomorrow."

I have no idea why Varick Dolion is making strange offers to me, but maybe this was his plan all along? Is there a possibility that he was offering his help when he didn't hit me that day in Agility Skills? Or that he was trying to save me when he volunteered to take my place right before I got hurt? Even if that's not the case, what's the worst that could happen? It's not like he could make my fighting worse, and if he was going to hurt me, then he probably would have already done so. I gnaw on my lower lip while I contemplate his offer.

"Fine," I agree, already feeling like I trapped myself in a less-than-ideal situation. The feeling of uncertainty boils in the pit of my stomach.

He gives a curt nod and moves to the bag, the tension leaving his shoulders.

"You need to focus on your strengths, no matter what you're doing," he explains. I'm a little taken aback by his quick transition. Evidently, nothing more will be said about our strange agreement. "You're fast and determined. If you learned a few skills, you could actually be a decent fighter."

I have no idea if his words are a compliment or insult, and at both notions, the heat returns to my cheeks.

He laughs again. I'm not sure if it's at my blush or his words, and he doesn't offer an explanation. Instead, he lightly jogs to the table with all the draws and opens one without hesitation.

"First, you need to wear boxing gloves or wrap your hands while training. Always." He shoves one on my single good hand. "It's bad enough that you get injured like you do in the Ring. Protect yourself as much as possible outside class hours."

"Okay." My voice sounds dazed at his accurate advice. He has a point, but I can't get past the fact that Varick is the one offering it.

"Come over here." He motions to the same black leather that knocked me backward. "You should keep your feet farther apart. You have to distribute your weight, or you'll be too easy to knock over. Look."

He pushes my good shoulder. With my feet the same distance from the bag, I have to move one of my legs to catch myself. Before long, he continues, "Now spread your feet apart. Put this one back here."

He repositions my right leg behind me while he keeps the other near the bag.

"Watch." He pushes me again, but I am able to stay standing after tightening my abdomen. The muscles wince at being used, but not in a bad way. "Before you actually try and punch, face your hips like this."

His fingers gently grasp me, turning my body to face the bag. My cheeks grow hot at his touch, but I turn my face away so he won't notice.

"Good." He takes a few steps to the side as he analyzes my stance. A smile tugs at the corner of his mouth. "Now, you can't forget that while you're on the floor. Always keep your feet apart."

I nod.

"Don't drop your arm."

I put my right hand back up.

"Okay, put your left arm here when you can use it again. This is to block your face." His jaw tightens at his words and for a brief moment, his eyes harden again.

"I'm not very good at blocking my face," I admit, guessing where his train of thought had gone. I bite my lower lip again to keep my voice from shaking at the memories.

"Yeah, no kidding," he mumbles to himself, so low that I'm not entirely sure I was meant to hear it. "You need to learn how or you're going to die here."

His statement hangs between us, begging to be addressed, but neither of us say anything more on it.

"You need to swing from here," he says while putting a hand on my stomach. The touch surprises me, and I accidently lower my right arm.

"Sorry," I mutter as I raise it again.

He tries to fight a smile, then lifts a hand to rub his mouth and chin, concealing the reaction.

"Swing right here." He points to a spot on the bag. I lock my left arm in the sling by my side and brace myself for the sting that will follow. I raise my right hand and swing it forward with as much force as I can.

The bag hardly moves from the impact, but my body stays upright. I shake my hand to alleviate the stinging that spreads across my knuckles underneath the glove. My left arm aches, but the pain is tolerable.

"Maybe we should wait until you're feeling better." His brow wrinkles.

"No, I'm fine," I tell him with a shrug. He studies me closely before finally agreeing.

Varick continues to teach me different ways to punch the bag. It's the first time in months that I let myself get distracted in my exercise. We work through a few different movements, and he shows me how to walk around an opponent by matching their steps. He points out things that I don't do right in a fight, making me realize he's been paying closer attention to me than I ever knew. Maybe he watches everyone closely, which would explain how he's so skilled at fighting.

He tells me that we'll need to rehab my arm when it's out of the sling, but that I'll be able to do a lot more with both arms working. I can't help but wonder how long he intends to keep up this strange alliance.

Sweat drips down the sides of my face and my long hair sticks to the back of my neck. I want to put it up but can't with only one good arm. I haven't worked this hard in a long time and my left arm aches deeply. I keep trying to put pressure on it to alleviate the sharp stabs of pain, but it hardly helps.

"We need to be done," Varick says after another round of hits. He's out of breath from barking orders.

"No, I want to keep going," I argue, using my hand to fan my face.

"You're in too much pain," he says as his shoulders tense and he absentmindedly rubs his own left bicep.

"I'm fine." I try to add more persuasion to my voice. Who knows if this is just a one-time deal?

"Mercer," he says, shaking his head, "you're not."

He helps me out of the single boxing glove, despite my protests.

"Let's meet here again after dinner tomorrow. It's usually empty," he says like it's obvious we'll be doing this again. He doesn't look at me as he cleans up the small mess we've made.

I guess I can agree to end things today if he's already making plans to continue.

"Okay," I mumble.

"It's probably best if we don't tell anybody about our arrangement." His eyes refuse to meet mine.

My gut clenches tightly at the memory of Breyson and Trinka kissing, and I shove aside the desire to tell Brey anything at the moment. Besides, I have no idea how he'd react to the information that I've struck an alliance with his ex-best friend. If Varick is going to help me, I'm not going to say no just because it might hurt Brey's feelings.

"Agreed," I say through tightness in my voice.

Varick quickly studies me, obviously hearing the strain in my tone.

"Aren't you coming?" I ask him on my way to the door.

He raises a single eyebrow and smirks. "I need to finish my workout, or I'll be as bad as you are in class."

I shake my head, the uncomfortable feeling still gnawing at my stomach. How have things changed so much in only a few hours?

Before I reach the dorm, Brey finds me in the Eye. I'm relieved to see he's alone.

"When did they discharge you?" he asks me silently, the look of overbearing concern on his face.

"A few hours ago." I clench my teeth together. I'm not ready to ask him about Trinka, and the lump in my throat forms at the reminder that he prioritized her over what happened to me.

"Were you working out?" His eyes trace my sweaty forehead and flushed cheeks.

"I'll explain later," I mumble without any real conviction. I say something about exhaustion and scurry away from him before he can press further.

My racing thoughts make me forget about Brey the second I walk away from him. I just can't fathom how or why Varick Dolion wants to help me.

I do have to admit the truth, though. Varick is the best trainee in class. I don't know if it's supernatural or just skill, but it seems foolish to turn down that kind of help if he's offering. So, maybe this is how I survive.

Chapter Fourteen

Trinka is already asleep by the time I get to our room, though I have no idea if she'd even realize something is wrong with me if we spoke.

My bed has a chill between the covers and I sigh as my body sags into it. After two weeks in the infirmary, these blankets feel like heaven.

Across the room, Jaylee is sitting up in her own bed with a small light highlighting a book that she's reading. She glances up in my direction and I quickly try to look away, but before I do, I see a small, sad smile.

Strange.

She hasn't spoken to me since she demanded I leave Lottie alone. I try not to let it unnerve me. I'm starting to think that everyone is out to get me and there's just no way that's true.

Unfortunately, the time and space away from Varick and our odd situation doesn't help my anxiety. I can't stop thinking about the fact that if I'm right, and if Stealth does want me dead, Varick could be part of his plan.

Although I'm not sure that changes anything.

Varick might be my only option, trap or no trap. I can't deny that his help made a difference, even in just one night. If he's going to try to hurt me, why don't I get as much out of it as I can first?

The idea of talking to Brey makes my stomach clench. It

almost feels like it's wishful thinking to believe he'll see things the way I do. But do I owe Brey more credit than that? I haven't even attempted to hear him out, and he's been my best friend for as long as I can remember.

I need to talk to Brey. I have to at least give him a chance. Maybe he'll even agree to help me get stronger, which would allow me to forget everything with Varick and solve two problems.

It's settled. I'm going to tell Brey what I suspect, and based on how he responds, I'll either embrace the strange thing with Varick or I'll skip tomorrow's planned training session.

My mind finally relaxes enough to slip into a deep sleep and I don't wake until Trinka nudges my foot.

"We're going to be late," she says while I force open my eyes. Her voice still sounds cheerful, but the happiness is almost pinched, which isn't like her.

We wait for Brey at our purple loveseat while Trinka asks if I'm excited to be back. It feels so normal that I start to wonder if what I saw last night was even real.

"How are you feeling, Merc?" Brey asks out loud, drawing our attention. He gives Trinka a small look that I can't decipher as I answer.

"Fine. Just tired."

"Did you not sleep well?" His response is silent and I don't think anything of it, but Trinka shifts uncomfortably next to me during the pause that it takes for Brey to get the words out.

"I did. I think I'm just still recovering." I stand as my answer spills from me so we can start making our way to the dining hall. It doesn't take me long to notice that both of them are a few steps behind, and when I glance around to look for them, I catch the end of a tense conversation. "Everything okay?"

"Fine," Trinka says, taking a few steps to catch up with me and leaving Brey behind. "I'm starving. Let's go."

I try to meet Brey's eyes as Trinka grabs my arm to whirl me around but he avoids my gaze.

I can't find the courage to tell them about my suspicions during breakfast. They don't bring up their kiss, and I don't ask about it. I also don't mention the weird alliance I made with Varick last night.

Agility Skills is strange. Nick isn't necessarily hostile, but he definitely isn't friendly either, and part of me wants to remind him that between the two of us, I should be the angry one. His lack of intervention is what landed me in the infirmary for two weeks.

JC, on the other hand, radiates hostility. The look he gives me is enough to set my nerves on fire.

My body aches after training with Varick last night, and although I could use the bike while wearing my sling, I choose to sit on the steps and watch the fights instead.

Nick announces that I'm excused until further notice, so nobody pays me any attention. Brey sits with me for a bit, but after a few warning glances from Nick, goes to a bike. Although he's been keeping up a one-sided conversation from there… not that he's said anything about Trinka or my injury.

"Hey," a voice calls from nearby. It's not Brey, so I just assume it isn't meant for me, but then a body slinks down the steps and sits right next to me.

I work to hide my shock at Cynthia's sudden appearance, or even her willingness to talk to me, but she continues before I can say anything.

"How are you feeling?" she asks like we've been friends for months. Her eyes watch mine closely, waiting for an answer.

Meanwhile, I'm still working on closing my mouth.

"Are you okay? What's going on?" Brey's voice interrupts my shock.

"I'm fine," I say loudly enough that Brey can hear me. I can see him mount the bike again out of the corner of my eye, seemingly having gotten off it to come help me in case Cynthia was being aggressive.

"Are you really?" Cynthia presses, not realizing I was also answering Brey. Her eyebrows push together and I can't help but feel there's genuine concern behind her question, though I have no idea why.

For the briefest moment, I want to tell her that I'm far from fine. I want to explain that my problems go so much deeper than my physical injuries, and that I don't know how I'm supposed to survive here.

"Yes," I say, through a weak smile. "Happy to be back."

"Liar." She gives a forced chuckle. "But I won't tell anybody how you really feel."

I cough, but no words come out. She looks at me in a way that's clear she's trying to read my body language, so I sit up straighter and direct my eyes back to the Ring where JC is pummeling a boy he hangs out with.

Cynthia doesn't leave, but she also doesn't say anything else. She just sits beside me in silence.

I try not to appear uneasy at her presence, but I have no idea what she wants from me. Then, almost as if she's answering my unspoken thoughts, she continues.

"I'm beginning to think you were right. Stealth isn't the savior we all thought he was."

My head turns to her so I can read her face, but there's nothing to indicate that she's messing with me. Instead, she gives a sad smile and stands.

"Don't let them take your voice away." She sounds so strong, determined, and unbothered about the fact that anybody might hear her.

"I—" but nothing else comes out. What am I going to say?

As I watch her cross to the other side of the room, I can't help but wonder if this change in her behavior is because of what happened with JC. Did she finally see that we could be pushed too far?

I tell Brey about the interaction on our way to lunch, but he doesn't offer any insights. Trinka meets us in the cafeteria and Brey ends the conversation before she can get involved. I consider bringing it up again, but I had promised myself I would tell them what I think about Stealth, and if I don't do it now, I won't do it at all.

"I need to tell you something," I say after fidgeting with my fork. They both sit in silence, waiting for me to continue. I take a drink of water and clear my throat. "I've been going through the fight with JC, and I think that it was on purpose."

I continue to stare at my plate and I hate how much my insides are squirming at the idea that they might not believe me. I'm almost embarrassed to voice these things out loud, but I'm not sure why. I try to focus on my fork, spinning it around with my fingers while I wait for a response.

"Of course it was on purpose. He hates us," Brey says as I snap my head up, almost relieved at his words, before I realize he doesn't fully understand yet. Trinka just continues to watch.

"It's not just that," I push. My heart feels like it's jumped into my throat and I hate how difficult it is to talk, but I need to get this out. I've already started the explanation and I can't just let it go unfinished. "I think that Stealth put him up to it."

They just sit and stare at me. I risk a glance upward to meet their eyes, while also wiping my palms off.

"You think the director of this entire facility tried to get another student, a child, to kill you?" Trinka finally asks. Her voice is calm, but it's so condescending that I balk from it. When she says it like that, I can hear the ridiculousness behind the theory, but I still know I'm right.

"I do," I say slowly and more determinedly, realizing now that my hesitancy is thanks to my fear that they won't believe me. "We know that death happens in Agility Skills, but maybe it isn't always accidental."

Again, silence greets me. I start thinking about what more I can say on the subject when she huffs so loudly that it draws my attention.

"I told you this would happen," she says under her breath to Brey. She shoves her chair away from the table and gets up, not bothering to lower her voice. "I'm not letting her ruin my chances of getting out of here. You need to speak to her."

I work to control my stunned reaction as she strides away with her nose high in the air.

"What—what was that?" I ask Brey dumbfounded. He rubs his hand across his forehead, pushing it into his hair and making it flop around. It's much longer than it was when we got here; it's not sticking up in strange directions after he messes with it anymore.

"The person who works here who knows her mom... they warned her to stay away from you," Brey tells me. He meets my eyes, and I can only see sympathy behind his gaze, but that just makes it worse.

I fight through the hurt behind his words. "Doesn't that just prove it even more? Stealth clearly doesn't want me here."

He waits before answering me, and I can't tell if he's considering his next statement or if he's trying to give me a chance to cool down.

"I think the only thing it proves is that you're making your situation worse here by being so determined to find something wrong with this place," Brey says to me out loud, as if he wants his words to really resonate. "Trinka is just worried it's going to ruin her chances of graduating."

"And Trinka is eager to graduate? Just like that?" I demand. Part of me feels guilty for not fully disclosing the graduation I saw to him, but now's not the time to consider that. I made my decision and I can't tell him about the boy until I know I can trust that he won't judge me for it.

He takes a deep breath, watching me carefully before he says silently, *"I don't doubt your abilities, but I think that you're wrong here. We've been given no reason to believe they don't have our best interests at heart. I'm going to trust them until they give me a reason not to. So, no. I don't think Stealth is trying to get someone to kill you."*

"Oh, and that incident with JC, I suppose that was just Stealth having my best interests at heart?" My hands start to shake with anger and I clench them so tightly that my body seems to pulse in response. I push my chair back from the table and when Brey opens his mouth to answer, I cut him off. "You know what? Forget it. Just forget all of it."

My steps carry me away. I'm not even sure where to go; I just know that I need to get away from Brey. I yank open the stairwell door, praying that he isn't following me.

The cold space is empty as my first shaky breath echoes around.

It shouldn't matter. It really shouldn't matter.

Brey has been there for me almost my entire life. He's still the same person he always was.

Right?

Even as I try to convince myself of those words, I can't help the crumbling feeling that's taking place inside me, as if my heart is shattering and falling into pieces all around me on the floor, impossible to pick up.

Voices filter into the stairwell from every direction as my peers are bustling around with their free time before our afternoon sessions start.

I stand in the stairwell with my hand on the railing, looking for an answer as to where I should go. The door to the Eye opens below me, laughter filling the cold space, and I start to move up the next several levels, just to avoid being seen.

Since our first day here, I've had no reason to go upstairs beyond the classroom corridor. Besides Stealth's office and our first orientation, I haven't seen what's on any of these levels.

But that hardly matters now. The only thing I care about is that these floors are rarely used.

It hits me all at once.

I'm so alone. I would give anything to simply be worried about making it to ethics class on time. Maybe I'd be enjoying lunch. Brey and Trinka could awkwardly break the news that they're dating. I would congratulate them, laugh off how weird they were being all morning, and we'd talk about our weekend plans of trying to watch a movie in one of the always-populated television areas.

Even just thinking of that reality makes my stomach hurt. It's so far from my reach, an impossibility that will never be met. Instead, there seems to be an ever-growing list of reasons why my life will never be that carefree, starting with a graduation that may or may not be in my future.

My dream hasn't become a reality yet, which means I can still keep it from happening. Nobody even needs to know about that version of the future. I can keep this as my darkest secret, never to be shared with anybody. Because the fact of the matter is that ever since that dream, I've felt like I lost a piece of myself.

I've always been fairly confident in who I am, but the person I believe myself to be would never kill a child. That dream of my future… I don't know that person. I don't want to become her.

But that dream is just one of the reasons why my life is so messed up.

I've had one ally my entire life. When I woke up here, I felt lucky that I had found another in Trinka. But just like that, two weeks without me around, and now I can't count on either of them.

I know I'm right about Stealth. I know I'm in danger. And if Brey and Trinka won't believe me, then I'm just going to have to figure things out on my own.

I hadn't realized how much I was crying but it's almost painful to force air into my lungs as my breaths are jerky and shallow.

"Mercer?" A voice descends the stairs from above me, and there's relief in it, like the person had been searching for me, but that wouldn't make any sense. I hadn't heard a door open, but I can't exactly say that I'm paying attention.

I wipe the back of my hands against both cheeks, and they come away streaked with my tears. I'm certain my face looks red and puffy, and my breathing still hasn't stabilized.

"What are you doing" There's a demand in the question, and the voice is closer this time, close enough for me to recognize who it is.

That realization sends a new wave of dread through me. I haven't even gotten to the part of my self-analysis where I considered what my new agreement with Varick means. Do I train with the person who I think might be setting me up? Can I use him for his knowledge before he uses his time with me to do what he's supposed to do?

Varick almost reaches me but I stand in a hurry and start the descent down to the classroom corridor. I might be able to duck into a bathroom and fix my face before anybody sees me, but if Varick gets even a little closer, he's going to see the tears, and that's not something I want to risk.

"Mercer," he says again, sounding frustrated. Our first night here, Varick was also on the top floor. Perhaps he just came from a meeting with Stealth. Perhaps that meeting was about what to do to me.

"I'm fine," I say weakly. My voice cracks and I have to take a gasp of air as my lungs try to work normally after how much I have been crying.

"You're not fine. You're freaking out," he continues. "What happened?"

He steps in front of me and cuts off my fast-paced race back down the stairs, forcing me to stop. He's nearly at my level as he looks into my eyes while standing a few steps below me.

"Nothing," I say automatically. "It just still hurts." He glances to my arm in the sling before looking back at me.

His jaw tightens and he narrows his eyes as we stand like this for several seconds. He opens his mouth to say something, then closes it and seems to think twice about his answer before finally responding.

"I hope the pain doesn't keep you from training tonight. I have something good planned." He smirks like he just said an inside joke that only he understands, but all I can wonder is whether or not what he has planned is something Stealth has asked him to do.

"I'll be there." Some of my determination is coming back and my voice sounds more sure as I remind myself that training with Varick is going to help me no matter what the outcome. "Excuse me."

I don't give him a chance to stop me a second time, racing down the steps to the classroom corridor.

A quick inspection in the bathroom has me wincing at how red my face is, but there's not much more I can do other than splash some cold water on it.

As I walk into ethics, Varick is already there and he doesn't even acknowledge me. Brey on the other hand…

"What happened? What's wrong?" His voice comes out in panicked silence and he stands from his desk as I walk by.

Nothing. I'm fine," I mumble to him as I pass. I've been sitting in the back row since that first day, not that it helps keep me from Mr. Clayton's line of fire.

As I take my seat, I watch as Brey gathers his things from his desk and walks the distance between us, plopping down next to me. I don't miss the judgmental look that Varick gives him, but I don't have it in me to analyze why.

"What is going on?" Brey's voice flies into my head again. This time he stares at me while waiting for a response.

"I'm fine," I say again, and I can't help but notice that I'm saying those words more and more, not that it's ever true. I want to tell him everything. I want to tell him that I know I'm right about Stealth, but I can't do that in a room full of other people, and even if I could, I just keep hearing his response to me earlier.

"Is this about what I said to you at lunch?" he thinks to me,

but Mr. Clayton walks into the classroom from his spot at the door, saving me from having to answer.

The class is much like the rest of them, although even Mr. Clayton must notice something is wrong with me because he doesn't single me out at all.

In history, we discuss the population crisis and ailments that took most of our world, including my parents. It's still unclear whether their deaths were caused by the food, chemicals or something else entirely. Perhaps the human body just couldn't adapt to all the new realities it was up against.

We're about to be released and I'm already contemplating how I can skip dinner. I don't want to see Trinka. I can't have a repeat of lunch. But before we can go, Mr. Regis closes his book and stands directly in front of us.

He addresses us all, but his eyes seem to linger longer on JC and then on me, when he says, "Though it's unclear what may have caused us to be in this predicament, there is something for certain that we must always focus on. Cowardice is an option in today's world, yesterday's world, and tomorrow's world. You are here because you are different. Being different can set you apart in both good and bad ways. The only person who can choose whether you are a coward is you. Remember that."

Nobody speaks and it takes a while for the first person to stand up and leave the classroom.

I can't help but feel like the message was for me, but what could it mean? Was he criticizing JC's actions toward me? Or does he somehow know the thoughts that I'm conflicted with now about my future graduation?

"That was weird," Brey thinks to me. It's forced conversation and I know him well enough to know that he's just trying to test the waters and make things more normal.

"Yeah," I reply, but it comes out bitter and we both hear it. I'm not ready to talk to Brey. The words he spoke to me at lunch still sting. I can't help but imagine that if he wasn't kissing Trinka these last two weeks, he'd likely have heard me out more than he did. I'm not sure when this became a division of sides, but evidently it's more important for him to take Trinka's, even though mine is quite literally life and death.

"I'm starving. Ready for dinner?" The phrasing of his question makes it clear that he's wondering how deep this tiff runs. Brey and I don't fight, not really. I don't want to deliver my response, but I cannot stomach another meal with them. As badly as I want to protect this friendship, I can't. Not this time.

"I'm not hungry," I say grimly, trying to avoid eye contact, but I can still see his face drop at my words. He knows. "I'll see you."

I'll have to find time to eat later, once Brey and Trinka clear away from the dining hall. My appetite has grown since I've been here, and it's not surprising, given the amount of physical activity we get. But, in this moment, there's really only one place I want to be.

I haven't stopped thinking about the high I felt last night when Varick taught me how to actually defend myself. There's power in knowledge, and I've spent months here giving up the opportunity to learn. I won't do that again.

As soon as I open the Pitch doors, the smell of sweat is strong, the last class having just vacated. It may be dangerous to be in this room alone, a waiting target if JC or anyone else working for Stealth were to join me, but after today, I can't find it in me to care.

Instead, I walk over to a punching bag and line myself up, practicing the things that Varick walked me through last night. I had been itching to do this in Agility Skills, but I didn't want anybody to notice.

I stick with it for thirty minutes or so before the door opens. My heart jumps into my throat at the idea that it very likely could be JC.

"You're early," Varick calls over to me. His eyebrows are drawn together and even from this far away, I can see how worried he is, though I have no idea why.

"I ate quickly," I call back. It's not the truth, but he doesn't need to know that.

His lips turn to a frown as he gets closer to me, but whatever is on his mind must become an afterthought because he motions for me to continue.

"Let's pick up where we left off yesterday," he says while I start again. "When you're out of your sling, I want to work on your speed, but that requires more than a treadmill. You're easily the fastest person from our class back home and I think you're the fastest person here." He hesitates, and it serves as a reminder that he's likely working for Stealth right now.

I have to breathe through my nose and remind myself that it doesn't matter; I'm going to get what I can from training before Stealth tries to kill me again.

"What are you thinking?" Varick's voice turns cold and serious. He stands directly in front of me, demanding an answer. I don't know what my face reads, but I scold myself for not better masking what I was thinking. I don't need Varick learning how to interpret my reactions.

"Just ready to start," I lie feebly. He looks like he wants to press the issue, but after watching me closely, he sighs and shifts his eyes to the punching bag.

I let myself get lost in the movements, relishing the feeling as I put all my aggression into the black leather bag hanging in front of me.

By the time eight o'clock hits, my entire body is heavy with fatigue. While sweat drips down my face, I hunch over to catch my breath. The pause makes my left arm throb in protest.

"That's probably enough for today," he says, gingerly rubbing his own left arm.

He looks up at my confused expression and drops his hand immediately.

"Same time tomorrow, he says to me. "Although by that, I mean same time as planned. You need to eat dinner if you're going to train this hard."

I open my mouth to say something but his knowing look stops me short, so instead, I just answer, "Fine."

Confusion has plagued my day from start to finish, but at least one thing seems to be more certain. I was already confident that I would give Varick this chance to train me, knowing that his ulterior motives might not be great. But now I'm positive that it was the right choice. Whether Varick turns on me this week or a month from now, it won't matter because I'll take all that time getting better at fighting back.

The following day is still strange with Brey and Trinka. I can't tell if it's because of them or me at this point, but I take Varick's advice and scarf down dinner before meeting him in the Pitch.

Just like the first two nights, I learn things that I've never known before. I become a better fighter, even if it's just by a little. The trainings with Varick usually exhaust me so thoroughly that sleep is easy after I fall into bed.

My mind is free from the drama with Brey and Trinka and my body is so tired that I don't feel compelled to worry about how I'm going to get out of the Domain or what Stealth's plan is.

Blissfully, I fall asleep, only to wake up to another dream.

What's strange is that as soon as I realize I'm dreaming, I

also realize that I've seen this before.

I watch as dream-Mercer runs to the curtains in Brey's living room, calling out that someone is coming.

I barely have a chance to glance beyond the window to see those two men she's afraid of before my consciousness tugs at me.

Before I wake up fully, though, I do take note of the attire of the men who are clad in the same black uniforms I've seen before. It's familiar and now I know why. I try to calm my racing heart as I comprehend what it means because the truth behind the dream is bittersweet.

I am going to successfully escape the Domain, and when I do, I'm going to go to Brey's house for some reason.

But despite getting out, things won't be easy.

Stealth is going to hunt me.

Chapter Fifteen

It isn't until one week after I'm discharged from the infirmary that Trinka finally tries to speak to me. It's an awkward conversation and I can hear Brey's influence behind her words, but I take the olive branch that she's offering.

I sit with them for breakfast and lunch, although the conversation is forced and none of us enjoy it. Brey doesn't speak to me using his ability, but that's hardly surprising given how awkward things are even when he speaks out loud.

Varick and I continue to train in secret. I keep waiting for him to end our alliance, or try to hurt me in some way, but he doesn't. So, just like I had decided, I continue taking as much knowledge as I can from him.

"I think I'm fine," I tell Ms. Williams the second week after I was discharged. I show her my range of motion to prove it. My arm has never felt better and I can't imagine why I'd still need the sling. Even though I had a broken bone, I can't deny how much better I feel. It may be irrational, but I know I'm healed.

"One more week," she says through pursed lips. I start to argue with her assessment but she doesn't even hear me out before moving on to another student. I'm starting to think that her diagnosis has less to do with my recovery and more to do with keeping me out of the Ring. I consider telling her about my training with Varick but decide not to.

Hunger claws at my stomach from the long day as I walk to the dining hall. If I thought I was hungry before, it's nothing compared to now. I've noticed my appetite increase substantially since I started working with Varick.

Unfortunately, it becomes clear as soon as I enter the giant hall, that I can't avoid Brey and Trinka, who sit at a table right near the entrance and wave me over. They sit side by side, even when dining without others, which is so strange to me. The arms closest to each other are both under the table, and I fight the urge to gag at the idea that they hold hands while eating. I want to tell them that I don't care, or that they look stupid, but I just say nothing. Instead, I try to finish my dinner quickly so that I can spend some time alone.

After several tense minutes of me shoving food into my mouth, Brey raises his eyebrows but doesn't say anything as I stand from the table. Almost daily, a stab in my chest makes me think about how much I miss him. To be honest, I also miss Trinka. Even when I'm physically with them, it just doesn't feel the same.

Neither of them demands to know why I'm leaving so quickly, and I don't offer a reason. The hallway back to the stairwell is empty, the smell of disinfectant stronger when nobody is around.

Truthfully, I'm not in a hurry to be anywhere tonight. My urgency was simply to get away from them. Varick insists on taking days for rest between our training sessions. I hate our off days.

I find my way to the purple loveseat in the Eye. It's so strange how different everyone looks from when we first arrived, something I don't think I'd notice unless I was intentionally looking.

My legs fold under me on the sofa so I can recline comfortably. The Eye is always busy, even when students are eating. The strong, buttery smell of popcorn wafts through the air from the group watching a movie nearby. It's an animated film that I've seen played on that screen before but haven't watched myself. In fact, I haven't really utilized any of the activities in the Eye. Before JC had landed me in the infirmary, Trinka, Brey and I were planning to wake up early on a Saturday to get one of the television areas before anybody else could. I wonder if they did that without me.

Jaylee enters the room, likely coming from the dining hall, her arms wrapped around her stomach and her eyes distracted. She looks up at the pool table, the spot that her friends usually occupy, but it's empty. She must feel my gaze because she glances at me, but I look away and my ears grow hot at getting caught. I try to look fascinated by something on my nail beds.

"Hey." Her high-pitched voice pulls me out of my forced distraction.

She doesn't wait for an invitation, but just sits in Trinka's armchair. First Cynthia, now this. Could Stealth be using these girls to get to me? But no, Cynthia insinuated that she was as wary of Stealth as I am.

"So, Brey and Trinka," Jaylee says, as if we'd been mid-conversation.

"Yep," I answer, feeling my eyebrows pull together in skepticism.

"Interesting combination," Jaylee continues. I'm not sure why she cares. Then again, Jaylee shares every class with Trinka; there's a very good chance she knows a side to Trinka that I don't. Jaylee doesn't move to get up, but instead leans back even more, settling into the chair. "You know, I accidentally showed him my ability in school once. He cut his hand in class; I used my ability before I even realized what I was doing. I spent weeks afraid of when they'd come for me. I guess he didn't tell anyone." She watches me and adds, "Including you, judging by how surprised you look." A thousand thoughts race through my brain, but the one taking priority is that my best friend hasn't been as honest as I had thought, which seems like a habit he's carried here.

Before I can answer, Valor strolls toward us and flops into the other armchair.

"Is it just me," he says with a wave of his hand, "or is everyone here focused more on dating and less on training?" He shakes his head and starts tapping his fingers on the chair.

"It's so inappropriate," Jaylee agrees in a whiney voice, switching her attention to her friend. She shifts her entire, small body to square herself to him when she responds.

"I—" I start to stutter but my mind goes blank, "what?"

"Have you really not noticed anybody else?" Valor asks, eyebrows raised, with a spark of amusement in his eyes. There seems to be a double meaning to his question that I ignore.

Looking beyond the chairs where they sit, a boy and girl walk by, holding hands. In an area nearby, several couples sit across from each other, leaning their heads together. And now that I'm looking for it, I notice the group watching the movie is full of pairs sitting too close to just be friendly.

"When did that happen?" I ask, my jaw still hanging open. My fists start shaking and I have to dig my fingernails into my palms to control myself. That little boy from my dream seems to always be on my mind, begging for me to find an alternative to the future I saw. How can so many people spend their time so trivially when that's my reality?

"You're so blind, Lewis," Valor says, shaking his head.

Cynthia and Lottie walk up to us while continuing whatever conversation they were having. Cynthia plops down on the purple sofa next to me without hesitation.

"Here, Lots," Valor says, jumping up. He runs over to another section and grabs a small chair. My stomach twists in discomfort at whatever is happening.

"It's okay," I say. "I can go." I'm sure they didn't mean to overrun my spot, but it makes more sense for me to leave than it does for them to relocate.

All four of them turn to look at me like I said something stupid. As I stand, Cynthia grabs my wrist and pulls me back down.

"Why would you go?" Cynthia leans deep into the edge of the couch and puts her feet up so they're inches away from me.

"Don't you know, Livingston, she's only happy if she's being a loner," Valor address Cynthia with a smirk. I open my mouth to argue with him, but his returning wink stops me.

"Just stay," Jaylee urges with a sincerity that I haven't before heard from her.

"I meant what I said to you," Cynthia murmurs close to me. "I shouldn't have believed what he told us. I was wrong about you and I'm sorry."

The others seem to watch me closely, clearly allowing Cynthia to speak for them as well.

"Well, I always liked you," Valor declares before moving the conversation to another topic.

Cynthia must have changed her opinion of me after the fight with JC. Nothing else makes sense.

I hesitantly settle back into the velvet and watch them, still in disbelief at what's happening. Sometimes I join the conversation, but for the most part I just listen.

When Breyson and Trinka come down from dinner, they both give me a look. Brey raises his eyebrows, but Trinka grabs his hand before he can slow down. She ushers him to a set of chairs not far from us. I expect them to bring the chairs over and join our circle, but they don't.

After a while, Valor stands. "Why are we sitting here? Is it because you don't want to lose again?" He lightly kicks Jaylee's foot off the coffee table.

"I'll play you, but you have to agree to my handicap," Jaylee says as she stands.

Valor's laugh is contagious. "Fine, let's go." He runs a hand through his hair and follows her.

The group gets up and they start walking to the pool table, which I figure out is what they are talking about. I shift in my seat, more upset than I'd like to admit at their departure. It was nice to have people to talk to again.

"Aren't you coming?" Cynthia asks before following her friends.

I open my mouth to answer but close it. Confusion acts like cobwebs, clouding my normal analytical processing. I try to run through why they'd invite me. An apology is one thing, but being sorry doesn't necessitate a friendship, does it?

"Oh, come on," she continues. "It's better than sitting here by yourself." Her mouth presses into a thin line and I have a feeling she wants to say something else but isn't.

"Okay, sure," I mumble, finding myself once again curious about the sudden change in them.

I follow the short distance, forcing my focus on the floor in front of me so I won't look at Brey and Trinka. I can feel his gaze following my back, confused by this new dynamic, but I don't ever meet his eyes.

After Jaylee loses to Valor, despite the handicap, I watch as Cynthia takes a turn.

Jaylee sits by me, her arm brushing against mine. It's clear that she's filling out the long-sleeved gray shirt much better than she did when we first arrived.

"How's the arm?" she asks me.

"It's good," I say to her, lifting it in the sling. "I feel like I'm better, but I'm not allowed to ditch the sling yet." I sigh heavily, the frustration from my earlier visit with Ms. Williams at the forefront of my mind.

Jaylee laughs and it sounds like bells in the wind. I don't think I've ever heard such a carefree sound, and it seems so out of place here.

"You are better," she says through a smile. "You have been for a while." She looks to my curious face before continuing, "My ability is to heal. I helped Ms. Williams with your arm. And your foot."

My mouth falls open with an audible pop as Valor knocks another ball in.

"I… thank you," I stammer at this new information.

She smiles at me, and the genuineness reaches her dark brown eyes.

"I'm just glad you were passed out for it. My ability is helpful, but painful, unfortunately." She winces at her words.

"I guess you have JC to thank for the unconscious thing," I say through a tense jaw, and I'm surprised to see that Jaylee seems almost as displeased by him as I feel.

"Well, it substantially speeds up the process versus healing with conventional medicine, but it isn't foolproof. I suppose in your case, you likely had some lingering pain for a week or so."

Everything makes much more sense now. Normal healing does take a long time, considering how many medications were outlawed because the side effects.

"That's such a useful ability." I sound stunned. The words kind of spill out of me, never having heard of another ability that would be so beneficial. It's hard not to envy her.

"I'm hoping I can get to the point where it isn't painful, or maybe decrease the amount of time it *is* painful. Ms. Williams is helping me grow my ability." Her eyes become distant for a moment before she looks down at my arm. "Anyway, she must have some other reason for keeping you in that thing." Her knowing eyes glint but she doesn't reveal anything further.

"Oh," is all I manage. She seems comfortable letting the silence hang between us for several minutes.

"Sorry I was so mean to you those first few days," she finally says, giving a sad half-smile. Her small fingers comb through her hair, which is now past her shoulders.

"It's okay," I reply, surprising myself at how much I mean it. I shift in my seat, uncomfortable at the new direction of this conversation, and glance around for a distraction.

I spot Varick across the Eye. He's sitting near the dartboard while JC plays against someone who's in the afternoon Agility Skills class. I feel like it's reckless to put a weapon in JC's hands, regardless of how small the dart is.

Varick laughs, and I'm too far away to actually see the dimples, but I know him well enough to know that his laughter brings them out. I keep looking for signs that our new relationship will end, but instead, it surprises me. He plans my personal training sessions weeks in advance.

As if he can hear what I'm thinking, he meets my gaze. He still has the smile on his face from whatever joke was just told, and there's a sparkle in his eyes. He raises a single eyebrow, as if to ask what I'm thinking. Then almost immediately, he snaps his head back to JC just in time to meet JC's glance. Keeping our friendship a secret is difficult, but necessary.

Valor takes a seat on the other side of me, plopping down in feigned exhaustion. He looks to his brother and then to me, and I cough to cover the uncomfortable silence at the fact that he likely just saw that interaction. Valor simply cocks his head and smiles. He has the same dimples as his brother.

"I've been asking my brother to train me for years," he says with an exaggerated sigh. He whispers the words close to me. Even still, I can't help but check to see if Jaylee is listening.

My cheeks grow warm, and I look down to the floor while something uncertain grows in my stomach, turning over and over. Suddenly, the smell of popcorn makes me nauseous. I didn't think Varick would tell anyone about our arrangement, including his brother.

"I don't know what you're talking about, Valor," I lie, refusing to glance at him. I silently curse myself for how quickly my cheeks must be turning red.

Again, he looks at Varick and then at me. Varick sits with a determined look at JC, but he's fighting a smile.

"Yeah, yeah, whatever," Valor says. "That's why you both conveniently disappear at the same time most days."

My eyes narrow at his words, and I can feel the heat rising on my face even more. I refuse to look down again and give Valor the satisfaction.

"If he's not training you," Valor continues, "I can come up with some… better… reasons why you might be running off together." He winks at the insinuation and I'm too dumbfounded to respond. Thankfully, I'm saved from the conversation.

"So, I heard there's another guy with strength in the next incoming class," Cynthia announces to nobody in particular.

"How the heck did you hear that?" Valor answers, unable to

hide how impressed he is.

"What do you mean incoming class?" I look between the two of them.

Jaylee and Lottie look equally confused as Cynthia offers, "They bring in new students twice a year but they plan for it year round. I just happened to find out one of the Unnaturals they were targeting." Her accompanying smirk reveals the pride in her ability to access this type of information, and I have to admit that I'm impressed at how much she knows. "That's also when we change class schedules."

How had I not considered newcomers? Obviously, there were students before we joined. I open my mouth to ask more, but Cynthia interrupts my spiral by dropping her pool stick.

"I need to finish my essay," she declares. "I hate Infantry."

I really haven't been paying attention. I've never even heard of Infantry as a class. I want to dissect this information more, but pure exhaustion wins out.

Sleep finds me easier than most nights. I think it's because of the warmth that encompassed me all evening. I hadn't realized how lonely I was from the strained relationships with Brey and Trinka.

As wonderful as last evening was, I'm not expecting the strangeness to continue. For that reason, I can't hide my surprise as Cynthia and Lottie sit down with me for breakfast. Valor joins us shortly after and lets us know that Jaylee is working with Ms. Williams, despite the early hour.

Brey doesn't acknowledge me when he walks by with Trinka, but the hollow feeling in my chest isn't as painful since I'm surrounded by other people. I let myself get lost in the conversation, ignoring Brey completely as Valor mocks Cynthia's choice of putting olives in her eggs.

In Agility Skills, Cynthia takes the bike next to me, and I have to force myself not to look surprised. When Brey walks in, I can't fight the stabbing pain in my chest at his look of confusion and sadness. He warms up alone on a treadmill.

I ditch the sling since Jaylee confirmed my suspicions of being completely healed. My body doesn't feel nearly as awkward as it did those first few months in Agility Skills. I know what I'm doing now, even though nobody sees that.

My first day back gives me a rush that I've never felt. My fight is against a passive ability, but since I don't know how to use my abilities on command, we're on an even playing field. We circle each other and I get a few good hits in. I still lose, but I fight back, and that's a huge improvement.

Life continues and I settle into this new, and very strange, normal. Days turn into weeks and the time seems to put an even bigger wedge between Brey and me.

I'm grateful that I have other friends now, and an unlikely alliance in Varick, but I miss Breyson.

I spend the day waiting for the evening, just like I often do. When everyone else goes to dinner, I remove myself with an excuse of homework that needs to be finished. Especially now that I have new friends, I have to take precautions to make sure nobody can see where I disappear to while praying that Valor won't give away our secret.

Unfortunately, training is anything but productive. Varick's mood is foul and he refuses to tell me why.

"Raise your left elbow," he growls. "You have to do better or this is all for nothing." He pushes my arm up aggressively and I shoot him a look.

"I'm trying," I huff, annoyed.

"That's not good enough. Mercer, I'm not kidding."

Something is clearly going on with him; something that's putting the edge of urgency into his training. Although I'm sure I've been on edge myself several times these last few months. Brey's face drifts to my mind as the primary reason, and the sadness of our distance feels impossibly heavy.

"Hey, can I ask you a question?" I stop the training completely and square to him. The image of Brey and Trinka is at the front of my thoughts.

"Sure."

I hesitate before asking. This feels like it's overstepping in multiple ways, but I need to do something to keep myself from collapsing from the sadness.

"Why did you stop talking to Brey?" I blurt out before I can change my mind. Back home, it was always obvious to me why they weren't friends. In my mind, Varick was just as bad as JC. But things have changed now.

His eyes widen a small amount before he gains control of himself.

I continue quickly, "I mean, from what he's told me, it's like you picked JC over him. I get that you think JC is a good guy… but better than Brey? It doesn't make sense." The words come faster as I unload my thoughts from the last few weeks. He just rubs his jaw and continues to stare at me.

I have to consider that my question might have made him angry or uncomfortable. I turn back to the equipment, ready to let it go.

"Mercer, why haven't you asked me what my ability is?"

The air becomes tight as I try to hide the shock on my face.

"I… uh," I stammer, shocked by his topic change. "I guess I didn't think you would tell me."

He narrows his eyes and watches me for several beats.

"I'm an empath," he finally says with a frustrated sigh. "I can feel what other people are feeling. It's particularly strong if," he pauses and tries to search for the words, "if the feeling is about me."

My eyes widen as multiple emotions course through me. He's *felt* everything that I've felt about him in the last few weeks. My cheeks grow warm as I fight the urge to bolt from the room. I shake my head, turning around so he can't see me.

Finally, he continues quietly, "To answer your question, learning how to be an empath was hard. I didn't think I'd survive it. There were just too many emotions." I turn back so I can see him as he explains. He stares into the distance so I don't say anything, waiting for him to continue. "The only way I could do it was by surrounding myself with people who don't feel… as deeply… as others," he finishes.

"Oh." I'm overwhelmed by his admission, unable to fully unpack it.

"I could nearly turn my ability off around JC." He gives a sad smile that doesn't reach his dimples or eyes. "I couldn't do that with Brey. Especially not when his voice *and* his emotions were in my head."

I huff a quick laugh; I can understand that well enough. "Do you miss him?" I ask, looking off to the other side of the room as a lump forms in my throat.

"Sure," he answers. "But you already know that. You feel the same."

Chapter Sixteen

According to my calculations, fall is starting, and that fact creates an empty vacuum in my chest. Time has been flying by while we're held captive, and part of me longs for the summer Brey and I would have enjoyed if our lives weren't flipped upside down.

I can't help but wonder if my family will participate in their normal fall activities, despite my absence. Are they happier because I'm gone? Or does it feel like there's a void without me there? Will Aunt Pam still put the Christmas decorations up too early or will they spend this year somber? What have they even been told about my sudden disappearance?

It's bittersweet that time seems to be passing faster now. On the one hand, every day that goes by is one day closer to my freedom because somehow, although I'm not sure how, I'm going to get out of here. I've seen it. But on the other hand, it's physically painful to think about how the outside world is continuing without any of us in it, and even when I do escape, how am I going to make sure they don't find me?

There are so many terrible parts to my day that it's surprising to see time pass as quickly as it is. Even my seat in the corner of the very back row doesn't protect me from Mr. Clayton's rage, which is usually only directed at me.

"Ms. Lewis," he says in his nasally voice. Nobody even bothers to turn around and look at my reaction, since it's become so common for him to single me out, "let's consider your life after graduation when you're serving the Domain. If you were to have an opportunity to save thousands of people, would you do it?"

"Of course," I reply while tilting my head and maintaining eye contact.

We've both been through this enough to both know that his responding smile isn't genuine.

"Now, let's continue and say that you have to sacrifice someone you know to make it happen. Would you still make that choice?" His voice almost ends the question in a plea. I don't know why he's so focused on this particular scenario, but it's like he can't mentally move on with the class until I agree with him.

"No, I would not." There's smugness to my voice that I can't seem to hide as I cross my arms in defiance.

"And you would be content with your unethical actions?" He presses. I'm not even sure what relevance this class has for our lives. My best guess is that they're trying to brainwash us so Unnaturals default to blindly following Stealth's orders after graduation. If you talk about killing people often enough in a classroom setting, does it desensitize you to it?

"I wouldn't have a problem with my decision," I answer flatly.

Brey twitches from his seat next to me, although I don't know why he even bothers to sit beside me anymore, it's not like we really talk. Maybe he knows I'd sacrifice a stadium full of people to save him, even when we aren't speaking.

"It's such a pity to see someone so young and talented ruined by their own selfish ego." Mr. Clayton smirks while pushing his glasses back up his nose. Little does he know that his words are meaningless to me. I'm proud that my dreams have been able to keep me from being brainwashed by them. I'm proud to know that I'll always stand by my loved ones, even if the odds are against us.

After class, Varick gives me a sad and secret smile, not in support of my answer but in solidarity of my continued abuse here. Even though we can't be openly friendly, it's nice to know I have him.

I must admit that over the last few weeks, my feelings about our alliance have shifted. I'm starting to wonder if he actually cares about my improvement. Maybe Stealth didn't send him to train me.

Later in the evening, Mr. Clayton's words are still cycling through my thoughts as I sit in the Eye with my foot resting on one of the stools.

From where I'm positioned, it looks like I'm simply watching Valor beat Cynthia at a game of pool, but in reality, I can't look away from a scene playing out behind them on the purple loveseat that I used to frequent.

Trinka leans toward Brey, her cheek right next to his. I clench my jaw and focus on breathing in through my nose to alleviate the tension in my chest, while Brey's fingers neatly tuck a piece of her curly hair behind her ear. I can't seem to look away as their lips touch, and I can feel the grimace on my face.

I know that neither of them want a strained friendship with me, but I just can't seem to let go of my anger at how cavalier they were over JC trying to kill me.

In an effort to smooth things over, Trinka has been showing more of an interest in me and how I'm doing, which feels strange and out of place when we hardly speak outside of those conversations.

"Hello?" Valor appears directly in front of me, blocking my line of sight. Before I can help myself, I glare up at him with hostility for getting in my way. "Do you want to play again or be a stalker all day?" he asks. I know he's trying to be funny, but the comment makes me want to take the wooden stick he's holding and whack him over the head with it. He must read my reaction because an apologetic smile creeps on his lips.

"I'm good," I tell him through clenched teeth.

He turns around and I follow his gaze to see Trinka place a delicate kiss on Brey's lips. My cheeks grow warm, so I look down at my hands.

"Maybe you should stop playing defense and start playing offense," Valor says in a low voice. At first, I think he's talking to Cynthia about the game, but his mischievous eyes bore into mine and he raises a single eyebrow before nodding his head to the other end of the Eye.

I feel the confusion on my face while I turn around to follow his movement.

Varick. He means Varick.

As we watch, Rose, the girl from our Agility Skills class with a buzz cut, leans into Varick's side to speak to him, but he seems to be distracted by something else, disengaged and leaning away from her. She grabs his hand to get his attention.

"Well, that was awkward timing," Valor says in the same low whisper. I hear him move away from me, but I can't seem to take my eyes off Varick and Rose.

Varick smiles, but it's a smile to himself, not to her. Then he yanks his hand away.

I can feel my eyebrows pull together as I continue watching them, trying to figure out what he's thinking, or maybe his reaction is just in response to what he knows Rose is feeling.

Almost immediately, his eyes meet mine with humor. I turn around so suddenly, that my hair whips myself in the face.

I wipe my hands on my pants and curse under my breath. I

hate that he caught me watching him.

It's a vicious cycle now that I know what Varick can do. My embarrassment makes my cheeks grow warm, then my frustration claws at me at the fact that Varick can feel everything I'm experiencing. The frustration makes me desperate to end the embarrassment, but instead it just makes it worse. When things like this happen, I try and shift my focus. It's not easy, and I'm sure he's already gotten quite the show from me, but I can't just sit here like this.

Breyson and Trinka get up from the loveseat. They must be going to dinner. I've joined them occasionally, but mostly choose to eat with my new friend group. Cynthia, Valor, Jaylee and Lottie make the pain in my chest more bearable. I won't be eating with any of them tonight, though. Tonight is a training night.

As everyone leaves, I make up another excuse to not join them. Valor gives me a knowing smirk before whispering, "Offense."

They all walk away together, and I'm just glad that nobody else heard him.

I wait a few more minutes to be sure that I won't be seen. Varick has already disappeared, his friends likely going their separate ways, so I know he's waiting for me.

Finally, after an eternity, my feet bounce down the stairs with familiarity as my hand runs along the metal railing. The warmth in my chest wards off the chill that surrounds me in this place. I already shed my gray jacket, leaving just a gray tank, knowing that the workout will make me sweat. I'm eager for the distraction Varick's trainings always give me, leaving me exhausted with no ability to think about the bad in my life.

I pull open the Pitch door with a hard wrench, but what's waiting on the other side has my stomach dropping, leaving an empty feeling in my chest as I try to catch my breath. I'm not fully in the Pitch yet, and my feet take hesitant steps back to the door that I just came through.

I realize I'm foolishly hoping that if I go slowly, nobody will notice me. Complete and utter fear has replaced excitement as I try to come up with a plan. We've always had the place to ourselves; I don't know what went wrong. The door clicks behind me as an ominous announcement that I'm here.

JC stands a few feet from me, so close that his uneven teeth are noticeable in his grin. Out of the corner of my eye I see a few of his other friends, including Rose and Phillip, look to me and then to him.

My wide eyes find Varick, and he shakes his head slowly from side to side, unnoticed by the rest of them.

My legs feel weak and a dizziness starts clouding my vision as survival instincts shout at me. I haven't been in a room where JC could target me since our last match in the Ring and my entire body is screaming at me to run.

I take a step to the door and reach a hand behind me to grab the handle, while refusing to turn my back on JC.

He notices my movement. Of course he does, he's watching me carefully.

He bounds over in two steps, his eagerness propelling him.

I turn and try to wrench the handle, somehow thinking that getting the door open will save me, but I'm too late.

JC's hand is faster. It slams against the metal, leaving a palm indentation directly in the middle of the Pitch door thanks to his strength. The noise of bending metal is like nails on a chalkboard in the open space.

I look from his hand to his face to see him grinning down at me like I just single-handedly made his day.

My brain doesn't slow down to think through what I'm doing. I simply shift my weight and attempt to sprint out of his reach. I'm not sure where I'm trying to go, just anywhere away from him, anywhere to put distance between us.

He must anticipate my reaction.

A small yelp escapes my lips as his fingers encircle me in the same spot that he hurt me before.

I meet his hungry eyes once more, unsure of what he sees in return. Whatever it is, it makes the smile deepen, showing a few yellowing teeth.

A buzzing enters my ears, which can only mean that my disarming ability is starting to work. I try to focus on the noise, knowing in the back of my mind that it's my only chance right now. My eyes close to allow the buzzing to take over, and JC's grip loosens in response.

I try to yank my arm free, but despite disarming his ability, he's still stronger than I am. Unfortunately, I don't have the factor of surprise that helped me last time. He almost expected this outcome. His eyebrows pull together and his face is an alarming shade of scarlet, as if he's holding his breath out of concentration.

We seem frozen in place while I keep his strength at bay through the buzzing. I try to keep my breathing steady, and JC keeps trying to tighten his hold to inhuman levels.

"Let go of her." Varick's voice interrupts my focus. I had forgotten he was here. I seek Varick's wild, intense eyes. But he isn't watching me, he's watching his friend.

The moment my eyes shift, the buzzing disappears and the pain in JC's grip returns with a vengeance. I can't hide a whimper that I let out as my body sags, held up only by JC's hold. I try to bring back the buzzing, but I can't focus… can't see straight enough to get it to return.

Varick's voice gets closer and he repeats, "Let her go." There's something in his tone, an authority that would seemingly make it impossible not to do what he says.

The grip on my arm loosens. I can't imagine JC would ever take orders from Varick, so I can't help but wonder for a moment if my ability returned. But no, I don't hear the buzzing, so that wouldn't be it.

"Why?" JC asks. Without the pressure, I'm able to really take in his demeanor. He's visibly shaking from head to toe, and the red shade on his face has now extended to his ears, neck, and arms. "You want a turn?"

I'm not able to voice my indignation at the suggestion of JC's words, because before I can, Varick does something to JC's neck, making him release me.

In just seconds, Varick pushes me behind his body so that he now stands between me and all the bullies in the room. In that simple action, everything seems to have shifted. The air is tense, no longer filled with JC's excitement.

"Is there something here that I don't know about?" JC asks, his eyebrows raising at the idea. His fury seems to increase with each second that Varick doesn't announce it all as a joke. His feelings are so big, so consuming, that they take up the entire space. Every inch of me is terrified about what JC will do, and I'm not crazy enough to think that Varick can somehow take on JC and all his friends.

Varick doesn't answer, but his left hand reaches back and grips my hip. I'm unsure whether he's trying to tell me something or reassure himself that I'm here, but the pressure increases as JC steps forward. Meanwhile, the panic inside me is roaring, screaming at me to run, get out of here, do anything to protect myself.

"Is this why you tried to talk me out of graduating?" JC asks.

To my left, Rose takes a step forward, inching closer to us from the side. Varick must have noticed too, because his hand shifts me toward the wall and away from Rose.

"It all makes sense now," JC continues to sneer. I try to peek at him under Varick's arm. "You're an idiot. You know he has other plans."

Everyone was already listening, but something in JC's statement makes the entire room pause. Silence follows until finally, Varick answers.

"Go." Varick's voice is pinched. "Before I make you go."

I want to find out what JC is talking about, but something in Varick's tone makes me stop. They must know that they can take Varick if it's just him, but maybe they heard the same warning in his voice that just made me shudder. Or perhaps they can hear the direct instruction like I did. Maybe they have no choice but to leave.

My left bicep is pulsing. Unlike last time when I passed out, I'm conscious enough to feel the deformity JC made. More out of curiosity than pain, I run my right fingers gently over the unnatural dent still pressed into my arm.

Varick moves my hip so that he can face me without having his back to the door, likely in case our visitors return.

"Your arm, we need to get you to the infirmary." His jaw is clenched, and I have to fight the instinct to be afraid of him. I think I can stop worrying about him turning on me.

"I think it's fine," I tell him, out of wishful thinking. I curl my hand into a fist. There's a sting of pain, but not the worst thing I've felt since being here. I'm sick of being in the hospital, and I don't trust my legs to carry me up the stairs right now. I know fear and panic will hit me any second and I don't want to fall apart in front of Varick.

He eyes me carefully, raising a single eyebrow, and I figure out what he's doing, so I try to channel a certain calmness, taking a deep breath and focusing on anything but what just happened, while letting him stare into my soul, reading those feelings.

After thirty seconds of staring at each other, Varick grabs me, careful to leave my arm alone, and leads me to the door.

Apparently, the pain he felt was enough to end the conversation.

There's another person sitting in one the beds in the infirmary. They look at us just in time to see me gag at the strong antiseptic smell. Ms. Williams is fidgeting with the dial on the machine by their station and she looks up when we walk in.

"It's her arm," Varick says to Ms. Williams in the same growl that he's carried since I walked into the Pitch.

Ms. Williams frowns, and the movement creates wrinkles in her forehead.

"Come here," she says to me, her thin fingers patting a bed next to her.

I follow and gingerly sit down. Every movement is making a jolt of pain shoot through my arm.

Ms. Williams examines me quickly.

"Looks like it's fractured again. I'll take some images to confirm while we wait for help," she mumbles more to herself than to me. Without looking to Varick, she addresses him, "Would you mind going to get Jaylee Nguyen? Do you know who that is?"

He nods and quickly crosses the room, putting his long hair back into a bun while leaving. It doesn't bother me like it used to.

"Here, take this pain medication. I wish I could tell you that it won't hurt. Very worth it though."

"Thanks," I mumble, swallowing the pill. I can't imagine the pain getting worse than it feels right now.

She smiles, still not meeting my eyes as she guides me into an adjoining room for imaging. "I'm glad he stopped sneaking around," she says.

Her words rattle around my mind but no matter what way I consider them, it doesn't make sense, and I'm not sure I care enough to ask for clarification.

She guides me back to the bed after taking some x-rays and I let the heaviness settle into my eyelids. I don't know how much time passes before the door opens, and Varick rushes in followed by Jaylee… and Brey.

"What happened?" Jaylee asks. Her eyebrows are knit together and the concern warms my heart, given how much she hated me just a few months ago.

"I… my…" I stutter to get my words out, but my tongue feels heavy. The sensation seems to be working its way down my chest and into my hands.

"It's broken," Ms. Williams answers for me. Her eyes narrow at my arm while she speaks to Jaylee. "Images confirmed. Best to start now," she finishes gravely.

"Why?" Brey steps forward and puts a hand on Jaylee's shoulder. "Jaylee's just told me it's painful. Can't you wait until she's asleep?" My tongue is still too heavy to ask the questions swirling in my head.

"The longer I wait, the higher the risk that I don't heal it right the first time," Jaylee says to Breyson with a small grimace. "The last time I tried, it had been too long, and we had to rebreak the arm to get it right, which resulted in a longer recovery than it should've been and undoubtedly more pain."

My jaw falls open at this new information. Varick's eyes haven't left me since he returned. I meet his gaze and try to say something, but instead I just open and close my mouth a few times, getting reacquainted with my tongue. The feeling is thick and foreign.

Jaylee hovers over me with her palms covering my left bicep. She closes her eyes and a gold light emits from her hands into my arm.

I try to say that it looks pretty, but all I can get out is "Th-preddy." I don't bother meeting the gazes around me at my words, or lack thereof, because I don't want to look away from the light.

My fascination is short-lived, however, because the burning takes over. It grows so hot that I'm convinced the entire room is on fire. I want to scream but when I open my mouth, my tongue pushes its way down my throat and threatens to choke me. My eyes pinch together as I try to breathe through the pain coursing through me. Every nerve ending is screaming with the sensation, and I'm nearly convinced that something went wrong and I'm going to die right here.

I don't remember how I opened my eyes, but I'm relieved that there aren't actual flames. Then I realize the burning has lessened considerably. Brey's face distracts me from the lingering agony, but it's not right. He's frowning and he doesn't usually frown. I reach my right hand up and trace his mouth with my finger.

What's wrong with her?" I hear Varick ask, and I try to listen to his words, but it's difficult to focus on anything other than what I'm looking at.

"Pain medication," Ms. Williams responds.

"Mercer," Brey says. The movement of his mouth startles

me while my finger is on his lips. I giggle at myself for getting scared so easily."

I want to ask him why he's here, but it comes out as a gurgled, "Why here?"

His frown deepens, which I wouldn't have imagined was possible. I keep pushing his lips to try to force them back to their normal state.

"Varick told me you were hurt. Of course I'd be here," he says. His hand grabs mine from his mouth and forces it back to the bed.

"Guess wha" I ask, slurring it together to sound like one long word.

"What's that?" Brey's mouth finally tilts into a twitch of a smile as he listens to me.

"I wasn't only one misses you." Each word feels like concrete coming out of my mouth and I'm not even sure I got the point across.

Brey's eyes dart up to the other side of the room and I shift my focus to see what he's looking at, but the fuzziness comes back so I close my eyes before I can get my answer.

I want to ask Ms. Williams a question about how they rebroke my arm last time, but my mouth isn't cooperating, and I can't force myself awake. Not to mention, I don't even remember what question felt so pressing just moments ago.

The black almost pulls me under before I decide I want to be awake. My eyes finally work and I wrench them open.

Except, I'm not in the hospital anymore.

In fact, I'm back in Brey's living room. My mouth pulls down at the corners. I've seen this before, twice. Why am I watching it again?

"Okay, they're coming!" dream-Mercer yells. I usually wake

up before seeing what happens next. I move to the window to gain more clarity about why my subconscious has shown me this three times.

Dream-Mercer is nearly shaking with nervousness and seeing how scared I'll be in the future makes my stomach roil uncomfortably. I try to follow her gaze, but as soon as I do, an audible gasp escapes me.

For the first time, I get a good look at the men walking toward the house. My hands start shaking as I watch. These men, they aren't just any guards from the Domain.

Stealth is going to send Nick and JC to come find me.

Why would Stealth send them after me? And if I'm so lucky as to get away from the Domain, why would they think to look for me at Brey's house, of all places?

It just doesn't make sense.

I close my eyes and shake my head to try and clear my thoughts, but in doing so, I must wake myself up, because I'm out of his living room and back in the infirmary.

Reality comes crashing back.

"Ugh," I groan at the wires hooked up to me as they tug on my skin.

"What is it?" Brey flutters beside me and raises a hand in my direction like he wants to fix whatever pain I might be feeling.

"Just reminding myself about everything that happened before I passed out." I give him a small grimace and hope that he believes me. It's not that I'm keeping the dream a secret, but I need to figure out what it means before I tell him. If that was JC's graduation and they were at Brey's house, then they may be targeting Mrs. Jones for some reason.

"Does it hurt?" he asks, his brows pushed together. He smiles his half-smile, but it doesn't reach his blue eyes. His fingers still haven't found something to touch on my body, so he just lowers his hands until they awkwardly sit on the edge of the bed.

"Where's Trinka?" It occurs to me that my question sounds accusatory, but I don't know how to ask him the questions I really want to voice, like how he could turn his back on me for so long. As grateful as I am to see him here, I can't deny the resentment boiling inside me.

The door opens and Varick walks in, carrying coffees from the dining hall and saving Brey from answering.

"Hey," Varick says. He shakes the brown hair out of his eyes, showing the anger still lurking beneath "Welcome back."

"What happened after—" My voice sounds weak and I hate that. I can't stand that JC has made me fearful. The look they exchange makes me clench my jaw as I wait.

"JC met with Stealth, but we have no idea what was said." Brey's mouth is drawn down and there's pity in his eyes.

Varick looks between us both before sighing and adding, "JC is furious. I haven't felt him this angry in a while. Whatever happens, I have a feeling it's going to get worse before it gets better."

Chapter Seventeen

As soon as the grogginess wears off, I feel great. My speedy recovery makes so much more sense now that I know about Jaylee's ability. Ms. Williams isn't able to convince me to wear a sling this time, not now that I suspect her only reason is to keep me out of the Ring in Agility Skills.

I'm so grateful to be discharged quickly, having only needed to spend one day in the infirmary. As I make my way down to the Eye, my feet are hesitant on the steps. It's one thing for JC to attack me under the guise of Agility Skills, but another thing entirely for him to do it out in the open, outside of class hours. Does that mean I'm not safe anywhere anymore? Ms. Williams gave me dinner before discharging me, but what if my friends are in the dining hall? Do I dare risk being caught alone in the Eye?

As soon as I step into the Eye, my eyes jump to the dartboard area. It's almost like JC can sense that I'm here because he looks my way immediately as his lip curls up in a sneer. I can't help but wonder if Varick tried to repair that friendship, or if the scene in the Pitch was enough to end things between them permanently.

Lucky for me, the pool table is closer than the dartboard, and my chest releases some of the pressure at the sight of the girls.

I don't hesitate as my steps quickly steer toward them, though the more I think about JC, the less muted my fear becomes and the more I want to try and fight him again.

It doesn't take them long to notice me, and they all stand right away. Lottie gets my attention as she takes a step toward me, her hands clutching her chest at my appearance.

"Mercer," she says in her quiet voice. She eyes me closely and her lip quivers like she's about to cry. Lottie doesn't say much, but she's the most compassionate person I've ever met. She doesn't continue, but instead, throws her arms around me, making me flinch at the sudden contact. She doesn't let go, so I reach a hand around and give her a few pats on the back.

"Are you okay?" Cynthia asks from behind Lottie. She pulls on a strand of her hair while watching me and it looks like she has dark circles underneath her eyes. "Jaylee told us what happened. We were going to come see you, but I wanted to keep JC in my sights to make sure he didn't go up there." Her eyes glance to the area with the dartboard but I don't follow her gaze.

My heart warms instantly at her sincerity and whatever tension I was still carrying falls away. I never really had more friends than Brey, and I'm still not used to people caring about me.

"I'm fine, feeling back to normal," I say with a tight smile and a nod of thanks to Jaylee.

She just lifts one side of her mouth, but the worry in her eyes doesn't leave.

"How can they not do anything about him?" Lottie says quietly as she releases me from her hold.

JC isn't watching me, but I can feel his anger from here.

My mouth opens to answer her, but then I close it again, not exactly sure what to say.

Luckily, I'm saved from having to find the words because in that same moment, Brey and Varick approach our group and they don't seem surprised that I'm out of the infirmary. It's so strange to see them together. I have no idea what they said to one another after I fell asleep, but the way they walk close to each other… it almost looks like they're friends.

Before I can react to them, Cynthia pushes me aside with so much force that my feet trip over each other. My stomach drops at the realization that she senses a threat that I've yet to see, but then I realize that the threat is my friends. I suddenly feel too hot in my clothes as I try to edge my way into her vision.

"Cynthia," Varick greets her in a tight voice. The twitching of his fists is alarming, but his eyes appear calm.

"Can we help you?" Cynthia snaps. Her arms are pressed to her body, like she's trying to keep herself from fighting.

"Cynthia—" I start to explain, but Varick cuts me off.

"She doesn't trust me," he says with a frustrated huff. "And she's mad at Brey for… well… she can tell you why she's mad at Brey."

Breyson hunches his shoulders as he looks at his shoes.

"Varick's been secretly training me for months," I rush to say as I put a hand on Cynthia's arm. "He's not as bad as you think." I consider telling her that he's still annoying at times, but it doesn't seem appropriate at the moment. As for Brey, well I'm not sure I disagree with her anger there, so I don't say anything.

I can tell she hears me because her body relaxes just a fraction, but she doesn't answer me, directing her question to Varick instead.

"Are you still friends with him?" she demands with a nod to JC. Everyone seems to know who she's talking about, but I can't help but glance over to where JC is glowering from a chair as he watches us.

"No, Cynthia," Varick replies grimly. "I'm not."

"And you…" she scolds, as she shifts to Brey without even acknowledging Varick's answer. "How could you just leave her when she had nobody else? I bite my lip as her accusation very clearly burns into Brey, but I can't find myself disagreeing.

"I'm so sorry," he thinks to me. His jaw quivers and I find it breaking down a small part of the wall I built up to keep him out.

"It'll be okay," I say to him, knowing it's true. It might not be okay right now, but Brey and I are family, so it will get better.

Cynthia watches the interaction, before seemingly accepting them into our circle, but her shoulders are still raised and she glances their way often without being subtle.

Part of me wants to remind her how she treated me not too long ago, but I don't want to risk ruining this moment, so instead I laugh under my breath. Jaylee finds my eyes, giving me a small shrug before returning her attention back to the boys.

Before too long, Valor joins our group, too.

"So," Valor says as he bats his eyelashes and motions between Brey and Varick, "when did this happen?" He raises a single eyebrow and flicks his hair out of his eyes. It's not as graceful as when Varick does it, but it's clear who his inspiration is.

Nobody answers, but Cynthia clears her throat and narrows her eyes at Varick, despite having let him into the group.

"Well," Valor continues with a sigh, "I, for one, am happy about it. Varick's been a moping mess since the first grade because of your breakup." He frowns at Brey.

For the first time since waking up in the Domain, my heart feels whole. We have so many things to worry about, so many things that we need to face, but for now, we have a sliver of peace in the worry. Things feel right.

Valor and Varick play each other in a game of pool while Brey sits between Jaylee and me. It surprises me how well they fit into our dynamic, like they were missing this entire time.

When the girls stand to head to bed, my heart squeezes uncomfortably and I stay seated.

"You coming, Merc?" Jaylee asks me, but I just shake my head. I've been avoiding several thoughts, and the second I close my eyes, they're going to force their way in.

"I'll be there in a bit," I say with a smile, wanting a few more minutes of peace despite the late hour.

Cynthia's eyes find the dartboard again before she looks at Varick, Brey and finally Valor, while she says, "Make sure she gets to the dorm safely, yeah?

"We will," Brey answers with a bit more determination than is needed. It's clear that he's overcompensating for his months of distance as his arm tightens next to me.

After the girls leave, I try to give Brey a reassuring smile, but instead of looking at me, he watches just behind my back and I have to turn around to track what he's focused on.

Varick and Valor seem to be in an intense and silent conversation, neither of them having noticed us.

"What?" Brey finally asks. "What's going on?"

Valor looks to Varick, as if to defer to him in deciding whether or not to answer Brey's question.

Varick's jaw tightens as he communicates silently in response. He raises an eyebrow just a fraction, which wouldn't be noticeable if I hadn't already been watching.

Valor nods again, a quick and succinct nod.

Varick finally turns to us and says, "Valor felt something."

"What do you mean, felt something?" Brey asks in a strained voice.

But I talk over him when I ask Valor directly, "Felt what?"

Varick looks to me first, but then faces Brey.

"Valor can sense danger—when someone is going to cause

danger or when someone is in danger, but it's not always a sure thing," Varick explains to Brey.

I know about Valor's ability, but I didn't know the details. Valor had said it was worthless, but I would love to be able to protect my people with a warning like that.

"So, what did you feel?" I ask again as I tap my fingers on my leg. Something inside me tightens uncomfortably as I wait for him to answer.

Valor looks to Varick once more, seemingly asking permission to tell us, and Varick gives a single nod as Brey releases a heavy sigh of frustration.

"It's JC," Valor says in a hushed tone. "He's usually not too dangerous. I'm not really sure how to describe it, but let's just say I usually feel him giving off danger vibes of like a six out of ten. Right now, he's a full-blown ten."

Brey turns his head to where JC and his friends are sitting on a group of couches near the other side of the Eye. I can feel Brey tense next to me, as if JC might rush over here any second and Brey is ready to throw himself in between us.

"It could be nothing," I try to rationalize, knowing in my gut that I'm wrong.

"I wouldn't say that," Valor says with a huff. "I stay away from people giving off level ten vibes. It's usually only that high right before something bad happens, so it's best to steer clear. And I doubt it's his ability. The only person I've met who reads that high consistently is… well… you."

I swallow and bite my lower lip as Varick and Brey both turn to me, shocked. This isn't necessarily news to me, since Valor told me he thought I was dangerous our first night here, but he clearly kept that to himself.

"Sorry," Valor mumbles at the realization that my friends

didn't know. "I just figured you had told them since, you know, you were always with Brey and you've been with Varick so much. I wouldn't have said—"

"It's fine," I cut Valor's apology short. Before anybody can ask about it, I cough and change the subject. "Okay, so JC is dangerous. What does that mean?"

Once more, the brothers look at each other as something passes between them.

"No," Varick says through a clenched jaw. "Absolutely not."

"I already told him I was stopping by before bed," Valor says as he squints his face like he's expecting Varick to hit him.

Varick takes a step away from Valor and pinches the bridge of his nose.

"Someone tell us what's going on," I demand through my frustration.

Valor gives Varick another sheepish look before turning to me and saying, "It's messy. I guess the best way to explain it is that if I ask Stealth about JC, I'll be able to read whether Stealth's levels change in his answer. That'll tell me if Stealth ordered something to make JC more dangerous."

Varick doesn't relax at all but looks up at the ceiling like he can't believe how much of an idiot his brother is. In this moment, I think I agree.

"Won't he think it's strange that you're asking for a meeting so late?" Brey asks, always the one to bring common sense into things.

"Nah," Valor replies, relieved that the conversation isn't allowing Varick a moment to scold him. "That man never sleeps. He might not even know what time it is."

Brey reacts as if somehow this gives him insight into a bigger problem. Varick finally composes himself enough to answer, and despite the last few minutes, he sounds calm and focused.

"He'll be watching you after you leave. You can't come down here to tell me what you find out," he says.

They stare at each other again, this time without the anger from earlier. It's like they're trying to solve a problem together and I can't help but feel a stab of jealousy. It makes me miss Lizzy and what we could've had.

"Why don't you go to the storage room, and I'll meet you there?" Valor suggests. I have no idea what that means but I don't interrupt them to ask.

Varick nods once before instructing, "Be careful. Do not let him know what you're doing."

"Obviously," Valor replies with a smirk. "Stop worrying so much. You won't look good with wrinkles." With that, he turns on his heel and heads to the elevator on the other side of the Eye, the one closest to Stealth's office.

I can feel both Brey and my questions bubbling to the surface, but before we have a chance to ask, Varick raises a hand and stops us.

"I'll tell you, but let's get to the storage room first. If Stealth has his people watching, I want to try and mitigate how much trouble Valor could get into." His jaw doesn't relax at all through his answer.

Brey and I don't fight him. Helping Valor is more pressing than our curiosity. Instead, we wordlessly follow Varick. I have no idea how he knows about this storage room, but it sounds like he and Valor have found it to be a safe place to talk, so that's all that matters.

Varick leads us up the other stairwell to the eighth floor. I haven't been on this level, and I have no idea what we're going to find.

Unfortunately, the answer is not much. The hall consists of several doors with no indication of what lies beyond them.

Many of the doors have a keypad next to it, and Varick leads us to the fourth door on the left. He types a code in quickly, glancing both ways before hitting the last button. The pad beeps and a green light flashes, letting Varick open the heavy door while he stands to the side and motions for us to enter.

How does Varick know about this place? And how does he have the code? The questions swarm around my mind.

But then they stop immediately as I step into the room.

All my curiosity fades, only to be replaced by something else.

How many times have I thought of this room?

"How do you have the code to this room?" I distantly hear Brey ask Varick.

"Valor saw it on Stealth's desk. We tried it on every keypad until it worked," Varick says as he closes the door behind us. Someone bumps into me from behind.

"What is it?" Brey asks. I hadn't realized I had halted so abruptly. I can feel my heartbeat in my ears. I want to make my feet move forward, but my brain doesn't seem to be working fast enough and I'm having a hard time catching up. "Mercer?" Breyson pushes further. He places his hand on the small of my back and the contact makes me jump forward.

How can I tell him that I've seen this place before without telling him that I saw him kiss me in this room?

I cough into my hand to gain some composure and walk over to the same spot that I saw Brey lean in.

I had convinced myself the dream of our kiss wasn't in my future anymore. I swallow, wondering if the boys can hear it, given how dry my throat is. I nearly collapse into one of the newer looking desks before my knees can give out on me. This is clearly a storage room, just like I thought. I just hadn't known it was a storage room in the Domain.

Varick's eyes meet mine. His fear for Valor and determination to fill us in is momentarily replaced with genuine curiosity. One of his eyebrows raises fractionally, but I know it's not meant for me to answer. It's a question to himself. He wants to know the reason behind the chaos of my recent emotions.

Brey's eyes are also on me, asking a silent question about my reaction.

"So, what now?" I ask, regaining my composure and breaking the tension, hoping that I can steer the conversation away from them asking about my reaction to this space.

"We wait for Valor," Varick says. He eyes me one more time before evidently letting go of his questions. He hops on the table that's pushed into the corner so that his legs swing off the end.

I start to chew on my nails as countless emotions bounce around inside me.

"Since we have time to kill," Varick says while looking at me, and my stomach drops as I pray that he doesn't ask about my reaction to entering this room, "maybe you could let us know why you're such a dangerous person, according to Valor."

I let out a huff that's meant to sound like a laugh but carries too much stress.

"*He doesn't know you have multiple abilities?*" Brey asks me silently. He doesn't sound like he's scolding me, but almost like he's relieved that we still had that secret just between us, even if it's going to be shared now.

"I didn't mean to keep it from him," I answer Brey out loud, and it's true. Somehow in the last few months, I've started to trust

Varick. "It just never came up."

"What did you keep from me?" Varick doesn't look angry, just curious.

I rub my eyes, trying to relieve a headache that's begun forming. So much has changed in just a few hours.

"I have multiple abilities."

Chapter Eighteen

"How is that possible?" Varick gapes at me. Meanwhile, Brey has a gleam in his eye. "I've never seen that before."

"Well, it's not like you've met every Unnatural in the world. It might be more common than we think," I try to defend myself, feeling suddenly hot and uncomfortable but knowing that he's not actually accusing me of anything.

He seems to be at a loss for words while he scratches his chin before finally asking, "Well are you sure they're not all related? Could it be one ability, but it shows itself in different ways? What are they?"

Interesting. Could they all be one ability? I'd never really thought of it like that before.

"I can make people do things. We call it compulsion."

That's what Stealth knows you can do," Varick says in a sure voice, leaning forward on his knees to hear my response. I don't bother asking him how he knows that, but I'm not sure I ever mentioned it.

"Right." My word is drawn out while I eye him carefully. "I used it against the guards who took me. I can also stop another Unnatural from using their ability. We call that my disarming ability."

"Those could be related" Varick tilts his head to the side. "They're essentially both ways to control another person, and an active ability grows over time. Take me, for instance. I started by feeling the emotions of others, but eventually I was able to actually manipulate what others are feeling. I bet your ability just grew."

"You can do what?" I recoil from his admission, and he must notice the change in how I'm feeling because he looks to the floor and clenches his jaw.

"Perhaps." Brey chuckles and rubs the back of his neck. "But then how do you explain the dreams?"

"Dreams?" Varick's head snaps up and he looks from Brey to me. I sigh, letting go of what he had just said. There's really no easy way to explain this, so I decide to just rip the band-aid off.

"My dreams come true. I dream the future." I tap my fingers on the surface of the desk, hating that I can't hide the flush that creeps up my cheeks.

Varick opens his mouth but before saying anything, he closes it again. He lifts an eyebrow while watching me closely, making my insides squirm. I'm about to say something, change the subject or tell him it was all a joke, but I don't have to. The keypad outside the door beeps and it changes the air in the room as we turn to see the door open.

Valor's body snakes in quickly.

Varick looks like he wants to run to Valor, but instead he stays where he is, wringing his hands and waiting for Valor to speak.

"He's definitely in on it," Valor says with a grim expression, which is unusual for him.

"What did you feel? What did you ask?" Varick steps forward, reaching an arm out to Valor before dropping it back to his side.

Valor backs up sheepishly and his eyes dart to the floor.

"Valor," Varick warns, following Valor's retreat.

"Yeah, well, he was being super cagey, so I just came out and asked," Valor says with a wince. Varick's fist clenches so tightly that I'm sure he's going to be in pain. "And when I brought up Mercer and JC, his energy shifted. He went from like a seven, which is his usual," Valor says for our benefit, "to a full ten."

"And that's supposed to mean he's involved with JC?" Brey clearly doesn't appreciate Valor's ability as much as I do.

Valor sighs and rubs the back of his neck. "It's not like I can always read simple decisions. Based on your daily decisions, your 'danger level' changes to reflect if you're more or less dangerous based on those decisions. Usually the fluctuation isn't by that much.

"Stealth's levels went up by a lot when I asked about Mercer and JC, which makes me think that he's involved in JC's new reading." Valor's ability would give me a headache.

"Valor," Varick growls. There's a vein in his neck pulsing at a dangerous tempo.

"Wouldn't Stealth think it's strange that you're asking about something that has nothing to do with you?" I'm curious, but also interested in buying him a few more seconds from Varick's rage.

Valor looks to me and narrows his eyes, then glances at Varick as if to ask him a silent question. But instead of answering, Varick just says, "You need to get out of here. Now. He can't know you came straight to us."

Valor takes a deep breath, and I can tell he's considering an argument with Varick.

"He's right," I say, letting go of my curiosity. "Things are bad enough as is."

Brey reaches for the door and opens it, showing him that we're all in agreement. Valor looks between us, seeming to accept that it's three against one, and walks out.

Varick doesn't move for a while, and I can't imagine how he's sorting through everything he's just learned.

"It's a lot to digest," Brey echoes my thoughts. *"Give him a second."*

I nod, and the movement gets Varick's attention.

"You good?" Brey finally asks him.

Varick takes a deep breath through his nose, then says, "Tell me about the dreams." His transition surprises me, so I stutter when I answer him.

"When I have a dream, it comes true at some point in the future unless I do something to change it. I dreamt that I would get taken from the school, which is how I knew it was coming." I intentionally don't mention the dream of the kiss with Brey because it's embarrassing, the dream of my graduation because I'm too ashamed to tell them about my involvement in the murder of the boy, or my dream about Brey's living room because I'm still not sure how to let Brey know his mother could be in danger. My secrets seem to just be stacking up to levels that I can't handle.

"Multiple abilities," Varick shakes his head and rubs his arm, "I never knew it was possible."

"Do you think Stealth knows?" Brey gives Varick a pointed look but doesn't explain why he thinks Varick would be able to answer that question.

"I'm not sure," Varick says while I chew on my lower lip.

We try to think of any and every reason that JC and Stealth could be more dangerous right now.

It's impossible to make plans when we don't even know what we're planning for. Ultimately, we have to concede that our only path forward is to return to our dorms, hoping that we somehow find more answers tomorrow. My body is exhausted, even though I spent most of the last day sleeping in the infirmary. Given the late hour, nobody says much as we trudge to bed, wishing for just a few hours of sleep.

The next morning, Jaylee, Lottie and I find the boys standing right outside our dormitory. Evidently, their paranoia grew with the distance from me.

Discomfort becomes our new normal as we navigate the following week. We seem to jump at every cough and noise, waiting to see why Stealth is more dangerous.

Day after day goes by and we have yet to figure anything out. It feels like we're just walking around the Domain blind, and that creates so much helplessness in all of us, something that I know Varick is struggling with the most.

It feels like it's been months since the incident with JC, when it was just last week. Every bone in my body is tired as I sit between Brey and Varick in Agility Skills. We're on the mats and they're discussing sparring as part of their training with Cynthia. It's so strange to be surrounded by the three of them.

In response to my thoughts, I glance over to where JC is lifting a heavy weight. His eyes find mine and the accompanying smirk gives me chills. Whatever JC is feeling is enough to catch Varick's attention. He abruptly ends the conversation with Brey.

"Ignore him," Varick says close to my ear. I'm trying.

Nick reaches the bottom of the Ring. He looks to me and tilts his head to the side, as if I'm a problem to be solved. Then, he continues class normally. His eyes glance my way more often than usual and I know that he's up to something.

Name after name is called while I train with my friends. My anxiety ramps up, waiting to see what Nick is going to do.

Finally, as we near the end of class, Nick meets my gaze and smiles again.

"Lewis." I rise from my place on the mat while watching him closely.

"Craw," he continues, his eyes never leaving mine.

My jaw clenches so tightly that it hurts. Of course this is happening. I should've expected it, although I never thought they would be this obvious.

They're making me fight JC again. This must be what Valor felt. Stealth is going to try to kill me again today, and he's going to use JC to do it.

"You don't have to fight," Brey says from beside me. "Tell them your arm still hurts."

"It'll be worse if she says no." Varick's throat bobs as he watches Nick from my other side.

"Screw that." Cynthia steps in front of me. "It can't be worse if she's dead."

My heart pounds loudly, but it's not fear that's making me shake. It's anger. Stealth is going to win, and I hate that more than anything else.

I step around Cynthia and none of them physically stop me, but I can hear them following me down the steps.

Nick meets me on the step first. I try to keep my chin up as he smirks at me.

"I need you to use your ability." He doesn't offer any other explanation about what could be happening or who ordered it.

"You already know about my compulsion." Emotion chokes my voice, but my ability of compulsion is a silly thing to face death over.

I expect a response, but he doesn't give one. Instead, his smile tightens like he expected that answer.

You would think that I'd be afraid, knowing that my death

could be close, but I'm too angry.

JC has already assumed his spot on the other side, and I hear the clicks of Nick's remote. The plastic enclosure begins to rise, putting a barrier between safety and me.

"Don't stop fighting, even if you feel like it." Varick warns in a low voice with a knowing look. I don't have time to analyze what he said and the enclosure lifts fully, cutting off my contact to him.

My entire body buzzes with adrenaline as I face the person I'm the most terrified of. I hold my elbow up, just like I was taught. When we start, I watch JC's footwork instead of his face. My heart flutters, urging me to embrace the unlikely: maybe I can do this. I'm stronger than the last time I faced him. I know more.

Several minutes pass and not much happens. It's obvious that I'm going to have to do something, because Nick won't let this stop until I do.

I'm stuck in this cage until JC either hurts me or I use an ability that I can't seem to control. That realization forces the wind from my lungs, taking away an ounce of my anger as I feel my shoulder hunch over.

My eye catches Varick's and it makes me miss a step. He's angry with me and I can see it. He must have felt my momentary lapse in determination and his instructions rush back. *"Don't stop fighting, even if you feel like it."* He shakes his head back and forth, as if to confirm what I'm thinking.

The distraction almost makes me miss JC rushing forward, seemingly about to accomplish what he's been considering for weeks.

"Stop!" I yell, completely overwhelmed. My entire body vibrates as it delivers the words, tingling from head to toe. It's immediately obvious that my ability is working as JC freezes mid-step. A thrill rushes through me at finally succeeding. Not only did I stop JC, but I did the very thing Nick asked me to do. Which means I survived. I won. I beat Stealth.

"Craw, what are you doing?" Nick calls out, interrupting my silent celebration.

JC stays frozen, rooted in place with one foot in the air as he quite literally stopped when I told him to. His eyebrows push together, and his face reddens like he's trying to solve a difficult math problem.

"I… I… she made me do it, I don't know what she did, but she did something to me," he says through clenched teeth.

I can't help the laugh that escapes me as he tries to force his leg to lower. We both stay like that for a few seconds.

My exhilaration doesn't let me see the warning signs before it's too late.

Not only does JC regain control of his leg, but the walls of the Ring are still up and I'm alone with him. His foot doesn't just return to the floor, but it takes a significant step in my direction, closing the space in no time.

His fist grazes my face, leaving a sharp sting on my lower lip. My heart hammers in my chest and I look to Nick, ready to beg him to stop this. I did what he asked.

JC pulls back and reaches for my left arm. I'm certain that he could grab hold of another part of me more easily, but he doesn't want to. He wants to continue hurting me in the same spot that he has before.

Nick doesn't do anything, and the panic in my chest rises.

A buzzing fills my ears just as JC's hand closes around my arm. I watch his fingers, but the pain never comes. There's a slight pressure, but nothing supernatural, although it prevents me from pulling away from him.

I look up and meet JC's eyes, unable to hide the grin that spreads across my face.

Upon seeing my smug reaction, he lets go immediately like I burned him, and his head whips around to stare at Nick.

"See! What the hell was that!" he yells and points in my direction. "My strength was gone! She didn't say anything, it was just gone."

The excitement from my momentary win vanishes as quickly as it came. My knees start to shake at the realization of what I just did, and my chest constricts while I try to swallow. Nausea threatens to choke me as the smell of sweat and coppery metal is even stronger now.

I turn my head to look at Brey just as Nick lowers the walls. I have to clench my jaw to stop it from quivering.

Varick leans close to Brey and whispers something in his ear. Brey meets his gaze in a look I recognize. Whatever Varick said, Brey is answering silently.

"Phillip," Nick breaks the silence, "go get Tanner. He's in the Eye waiting."

I hadn't realized that most of the class had stopped what they were doing to watch. Cynthia stands behind the boys, though she's not part of whatever conversation they're having.

Nick's words mean nothing to me, but judging by Varick's reaction, it can't be a good thing. Brey makes a move to join me in the middle, but Varick's arm reaches out to stop him. Varick leans over and whispers something else.

The seconds pass so slowly it's painful.

"Are you okay?" Brey interrupts my panic. *"Your lip is bleeding a lot."*

I use the gray sleeve of my shirt to smear my face, staining the edge of the fabric. It isn't a bad injury, but I can feel a puffiness setting in. I start to gnaw at my lower lip to keep myself distracted.

What feels like an eternity later, the door bangs open and Phillip walks in with a familiar looking chubby boy, who I can only assume is Tanner. The kid has flaming red hair but it's his condescending face that brings back a specific memory that I can't quite place.

"*Are you kidding me?*" Brey interrupts my pondering.

"Finally," Nick says, standing up. "You sure took your time for someone on standby," he mumbles.

The boy named Tanner walks down the Pitch stairs. His eyes scan the room before finally landing on me, a single eyebrow raising on his freckled face.

"I need you to test her again," Nick says with a casual wave of his hand in my direction.

"Fine," Tanner answers. He scurries into the Ring to meet me in the middle.

My eyes rest on his hand, held out for a handshake. The memory comes back fully as I look at his chubby, sausage fingers, waiting expectantly for mine.

It seems like another lifetime when I flinched under his hand as he grabbed my shoulder in Mr. Miller's class.

The images rush back from that day. From home.

I stare at the fingers and continue to gnaw on my lip. Confusion is making my brain fuzzy, but the answer seems so obvious in front of me, begging to bridge my misunderstanding. Why are they letting someone who isn't one of us in here? If this Tanner knows about the Domain, why doesn't he try to get us out?

Tanner wiggles his fingers back and forth and sighs loudly.

Why would he want me to shake his hand? Why here? Why is *he* here? How did he get here?

There must be another reason why he would be here.

And then it clicks. Those of us here are either guards or Unnaturals.

If he isn't a guard, then he must be one of us. He's an Unnatural.

He was in our classroom the day before we were taken. He walked around and touched each of us. He had laid his hands on every student. I thought it was weird, but I never considered it to be something more. A betrayal. Nick asked him to "test" me.

Tanner is how Stealth locates Unnaturals. This boy in front of me is the reason I'm here.

Something flutters in my chest and my fists clench. I start a list of crimes that this boy has committed against me in one way or another: being taken, being dropped off a roof, Brey dating Trinka, getting hurt by JC, the fact that I haven't seen Lizzy. All my problems started with him.

My feet take small steps in his direction before I know what I'm going to do.

I no longer feel like myself. It's like there's cloudiness in my vision except when it comes to Tanner and this immediate moment. All I can think about is the intense burning inside my chest.

I close the distance between us. Despite my size, I lunge at him. The force of my jump rocks him backward, and I collapse on top of him, pinning him to the floor. I know I'm stronger than I was when I got here, which empowers me and pushes me further.

The list of what he took from me runs through my mind over and over: *Lizzy, the roof, losing Brey, JC hurting me, Lizzy, taken, losing Brey...*

I perch myself on Tanner's body, forcing him to stay on the ground. My fingers are pressed firmly against his throat, while his own hands try to pry my grasp away. His neck is chubby, flesh puffing out around my grip.

His strength is enough to slowly overpower me, making it nearly impossible to achieve what I need.

Drops of blood land near his face, but I don't care that my lip is bleeding; nothing matters but winning this battle.

There's power in my chest, radiating outward as my compulsion takes over once more. My body tingles as I say through struggled breaths, "Stop… fighting… me."

Tanner's hands drop next to his body immediately, eyes widening even further with terror.

Now that I have all the power on my side, it dawns on me that I don't know what I am going to do to this boy. I didn't come over here to kill him, but if I don't stop soon, he will die because of me.

Can I do that? Can I take someone's life? *Lizzy, the roof, losing Brey, JC...* the thoughts continue cycling through my mind. Do any of his crimes warrant a death sentence?

His face is turning white, making the freckles even more pronounced. The color is odd under the flaming hair, and it pulls at my stomach.

I still haven't made my decision, but my grip hasn't loosened.

His eyes roll back. I wonder if that means life is leaving them.

Stealth wouldn't hesitate to kill him if he were in my position. But do I want to be like Stealth?

My hold loosens ever so slightly at that idea, at the

comparison to Stealth, but before I can decide either way, someone grabs my hips, pulling me into the air and forcing my grip from Tanner's throat.

I should have known Varick would be close behind me. I can't imagine what he must think of me after the intensity of what I just felt. He likely rushed over before I even reached Tanner, already understanding what my feelings meant.

I take a deep breath and Varick puts me down. I'm still shaking, feeling like I'm losing my mind and wondering how nobody else here is sharing this fury inside me.

My eyes scan the room to see every person staring. Some with fear, some in awe. It makes me feel worse to realize that those in awe are the ones who I would never associate with, like JC.

Nick, who I didn't realize was casually sitting on the steps of the Pitch, stands and starts to clap slowly before saying, "Finally, we see some real fight in you."

His approval is the last thing I want. It seems to trigger something deep inside me that feels like poison and I get sick all over the floor.

Varick shifts my body, continuing to hold me upright. I see him glance beyond me to Breyson before he leans close to my ear and says something about a concussion and going upstairs, but Nick has other plans.

He lets me finish and calls someone to clean up the mess I made. Without waiting for everything to calm down, he turns to Tanner again.

"Tanner, if you would, please," he gestures one hand over to me. His indifference to what just happened is disgusting.

"She tried to kill me! I'm not going near her!" Tanner protests with fear coating his plea while he rubs his throat. I try to find remorse in myself, but my anger toward this boy is too strong.

"Varick, hold her arms, please." Nick runs a hand through his buzzed hair.

Strong arms grab my wrists. I know he's not doing it because Nick asked, but to save me from myself.

"There, you'll be fine." Nick nods to Tanner.

My nostrils flare and my teeth make an audible snap as I grind them.

Tanner shakes his head as he takes a step closer but stops as far away as he can, while still within reach. He grabs my upper arm, which is pinned to my side.

We stand there for a full minute while Tanner bows his head, eyebrows pulled together. His hand doesn't move from my arm.

Nobody speaks but everyone watches.

It feels like an eternity in which every breath, cough and movement echoes through the space while we wait.

Tanner finally opens his eyes, but the furrowed brows don't move.

"There's something there," he says as his face scrunches up, "but it's not something I've ever seen before."

"Like an ability you haven't seen?" Nick asks Tanner. He walks to us so that he's only a few feet away.

"No." Tanner hesitates but doesn't pull his eyes away from mine. "I know what it looks like to see a new ability. And I do see that here, but there's still something different."

"Different how?" Nick presses. He rubs his temples but doesn't lose his temper with Tanner. It's as if he isn't surprised by this assessment.

"Since I've never seen it, how am I supposed to tell you what it is?" Tanner snaps back. Based on how scared he was just minutes ago, I'd say this tough-guy routine is just an act.

Nick takes a deep breath and rolls his eyes.

"Could it be more than one ability?" Nick finally asks Tanner.

The silence permeates every inch of the room.

"That's not possible," Tanner replies with weak resolve. "Is it?"

I can feel my breath hitch like it got caught in my chest and won't come out. My head swivels and I meet Brey's eyes, only to see my own fear reflected.

"Try again. This time look for more than one," Nick says to Tanner, having seen my interaction with Brey.

I don't know what to do. It crosses my mind to run, but where would I go?

Tanner reaches for my arm again. His eyes close much longer this time.

When he finally opens them, he doesn't speak. He just stares at me with one eyebrow raised.

"Well?" Nick huffs. He may have expected this but he's eager for confirmation.

Tanner stares, mouth open.

"There's more than one."

Chapter Nineteen

The silence ends abruptly, making me jump as voices boom. I swallow and hunch my shoulders, wishing I could disappear. In a world where the biggest uncertainty was at least somewhat known, my entire existence just shook everyone's foundation.

Varick's hands have moved to my sides, but he continues to touch me.

It's impossible to follow the various conversations. My gaze lands on JC who's seemingly yelling at Tanner. The ginger has lost his confidence as he cowers beneath JC's mass. I'm sure I could hear the words JC is screaming if I focused hard enough, but I don't care to. I just continue watching, grateful for something to occupy my mind in the chaos.

Nick steps in my direction, gaining my attention. He's not smiling, but there's a spark in his eyes that makes me uncomfortable.

"Lewis, come with me," he says. It's almost impossible to hear him, but he stretches a hand in my direction to emphasize the point.

The noise in the room starts to fade as everyone realizes something is about to happen.

"No," Varick says in a low voice. He shifts me away from Nick and I trip over my feet to follow his forceful guidance.

Nick doesn't seem at all surprised by Varick's defiance. "I'm not asking," he responds simply.

It's fine." I shove past Varick. Breyson is on his other side, though I have no idea when he came down to the Ring. They both look at me like I've lost my mind, but I start to walk forward anyway.

Varick reaches out and grabs my arm, the grip too tight. "It's fine," I repeat. My voice shakes, so I try to explain myself with my eyes. What other option do we have? We can't fight our way out of the Pitch, and even if we did, where would we go? Nick was obviously expecting this. I'm sure these next few moments were all premeditated, including what he'll do if Varick and Brey get in his way.

"You're not doing this," Varick says, like he can hear my reasoning and has no valid argument, but still disagrees with the plan. His jaw clenches and I can feel the hand around my arm tighten. My eyes find Brey's and I try to tell him everything I'm feeling. He watches me closely and I know he understands.

"Let go," Brey says as he approaches Varick. The twitch is present in his left eye, but he appears calm otherwise. "You know she's right. Let her go."

Varick doesn't break eye contact with me but his hand releases while his jaw tightens further.

"I'll find you," I mumble to them. "After…" my voice trails off. After what? None of us know.

Nick waits until I'm a step in front of him on the stairs before following me. He puts a hand on my back, but it doesn't have the same protective feel like Varick or Brey. This feels possessive and threatening. He follows me out the door and up the stairwell while I issue a silent prayer that Brey can keep Varick at bay. It's not that I'm eager for whatever I'm about to do, but it's not worth them getting in trouble as well.

As we walk, I feel clarity sink through me regarding the recent events. Nick said Tanner was waiting. Nick wasn't surprised. He even pushed Tanner to look for multiple abilities. JC has seen my disarming and he's also seen my compulsion. He must have told Stealth, and Stealth must not believe them to be related as one ability, because Nick knew. Somehow he knew I had multiple abilities. This has all been planned out because I wasn't careful enough.

Stealth wasn't planning on killing me. He was planning on catching me.

Nick doesn't direct my movements but doesn't stop me as I head to Stealth's office, so I assume I'm correct in where I'm supposed to be going.

Nick knocks three short times and Stealth's voice answers for us to enter.

"Ms. Lewis," Stealth says from inside his office. He doesn't appear surprised to see me, lending to the credibility of my theory, "sit."

Nothing has changed since my last visit except the stack of papers on his desk and the black circles under his eyes. The strong smell of his aftershave clouds the room, making my thoughts fuzzy and my lip sting.

Nick stands by the door as I file past him.

"Well?" Stealth asks Nick. The calmness he displays is unnerving.

"It's what we thought," Nick says with a nod, running a hand through his buzzed hair.

"Tanner confirmed?" Stealth presses, leaning his head forward over his interlaced hands.

"Yes, sir." Nick's eyes dart to me for a second before returning to Stealth's. "Multiple, and at least one that we haven't seen."

"Thank you, you're excused."

Silence doesn't usually bother me, but the long, drawn-out emptiness is making me uncomfortable. What's even more frustrating is that I think he's doing it on purpose. He wants me on edge before he starts asking questions. I grind my teeth together and shift in my seat.

"Ms. Lewis," he finally says, "I don't know how many times we have to have these conversations."

But that's ridiculous given our single other interaction. If anything, Stealth is just revealing how often he's spoken about me, how often I've been on his mind.

He stands, slowly circling the desk, before sitting on the edge closest to me and crossing his legs in front of his body. Despite the casual stance, his dark eyes bore into me, revealing the true frustration he feels.

"How exactly do you expect me to proceed when your behavior is so blatantly disrespectful?"

"I have no idea what you're talking about." My words are automatic. Seeing through his practiced calm gives me a boost of confidence.

He sighs, and the movement is remarkably similar, despite our minimal interactions.

"Multiple abilities. That's incredibly special." His eyes stare into mine and I do my best to reveal nothing. "How many abilities do you possess?" He tilts his head to the side, and his eyes don't stray from mine while he waits for my answer.

His desperation brings a small smile to my lips. I clench my jaw to stop, but the movement doesn't go unnoticed.

"Does your family know about this?" His sneer unsettles me as my breathing becomes shallow. I can't help but worry for their safety upon his question. I wouldn't put it past Stealth to find some way to bring them into this because of my behavior. Before

I answer, he continues, "I understand you shared a room at home, and that must put you in very close quarters."

"My sister doesn't know," I rush to say with a bite. "None of them know." I'm not sure why I defend my uncle, except it seems safer for Lizzy and Aunt Pam to just leave them all out of this. Not that I would mind Stealth going after Uncle Al.

"Your sister?" His mouth falls open and he stiffens but I simply tilt my chin a little and draw my eyebrows together. "I was under the impression she was your cousin."

"She took their last name when our parents died, but we're twins." His reaction makes no sense. He relaxes his posture as he watches me, perhaps surprised that he missed a piece of information when looking into my past. When he finally recovers, he moves on with the conversation.

"Very well, and your abilities?" There's something that has shifted in him since I arrived here, and I can't put my finger on what or why.

"I already told you about my ability." It's a weak attempt to stick to my old lie, but I stick to it nonetheless.

He smiles at me, though he should be frustrated by my lack of responses.

"Everyone has their breaking point, Ms. Lewis. I have no problem finding yours." He uncrosses his legs with a wave toward the door. Then he circles back to his chair and sits down.

"I'm free to leave?" My voice catches on the end. This was too easy and he's trying to unnerve me again.

"I much prefer to use my time efficiently, and that does not include whatever lies this conversation is revealing. Rest assured, we will pick this up at a later time." His promise sends chills down my spine. "I expect the truth from you the next time we speak."

I stand, still waiting for him to stop me.

"Ms. Lewis," he calls as my hand is on the doorknob. I turn my body so it only faces him a fraction, "I understand that my son has become rather fond of you. Please tell him that he'll be removed from the situation if he doesn't work on being a better influence."

I stare back into his hardened gaze as I replay the words he just said. I try to piece together what he could mean. He lowers his eyes, returning to his paperwork, as if my momentary shock is a completely normal occurrence. Without lifting his eyes again, he smiles to himself. It's genuine, showing the sparkle of his white teeth.

"No," I say in barely a whisper. My hand drops from the door.

Stealth ignores me, knowing he's already done what he intended. The smile fades, but his happiness stays plastered on his face—happiness that he's unravelling me.

Which he is. Because when I look at his face, the genuine smile covering his features, I see the familiar two dimples that I've recently grown so fond of.

Varick's dimples.

I can't wait for my breathing to return before I shove the door open and walk the short distance of the hallway. I just know I won't be able to get a full breath while I'm in the same room as that monster. My head spins, making the walls appear like they're closing in on me.

How can this be? How could I have missed this?

Varick's parents weren't around when we were kids. They had important government jobs. He was raised by a nanny. Is this what his dad was doing the entire time? His dad was absent because he was creating the Domain. Varick, *my friend,* is the son of the man who will send me to kill a woman and child. I clench my teeth and ball my hands into fists. The pressure stings my palms, but I welcome the pain.

My original plan was to go to lunch and find my friends, but that was before Stealth's unsolicited information. Now, I can't go there. I can't be anywhere near people while I try to work through this. That means the Eye is out of the question, as well.

I open the Pitch door. My body is on autopilot while I fend off the intense and deeply rooted betrayal coursing through me. I ignore the gloves that I know are sitting in one of the drawers and square my feet in front of the hanging leather. My fist flies forward while my brain reels. I throw myself into the bag, over and over, waiting for the motion to numb the onslaught of emotions running through me.

The signs seem obvious now that I know.

Left fist, right fist, left foot, right foot. I let the sounds of the bag drown my sorrow.

Varick and Valor weren't in the principal's office. Is that because Stealth had more humane ways of transporting his own sons?

Left fist.

Right fist.

My knuckles sting but I ignore the pain. Tears are rolling down my face, blurring my vision, but I keep going.

The door opens and I use my sleeve to wipe my face. I'm sure it's red and blotchy from the tears. I have no idea how long I've been gone. If the next Agility Skills class is starting, I need to get out of here before Nick returns.

But it isn't Nick.

In fact, it's the one person I'd want to see even less.

Varick spots me immediately and Brey is with him. He knew

I'd be here, either by instinct or because he could feel me. I start my routine again but the stinging in my hands is much more prominent now that I was interrupted. I clench my jaw to keep the tears from returning.

I can feel their presence at my side before either makes a noise.

"What did he say?" Varick asks me in a soft voice. "Why are you so mad?"

I have nothing to say to him. I clench my jaw tighter and continue to focus on the bag. Breyson places a hand on my shoulder, but I can't seem to calm down enough to look at him either.

Varick reaches a hand around the bag and grabs my fist before I can make contact again.

"Let go," I hiss at him, trying to pull my hand, but his grip tightens as he analyzes the bloody knuckles. His forehead creases with frustration.

"What, you don't bleed enough in class?" Varick snaps at me.

The last thing I need from him is a lecture.

"You should wear gloves or at least wrap your hands. You'll get an infection." Varick pulls his hand away and a small spatter of blood lands on his shirt. "Not to mention, you'll get blood on my shirt," he mumbles as an afterthought.

I ignore him and walk in the other direction. There's no point in being in the Pitch if the one person I need to distract myself from is here with me. He's right, of course, but I don't care right now.

"*What's going on? You're freaking me out.*" Breyson's thoughts fill my mind while I storm away.

They both catch up to me, but I still don't stop.

"Mercer," Varick demands. He grabs my arm and pulls me around to face him. His eyebrows are knit together in confusion, but still hold the threatening darkness that I've become so used to.

My fist flies forward in the direction of his face. But he's faster. He lifts his own hand and grabs mine, stopping the momentum.

"Mercer, what are you doing?" Brey questions as he jerks back slightly.

I try to pull my hand away from Varick, but I can't. "Look at me," Varick demands.

I don't want to meet his gaze, too worried that the tears will come back.

"Why didn't you tell me?" I say while still staring at the floor. I'm frustrated that it sounds more like a whimper and less like an accusation.

I can't see his face, but I do see his other fist tighten.

"He told you." It's not a question, but a statement.

Finally, I look up to his eyes. His brown hair covers his forehead, but he hasn't bothered to push it away.

"Did he tell you to train me?" My voice is strained as I ask the very thing I suspected.

"What? No—that's not—" his voice cuts off while he takes a breath and gathers himself. "He didn't send me to train you. I did that on my own to try and help. I told you to keep it a secret so that he wouldn't find out."

"That's some apology," I huff at him, crossing my arms. Varick seems at a loss for words, despite Breyson's frantic gaze between the two of us.

"She found out Stealth is my father," Varick finally says to Breyson, likely in answer to something he silently asked.

I watch Brey, waiting for the same explosive reaction that's currently raging through me, but it never comes. Instead, his icy blue eyes just meet mine with sympathy.

He sighs, but it isn't filled with frustration. It sounds like he's almost feeling sorry for me. *"Mercer, is it really that big of a deal?"* he finally thinks silently.

"What!" I scream. "How can you say that? Why aren't you more upset?" Varick's eyes scan Brey like he also can't believe the calm reaction.

"Varick doesn't act anything like Stealth." Brey's voice is soothing, willing me to let go of my anger. "And I kind of suspected it. There were so many signs."

Fingernails dig into my palms as I shake with rage at what Brey is justifying.

"That still doesn't change things!" I yell over the pounding in my ears, directing my next words at Varick. "Here you are, acting like we're friends, yet you have the ability to stop this, or get me out of here, but you don't!"

"I don't know how to get out of here," he says simply, his shoulders hunched forward. "If I did, we'd have left by now." His voice carries something, like he's trying to be funny. But there's a truth to the words spoken, and it pulls me up short.

"You weren't in the van with us," I argue back. "You're telling me you don't know how you got in here?"

He raises an eyebrow before replying, "I wasn't in the van at the school. That doesn't mean I wasn't in the van. They drugged me just like they drugged you. I just held my arm out willingly, instead of being chased across a roof." My mouth pops open as I consider that statement. I tip my head to the side as I watch him. The anger still burns like a fire in my gut because of his secrets.

"You're telling me that your dad is Stealth and you don't

know the way out of here?" I say through the heaviness inside of me.

"That's right. I don't know." His voice is flat and defeated. "I know that the way up is through some obscure door and a passcode. It takes you to the garage."

"Up?" I can feel surprise replacing my anger for a second. "Why up?"

"We're underground," he says simply, like I should have already known. This entire time I was so sure that my senses were leading me in the right direction when I scoured the bottom floors for an exit. "I believe we're about a ten hour drive from home, but I'm not sure which direction. They didn't think that was important information to tell us. Valor believes we're in the D Region, though."

I haven't ever been outside of the B Region. We're told the D Region holds most of our troops and supplies because of its proximity to the A Region, which is where our government is located.

"Valor didn't want to come here, did he?" I ask, remembering Valor's reaction to being here on our first night.

Varick avoids meeting my gaze. The silence settles around us as we wait for a response.

"No," he answers, his voice thick. "He wasn't going to come here. He wanted to go with our mother, who disagrees with how Stealth is handling Unnaturals. I ended up talking Valor into coming." He's watching the floor, like his shame is keeping him from looking at either of us directly.

"By 'talking him into it—'" I start to ask, remembering what he admitted about manipulating the feelings of others. I have no idea how powerful that part of his ability is, but it terrifies me.

"I made him change his mind, yes," Varick admits, cutting

me off. "He knows I did it. We wouldn't have separated, but I won the argument easier than I should have."

"Whatever you did is in the past. We still need to worry about what's coming. Is there any chance of us finding the way out?" Brey interrupts the tension and Varick gives him a small smile. I want to voice my disagreement with Brey and tell Varick that he better not ever use his ability like that on me but Varick answers before I can.

"Without graduating?" Varick's voice suddenly holds no hope. "I have no idea, and I don't think graduation should be your goal. When you graduate here, you have to show your loyalty to the Domain by cancelling someone," Varick takes a deep breath and looks at us expectantly.

Brey answers with a small nod. I, on the other hand, have known this for months. When neither of us say anything, Varick continues.

"Usually, it's a threat in the world. But sometimes it's another student… if that student has become problematic." Varick's eyebrows raise again, questioning when we're going to catch on.

I can feel my pulse quicken as I realize where he's going with his explanation.

"He thought I was a threat." The words spill from my mouth in a hollow voice.

"My graduation was supposed to take place a few months ago during class. It's always made to look like an accident." He swallows and shifts a little. "I clearly didn't do it."

"You were supposed to kill her?" Brey finally seems to understand. His nostrils flare as he advances on Varick.

"I didn't do it, did I?" Varick snaps, one hand gesturing to me.

I think back to that day in the Pitch when Varick had faked the fight and told me to stay down.

"Why didn't you tell us this before? About Mercer and your failed graduation?" Brey interrupts him. I can tell that Varick's last statement bothers Brey more than it bothers me.

"He made me keep it a secret," Varick says while crossing his arms.

I look away from his face. That's not a good enough reason.

"He has ways of making people cooperate," Varick responds to my emotional reaction.

"Not me," I argue with my jaw tight. "He can't make me do anything."

"Why do you think you got such a long break after your injury?" Varick asks.

"Because Ms. Williams said I couldn't participate," I respond confidently.

"That's not why," he answers quietly, making me question everything I thought I knew.

Chapter Twenty

My hand reaches for the girl's dormitory door. I don't particularly want to crawl under my covers, but I need space from Brey and Varick to sort through my feelings.

The last week has been exhausting. I'm still upset with Brey. I can't just let go of how he abandoned me. I had always thought we were closer than that. I have to admit he's trying, though.

It's been several days since I learned of Varick's true identity and despite having a busy week of classes and a weekend full of friends and laughter, I can't stop thinking about how hurt I am by his lies. It's not that I blame him for his lineage, that would hardly be fair of me when I was raised by Uncle Al, but I'm hurt he didn't tell me. I'm upset he didn't trust me enough to confide that piece of information.

It's so difficult to hold onto my anger when Brey, the person who hated Varick, is ready to look past these lies so easily. Am I holding onto this for nothing?

It all just feels like too much. Being around Varick also means that he reads my emotions while I try to process everything, and that invasion of privacy isn't what I need right now.

"Oh," I mumble upon hearing someone else in our room. "Sorry." My first instinct is to turn around, but my steps falter at the idea of having to join everyone again. I haven't said anything to anyone else about Tanner's reading of me, but gossip travels fast, and the entire Domain seems to know. My friends have had enough courtesy not to mention it, but the attention I'm getting from the rest of the Domain leaves me on edge.

The person in our dorm doesn't answer me, but I realize it's a mound coming from under Trinka's blankets, not unlike that first week here when she was traumatized by her actions in the Pitch.

"Trinka?" I ask, distracted from my previous mission to be alone, "are you okay?" I haven't had a conversation with her since my second stay in the infirmary. I later learned that she asked Brey not to check on me, but he did anyway.

It hasn't been for lack of effort. I've been wanting to talk to Trinka, to tell her that I'm sorry about her and Brey. But I always stop myself because I'm not sure if I really am sorry; I just know I don't want her hurting. Trinka wormed her way into my heart when I didn't have space for anybody but Brey. That's not something I can easily forget.

"Hey, what's wrong?" I push further.

Her body stills under the blanket, letting out a muffled noise that sounds remarkably like, "Go away."

I sigh and turn back to the door. Granted, I wanted to be alone, but Brey and Varick's hovering is preferable over Trinka's animosity. My hand is about to reach the handle when the voice, much clearer now, grabs my attention.

"Why do you care?" It isn't aggressive, but sad, as if she genuinely can't understand why I would check on her. I take a breath and chew on my lower lip while I turn back to the mound on her bed.

I have no idea if she can hear me through the blanket fort she's created.

"Because you were kind to me when nobody else was." As soon as the words escape my mouth, I realize the truth to them that's been weighing me down. I've felt like I owed Trinka a debt for being there for me in the beginning when the rest of the Domain considered me an outcast.

The blankets slowly pull down to reveal her red and puffy face. Her brown curls, now longer than shoulder length, are matted to her cheeks.

"You shouldn't bother wasting your breath on me." She sighs, her bloodshot eyes meeting mine. I move to her bed, only hesitating a moment before sitting down.

"About what happened between you and Brey…" I stare at the floor. Brey and Trinka haven't spoken since my stay in the hospital, and even though I didn't cause their issues, I can't help but feel bad for her. For some reason, I can't meet her eyes, "I'm sorry."

"That's not even…" She struggles to inhale a full breath through her rattled sobs. "I'm not a good person, Mercer." Her sentence has a bite to it, an edge that she wants me to let go of instead of exploring further. I'm tempted to take her up on the warning. It might be selfish, but I don't need any more issues than I already have.

"Are any of us?" I whisper back, ready to end the conversation.

"I almost graduated today." Her words give me pause. I'm unsure if she intended to do that, to stop me, or if she simply felt she couldn't contain that secret any longer. But my chest suddenly feels tight again, and my own future graduation rushes to my mind along with Varick's words from earlier: *"You have to show your commitment to the Domain by cancelling someone. Usually, it's a threat in the world. But sometimes it's another student."* Do I even want to know who she almost killed?

"Congratulations," I mumble through gritted teeth.

"Mercer." Her voice is pleading. I don't want to be this outlet for her. I can't handle hearing about what she did.

"I have to go," I say in a tight voice. I don't want to discuss her graduation. I don't want to do anything that could lead to me thinking about my own graduation.

"I'm sorry," she whispers into the quiet awkwardness that surrounds us.

It's enough to keep me rooted. As I rack my brain, I can't figure out why she would be apologizing to me. Especially now that things with Brey are back to normal. But perhaps she's just sorry in general. After all, I can't imagine going through a graduation and *not* feeling remorse.

Her eyes search mine, willing me to understand some untold secret so she doesn't have to voice it herself.

"Sorry about what?" I finally ask, unable to help myself. Something starts clawing inside my chest and a shakiness takes over at whatever she's about to say. I have no idea why my body is trying to warn me against her next words, but it is.

"They wanted me to bring the targets back here." Her voice is ice cold as she doesn't answer my question. "Not a typical graduation, but he said that I could hurt them, so long as they came back alive."

This is new information, a part of graduation I hadn't known. I'm not sure why Stealth would need someone here injured but alive.

"Who were they?" I press, hoping for some kind of solution to my curiosity. Her eyes widen as she hears me ask the single question she was hoping I wouldn't.

"I messed up." Her voice is nearly a whimper. Frustration begins to grate at me because of her reluctance, despite being so keen to talk about this subject. "I killed one of them. The woman.

I don't know how to fully control my ability yet and she screamed when she saw me in the house. It scared me and I lost control." Her voice is so dull that she sounds anything but scared as she relives the moments. "Stealth says because I didn't do what he asked, it doesn't count as a graduation, and I can't see my mom. I didn't kill them both, though. The man is here. I suppose you'll see him soon."

"Why would I see the man soon?" The words come out slurred while my brain races to catch up.

"I think that's why he made me get him." Trinka finally looks me in the eye. There isn't a drop of malice in her features. "Since he's your uncle."

Cold fear washes through me, freezing my limbs in place as I continue to stand at an awkward distance between Trinka's bed and the door. Uncle Al is so close. The trauma he inflicted when I was a little girl is too deeply rooted for me to be rational, and it takes several seconds for me to realize that I can't run to put distance between us. If I could, I would have already.

Then the fear turns into sheer dread. My mouth dries up and I question if I'm going to get sick on the fluffy carpet. Trinka's words run through my mind once more.

"Who did you kill?" I manage to say through my clenched jaw. Neither answer is going to fix the pounding in my ears, but it can't be Lizzy. Lizzy has to be alive. Even as I think the words, I realize that means I'm hoping she'll say—

"Your aunt." Her emotionless tone is gone, instead, sobs start to rack her body again. If I took a moment to really consider the scene in front of me, I might feel sorry for her. But I don't take that moment.

Instinct comes over me as I leap across the space to jump on top of her. My fingers close around her throat, and despite the whites of her eyes bulging, the tears continue to wash down the sides of her face. I hold her as seconds go by. Did she watch as Aunt Pam's eyes became lifeless?

"Mercer, stop," Brey thinks to me from somewhere.

"She's not thinking straight. Something's wrong," Varick's voice murmurs, so low that I doubt it's for me to hear. I hadn't realized they had followed me in here, likely because of whatever emotion Varick felt coming from me after Trinka's confession.

Brey's strong arms wrap around my body, but I fight him and pull Trinka's neck with us as he yanks me away. Varick's hands force my fingers to unclench from around her. I fight him too.

I lash out in Brey's hold, my teeth gnash and spit flies around my face. Brey's arms simply tighten around me, forcing me to hear the pounding in my temples as I pant heavily.

"What—" Varick starts to ask.

"She killed my aunt," I say through my gasps for air. The intensity of my own voice scares me. It occurs to me that this is the second time I tried to kill someone with my hands, and I should feel embarrassed at what the Domain has turned me into, but all I feel is fire.

Both of their dumbstruck faces look to Trinka with silent requests to deny what I'm saying. But her responding sobs tell them my words are true.

Something inside me is screaming to let go of my emotions because there's a bigger issue. It's nagging me, pushing me to understand.

"Let go of me," I say to Brey. There isn't the added authority that my compulsion brings, and I realize now that I was too angry in the moment to even consider using compulsion. Trinka also refrained from using her ability, but perhaps that was intentional. Maybe she knew she deserved my anger. "I'm fine, put me down."

His grip tightens only a second while he looks to Varick for confirmation. I grind my teeth together as Varick reads me and gives a nod to his friend. Trinka watches, her face tear-stained and red from our interaction.

"Your sister," she whispers the answer to my unsolved problem, "wasn't there, but that was the whole point. I was supposed to get them out of the way so JC could get to her. Stealth said he wanted to give JC another chance."

There it is. The words hit me like a ton of bricks and my legs wobble underneath me. I know I need to ask more questions, for Lizzy's sake, but I can't bring myself to do it. I feel Varick's eyes on me, watching with an acute awareness. I clutch my stomach and Brey's arms grab me to keep me upright.

"When?" I manage to croak.

"Now. It's already happening," she squeaks before sobbing again.

Nothing she's said makes sense. Why is this happening? Why now?

"How—" I continue to ask something… anything, but Varick interrupts.

"Why didn't he send you with JC?" Varick asks through his clenched jaw.

"I don't know," she whispers to Varick.

My throat is thick as I try to swallow.

"Is there any way to stop it?" I ask in a defeated voice. I can't get out of the sinking feeling that's surrounding me.

Varick's eyes are shining with sadness as he looks at me. He doesn't answer my question. He doesn't have to. They're already on their way and we can't even get out of here to follow.

My heart is racing and the tightness in my chest is getting

worse. I try to fight through the desire to curl up in my bed and sob away the pain.

If I give up now, Stealth wins. I don't know where I'm going or what I'm doing, but Stealth winning is not an option. Maybe we fight whoever has her when they return. I don't bother glancing back at Trinka on my way out.

The walk through the Domain is excruciating while every second is one less moment of Lizzy's safety. Something in Breyson is turning more urgent with each step but he doesn't clue me in to what he's thinking and it's not the time to ask.

Nobody says anything as we all make our way to the storage closet, dodging other students all around.

When we finally reach the space, the defeat seems to feel more consuming. Varick is angrier and Brey is even more frantic than he was during our walk. His eyes dart around the room and he mutters to himself, as if trying to organize his thoughts.

"Brey," Varick says, while watching our friend. But Brey doesn't acknowledge him.

"Mercer, if Stealth is trying to find people close to you… people who he can use to get to you…" Brey struggles to finish his thought.

Varick and I don't answer, waiting for him to continue. He watches us, wishing we would catch on without him having to spell it out. His throat bobs and he's on the verge of losing himself to emotion.

"You weren't even close to your aunt and uncle," he continues. "If Stealth digs, he's going to learn where you spent all your time growing up."

"Your mom," I whisper. I had been so consumed with worry over Lizzy that I never even considered the safety of Mrs. Jones.

She doesn't deserve this. She's so good, so kind. I want to

cry as I picture her sitting in their living room, drinking a cup of coffee as JC bursts in. As I picture her living room…

"Wait," I mumble, staring into nothing. I was sure the dream I had was after my escape. But that must not be.

It never made sense to me why I would go to Brey's house after I left the Domain. Why would I make myself so easy to track down?

But I bet I don't physically go there at all.

In the dream of my graduation, JC had said that I could project, and while I haven't given it much consideration, that must mean that at some point, he witnesses me projecting. He's going to witness my fourth ability.

This makes sense.

I'm not going to escape the Domain and go to Brey's house. I'm going to project to Brey's house and save Lizzy and Mrs. Jones.

The air in the room seems to change as they both watch me closely. I can tell that Brey has a thousand questions, but he holds them all in as he waits for me to continue.

As the pieces fit together I can feel in my gut how right I am in this theory.

I set my jaw and look Brey in the eye as I finally say, "I can get them out."

Chapter Twenty-One

"I don't follow," Varick says as he scratches his jaw.

Now that I know what's going on, it feels like we don't have time to go through my explanation, but I owe them something.

"I had a dream of my own graduation." My voice is rushed, but I don't care as I continue, "And in that dream, JC said something about me projecting."

Neither of them are convinced, though Varick's brows do flick up in surprise as he lets me continue.

"I also had a dream that I was in your living room, Brey, as JC and Nick were coming to the house." He tightens his jaw and I know he's suppressing anger at the fact that I never mentioned this potential threat to his mom. "I thought it was a dream about what's going to happen after I escape, but that doesn't make sense, and I never connected the two, but they are connected. Don't you see?"

They don't answer. Varick tilts his head to the side and listens while Brey just frowns at my words.

"I'm going to project to your house. I'm going to get them out by warning them." I straighten my body, urging them to adopt the same confidence I feel in this plan.

"I don't like it," Varick finally says while shaking his head. "No, not that," he continues with a look to Brey. It takes me a moment to realize he must be answering a question that Brey asked silently as he continues, "I think something else is going on. Why did he send JC separately from Trinka? It doesn't make any sense unless Stealth wanted Mercer to find out."

"So what if he does want me to find out," I nearly scream the words. "He has no way of knowing I can get there first and save them."

Brey must answer him silently because Varick pauses as he listens before continuing to both of us, "It's dangerous when we don't have all the answers. We don't know his end game."

"She can do it," Brey says out loud, jaw tight.

"No, you want her to do it. There's a difference," Varick answers. The air becomes uncomfortable and awkward.

Brey's cheeks burn red and I know he agrees with Varick, but it's not enough to keep me from trying.

"I can do it," I defend myself, feeling my entire body shout in agreement as my pulse picks up.

Varick's fists seem to vibrate at his sides and Brey's eye twitches.

"This is ridiculous," I say through an exaggerated huff. "I'm doing it, Varick. Either help or leave us alone."

He looks between the two of us before taking a defeated breath, jaw clenched.

"You can't be seen. That's more important than saving either of them." He presses his lips together as he watches me and analyzes my reaction.

Brey shifts uncomfortably at Varick's direction, and I don't disagree with his frustration, but now is not the time. Varick must feel something in Brey's emotions, because he looks back to his friend.

"I would say the same thing if it were Valor's life on the line," Varick says as an answer to either Brey's silent question or avalanche of emotions. "There are some things more important than protecting the people we care about." Turning his attention to me, he continues, "Stealth doesn't understand the extent of what you can do. We need to keep it that way. If he realizes Unnaturals may exist with multiple abilities, he'll be an even bigger terror to the world. I know his ambitions better than anyone. This is more important than us, than Lizzy, even than the Domain. The world needs him to never find out. Do you understand me?"

A beat of silence follows while he stares at me with a heaviness that I don't want to acknowledge.

"Okay," I finally answer with what I hope is a reassuring smile.

The pressure in the room feels like it might swallow us, until finally Brey's urgency increases.

"How do you do it?" His words are rushed.

"I don't actually know," I admit. Heat fills my cheeks at the embarrassment of the statement, but I must be able to figure it out. I'm absolutely certain that's how I'll get to Brey's living room, although that idea brings another question to mind.

"If Lizzy is his target, why would I go to your house?" I process out loud.

"My mom has a car," Brey says while nodding through his analysis. "And if you saw them at my house, then Stealth instructed JC to get my mom, too. Go to your house first. Get Lizzy over to my house and they can leave together."

I nod while letting that sink in. It could work.

"Where do I tell them to go? The holes in this plan start to become overwhelming. How are we going to pull this off? I don't know how to project at all, and now I have to go to multiple places. Fear starts to grip my stomach but I can't give in. I just need to focus on the first step and get to Lizzy.

"Austin," Varick says through clenched teeth. His arms are

folded in front of him, but I can see the muscles rolling through his forearm as he flexes to maintain calm. Both of us look at him and I raise my eyebrows.

Texas seceded from what used to be the United States. It's nearly impossible to cross the border. Nobody I know has been to Texas.

"Valor told me about it," Varick says with a hint of regret. "We almost went there together before we were taken. Tell them to go to the Hut and that Valor sent them." His words make no sense to me but I'm out of time for an explanation.

My heartbeat pounds in my ears. I look up at them and feel instantly overwhelmed with the fear and hope radiating around this room.

I close my eyes, more to drown out the sensations around me than because I know what I'm doing. It takes a few minutes for me to ignore Brey's footsteps and Varick's obvious judgement, which I can feel burning into me from behind my eyelids. Instead, I try to focus on this key fact: I know I can do this. I wouldn't feel nearly as confident if I hadn't seen it. It's just a matter of how, but obviously I must figure it out.

Aunt Pam used to practice yoga with Lizzy. They had spent every day one summer trying to ground themselves. I didn't have the patience to join them, but I would hear their voices drift up through my bedroom window. It's like I can hear her voice now, *"Focus on the in-breath, then the out-breath. Nothing else matters. Nothing else is in this present moment."* I remember scoffing at that statement, bitter that my entire life revolved around fearing future moments too much to be in the present moment.

Perhaps my memories of Aunt Pam's voice are held more gingerly now that I know I'll never hear it again; it's as if she's coaxing me to follow her instructions. I breathe in, then out, until I'm no longer thinking about my fear or the two people in front of me.

It isn't until I'm satisfied with my control that I think about home, really think about it. I let my mind wander to the details of the pink wall that lines the stairs.

In my mind, I reach my fingertips out and graze the photos that adorn it. My favorite is one of Lizzy on a swing when she was nine, with the sun shining down on her brown, curly hair and her smile radiating. I don't remember what she was laughing at, but the picture often numbed the edge of bitterness that had become so normal.

I take a deep breath and a tear runs down my face.

I open my eyes, startled and embarrassed, a hand snapping up to my face to wipe it away, but my breath catches in my throat. I'm not in the Domain anymore. Instead, I'm standing in the very same hallway I was thinking of, directly in front of that picture. My fuzzy memory of the photo didn't do Lizzy's sparkle justice.

I swallow and the feeling is tight. I've never projected before, and I have no idea how this works. When I appear in a space in my dreams, I simply float along. But it feels like I'm actually here. Even the smells are remarkable, though the familiar scent of home has a slight tinge of lavender that doesn't belong.

A quick glance into the kitchen reveals it to be empty. My chest tightens as I remember that the only person who could be here is Lizzy. Uncle Al is at the Domain and Aunt Pam is dead. I shake my head to force the emotions back down. I can't fall apart now, but the thread of her death is sitting there, begging to be pulled. I know the second I give in to my sorrow over it, the grief will consume me.

There are no Christmas decorations out, which almost makes my heart hurt more.

I rush up the stairs, reaching for the railing for traction. My hand floats right through the wooden rail, then through the wall, but I only hesitate for a moment to consider how interesting it is. My feet can carry me on the ground, but I can't interact with objects.

As much as I thought about this house since being taken, physically being here still makes my skin crawl. I grit my teeth knowing Uncle Al is the reason for that. He ruined everything good about this place.

The bedroom I shared with Lizzy is the same as I remember it, with our old, wooden bunk bed pushed into the corner.

The blinds are open, letting the sun stream through. My heart jumps at seeing the outside world for the first time in months, but I shiver at the memory of the last time I was in this room and my foot groans in protest despite being fully healed.

Lizzy's bed on the bottom bunk is neatly made, and a frustrated huff escapes me. I hadn't thought about what I would do if Lizzy weren't here. Is she at school? I'm not sure why I figured she'd be here, but what else would she do if she realized her guardians were missing? Could I project to the school and get her? If I do that, I'll certainly be seen and that was Varick's one warning.

Panic starts to grab hold of me, the holes in the plan seeming even bigger than before I projected. What were we thinking?

There's movement on the top bunk, my bed, and it catches my attention.

"Lizzy?" I ask tentatively. The heaps of blankets move, and the covers pull back to expose the disoriented and splotchy face of my sister. I stand rooted in place, too stunned to do anything.

It's been months since I've seen her, but the piercing brown eyes are just as I remembered.

"Mercer! Oh my gosh! You're alive!" She half crawls, half falls out of the bed while she speaks.

"I—" I start to say but I close my mouth with an audible snap. I have no idea how to explain what's happened to me, not having planned any of this.

She doesn't wait for me to answer, instead rushing over and throwing herself at my form with her entire weight, arms outstretched.

Her petite body flies right through me and hits the wall. The impact knocks her backward and she falls. Brunette frizzy curls from days of not being manicured rest like a lion's mane around her face. When she finally looks up, hysterical tears are streaming down her cheeks.

"We realized," she whispers while looking at me as if I just proved a theory to her. "Mother and I realized what happened. I was worried I'd never see you again."

I have to clench my jaw to make the clawing at my stomach stop. I hadn't ever considered that my family would miss me. Especially if they found out the truth.

"I… just… can't," she gasps. She keeps speaking, but the words are entirely incoherent.

"Lizzy, it's okay, please." I try shushing her. I move over to her body in an attempt to comfort her, despite the inconvenient lack of contact.

Lizzy's sobs continue like she isn't listening at all. "Aunt Pam… and Uncle Al," she says through a deep and ragged breath, "they aren't here." I don't know the last time I heard her refer to them like that, as her aunt and uncle and not parents. It must be for my benefit.

"Aunt Pam is dead." I hope I sound calm and controlled. It may not be the right time, but I can't have her running around searching for Aunt Pam before leaving. Her eyes widen and her entire body starts to shake.

"Dead?" she mumbles in a hollow voice.

I merely nod my head.

"And Uncle Al?" Her voice is barely audible.

"He's not dead. He was taken by the same people who took me, but I wish they had killed him," I admit, my voice pinched. She glances to my fists clenched at my sides, then her eyes track up my arms to what must be muscles she's never seen. "It's not the time to explain," I say. "The same people are coming to take you. That's why I came. You need to leave."

Her eyes widen and her jaw trembles.

"Are you coming with me?" she finally asks with a glint of hope in her eyes.

My mouth presses into a thin line, not wanting to have to answer this question.

"No," I admit. Her fear starts to spill out in fresh tears. "I'm not really here, or I would. But Breyson's mom will, so you won't be alone. When I get out of the mess I'm currently in," I laugh at the impossibility of ever finding a way out of the Domain. "I'll come find you."

Her mouth quivers but she nods in agreement.

"Pack," I direct, trying to grab one of her bags myself and forgetting that I'm not really here. My hand floats right through it.

"How long will I be gone?" She finishes stuffing the bag and grabs another.

"Don't plan on coming back."

She doesn't break her momentum, but the flow of tears

increases.

"You should—" she stops what she's doing and looks up at me, "you should go look at the folder on the counter with your name on it."

My eyebrows pull together and she gives me a sad smile.

"When we realized what you were and why you were gone," Lizzy says while returning to the contents of the dresser. "Aunt Pam was miserable for a long time. She felt terrible. She wrote you a letter in case you ever came back."

"Oh." It's all I can think of responding. Her words leave an emptiness inside me that I can't address right now, so I respect my earlier decision and force the feelings down.

I take a deep breath, trying to focus on the task at hand.

"Can you jump the back fence?" I ask her. It's impossible to reach Breyson's house without going on the main roads. But at least we can minimize her exposure.

Her jaw tightens but she gives me a single nod. Lizzy isn't very athletic.

"Do you know which house is his?"

She nods again and we rush downstairs during my hurried instructions.

"I need to go there now and get Mrs. Jones to start packing. Stay off the main roads as much as possible; I don't know how much time we have."

She hesitates in the kitchen for a moment before running to the counter. Her fingertips grab a red folder that's neatly placed beside the television before she unceremoniously stuffs it into her backpack.

"For when you get out and come find me." She smiles weakly. My chest warms at the gesture but breaks at the idea that I may never see her again.

She opens the back patio door, allowing the chilled air into the space, and runs to the fence. Winter is creeping in based on the temperature. Lizzy throws her bags over the fence and then awkwardly grabs the top, climbing it without an ounce of agility or finesse.

Her body falls with a thud on the other side and I wince, knowing she's going to feel that tomorrow. I just hope she's not in the Domain when the pain hits.

I close my eyes and think of another longing. This time I'm more confident because it's the very scene I had already envisioned.

Focus, I tell myself, thinking about Breyson's living room, the place that gave me solace for so many years.

I open my eyes to Mrs. Jones standing right next to their blue couch. The small television is on, showcasing the current propaganda.

The sound of broken glass hitting the floor echoes off the walls, but she doesn't even seem to realize she dropped the glass of water she was holding. The familiar smell of detergent that I've missed fills my senses, waking up a part of me that's been dormant in the Domain, although that hint of lavender is still present, even here.

"Mrs. Jones, listen, Brey knows I'm here, he sent me. He's with my…" I hesitate, not knowing what to call my physical form in the Domain, "my body, waiting for me to return."

"Mercer, oh! Breyson? He's alive?" Her hands tremble. She doesn't bother cleaning up the mess. "Did you say he's alive? Are you both okay?"

"We are, but you aren't safe and we need to get you out of here." She starts nodding, but the movement looks almost robotic.

"You need to pack, fast. Only the essentials and some food. My sister, do you remember her?" Mrs. Jones' eyes still hold mine and she continues to nod, having not stopped at all. "She's on her way over here. I was just with her."

As she continues to nod, I start to question her state of shock.

"Mrs. Jones!" I yell. I approach her to slap her, shake her, something, before realizing I can't physically touch her. "Pack! Now!"

It only takes her another second to recover, though there's still something distant about how she runs down the hall and starts to pack. After a few minutes, there's knocking, but it comes from the back of the house.

"It's Lizzy," I try to reassure her frenzied look. She still doesn't know what threat she's packing to avoid, blindly following my instructions. She unlocks the door to let Lizzy in.

Lizzy's forehead is glistening and her breathing is heavy and erratic.

"Mercer, someone saw me," she whispers in panic.

It feels like lead was dropped into my gut, but I just swallow and try to ignore it. If I freak out, they'll both lose it.

"Can you help Mrs. Jones?" I try to keep my voice calm, but it isn't easy. I have a feeling I know who followed her and where I'll see them. "And Lizzy, can you take that photo album," I give a pointed look to the coffee table.

One glance to Mrs. Jones, and Lizzy gives me a meaningful look to say she'll take over. She grabs the album and leaves the room. I cover my stomach with my hand to stop the panic that's threatening to make me freeze.

I can't stop JC and Nick if I'm not physically here; I'm not even sure I could do it if I *were* here. And there's no way that Lizzy and Mrs. Jones can overpower them. Tears threaten to unleash themselves and the heat inside my chest is begging me to just give up.

It can't be that all this was for nothing. There has to be a way.

I hesitate to move to the front window as I stand in the living room alone. I know what my dreams showed me, and it almost feels like I'm manifesting them into reality by moving to the window.

But if I avoid looking out front simply to change the outcome, all it would do is leave us unprepared for when they show up.

With a deep breath, allowing Brey's familiar smell of detergent to calm me, I move to the front of the room and my eyes scan the front yard to confirm my suspicions. My promise to Varick not to be seen echoes in my mind. But now that I'm here, now that I've seen Lizzy again, I must get them out no matter the cost. Perhaps Brey knew I would reach this point once here. That would explain why he backed down as soon as Varick started making demands.

Guilt rips me apart as I consider the idea forming in my mind. Are saving Lizzy and Mrs. Jones worth my being seen? Varick said he would even sacrifice Valor, but Varick and I are fundamentally different people. I will always sacrifice the greater good to save those I love. It's why Mr. Clayton hates me so much. So, even if Varick's reasoning is for the greater good, that's not good enough.

"Okay!" I yell, my plan becoming solidified. "They're coming."

Nick and JC are too close now. My sister gasps next to me in recognition. After all, she went to school with JC.

"Go wait in the car until I come back to tell you it's safe," I say in a hushed whisper.

I can almost see Varick's dark gaze as I stand in front of the door, prepared to do the very thing he told me not to.

I have Lizzy open the front door from the inside while I keep my hand on the knob so that it looks as if I opened it myself. I listen to the door click behind me and know that Lizzy is rushing to the car to wait for my next instructions. My heart feels like it's lodged somewhere in my throat.

Nick's steps falter at the sight of me. JC takes a few more moments to understand, but then he stops, as well. Heat from the sun makes me squint, though it's freezing out here without a jacket.

"Hey," I yell in my best surprised voice. "What are you guys doing here?"

JC's face pinches together. I don't give them enough time to work through their shock. After all, I should be in the Domain, and something has gone wrong if I'm not. They have no idea what my abilities are, and no way of knowing if I escaped.

"Anyway, they left already," I continue. My voice shakes, and I know that I'm not conveying my words how I'd like. A strange rattling in my chest threatens to make anything I say sound unstable. I cough once. "Well, all right then."

I start with a walk that turns into a jog along the side of Brey's house, praying that Nick and JC choose to pursue me and not Lizzy.

When my body makes it to the fence, I test my hand to be sure I can go through the object, then I slide through it completely before they can see me.

"I'll just see you back at the Domain!" I yell from the other side.

I hear a rushed debate while they work through what's happening. One of them sounds like they're communicating with someone from the Domain, and my heart hammers in my chest as I hold my breath until I hear the words I'm looking for.

"She shouldn't be here," Nick says in a low voice. "We have to get her back."

JC growls in response, no doubt frustrated that I interrupted his graduation.

I rush across Brey's backyard and glide through the other fence. I slow long enough to call out to them, so they know the direction I've taken. Every time I almost lose them, I stop and call out, luring them for several miles.

When my breathing is ragged and a stab in my side makes running impossible, I finally stop. I'm so grateful I didn't have to jump all those fences and can't imagine how they're holding up. I close my eyes and try to focus. I can hear the boys jump the last fence between us. They're close to me; too close. It makes it difficult to picture Brey's garage.

I open my eyes, willing myself to have moved through space, but I'm still in the same yard. And what's worse is that Nick and JC are now directly in front of me, their own smell of sweat too close.

JC glares down at me, his biceps flexing and a vein throbbing in his forehead. Sweat drips down the sides of his face from the exertion of what I put him through. He's not an especially talented runner and he's been leaning so heavily on his abilities during Agility Skills that he hasn't trained like the rest of us.

I might not really be here, but the fear of JC is too deeply rooted for logic to have much of a say. JC reaches for me, and I take a step back out of habit.

But the step isn't big enough, and his hand brushes right through my body. They're seconds away from realizing I tricked them. How long will it take for them to get back to the house?

I close my eyes once more and take a deep breath. I try my hardest to block out the anger coming from Nick and JC in front of me, to not focus on their words as they realize what I've done. I know that if I open my eyes, I would see them swiping at me, trying to make contact.

I concentrate on Aunt Pam's voice, breathing in through my nose and out through my mouth. This present moment and nothing more. I picture Brey's garage.

"Mercer?" Lizzy's voice interrupts my concentration. I open my eyes and my chest feels like it's about to explode from relief.

"Go, now!" I scream through rapid breaths. Mrs. Jones turns the ignition on. "Head to Austin," I yell at them, my voice hysterical. "Don't stop until you have to and when you get there, go to the Hut. Tell them that Valor sent you."

Lizzy's mouth opens and closes, shock all over her face. I don't try to hide my frustration. Nick and JC are surely on their way back by now. I'm just grateful Mrs. Jones seems to be out of whatever stupor she was in.

"Go now," I demand, jabbing my finger toward the garage door.

Both have the common sense not to argue.

Mrs. Jones puts the vehicle in reverse and speeds down the driveway, hardly making sure the road is clear. I watch as she drives down the street, the sun reflecting onto the shiny hood of her blue car.

I sigh, my shoulders sagging with heaviness. My entire body aches, which is strange considering my physical form isn't actually here.

I don't want to face Varick and admit what I've done. I don't want to think about what's going to be waiting for me at the

Domain when JC and Nick report back. But despite all that, a smile fills my face.

I did it. They're safe.

Chapter Twenty-Two

Returning to my body doesn't take nearly the same amount of concentration and focus as projecting to other places. My soul practically drags me through the space as soon as my eyes close, too tired to do anything except return to my physical form.

The aches are more pointed, like they had been dulled by me not being here. Something like a fire alarm beeps loudly, only slightly muffled by our location.

Someone has laid me down on top of the table. Hair sticks to my neck and back as if I was truly running as hard as my projected form. I sit up, my muscles screaming from the movement.

Brey is pacing the room and hasn't noticed me yet, but Varick sits on the floor, his back to the wall and his legs bent. His forearms rest on his knees and his eyes bore into mine, making me wince.

"How long has it been?" I ask, not because I want to know, but because I need Brey to get involved before Varick can unleash those dark feelings onto me. My throat feels like sandpaper, so I cough to clear it.

"Did they get out?" Brey's head whips around as he asks. His eyes reveal the pain and panic that he must have been subjecting both himself and Varick to.

"It's been almost two hours," Varick answers from the ground. His mouth presses into a thin line and he raises a single eyebrow to tell me he knows why I really asked.

"They got out," I say to Brey. My throat still aches, so I rub it while coughing.

"Thank God," Brey sighs as he collapses into a chair.

"What's that noise?" It's starting to give me a headache. I don't know how long they've been dealing with it. Varick stands and clenches his fists to keep them from shaking; that was the wrong question to ask.

I knew Varick would be upset that I was seen by JC and Nick, but I had also decided it was worth it.

Brey lifts his head and gives me a sad but meaningful nod, apparently leaving the answer to Varick.

"I'm assuming," Varick says, voice laced with so much fury that even Brey flinches from it, "that they sounded the alarm upon seeing you."

He holds my gaze, daring me to challenge his assumption. We stare at each other as the silence builds around us and Brey coughs uncomfortably.

"How could you," Varick demands, finally speaking. I grit my teeth and lower my eyes to avoid him. No amount of explanation will appease him right now.

"I didn't have a choice," I finally mumble. I can't look at Varick, so I shift my eyes to Brey.

Varick doesn't wait for me to elaborate. He walks to a nearby desk and picks it up before throwing it at the wall with a grunt. The resulting crash hurts my ears worse than the obnoxious alarm and I flinch away from him.

"You have no idea what you've done," he yells, his chest visibly moving with his gulps of air. "Stealth was basing his entire theory about you having multiple abilities on a loose reading from someone he can't even stand. We could have convinced him Tanner was wrong. He's irate right now, Mercer! I can feel him from here."

I set my jaw, realizing that Varick and I will never agree about this.

"I'm going to protect my family, no matter the cost." My voice is hoarse, but it doesn't stop me from explaining the conclusion I had reached during my projection.

Sadness flashes in his eyes, letting the anger drop for a moment. He grits his teeth and moves back and forth across the room.

"It's not that she doesn't trust you," Brey voices softly in answer to something he must have picked up that I missed. "Nothing would have been more important to her than saving them."

I give Brey a weak smile of gratitude. When I rise from my place on the table, the muscles in my legs seize up. It's fascinating; my body is responding as if it physically went through everything I experienced in my projection, despite being stationary here. I start inching for the door, testing the pain as I walk.

"What are you doing?" Varick demands when it becomes clear that I plan to leave.

"What do you mean?" I ask dumbfounded. "I can't stay in here just because they know."

"Sure you can." Varick grabs my arm and pulls me around so that he's standing in front of the only exit.

A yelp escapes me and I look to Brey for support. He must feel my shock because he takes a step toward us while shaking his head.

"She can't stay here forever," Breyson says with an edge to his tone.

Varick stares at him with one arm still holding me in place.

"I think your input has helped enough for one day," Varick

snaps.

"Or maybe you need to believe in her the way I do, instead of doubting her every decision," Brey barks back.

Varick's hand is still around my arm as they watch each other. Varick stares at Brey, almost willing him to keep going. When it's clear that Brey isn't going to push further, Varick takes a deep breath and pinches the bridge of his nose. The movement makes him look like Stealth.

"What do you want to do, Merc?" Brey asks as soon as Varick breaks, emphasizing that he trusts my decisions. Varick visibly tenses, waiting for my answer.

"I'm going talk to Stealth," I say with as much conviction as I can muster. Varick must feel my resolution and know that he can't talk me out of it. Either that or he understands what Brey and I are saying. We don't have any other options. Besides, what's the worst that can happen? Lizzy is safe.

"This is a bad idea," Varick answers, finally moving aside to let me out. "Let's go." Before I can even take a step, Brey shifts, as well.

"I'm coming too," Brey says. But something in my gut churns at that idea.

"You shouldn't." I try to sound as convincing as I can and his shoulders drop at my denial. "Stealth won't hurt Varick, but he might use you. It's safer if you act like you weren't part of this."

"She's right," Varick contributes. "He's not going to kill her now that he knows she's the only Unnatural with multiple abilities. And he won't kill me no matter how badly he may want to."

Nobody has to mention how Stealth wouldn't hesitate to kill Brey just to prove a point.

Once out of the room, I try to swallow the nausea down as my hands shake by my sides. I'm surprised that Varick, who walks next to me without so much as a glance to acknowledge that I'm falling apart, doesn't change his mind and race us back to that storage closet.

Instead, I try to focus on the small ray of happiness inside me. Lizzy and Mrs. Jones are fine. I never considered myself a martyr, but Stealth can do whatever he wants to me, and it doesn't change the fact that they're alive. I walk close to Varick, letting the smell of moss and wood become stronger than the disinfectant in the hall.

The blaring sound of the alarm is louder in the public areas. It seems like such an overreaction to the fact that one of us goes missing, but I guess that's Stealth for you.

I approach Stealth's door and only hesitate for a moment before knocking. I don't have any other options and Varick's hand keeps twitching, like he's fighting against his own instincts to grab me and run.

Stealth can't cover the surprise in his reaction as he opens the door. For a man who usually plans ten moves ahead, he couldn't see this one coming. I hadn't realized what my sudden appearance would mean to him. After all, I was just spotted miles from here.

"Ms. Lewis," he says coolly, "come in."

He holds the door open for me, but as soon I pass, he steps in the way to prevent Varick from following.

"You can wait out here, son," he says.

I turn around to give Varick a nod, but he doesn't look at me. His hardened gaze simply stares at his father with an intensity that scares me.

"No," Varick responds. They glare at each other without

words until finally, Stealth moves to the side and allows Varick to come in. I have no idea what kind of sway Varick might have to get his father to listen, but now is not the time to ask.

"Sit," Stealth directs me, not even bothering with the friendly façade that he's used in several of our meetings. At his desk, he reaches over and taps a button, finally ending the incessant alarm.

Then he picks up a phone. "She's here," he says in a crisp tone. He hangs up before whoever is on the other end can respond. I stare into his eyes. He stares back, his aftershave threatening to make me sick. Finally, after far too long, he breaks the silence. "You're very special, Ms. Lewis."

Varick shifts in his seat next to me. Of all the things I considered Stealth would say, that was not it.

"I feel that somewhere along the way, you began to think of me as the bad guy. I'm afraid that my son's recent feelings about my leadership only made things worse. But perhaps it's best that you're both here so we can clear the air." Stealth leans back in his chair and it squeaks at the movement.

I turn to Varick to see his reaction, but his eyes are narrowed at Stealth in a very obvious way. He doesn't trust this. Neither do I, but nobody knows the future I saw that made me so wary of Stealth and the Domain in the first place.

"I would like to help you, Ms. Lewis. We can teach you how to use each of your abilities on command. We can help you learn what it means to have more than one. I'm not sure why you got the idea that I'm against you, but I think it's time we put that behind us and move forward together." His voice is slick and if I hadn't had that dream of my graduation, I could see how easy it'd be to believe him.

But I did have that dream.

Because of that dream, I can't ever work with Stealth. I can't ever let him help me because I know what he's truly capable of, and even worse, I know what he can turn me into, and that's something that's haunted me for months.

He watches me closely, reading my face and dying for answers.

If only I were able to recognize then what I know now as I watch Stealth succumb to his irritation. Stealth is afraid of me. I, myself, am the unknown. He can't control me; he can't kill me, and he can't seem to find a way to get me to cooperate.

Stealth must see the shift in me, my newfound realization. Varick must sense it too, but his words aren't directed to me.

"I'm not going to let you force her into anything," Varick says through his teeth. I don't know what he's feeling from Stealth, but the edge to his tone sends a shiver down my spine. I wipe my clammy hands on my gray pants.

Stealth, on the other hand, isn't scared of Varick. Instead, a slow smile creeps up his face.

"Son," he says darkly, "you, out of anyone, should know that's not quite what I would resort to. Anything she does will be because she chooses to." The comment makes me relax, as I take a breath and loosen my shoulders, but Varick seems to have the opposite reaction.

He clenches his jaw and leans forward in his chair like he's about to jump up and strangle his father.

"Find Brey, now," Varick whispers to me, but it's loud enough that Stealth hears him.

My body doesn't react to what he's saying. I know Varick is in a better position to understand what's going on, but my mind feels like it's ten steps behind and I don't understand.

Stealth simply reaches down to his desk and presses a button before I can even stand.

In response to Stealth's call, the door creaks open and six guards walk into the office. The space is big enough to accommodate all the bodies, but the tension seems to fill the gaps in an uncomfortable and suffocating way. They seemed to have brought the smell of cigarette smoke with them, which is nauseating and not helping my panic. So, instead I focus on my heartbeat, which I'm sure the entire room can hear.

Varick's eyes dart between our joiners and his father as we all stand at the same time. Varick takes several steps to push me back into a wall, shielding me from everyone else in the room. His fists shake at his sides and his shoulders tense, ready to fight.

Stealth surprises me again by laughing at Varick instead of feeling threatened by his obvious declaration.

"Is it done?" Stealth asks a guard, who gives a single nod in return. "Ms. Lewis, I'd like you to come with me," Stealth says. He strolls past Varick with a casual arrogance that makes me want to punch his face. "Son, you can either stay here or return downstairs. The choice is yours."

"No," Varick says, and I can hear the determination behind it, but I don't think his insistence is enough this time.

Just as I thought, Stealth motions to the guards and they surround Varick, preventing him from following. Stealth said he would never make me do anything, so Varick's response is an overreaction. I try to give him a reassuring smile, but either he doesn't notice or it doesn't change his anger.

Stealth guides me to an elevator and steps in. The space is tight, much different than his office, and the aftershave is suffocating. Thankfully, Stealth's long fingers press the button for only one floor beneath us, making the ride short.

I release a sigh of relief when the doors open.

Stealth ignores me as he walks us through the hallway. There aren't any other doors here, apart from the one at the end of the hall. Interesting. None of the other floors look quite like this. Stealth reaches into the pocket of his designer suit and pulls out a single, long key. This door has a lock instead of a keypad.

Whatever it is Stealth wants to show me or do to me, my survival instincts are screaming at me to run. I have to keep reminding myself that Lizzy is safe. Stealth can do what he wants to me, but Lizzy will still be safe.

The new hallway is dark when we enter, but lights turn on as Stealth's shoes walk across the tiled floor. Windows line the walls, but they must show something other than the outside world since we're underground. Moments later I realize that the windows only separate the hall from several smaller rooms beyond them. Each space has a single cot and toilet.

They're jail cells. Stealth has a prison in the Domain.

My eyebrows furrow and I'm frustrated that I don't understand what's going on.

Stealth stops at one of the windows in the middle of the hall. My eyes take too long to understand what I'm looking at as I stare at the man in the cell. He's put on weight since I've last seen him, like my presence was the reason he was always malnourished.

Despite being in this place, seemingly as a prisoner, Uncle Al looks healthier than I've ever seen him. His face is puffy and it's clear he's been crying. Is it because of Aunt Pam's death? Or because of his unfortunate circumstances?

The nausea that was building makes me cross my arms over my chest to try and keep it inside. The sight of Uncle Al brings back the fury that I've always felt around him. Being free from him all these months just emphasizes how much I hate him.

Stealth pushes a single button that I hadn't noticed on the side of the glass. The color of the divider in front of us shifts, and it must have prevented Uncle Al from seeing us before, but now that's changed.

My guardian's eyes, wide with terror, find mine. Perhaps he thinks I'm behind this kidnapping because his lips turn to a small snarl.

I suppose I'm expected to be happy to see my guardian, or perhaps scared of what Stealth plans on doing with him. I don't feel either of those things.

"Bring her in," Stealth says calmly.

I set my jaw and continue to stare at my uncle. I hope that my gaze says everything I was never able to for fear that Uncle Al would turn me in. I hope he can read my anger and hatred.

The door on the other side of the cell opens and Trinka walks in. Her face is even puffier than it was in our dorm just a few hours ago and there's a ring of bruises around her throat. She gives me a pained expression.

Guilt rips through me at our last interaction. I almost killed her, but then the sorrow from what she did threatens to replace it, tearing at my chest. She deserves to die. Aunt Pam deserved better. I swallow, hoping the feelings get pushed down in the movement.

"I'm sorry," Trinka says through the glass while her chin quivers.

"Go on," Stealth answers, ignoring Trinka completely.

Trinka walks up to Uncle Al, who seems to have recognized his visitor. He starts to back away, aware of what Trinka can do. I wonder if he even tried to protect Aunt Pam from Trinka, or if he simply hid.

Trinka reaches out a hand, her eyebrows pulled together and a frown on her face, but Uncle Al continues to retreat. She clearly doesn't want to be participating in Stealth's game like this, her footsteps short and uncertain. She follows Uncle Al into the corner before finally reaching him, placing a hand on his arm.

The responding screams are shattering as Uncle Al crumples into a heap in front of her. His face contorts in agony and his limbs start to flail in strange directions. I've never seen what Trinka can do in person, but I understand why that first day in Agility Skills had traumatized her so badly.

"Stop," Stealth says into the room. He'd been watching me the entire time, and my face must have looked void of emotion as I witnessed my guardian being tortured at the hands of someone who was once my friend. He watches me closely, waiting for me to break, to beg him to stop.

I let out a small huff, then look back to Uncle Al, whose eyes plead with me to end this. I grind my teeth and remember his words all those years ago.

"By all means," I finally say in a dead voice, waving my hand toward Uncle Al to let them know they should carry on.

Stealth doesn't try to hide the shock on his face and rubs his hand over his freshly shaven chin.

"You must be more heartless than I gave you credit for," Stealth sneers at me. "You don't care to save your family?"

I release a humorless laugh. "He's not my family."

Stealth looks between my uncle and myself. Uncle Al just continues to stare at me. He opens his mouth but then closes it again. Trinka, waiting for an order, simply stands above him.

"I'm sorry," Uncle Al mumbles, his voice revealing how weak he is after just those few seconds with Trinka. "Mercer…"

Stealth looks to me, questioning if Uncle Al's pleas will garnish loyalty. I simply meet Stealth's black eyes. This is stupid. I'm never going to help Stealth to save a man I hate.

"Mercer, please," Uncle Al continues to beg. "I'm so sorry for what I did. We couldn't afford—we had no other—"

Stealth watches me closely. I don't know what he can see, but I feel empty of any emotion at all.

"What are you sorry for?" Stealth finally asks, trying to understand why this isn't having the impact he wanted. If I've learned anything about Stealth, it's that he hates not knowing something.

Uncle Al opens his mouth, but no words come out, likely choked by his own shame.

"He tried to sell us when we were kids," I say in a flat voice. I know Stealth will understand what I mean. After the population crisis, illegal adoption rings became incredibly popular. They're more profitable now than they were before the Censorship because of the hope that the child might have a freakish ability. "He was going to separate us and give us to the highest bidder right after we lost our parents. Do whatever you want to him."

Nobody knows about that aside from Brey. I kept it to myself, out of fear that Uncle Al would tell everyone about my abilities. It was a dream that warned me of his plans in the first place—up until recently, that had been the worst dream of my life. Stopping him meant admitting I was an Unnatural, admitting how I knew.

I don't want pity, but Stealth isn't one to offer it anyway. His jaw tenses and he slowly nods his head.

"Very well," he mumbles, more to himself than to me. "This way."

I have no choice but to follow him farther down the hall, deeper into this prison. The lights don't turn on in the cells we walk past, keeping the contents a mystery. It isn't until we reach the very end that he turns to a window and pushes the button that changes the color of the glass. I look inside, curiosity burning through me at whatever Stealth seems to think will force me into cooperation.

As soon as I do, I wish I could take back everything.

I can feel the blood drain from my face. A gasp leaves me, and I take several quick breaths to try and get air into my lungs. It occurs to me that I'm hyperventilating but I can't stop. I hunch over to try and fix the suffocation.

Stealth waits for me to stand back up before instructing

Trinka to come into the room.

She has the decency to look apologetic.

"I'm sorry. He has my mom," she says through a whimper. I don't know if she's speaking to me or him.

I don't bother giving her a response. Instead, I watch as realization sinks in. He knows what Trinka is going to do.

"I'll be fine," Brey says to me silently. *"This isn't your fault."*

But he's wrong. It is.

Chapter Twenty-Three

I force myself to watch once the screaming starts, out of respect for him. I haven't heard him make noises like this in as long as I've known him. I open my mouth to tell Stealth I'll do anything, but he speaks before I can.

"Enough," Stealth dictates calmly.

Trinka stops and I want to kill her, almost as much as I want to kill Stealth. The burning desire to end their lives courses through me and I focus on the obsession, knowing it's easier than letting myself think about Brey, who's still curled up in a ball on the floor.

"Well?" Stealth asks. It's already clear that the exercise had the desired impact on me.

I'm not sure why Stealth brought me to Uncle Al first. Perhaps he thought it would hurt me more. He would have no way of understanding that Brey has always been my real family.

It's too late when I finally realize that Stealth is waiting for me. My heart is shattered into so many pieces that it feels like I'm not even capable of speaking.

"Continue," Stealth says to Trinka, and I whip my head around in response. I thought it was obvious that Stealth won, that I would do anything to make it stop.

The screams don't come. At first, I feel relief at the absence of the sound, then I realize it must be because Brey has passed out from the pain.

"Stop!" I say through a tingling that has taken over my entire body. Trinka freezes immediately and I know my compulsion is responsible, although I hadn't necessarily been trying to use it when I spoke. It's almost as if the floodgates opened and all my emotion was poured into that single word.

"Ms. Lewis," Stealth gets my attention and I tear my eyes away from Breyson, "it's my understanding that you cannot hold your ability for long. Would you like us to wait it out, or do you want to discuss my offer?"

"I—what?" I sputter, unable to comprehend what's really happening.

His returning smile is nothing but sinister and I want to crawl into a hole and hide from him.

"I own you, Ms. Lewis," he says simply. He stands tall with his hands folded in front of his body. There isn't an ounce of worry in him. He knew that we would reach this point and he was ready for it. I'd even be willing to bet that if I said 'no' to this offer, he'd reveal another step in his plan. "Whether you agree or disagree is irrelevant. The fact remains: I can either make you cooperate by slowly picking off the people you care about, or we can put this entire day behind us and move forward, united." He seems to hesitate for a moment, shifting his weight from one foot to the other, before continuing, "I want you to work with me instead of against me. Understand that I'm not the bad guy. I have done nothing but help you in a world that was out to get you."

I look at Brey on the floor and Stealth must see my incredulous expression.

He tightens his jaw and gives a sad smile. "I was hoping you would hear me before I would have to take these steps. I can make a promise to you here and now, however, that if you give me your loyalty and start working with me, Mr. Jones will be safe."

"And if I don't?" It's hard to speak through the pain in my chest. We both already know the answer.

He swallows, waiting a beat.

"Ms. Lewis, I don't take lives because I want to. I do not enjoy that part of my job. However, I will protect what I've built here."

His indirect response doesn't need translating. Brey's life is on the line if I don't cooperate with whatever Stealth wants.

"What does loyalty look like?" My voice sounds broken.

"That's a great question," he replies, suddenly more cheerful than the past several minutes. "I think this exercise is enough for today. We will circle back to how we can both benefit from a friendship with each other." His eyes bore into mine, willing me to both believe him and accept this.

I look to Brey and think about demanding that he be let go, but Stealth seems to want me to ask that. Perhaps Brey is safer if he's locked away instead of roaming around with me.

"Fine," I say.

Tears stream down my face but I don't bother to wipe them. My throat is thick with sadness, and I know it's not just for Brey, but also for Aunt Pam, Lizzy and having to see Uncle Al. There are so many emotions I've been forcing down for these last few hours.

I follow Stealth down back down the prison hallway. I don't analyze his steps. I don't wonder who else is contained in these cells. And I'm no longer thinking about how to escape the Domain. I feel nothing.

Stealth doesn't force me back into the elevator. He doesn't even give me departing words. Instead, he locks the door behind him and walks to the stairwell.

Alone in the hallway, I let out the air that's suffocating me. I turn to the locked door that holds Brey inside and shake the silver handle. It doesn't budge even a small amount. If I had JC's power, I would rip the door off the hinges and get Brey out of there.

Brey's voice doesn't come to me and the realization of what that means has me sinking to my knees. I hold the doorknob to my forehead, knees on the floor, crying for the door to somehow open.

I was hoping that leaving Stealth's presence would make it easier to breathe, but the air is just as tight as it was around him. It isn't his presence, but his control, that suffocates me. And unfortunately, it doesn't appear like that's going to improve anytime soon.

I never heard the stairwell door open again after Stealth's departure, but strong hands lift me from the floor, signifying someone's appearance.

"Come on," Varick says in my ear.

"Brey?" I croak. He knows what I'm asking.

"Stealth called Ms. Williams up. She should be on her way to see him." His posture is rigid, and I can see he's fighting something inside himself.

"He said—he said he owns me," I say through sobs that are shaking my entire body. Perhaps I shouldn't be admitting what Stealth just told me. What if it makes Stealth angry and he retaliates by using Brey? But he never said it was a secret and I feel like if I keep it to myself, I might explode.

"Let's go find the others," Varick says as he helps me stand. He keeps one hand on my elbow and another on my back as he guides me to the stairs. The warmth helps calm the shakiness that's taken over my body.

"What did I do, Varick?" It's a rhetorical question. I know exactly what I did. I pushed and fought Stealth because I never considered that he could actually break me. I was so very wrong.

"This isn't your fault, Mercer." Varick guides me down the cold stairwell. But he's wrong. We both know he's wrong. He warned me against provoking Stealth, and I didn't listen. I thought I could pay the price of whatever Stealth's anger would mean, but I can't, because Stealth isn't asking me to pay the price, he's demanding it from Brey.

When we don't exit the stairwell for the Eye, I give Varick a questioning look.

"I think it's time to admit that we need help," he says with a quick glance at my face, and I have to imagine that I look like a mess. "Stay here."

He leaves me in the stairwell for less than a minute while he enters the Eye and rounds up our friends. I'm not sure where he's been since getting kicked out of Stealth's office, but by the way everyone is looking puzzled, he wasn't filling them in.

Whatever my face is showing, it must be signaling the others of the seriousness of the situation, because even Valor looks worried.

"What's going on," Cynthia asks as soon as the Pitch door closes behind us. It's completely empty, giving us the privacy that Varick was looking for. "Are you okay?" Her last question is directed at me.

"Stealth took Brey," I choke out. I know as I say it that the statement is completely without context for my friends, but I've been slowly unravelling since the second I met Brey's eyes in that room upstairs.

"Why would he—" Jaylee starts to ask but I interrupt her.

"The rumors about me are true." I need to start from the beginning, but my statement is just as random, so their confusion doesn't dissipate. "I have multiple abilities. That's what started all this."

Everyone watches me closely. I look at the punching bags, wishing we could reverse time and go back to when things were easier. My throat feels thick as each devastating emotion tries to take priority.

Varick must sense my struggle because he continues for me, "Tanner's reading of Mercer was just the start. Stealth has been furious. Actually, it probably started when she used two abilities against JC."

"How would you even know that?" Cynthia questions him.

Valor and Varick give each other a meaningful look and I know that they're debating how truthful to be in this moment. I'm not sure how they communicate so seamlessly, but apparently they reach the same conclusion, because Valor turns to the girls and says, "Stealth is our father."

Silence follows and the tension in the room is almost too much.

Cynthia glares at the brothers; her eyes are cold and locked on them. Jaylee takes the smallest of steps to put herself between Valor and Lottie, a movement that Valor notices and sighs at.

"Look," Valor says with his hands extended toward her, "I can understand your anger, but think about your anger compared to ours. At least you're not related to him. We got the short end here."

Cynthia's body is nearly vibrating as she shakes her head. Whatever is going through her mind, it's clearly not forgiveness, although after another look at my tear-stained face, she seems to understand that now is not the time and says, "Just keep going."

"He messed up by using Trinka," Varick continues for me, and even though Cynthia was talking to me, she turns to Varick and lets him speak.

"Trinka?" Jaylee's disdain for my old friend is clear in her voice.

"Trinka killed my aunt," I say in a dead voice. I realize that my statement isn't contributing to the conversation, but it feels like I'm on autopilot, and that pronouncement felt important. For Aunt Pam.

Nobody says anything to me, evidently still too confused to even offer condolences.

"Trinka was sent on her graduation to apprehend my aunt and uncle," I continue with a bit more sureness in my voice. "Stealth was going to use them to force me to cooperate. And if that didn't work, he was also sending JC to get my sister."

"But you said your aunt was killed." Cynthia raises an eyebrow and I finally start to feel frustrated at how long this is taking us. It's too much information. Catching them up is wasting precious minutes that we could instead spend trying to break Breyson out.

Varick must feel my frustration because he gives me a quick nod and speaks in a rush, "Trinka was sent to get them, got scared, killed Mercer's aunt, and brought her uncle back here. It's hard to know for certain what Stealth's plan was or is."

His voice trails off as his eyes become distant. He doesn't understand his father's motivations and that bothers him more than anything else, because not understanding means Stealth is more difficult to predict.

Valor, Jaylee and Lottie all react to that information visibly. They grew up with Lizzy, after all.

"She's safe," I tell them. "She's on the run with Brey's mom." But the mention of Brey has my insides turning so suddenly that I have to sit on the floor to keep the dizziness at bay. I'm sure they're giving me strange and concerning looks, but

I don't care in this moment. "He took Brey," I say again.

Varick jumps in, sensing that I'm falling apart. "Since her first day here—no, since the day we were taken to come here, Mercer has been a problem for Stealth because he doesn't know how to control her. He realized she was a liability and tried to eliminate her instead." Nobody even flinches at the casual way in which Varick talks about how I was almost murdered. "He sent several people to graduate by killing you," he says while looking at me. "I refused; JC failed; Cynthia refused."

My eyes open wide as I replay what he just said. Cynthia returns my look of shock, only hers is at the fact that Varick knows such things.

"Mercer, I—" Cynthia starts to either explain or defend herself.

"It's fine," I say through a half-hearted smile at her. And I mean it. I don't have the capacity to be upset about it.

She gives me a look of utter appreciation and a sad smile.

Varick must obviously feel both of our emotions, but chooses to ignore them as he continues, "When you stopped JC the second time, that's when Stealth called off the attempts to take your life because it was the first time he suspected you might have more than one ability. You went from being a problem that needed to be handled to an asset that needed to be figured out."

"But why Brey?" Jaylee's emotion makes her words come out choked.

I don't blame her for the reaction, as I also share the same feelings.

Varick doesn't hesitate to continue being the voice of reason as he says, "Stealth doesn't want to kill Mercer anymore. He tried to coerce her to trust him and she basically laughed in his face. That leaves one option. He'll force her hand."

"I own you, Ms. Lewis," his words are in my head just as clearly as if he said them to my face. I shiver involuntarily and Varick gives me a knowing look.

"What does holding onto Brey force?" Jaylee pushes, and I also look to Varick because I want to know the answer.

Unfortunately, I'm not prepared for his words when he says, "Whatever Stealth wants."

Chapter Twenty-Four

The room falls silent while several eyes find me.

"He told me he owns me." My jaw barely moves as I speak. "He has dozens, if not hundreds, of Unnaturals at his disposal. He doesn't need me." My voice sounds whiny, and I know that I'm trying to convince them in the hopes that it'll somehow change my fate.

"Unless we can find a solution for Brey, I'm afraid he's right." Varick's words are harsh and he doesn't bother to mention the fact that while Stealth has all the Unnaturals he could need, none of them are like me. None of them have multiple abilities.

"Any chance of us breaking him out?" Cynthia asks Varick, but I already know the answer. That place was impenetrable by anybody but the top leadership of the Domain.

"I can probably get him out of the cell, but unless we find a way to get out of the Domain, it won't matter." Varick responds, surprising me. Perhaps the key Stealth had is not the only copy.

Cynthia's stance widens as she addresses Varick. "What's his goal here? What is he going to make her do?"

Valor and Varick exchange a look that I can't interpret.

"He wants her to do whatever he asks. But to get there, he'll likely test her," Valor answers.

"Test her how?" Cynthia's voice gets harsher with each passing second.

"Some way that proves his control," Valor says. "Something she won't want to do but will have to."

Cynthia answers him but her words are drowned out.

"What did you just say?" My voice is a whisper, but I don't actually need Valor to repeat his question. I heard him and it replays in my mind over and over. What was it that JC said to me in my dream?

"How stupid are you to think it'd be your death. We both know that's not who he'll kill."

Brey.

That's who he'll kill.

"Graduation," I whisper. But a whisper in this large space can be heard when confusion silences everything else.

Stealth is going to make me graduate. He's going to send me to that mother and her son. I'm going to have to kill them. And despite my determination to say no, I realize Stealth has already won. Because if I don't, he's going to kill Brey. I can't change what I saw. I can't prevent that woman's death. Not if I want Brey to live.

"What happened?" Varick grabs my shoulders and he shakes me, bringing me back to the Pitch and this moment.

"He's going to make me graduate." I look into Varick's eyes, without an ounce of awareness for the others. "I saw it. I saw what he'll make me do. I can't—I can't do that—I—"

Tears choke me and it's impossible to continue my explanation. I don't even know how I could explain what happened in that dream. I've kept it a secret for so long, too ashamed to reiterate the details.

Varick closes his eyes as he keeps his hands on my shoulders and a sense of calm makes its way down my body. I know it's his doing. I can't help but embrace it for a moment as the panic subsides.

Tell us," he says close to my ear. "We can't help you if we don't know."

I clutch my stomach and my words come out quietly as I say, "He's going to send me on my graduation with JC. JC is going to kill someone." My voice sounds dead even with Varick's help. I don't mention the part of the boy, or that I'll be the one to kill him. I can't.

This isn't what Varick expected. Even worse, I can tell that he doesn't know what to do. "Varick…" Cynthia starts to ask, but she doesn't finish whatever question she started, because Varick cuts her off.

"We need to get Brey out before Stealth sends Mercer on her graduation," he tells the group. None of them bother to ask about how I know of my graduation. They must be confused or curious, but they're taking my word for it.

"Ms. Williams will help if we ask her," Jaylee says to us quietly.

"I think Mr. Regis might, too," I add, unsure if I'm actually right but also feeling desperate enough to risk it.

"Varick," Valor warns. Whatever direction he senses his brother's thoughts taking, he's not a fan.

"What other option do we have?" Varick asks his brother, knowing that Valor is ahead of us.

"What? What are you thinking?" My desperation is overflowing at this point. I just need something to hold onto.

"I think we have to stand up to Stealth." Varick's voice is determined and serious as he looks at Valor again. My brain spins while trying to comprehend his words. He watches me closely as he continues, "I've been thinking about it, regardless of the situation with Brey. It was clear you weren't safe and Stealth needs to be stopped. He may be able to dispose of an Unnatural here and there, but he can't get rid of a whole group of us, at least not while maintaining control."

"You want us to stand up to him? Like fight him? Stealth? His guards?" Cynthia sounds surprised but not altogether against the idea and I take note of her hands, vibrating even harder.

"It might not become a fight." Varick turns to address the rest of our friends. "Hopefully it won't. We just need to show enough strength in numbers to make him hesitate. And we have some guards; several of them are on our side. So are many of the teachers and most of the students."

My stomach starts turning as I think about every option in front of us. Either Brey dies, that woman and her son die, or we pray that they listen to us. How is this our reality?

Varick spends another hour telling our friends what everyone should be doing to prepare. We need to get people on our side, and quick.

We don't have a timeline apart from sometime before my graduation. And since we don't know when that will be, we're just loosely trying to make things happen sooner rather than later.

The more I hear, the more I can't help but wonder if this is a foolish plan. Won't more lives be lost if they don't listen to us?

Although those lives won't be lost in vain. Stealth does need to be stopped. How many women and children will he continue to target because he can?

By the time we finally part, it's nearly morning and the Eye is empty. We're all exhausted and I feel unsure about the plan. But at this point, it's all we have to save Brey unless I'm okay with the dream of my graduation coming true.

Throughout the night and thanks to my fatigue, I'm all but convinced Stealth's threat was a lie and that Brey is going to join us at any second, assuring me that none of it happened.

But I'm wrong. In fact, his absence is so loud that I find myself fighting back tears.

Before I can even make it to the dining hall for breakfast, a guard intercepts me as I walk with the girls. I have no choice but to follow him.

I tug on my shirt during the elevator ride. My stomach feels like it's inside out as I think about what's coming.

The guard escorts me the entire way to Stealth's office.

"Ms. Lewis," Stealth greets me at the door. I can't help but lean away from him, though it does nothing to give me space from the toxic smell of aftershave. I follow him in, too afraid for Brey's sake to do anything else. Stealth dismisses the guard and motions for me to sit. My stomach roils and it feels like a weight is sitting on my chest.

"I'm so pleased with how we ended things yesterday," Stealth says through a forced smile. Despite his relaxed posture, his hands twitch like he can't decide what he wants to be doing.

"Right," I say, hardly able to put any emotion into the word.

"And I've decided how to test this new relationship between us… to see where your loyalties lie." He grins at me. "I'm going to send you on a graduation."

It takes me a second to remember that I should be surprised and that this is the first he thinks I'm hearing of this. He notices my reaction.

"Graduation," he continues, "as you may know, will allow you to eliminate a threat to society and prove your loyalty in one mission." He folds his hands on the desk and stares into my soul. "I believe that you have incentive enough knowing that Mr. Jones is here with me, but just for your own peace of mind, the target is a threat, Ms. Lewis,"

I can picture the woman, her brown hair in a mess because she had been fast asleep.

"Why?" My voice shakes.

He continues to study me without answering. But when I don't say anything more, making it clear that I won't continue this conversation without a response, he puffs his chest out and says, "She wants to dismantle what I've built and end the Domain."

I don't know how I maintain a straight face at this information, but my insides feel like they're twisting into knots that will never be undone. The woman whose death I've dreaded for months is being killed because she wants to do the very thing that I've been praying for since waking up here.

"Unnaturals would have nowhere to go," Stealth continues. "When people have been caged their entire lives, they don't know how to be free. I'm afraid you and your peers don't know how to live without direction."

The hole in my chest threatens to get so big that it'll consume me, him, and everything in this office. I push my fist into my stomach to relieve the pressure. He stands and comes around the other side of his desk, sitting on the edge in front of me.

"If this woman successfully tears down the Domain, Unnaturals won't know any better than to look for another leader. Who do you think they'd choose? Because I would imagine they would choose the person who set them free. And her leadership will be much worse than anything you've lived through with me."

His words cause me to shiver. I don't want to believe him. I know that he's reading my reactions, but I can't hide my fear as I watch him in return. Could what he's saying be true? If we were all free to leave, would we be lost?

If we get rid of Stealth, will another person simply take his place? How can we ever truly be free if that's the cycle we're stuck in? My lower jaw quivers, but I don't want to cry.

"You will go early tomorrow," he finishes and waves to the door, his trademark dismissal.

My feet drag along the corridor while I reconsider Stealth's words.

I take the stairs to the Eye, but my friends are nowhere to be found. Come to think of it, the Eye is empty.

Which makes sense given the hour. I've been too caught up in my own problems to realize everyone is in class.

I trudge down to the Pitch for my morning session, all the while trying to convince myself that I can survive what's coming.

JC and Nick both look my way upon my entrance. JC isn't as furious as I would've expected, although maybe he knows that he's likely going to get another chance at graduation tomorrow.

Third time's the charm. It makes sense now.

"Thank goodness," Cynthia reaches me. Jaylee, Lottie and Valor are in their morning classes, and Brey is still in Stealth's prison.

"Where's Varick?" I look around the space behind her but he's nowhere to be seen.

"I thought he'd be with you. He ran out of here and said something about needing to get Valor." Cynthia has a pained expression.

I have no idea where Varick went but he doesn't return for the remainder of class. Cynthia and I try to look like we're busy, but after I let her know that my graduation is tomorrow morning, neither of us can focus.

We meet Jaylee and Lottie for lunch, but Varick and Valor are still missing. None of us have much of an appetite, which is hardly surprising given our current situation. I didn't think anything else could possibly add to our problems, but Varick misses afternoon classes and I find myself realizing I was wrong.

When we meet in the evening, the worry seems even heavier.

"Valor didn't come to Agility Skills," Jaylee reports through a clenched jaw.

"Varick missed ethics and history." My voice sounds equally defeated.

"Do you think their dad took them?" Lottie whispers from next to Jaylee.

It's what I've worried about all day. It's too coincidental. If they're gone…

I take a ragged breath in, refusing to think about what I'm going to do if they aren't here.

"Let's say Stealth did take them…" Jaylee begins, looking between Cynthia and me. "What exactly would we do to help?"

Nothing. We can't do anything, especially when Stealth still has Brey.

"Is there anywhere we haven't thought of looking?" Cynthia puts a hand on my elbow to urge me to think. I'm about to shake my head when I realize there is.

"Maybe," I say slowly.

The air is chilled as we climb the stairs to the level of the storage closet. Each step I take feels like one more inch closer to admitting defeat.

Outside the door, I try to listen for voices on the other side, but the door is too thick and it's impossible. Instead, I bang my fists on the metal, perhaps a bit too hard, but my anxiety is fueling my actions.

It feels like an eternity that we wait. My stomach is in knots and we still have so much to resolve before tomorrow morning. We're about to turn away when the door finally opens a crack.

Familiar brown eyes meet mine and my heart feels like it's relaxing from being tightly wound all day.

“Where have you been?” I demand without bothering to keep my voice down. My emotions are too powerful and they’re pouring into my actions.

Varick looks behind me to see the girls and his jaw clenches.

“Just come in here,” he says quietly. His voice is laced with something I’ve never heard from him before. “Before anybody sees you.”

I glance at the others as we follow him into the small room.

Valor is the only other occupant. He sits on the desk with his back against the wall and his feet planted on the middle of the surface. His face is red and puffy and he’s wringing his hands.

“What happened?” Jaylee sounds stunned after one look at Valor.

“I’m sorry that we just left,” Varick says, ignoring her. His face doesn’t show any sign of tears, but his shoulders are tense and he looks like he hasn’t slept for days even though I just saw him last night.

“What happened?” I repeat Jaylee’s question.

“It’s nothing to do with you,” Valor’s quick to say.

“Then one of you tell us what it does have to do with!” Cynthia’s patience snaps and I don’t blame her after the day we’ve had.

“It’s our mother,” Varick continues. “Valor can tell that she’s in danger. It’s bad. We came in here to watch it.”

“How—” Lottie starts to ask, but then she closes her mouth before finishing the question. She’s always the quiet one and her eyes widen like she can’t believe she was going to insert herself.

“Valor’s ability,” Varick answers even though she didn’t get the full question out. “He’s always watching the people close to him to make sure they’re safe.” Varick’s voice is pinched at the end and he swallows to gain control.

“Not to brush past what you’re both dealing with,” Cynthia says, trying to sound empathetic and failing, “because I’m sorry about your mom, but what can you do from here? Shouldn’t you be spending your time helping Mercer and Brey?”

The boys look at each other and a flash of guilt shows on each of their faces.

“Yes,” Varick answer Cynthia. “We should. But we figured we had more time. Whatever is happening to our mother is happening now.”

“My graduation is tomorrow,” I say through the building anxiety within me. My mouth is dry but nothing I do helps.

He stares at me as if he’s waiting for me to admit that I’m just joking. The longer I go without saying anything, the more his posture changes, as if he’s letting the realization slowly creep in.

“Mercer,” he says with a step in my direction, “I’m so sorry. I didn’t know. I wouldn’t have—I would’ve—”

“It’s fine.” I mean it as I say it, even though it feels like I’m still about to choke on my fear.

I can’t blame them for wanting to know if their mom is safe. Not when I would do anything to have my own mother back with me. An image of Varick, Valor and some unknown woman with dark hair pops to mind.

The image I conjure is the last woman with brown hair I thought of—the woman from my graduation. The reminder makes me shudder. I can’t believe Stealth will get his way and my dream will happen tomorrow.

If only that woman knew. She could run and solve everything. She has no idea of the danger coming.

Danger.

My body freezes as I try to force a ragged breath. I chew on my lip and flinch as Varick approaches me.

"What just happened?" he asks, eyebrows drawn together.

But I ignore his question.

"Is it just your mom who's in danger? Is there someone else too?" My question is directed at Valor as the whole room watches, confused.

"Why do you ask?" Varick tries to gain my attention but my eyes don't leave Valor's.

"It's also our little brother," Valor answers. "Our mom and little brother."

Chapter Twenty-Five

"You have a little brother? How did we not know?" Jaylee asks, though I hardly hear her.

"Half-brother. He doesn't live with us," Varick answers, but his eyes are on me as I spiral silently.

"Half-brother, but the better half, so worth claiming in conversations like these," Valor says with what sounds like forced humor.

"No, no, no, no…" My voice doesn't sound like my own but the answer is coming from me. "No, can't be…" I jerk my head back and forth, refusing to acknowledge the facts in front of me. I can't. I won't.

Someone's shaking me. It's Cynthia. Her face is close to mine but I hadn't noticed.

A hand grasps my shoulder and in the same moment, a wave of calm washes through my body, but it isn't enough.

"Stop!" I yell at Varick, flinching away from his touch. I don't want to confront this reality. I don't want to explain what I know.

"Mercer," Varick takes a step to follow me but I continue to back up.

"I can't do it." I start to sob as I speak, falling to my knees and covering my face with my hands. "I can't do it. I can't do any of it."

I had finally started to accept that a terrible part of me would allow my dream to come true. I would let that woman die to save

Brey. I would choose Brey over those strangers. Brey is family.

But they aren't strangers. I can't make the same decision if they aren't strangers, can I?

"Let me do this," Varick says as he puts his hand on my shoulder again. I feel the calmness rush through me as I take shaky breaths between my sobs.

It feels like both an eternity and no time at all when I finally feel like I can speak clearly. I know I can't run from this problem, but I still don't want to admit it to the people in front of me. Will they be my friends once they know?

"The dream of my graduation… there's more." I look into Varick's eyes and nowhere else, knowing I need him to keep me calm. "JC killed the woman. He told me I had to kill the boy. A young boy, maybe four or five. JC insinuated that Stealth would kill Brey if I didn't. I woke up before I saw what happened." My voice breaks at the end and I hope they don't read between the lines.

"You can't let them die, Mercer," Valor whispers close to me. I appreciate how he doesn't say that I can't kill them, which is what would happen.

"Brey," is all I answer. It's a choked response and fills the entire room with anguish.

Varick's throat bobs up and down, one hand still on my shoulder.

"Here's what we do…" Varick says with more determination. "Don't let them die. You'll be brought back here. We'll get Breyson out before you're back. He'll be safe. Then we either make them listen or we fight."

A small gasp escapes from Lottie in the corner, but I don't look away from Varick's eyes.

"Does anybody have any better ideas?" There's no sarcasm

in Varick's voice. In fact, he's almost begging for there to be another answer. This solution has too many chances for failure.

But nobody speaks up. This is our only option.

After we leave the Pitch, Valor continues to watch his mother and brother, who I learn is named Valiant. I almost wish I didn't have a name for the boy who I saw sobbing for his mother. It makes him more real.

Dinner is somber and none of us speak much.

"You're probably going to leave early," Varick says to me before we say goodnight. From my dream, I'd say he's right. "I might not see you before you go. We'll get Breyson out, don't worry about him. Try to get to the Pitch when you get back. Make any excuse to get there."

I can already feel my anxiety demanding attention. I'll be lucky to even survive the ride back if JC suspects I ruined his third graduation.

"Stealth won't let anyone hurt you," Varick continues, answering my thoughts. "You're too valuable to him. But Mercer, no matter what, please get them out. Keep them safe."

I give him a nod, understanding what my agreement means. If he doesn't get to Brey in time, this promise has consequences.

My hands tremble as I open the door to the dormitory. I play the dream over and over in my head, wondering how I'm going to keep it from happening.

Sleep never finds me, although I shouldn't be surprised. Trinka hasn't been back to her bed since the incident with Brey, and I can hear tossing and turning from Jaylee and Lottie's beds, though we don't dare say anything in case the ginger twins are awake and listening.

I spend my time trying to project to their mother. I saw that bedroom and I should be able to reach her. If I can warn her early,

I can save us from the heartache of tomorrow, but it doesn't work. I must need to have physically been in the space to project there. Or perhaps my emotions are too strong and I'm not able to ground myself enough to transport there.

It must be the early hours of the morning, too early to consider it acceptable to be awake, when a guard opens our door. I'm grateful that it's a woman, but it still feels like a violation to have her in the room we sleep in.

She requests I follow her, and it's unsurprising when she leads me to an elevator. It's the weekend, and the Eye is completely empty given the hour of the morning. Nobody sees her taking me and nobody knows what's happening. But it doesn't matter. I know where we're going. I've seen it.

We stop at a floor I've not been to, but it looks like most of the rest of the Domain.

"About time," a rough voice pulls my attention. Standing just to the side of one of the doors, a woman, not much older or taller than I am, stands back and watches the guard and me. "We're going to get you outfitted for the mission. Sweatshirt off." She has a scar that runs the length of her hairline, and hair that's so short it's gelled into a mohawk.

I strip out of the gray hoodie that I've been wearing to ward off the chill that always surrounds me in this place. My arms in the short-sleeved t-shirt are cold; I rub them with my hands for friction while she watches me with calculating eyes.

She doesn't introduce herself but grabs a vest and thick black belt from a rack. Her hands work swiftly as she walks over. Draping the belt over her own shoulder, she places the black vest over my head and my knees buckle under the unexpected weight. She doesn't react to my struggle, but places the belt around my waist. My stomach quivers and I try to swallow the feeling down.

"Your gun." She motions to the weapon that's holstered on the belt. I can feel my eyes widen at the trust Stealth has in me. He must really think my love for Brey is strong if he thinks I won't consider turning this gun on the people in front of me. "You'll need to come here first thing when you get back so we can check the weapon in." Her voice is crisp. This close, I can see strands of dark green in her jet-black hair.

"All right," I agree, wondering if that will actually happen. Will Nick demand I be locked up immediately upon return? I might just go straight to the prison floor. Hopefully not. I need to get to the Pitch somehow.

She finishes dressing me in tactical gear and the guard standing by the door turns on her heel as I'm dismissed.

I follow the guard down the hall, and we ride the elevator together in silence. The equipment is weighing me down, making each step heavy and difficult, which seems to emphasize what I'm walking to, the path that I'm about to take.

We ride all the way to the top floor, and I wonder if we're going to stop at Stealth's office before leaving. Instead, she goes to a door that's on the other end of the hall, one that has a pad of numbers to the side. I've walked past this door a few times, but I've never thought anything of it. She stands in front of me, blocking my view and forcing the stench of cigarette smoke to overwhelm my senses while I hear the subtle beeps indicating buttons being pressed. The door clicks open to reveal a second elevator that's hidden from anyone walking the hall.

Varick said the exit was up. I've been trying to get out for months with no luck. Now that I'm finally going to leave the Domain, the victory feels empty, hollow.

The elevator only has two buttons: the floor with Stealth's office and the exit.

My stomach drops during the short ride. The guard says nothing and I can't help but wonder how many times they do this. How often do they bring teenagers to murder innocent people in the world?

When the door opens, it takes my mind several seconds to catch up to what I'm seeing. We're in a garage that's big enough to be a hangar, surrounded by black vehicles of every kind: cars, trucks, 18-wheelers and even an airplane and helicopter. The vans and cars aren't like the ones that would patrol the B Region. Those had the Eramica symbol of an eye on the glass, clearly delineating their purpose and authority. As terrifying as those were, this seems even worse. The windows are so dark that I can't see inside a single one. Instead of demanding authority, these vehicles are like ghosts, ready to come and go without taking responsibility for the damage they leave behind.

Noises come from the far side of the space, echoing off the metal walls. The guard escorts me as we weave between a boat and a helicopter, all the way to the black van from my dream.

My heart fights against my instincts as I walk through the hangar. I want to run away from this place, get out and never look back. But I can't. Because Breyson is underneath us and his life depends on whether I can buy enough time to allow Varick to get him out.

We approach the van and Nick jumps down at the sight of me.

"Great. Let's go," he says. Another guard is sitting in the driver's seat and JC is already in the back.

I only hesitate for a moment before climbing in with them. The woman guard next to me says something to Nick but I don't listen to the details. Everything about this feels wrong.

We weren't told how far the drive would be, but based on

where Varick knows his mother resides and where they believe the Domain is, we're guessing it's only two hours.

I lean back and close my eyes, knowing it could be dangerous around Nick and JC to have my eyes closed, but also realizing that if they wanted to do something to me, keeping my eyes open wouldn't be enough to help. And I'm not sure I can keep up a calm façade for two hours, so it's best to limit how much I have to try.

Listening closely, I have to keep myself from reacting as Nick brags about the various missions he's been on. He must have been with the Domain for years based on his experiences. When it becomes too much to hear, I turn my mind instead to what's about to happen.

The sun is still down when the van pulls over and stops. The light in the back turns on and Nick stands. The van is littered with information about this woman and her house, but we haven't looked at it. Based on how JC navigated the house in my dream, I have to believe that he's reviewed everything. They probably don't trust me enough to look at it ahead of time.

"Congratulations on your graduation," Nick says to us, particularly focusing on JC. "After your success, you'll have independence and freedom. The Domain thanks you for your service."

Here goes nothing. I stand up from the bench in the van and when JC stands, I have to regain my balance since he shifted the vehicle so much.

Nick opens the side door and I hop out with JC close behind me. The air is freezing, but the crisp feeling against my face is just fueling my adrenaline.

JC walks with sure steps, lending to my theory that they prepped him while leaving me in the dark.

"No funny business, Lewis," JC says with a harsh bite.

"You know what they say, third time's the charm." I can't help but mock him, knowing he'll fail once more. At least, hopefully he will. "Kidding," I add when he turns to me with a look of murder in his eyes.

He'll find the truth out soon anyway.

Chapter Twenty-Six

As our feet crunch on the frost-bitten grass, JC approaches the door without an ounce of hesitation. His beefy hand wraps around the silver handle and he turns it. I can hear the small noises of the lock breaking from the inside before he pushes the door open, a detail I missed in my dream.

We step over the threshold and I wonder if he can hear how fast my breaths are. My hands shake as I hold my gun out in front of me, just like Nick taught us in Agility Skills.

Exactly as I remember, JC points to himself and the room on the left, then to me and the hallway. I nod and watch him disappear. I'm supposed to check the hall for any doors, then meet JC in the kitchen. From there, I know we'll go up the stairs together and start on the right, clearing the spaces one by one.

But I'm already running out of time if I want to change the outcome of my dream. This might be the only chance I'll have to get ahead of JC. So, as soon as his massive body is out of sight, I run like hell up the stairs.

I know exactly where I'm going, so I don't waste any time with the other doors. I try to listen for JC downstairs but I can't hear anything over the pounding of my heart and my frantic breathing.

The bedroom is dark, but I know where everything is from my last dream. I lock the door behind me, though it won't do any good to keep JC out.

"Hey," I whisper as loudly as I dare. Her body shifts but it takes her far too long to wake up. "Hey," I say again, "I need you to move."

This time she snaps awake, her body jolting upright.

"My name is Mercer, and I was sent by Stealth to kill you. Varick knows I'm here and he asked me to keep you safe. You need to leave. The person I'm with is too strong for me to stop. He's going to kill you if you don't get out." My voice is hysterical by the end of my confession.

She looks to the mound next to her, which is now stirring, then back to me.

"I hate to rush you, but you maybe have a minute before he's up here. You need to go right now." My words are hurried and my entire body shakes with adrenaline.

She opens her mouth to finally respond, but her words aren't to me as she leans over and whispers, "Valiant, get up now. We have to go."

The little boy with dark eyes who I've thought about for months snaps upright. He hops out of the bed quicker than I would have ever imagined possible, and I can't help but wonder if he's been through a routine like this before.

"Window," she says to him.

I start to stuff clothing into the first bag I can find. It isn't much and they'll need to go somewhere fast to get out of the freezing conditions, but at least they'll have something.

She helps Valiant through the window before climbing out herself. I rush over with the bag and throw the items into her arms.

"Where will you go?" I ask her. I can't fight the discomfort that's starting to build inside me. What if they just get caught outside?

"Your kindness won't be forgotten," she says to me instead

of answering. Again, I consider that maybe she had a plan for this. Maybe she's escaped Stealth before in the dead of night.

She and her son move into the darkness, disappearing around a part of the house that hides the other side. I want to listen for a sign that they got down from the roof or that they started a car, but there's no time.

Just as I close the window and turn around to the door, the noise of it smashing open vibrates through me, making me jump.

My heart hammers as JC walks into the room. His face is a color red that I can see even in the dark and there's spit flying about. His eyes are wide and trying to understand what he walked into as he scans the room looking at the bed first, then the window and finally to me.

His jaw clenches as his nostrils flare and his eyes seem to widen even more. I follow his gaze to see that when I closed the window, I closed it on some of the curtain, leaving a trail to show him where they went and marking myself as an accomplice in their escape.

"JC..." I hold my arm out as I try to reason with him. "Listen, do you know who they are? That's Varick's family." I'm not sure what kind of loyalty I'm hoping JC has to Varick, but he scoffs at my comment before his feet take giant, weighted steps toward me.

Even though the last thing I want to do is willingly put myself in JC's path, I know that Varick's mom and brother need more time, so I step to my right, just in front of the window.

The small movement seems to set him off. He becomes unrecognizable as he closes the gap between us.

He doesn't hesitate as he lifts his arm and swipes at me with the back of his hand. There's not enough time for me to summon any of my abilities and the speed of his movement takes me by surprise.

My body flies through the air after he makes contact with my shoulder. I land so hard on the rocking chair in the corner that the wood splinters beneath my fall. My head starts pounding and I try to move, but the breath hasn't returned to my lungs yet. When I lift myself up, my wrist protests, making me wince in pain.

I can hear the window open, followed by a chilling draft that fills the room, but there's no noise of him climbing out of the house.

I had expected him to chase them, so it surprises me when his beefy hands wrap around both of my arms and he lifts my body, evidently giving up on pursuing our targets.

This is it. This is how I'm going to die. I start shaking as I watch him. My knees buckle when he puts my feet on the ground, but he's still holding me up, so I don't fall.

I wait for the pain, closing my eyes as a tear moves down my face, but the pain never comes. Finally, I open my eyes and look at him.

JC's lips are pressed together in a grimace and his jaw is tight. I can feel his hands flexing and releasing around my arms, like he's trying to argue with himself about whether or not he should hurt me.

After what feels like several minutes, he removes his hands entirely and spits on the floor next to me.

"You're lucky I'm not allowed to kill you," he hisses. "Let's go." He steers me out of the bedroom and back down the stairs, keeping a hand on me the entire time. I try not to cradle my wrist in front of him, but it's difficult.

The street is empty and would appear almost peaceful if I hadn't known what just happened. I have no idea where Varick's mom and brother went, but they're nowhere in sight now.

Nick doesn't seem surprised when we return to the van with JC glowering.

"She got them out," JC snaps as soon as the door shuts behind us. I open my mouth to refute the statement, but there's no point. They already know the truth.

"Too bad. Jones had potential. Maybe I'll be the one to kill him." Nick juts out his chin and knocks on the divider between us and the driver. My stomach drops. I want to cry, scream or beg him to tell Stealth to take me instead, but none of those things will work. "I'll call it in."

What if it hasn't been long enough? What if they didn't get Brey out? I start shaking with panic and I clench my fists to try to regain control, but that was the wrong thing to do. My left hand throbs from the recent injury.

I have nothing to do but think about whether or not Brey got out and whether or not we're going to be successful. My rigid posture doesn't relax during the trip back. I want to just run away from them and from all of this, but there's too much riding on my involvement. If Stealth wants to keep me alive, then my position with the others will be heard the loudest. I just need to get to the Pitch.

There's a metal divider to the front of the van, so we can't see where we are, but the terrain changes to bumpy gravel, and then to a smooth surface. We stop suddenly and the lights turn on, illuminating the space.

"Craw, go check your weapon in. Do me a favor and take hers." Nick unholsters the gun from my belt, then lifts the vest off me; the movement feels uncomfortable and like he's way too close. "Lewis, you're with me."

My steps are fatigued as we walk through the hangar. I'm

barely keeping it together and a breakdown is just around the corner.

The three of us ride the elevator from the hangar to the top floor of the Domain. I want more than anything to get out of Nick's grasp and run. I've been trying to get out of the Domain for months, and now that I'm finally free, I'm almost willingly going back. I know it's because of my friends, but for the briefest moment, I consider how freeing it would be to have no one to care for and nothing to keep me here.

JC's anger seems to permeate the air even louder in the enclosed space of the elevator with the bright lights highlighting his aggression. His eyes keep flicking to my wrist and back to my face as his sneer builds. It's relieving when he leaves us to make his way to the armory room.

Nick grabs the shoulder of my tactical shirt while we walk the hall, as if he thinks I might bolt the other direction to avoid a confrontation with Stealth. Nick's fist knocking on the door is the only sound in the hall.

Every other time I've been brought here, Stealth has answered or called out for us to enter. As the seconds tick by, I can see Nick shift his weight and look behind us, like the answer to Stealth's quietness will be found in the hallway somewhere.

"Sir," Nick finally calls out while knocking again. He tries the handle, but it's locked. I can see the frustration threatening to make him lose control as he looks at me and glances back at the hall again. He clearly doesn't know what to do with me if Stealth isn't in his office. Does he let me go despite my transgressions? Does he walk me around the Domain in search of Stealth?

"Come on," he says to me, evidently choosing the latter. "We'll wait in the Pitch."

The Pitch. The one place I'm supposed to get to.

He insists on keeping ahold of me the entire descent in the stairwell. I have no idea why he didn't opt for the elevator, but instead we walk at an awkward angle while he pushes me slightly in front of him. My breaths are fast and I fight against his hold until we finally reach the bottom. The door is heavy and I struggle to open it with my good hand.

As soon as we walk into the Pitch, Nick's steps falter. He tightens his hold on my shirt and moves me directly in front of him so he's shielded.

All the talking stops immediately.

"What's going on?" He demands of the room. There are dozens of people here, with a clear separation of sides. The people closest to Nick and me are a handful of guards who seem to hesitate about what to do next. Those on the other side of the descending stairs are my friends, some teachers, and other students who I haven't spoken to. Breyson and Varick stand in the front of that group watching us closely.

My eyes meet Brey's and despite our current situation, I can't fight the relief that allows me to breathe for the first time in hours. He's alive and he's here. He flicks his eyes to my wrist, which I realize I'm cradling in my good hand. His brow creases with concern, but he doesn't say anything.

Nick seems to also notice Breyson, because his sneer turns cold at the sight.

"The Dolion boys broke out Jones," one of the guards closest to us says in answer to Nick's question. "We followed them down here but there are so many—"

"Your job is to maintain order. So, maintain it," Nick interrupts in a growl.

"Nick, it doesn't have to be a fight." Varick steps forward from the group. "We got Brey out so you would listen to us. Just hear us out."

We all seem to hold our collective breath. This is the very moment we were planning for. Of course, in all our meetings we thought we'd be having this conversation with Stealth, but it seems like Nick is going to be the one who needs to be talked down.

Nick seems to be doing an assessment of the odds in the room. We have at least fifty, most of whom have abilities, whereas there are only a handful of guards, and even though they have guns, Nick's side will lose if this turns into a fight.

"Nick," I say while trying to turn around in his grasp so I can look at him, "we just want to talk to you. The way things have been operating here aren't humane. We need to come to some kind of agreement."

His eyes find mine and there's nothing but cold anger reflected back in them. My jaw starts to quiver as I realize what his anger is already telling me.

He turns to the female guard who had previously spoken and whispers, "Go get the others. Everyone you can find."

She scurries out the door and I can hear her feet pounding on the stairs before the door closes behind her.

"Jones," Nick calls out, "you'll need to come with me. If you want us to listen, we can start with that."

My heart sinks at the idea. Nick is going to kill Brey if he gets the chance. My stomach turns and a tremor starts to build in my hands.

Brey takes a step toward us and hope is still in the air on that side of the room, but I know better.

"He's going to kill you, Brey." I say as loudly as I can through the terror washing through me. "He said so in the van just now. Stay where you are."

There are several murmurs in response to my statement, and the longer that Nick takes to answer, the more everyone in the room is understanding just how desperately we need to stand up to the Domain.

Nick tightens his hold on my shirt in response to my outburst, but he doesn't refute it.

The place where he holds me starts to get hotter under his hand. I try to find the source of the heat and it doesn't take long.

A scream builds in the back of my throat as I realize that Nick is causing the fire. He's burning my skin through my shirt.

"Jones, here, now," Nick says again. He holds his other hand in front of him and slowly opens the palm. Sitting in his hand, as if it were there the entire time, is a small ball of fire. It crackles and the flames lick at my skin.

"Nick, let go of Mercer," Varick demands, and the way he says his name makes me realize who this is.

We were told that Eramica killed Nick Rikter, the first Unnatural ever taken; the fire starter. We were told that they killed him even though he was so young.

As if he can hear my thoughts and wants to confirm his identify, his hand burns me again.

I've never been around burning flesh, and the smell is absolutely putrid. My disgust is magnified knowing that it's my own skin, and the accompanying pain makes me open my mouth to scream out.

Before a noise can leave me, though, a sharp stab of water hits Nick in the chest, forcing him to release his hold on me and take several steps back.

Cynthia stands just feet away from us, her mouth in a twisted smile of victory as she yells, "Mercer, run!"

I don't wait for Nick to react.

I dart out of his reach as fast as I can, running around the upper edge of the Pitch to where my friends are.

Chapter Twenty-Seven

Nick moves back slowly. His fist clenches for a second time before he peels open his fingers. As each digit moves aside, the bright ball of flames becomes more noticeable. He holds the fire like it's a baseball and tosses it in place one time, catching it in his hand again.

The room seems to be holding a combined breath. Maybe everybody is wondering the same thing I am: we came here with a plan. We have to at least try to talk our way out.

Nick's upper lip rises a small amount as he sneers at me. He doesn't pay any attention to the others around us, seeming to have eyes for me alone.

I force myself to swallow, but his eyes dart to the bob of my throat and I can't help but think the movement was a mistake. My fear is so tangible, I'm sure he can sense it, feed off it. Maybe he's also thinking that all this is because of me. These events happened because of my actions, and I need to be the one to make it better.

"Nick." I swallow again and reach out a hand toward him in a show of compromise.

His eyes narrow at the gesture and he scoffs.

Nick lifts the ball of flames once more, letting it soar above me.

I don't have time to panic, let alone move. My eyes are fixed on the ball of fire, which is so close that I can hear the crackling in the flames.

A force pulls on my right shoulder, yanking me to the ground. I land on my side with a sharp thud, pinning my arm beneath me, before glancing at Valor as he rises from where we landed. He doesn't meet my eyes, but his own reflect fear.

We both look back at the noise of the ball hitting just behind us, to see a circular hole being burned into one of the punching bags. The smell of something burning fills my nose, and Valor's hand pats at the side of my head over and over.

My stomach drops as I realize that my hair has been singed by Nick. The smell doesn't do anything to help the nausea and anxiety rising within me.

My mind feels like it's churning slowly, trying to make sense of what's happening, but I don't have the time it's demanding. The door of the Pitch opens and a rush of guards dressed in black swarm in. They're accompanied by several students, and to my dismay, JC.

Nick's fist clenches again, opening once more to reveal another ball of fire. An evil smile spreads on his face, but before he can launch his weapon, Cynthia douses him in another rush of water.

The movement is enough to shock the rest of us from our stupor as Varick screams and runs at one of the guards who had started advancing.

"Guess we're doing this," Valor says without even glancing at me.

He heads straight for Jaylee and Lottie, who are standing too close to those on the other side.

As everyone in the room starts to realize what's happening, several of the guards take out their guns. They don't seem sure of themselves as they point the weapons at those standing with us.

"No," I whisper to myself. This is exactly what I didn't want to happen. My stomach tightens and there's a burning sensation in my throat, but it only lasts for a second before I close the distance between some guards and myself.

In no time at all, it seems that everyone understands what's in front of us. There is no stopping it anymore. The only way to get my friends out safely is to win. The only way to end Stealth's reign of terror is to fight.

As I approach the edge of the Pitch, I find the man who drove the van to the house standing over a boy with curly, black hair. The boy is on his hands and knees, clearly already injured and desperately trying to crawl away from the guard. The guard simply takes a step to follow him, a sneer on his face.

I don't know the boy, but he's here because my friends convinced him that we could stand up to Stealth. This boy didn't sign up for the fight we're currently in. My gut churns as I watch the guard raise a metal pole from the weight room.

"No!" I scream. I reach an arm out in their direction and while my scream got the guard's attention, the momentum of his actions couldn't be stopped, and the pole comes crashing down on the boy's body. The guard's eyes, wild with fury, look up and meet mine while the boy collapses in front of him.

I don't think. I don't consider what I'm doing, I just run. Not away from the guard, but right at him. I don't know this boy, but I know he didn't deserve what just happened to him.

I let Varick's trainings manifest on autopilot. My steps aren't calculated like I know Varick would like, but the rage coursing through me won't allow for that type of precision. I launch myself at the guard without any forethought.

He's ready for me but doesn't use the pole to knock me down.

Instead, he grabs my arm and throws me to the ground. He

clearly isn't as strong as JC, but he's still strong enough.

The movement knocks the air from my lungs and makes my already injured wrist throb painfully, but I don't wait for a full breath before getting up. The guard faces me, eyes intent while I circle him. He seems to have forgotten about the weapon in his hand, but as he holds it, the bulkiness leaves part of his torso and neck exposed.

I shift one direction, then attack in another, landing my balled-up fist directly to the side of his neck. His eyes roll back for a moment as he falls to his knees, the metal pole leaving his grasp on his way down and rolling away from us with a clang.

When he's on the floor, I aim a few well-deserved kicks at his head. Varick told me it's considered poor fighting etiquette to continue beating someone once they're down, but that boy is still not moving just a few feet from us, fueling my actions.

I want to check if the boy is alive, but complete and utter chaos surrounds us, making it impossible for me to give him my attention. There's not much I can do for him either way.

It's impossible to know which side is winning. Bodies are scattered all around us, some guards, and some friends. My throat closes to think about those on our side who won't ever wake up.

Nearby, Valor grunts as two guards try to fight him at the same time. It's clear they're using more care than they had with the other students. My eyes narrow at the scene as I try to decipher what's happening. It isn't until one of the guards approaches Valor from behind, wrapping him in a tight grip, that I begin to understand. They're trying to move him, not hurt him.

The other guard reaches Valor's front and grabs his feet. Valor makes an effort to kick himself out of the hold, but the guards are too strong and unmoving.

They begin to walk to the door, carrying Valor with force,

despite Valor's attempt to wriggle out of the situation by contorting his entire body. I can see his panic from here.

"Varick!" Valor screams in the most blood curdling cry as he scans the room with fear. My eyes also dart around the space, trying to find his brother.

Varick hears Valor's scream, but he's stuck between five guards, all of them circling him in the same way they did with Valor. No doubt to bring him to the same place Valor is being taken. Varick tries to get past the circle, fighting three at once to make a hole, but they just push him back into their ranks and force him to stay. His eyes shift to his brother with anxious fear, so tangible that I feel I could reach out and touch it.

Valor's captors have nearly reached the door as I jump over the body of a small girl and dodge a guard fighting Mr. Regis. It takes all my self-control not to stop for either of them.

I use both arms to help propel me faster as I sprint to close the distance. The air is thick with smoke and blood. I swallow to keep from getting sick, even though the smell is trying to suffocate me while my lungs scream from how hard I'm pushing myself.

The guard carrying Valor's feet has already made it through the Pitch door despite Valor's flailing attempts to free himself. The other guard, the one holding his head, is struggling to get Valor's arms through the door, but he's close to succeeding. I don't have time to come up with a proper solution, and this might hurt Valor, but at least he'll be alive and here.

I launch myself at the guard still in the Pitch, clinging to his back and grabbing his face. My fingers claw at any skin I can find, stabbing his eye, scratching his cheeks, and jabbing inside his mouth. It feels like a part of me is being released as I release a scream.

And it works.

He howls with rage, dropping Valor's head and torso to get me to stop. I raise a fist and punch the side of his head, hoping the force is enough to cause damage. The guard's hands reach around the back of my head, and he begins pulling my hair and the top of my shirt.

Despite Valor's initial grunt of pain, he seems to be kicking the guard in the stairwell while clawing his way back into the Pitch. A smile of victory breaks across my face just as the man fighting me curses loudly.

He must have realized he won't get me off with his hands alone, because he turns and quickly runs backward to the wall, slamming my body in the process. A burst of pain shoots through me. The wind leaves my lungs, and I cough to try to recover. The movement is forced, like my body doesn't want me to get air right now.

He takes my momentary incapacitation as a sign and his thick hands grab me to haul me over his neck and to the floor. The impact makes whatever I was feeling in my lungs burn even hotter, and I squeeze my eyes to survive the pain as it seers through me.

I don't have time to recover how I'd like, though. Fat hands grip the collar of my shirt as the guard lifts me up. I'm happy to see several angry scratches along his face, but he doesn't seem impressed with my smile. He removes a gun from his holster while holding me and doesn't hesitate as he aims it at my face, just inches away.

A loud bang sounds out in the space, too close to my ear. I wait for the pain to come, but it doesn't. I continue to stare at the guard, confused, but his face mirrors mine, until he looks down at his chest.

I track the movement as we both realize who was really shot.

His hands release me and I fall to the ground with a jolting and painful thud. He reaches up to his chest and when he pulls it away, it's coated in a bright crimson. He falls to his knees while I turn to see who my savior is.

I don't even have time to fully comprehend my shock as my lungs beg for the breath that they've been craving for the last few seconds. Instead, an emotion-filled whimper escapes me as I sob at the sight of my best friend.

Brey lowers a gun and gives me a smile that doesn't reach his eyes.

"Stay smart. Don't go for the worst of them alone." His voice trails off as something across the Pitch gets his attention.

Hands lift me from where I still sit on the floor.

"Thanks for the assist," Valor says in my ear. He looks like he's taken a few too many hits to the face, but at least he's here.

Standing makes the feeling in my lungs even worse, but this battle is nowhere near over, so it's going to have to wait.

"Mercer…" Valor's tone is distraught. I follow his gaze to see Lottie lying unconscious near Jaylee, as Jaylee tries to disarm Phillip long enough to help her sister.

On the other side of the Pitch, Varick is in obvious need of help as well.

As Brey starts to make his way to Varick, I follow Valor, dodging and weaving through the space to get to Jaylee and Lottie. My gut wrenches as we sidestep others who are clearly losing their own battles.

"Go on," I say to Valor. "I'll meet you there." He looks at me with a moment's hesitation like he wants to insist I follow. "Go! They need you!"

I can't look away from JC and Mr. Clayton. They're working

in tandem against a cluster of students who may collapse at any second. JC raises his arm and backhands a girl so hard that her body flies across the Pitch, landing with a soft thud several feet away.

I grit my teeth, rage clouding my vision. It's difficult to run, each step resulting in a shooting pain to my ribs, wrist and the spot where Nick's hand burned me, but I clench my jaw tighter and cross the space as quickly as I can.

JC has turned his rage on another student, and I can't fathom watching him fling a single other person across the space.

"JC!" I scream, getting his sole attention. I'm the one he's really mad at, the true source of his anger. It's easy for him to shift focus when his sights are on me.

Knowing I won't be able to fight him physically, I fling my body toward a gun nearby. He runs after me, grasping my foot just as my fingers wrap around the weapon. I grip tightly as he pulls my ankle toward him, using too much pressure.

A strong sense of familiarity rushes through me from the last time he dragged me across the Pitch by my ankle. But I was weak then. I didn't know how to defend myself.

I do now.

That realization comes with a strong buzzing noise that fills my ears, and the pressure of his hold immediately lightens.

"Let go of me," I grunt.

He does, his fingers releasing immediately, and I watch as worry replaces rage in his eyes.

"Don't move," I say through the buzzing in my ears, a smile crawling up my face. He reads my reaction, his own fear tangible in the air, almost like I can taste it on my tongue.

I don't wait any longer, realizing my abilities might wear off any second, and while he was only sparing my life during our graduation because of Stealth's orders, I'm sure he would no longer give me the same courtesy. I aim the gun at him, but when it clicks, nothing happens.

It's empty. I don't allow myself the time to analyze what I almost just did. No matter JC's sins, I've never taken a life before. Despite Stealth's brainwashing, I never agreed to become a killer here, not really.

Instead, I lift the butt of the weapon and strike it down hard on his head. He slumps to the floor.

It feels like we've been fighting for hours. My body is weak and begging for a break, but the noises surrounding us suggest that we're nowhere near finished. I scan once more, trying to find who needs help.

"Mercer!" someone yells. I turn to see Trinka who's only a few feet away, her wide eyes locked on something beyond me. I hadn't seen her in days and I have no idea where she's been. Maybe she escaped the prison when Brey got out. My stomach turns at the sight of her. I take a step in her direction, without having decided how I want to proceed.

But the fear in her eyes stops me and I turn to follow the direction of her gaze.

I don't know how I missed him. I thought I had taken in my surroundings, noting where each of my friends are. Brey and Varick are safe on the other side of the room. Jaylee is hovering over Lottie. Valor is holding off guards to let her work, and Cynthia is winning her own battle nearby. I had looked around, I'm sure of it, but I hadn't seen this.

Of course, now that I know where everyone else is, I also know that nobody is coming to help me. Nobody can save me.

This isn't the first time tonight that death seemed close, but it is the first time that I let myself consider what it might be like to die. It's almost a relief, but maybe that's just because of how certain it is. I'm acutely aware of where everyone I love is. I'm aware of my breaths, coming in long, drawn-out waves. And I'm aware of the fact that I don't want this to be it for me, but I would also accept and welcome the ending, because it would also mean the end to this grief and fear.

Something else gnaws at me. Something familiar, and I realize it's Varick's voice because this very line of thinking goes against one of his instructions as I start to give up. But I can't seem to help it or turn it off.

My sense of relief is stronger than my fear as I look at Mr. Clayton's smile, his finger twitching on the trigger of the gun pointed at me.

Chapter Twenty-Eight

The world fades away as Mr. Clayton's finger pulls the trigger. I watch it happen, hearing the noise, too loud for this space.

I wait for the pain. But it doesn't come. His responding smirk tells me that he hit his mark, but all I feel is a slight sting in my stomach. I look down, my hand clutching at the sensation. When I pull my palm away, it's coated in red.

But Mr. Clayton isn't satisfied. He doesn't lower the weapon, but instead his finger twitches. If I thought it would be a slow ending, I was sadly mistaken. Maybe this is a blessing. This way I'll never have to wait for the pain to greet me.

A force rams into my side, shoving me into the floor just before another shot fires off, and that movement does bring pain. My hand still clutches my stomach, while I let out a frustrated gasp.

Before I can figure out what's going on, the loud bang of his gun sounds again and again, but it's not hitting me, it's hitting Trinka, who covers me.

"No," I mutter, my hand clawing at her to move her body. There's so much blood, sticky and coating everything. "Trinka."

Her lids are closed but I keep calling her name, desperate to see the round eyes look at me, reassure me. I still don't know how I feel about this girl, but my feelings don't matter at all as I work on autopilot. Blood is pooling out of her in too many spots to stop. I put a hand to her neck, covering both the blood and the bruises, and another on her abdomen, but her leg seems to be bleeding the fastest and I don't know how to stop that, too.

"Trinka!" I yell louder. I push my hands firmly, trying to force the red back in, but it just pours out faster.

It occurs to me that I should be worried about Mr. Clayton, that I need to make sure he doesn't keep firing. But I'm in no condition to fight him, and I'm terrified to glance away from Trinka.

"Trinka, can you hear me?" I plead. I drag my body on top of hers, praying the pressure will help stop the bleeding in the spots I don't have hands for, but the movement burns my body with pain. I have no idea what blood is mine and what is hers.

The bleeding is too rapid, too much is coming out for me to stop it. I don't know why I care so much when I had just thought about killing her myself, but sheer panic grips me at the idea that she might never open her eyes again.

She saved me.

"Trinka!" I sob into her chest while her eyes remain closed. My voice sounds more like a sad acceptance than a plea for her to wake up and I hate myself for it.

I lower my ear to her nose, listening for anything, but nothing comes out, not even a shallow breath. I sag on top of her, allowing myself to let up the pressure on her wounds, as sobs start to rack through my body. Each movement brings a terrifying trigger of pain, but I don't stop as I mourn this girl who was so woven into my life here that I never fully understood her loyalty until her dying act.

When she saved me.

Dizziness ebbs at my consciousness and my tears for this girl slow. It becomes more difficult to take a breath, although I don't know if it's from the bullet hole in my stomach, the injury to my ribs, or my sheer devastation. I continue to rest my head on her bleeding body, while I greet the emptiness of unconsciousness as it comes for me. I hadn't been aware of how much energy I was using trying to wake her up.

The noises around us grow faint, not like they're gone entirely but like I'm trapped inside the Ring and they're on the other side of the plastic enclosure. I can make out specific voices if I really listen, but I don't want to listen.

The pain has gotten worse in the last few moments. It's everywhere and seems to be spreading to each part of my body.

My only hope is that Trinka didn't have to wade through this pain on her way out. I hope it was faster for her. I welcome the unconsciousness; I want the final waves to greet me and pull me under. It's so close, my fingers claw at that darkness in my mind, guiding it forward.

A pair of arms wrap around me and the warmth from the body seeps into mine, making me realize I'm shaking. I don't feel cold, but my limbs are acting as if I were caught in a winter storm.

My breaths are shallow and fast. Too fast. I try to breathe in deeply, but it doesn't come. The smell of wood and moss is faint against the blood and sweat around me, but I cling to that scent, letting it embrace and comfort me.

There's a scream in the distance and I try to open my eyes to see who it is. At the same time, the strong arms lower me to the floor and the shakiness gets worse without the warmth surrounding me.

"Merc," Brey's voice thinks to me through the haziness that isn't allowing other noises to penetrate. I open my eyes this time so that I can find my best friend. The movement is exhausting, and I can feel my eyelids begging to be shut again. Brey is nowhere nearby.

My shirt is lifted to fully expose my abdomen while blood

continues to seep out. Varick leans over me, shirtless, holding gray fabric to the bullet hole.

"How bad is it?" Brey asks, out of breath. He must have just run over here. I want to thank him for pulling me out of the darkness, but when I open my mouth, I meet his blue eyes for a second and forget what I was going to say.

Instead, guilt tears through me.

Everything that happened today is my fault. It's always been my fault. I made things worse for everyone in my life by not finding a way to beat Stealth sooner. I had the knowledge of my graduation, yet I waited until the last second to do something about it.

A sob threatens to tear out of me, only dampened by the cloudiness that swarms around my mind. I embrace the numbness, approach it in my head. It'll be a relief to be done with the decisions. Every decision I make leads to death and destruction. If I do nothing right now, it can be my last decision. After all, inaction, in and of itself, is a decision. And this choice, I gladly walk into.

"Stop," Varick's voice whispers close to my ear. The heat from his breath tickles me, but my body can't move in reaction.

"Stop what," Brey demands. His voice is also very close to my head.

"She's giving up," Varick answers, and I can hear the grim realization in his tone, but I can't bring myself to try and reassure him.

"How long ago was she shot?" a girl's voice says weakly.

"I'm not sure," Varick answers her.

My mind drifts to Trinka. I hate to think that she's alone right now. If I'm not going to wake up, I want to be next to her.

My thoughts are interrupted by a sharp burning sensation,

and I wonder if Nick is trying to make sure my last moments are filled with pain. It starts in one spot on my stomach, but then seems to spread. It moves to every nerve ending until I'm convinced that my entire body is alight in flames. Perhaps Nick came back and he's finishing the fight.

I seek the fuzziness, yearning for it to make the excruciating pain better, but it doesn't greet me back.

The pain forces my eyelids to flutter open as I gasp for air.

Jaylee is kneeling over me, but her face is pale, too pale. Beads of sweat line her forehead. She stares at my stomach, her hands held out over me. Varick's blood-soaked shirt is next to her. I want to tell her thank you, but when I open my mouth, nothing comes out.

"That's all I can do," she says. But she isn't talking to me and her lips look white. "Take her upstairs."

I can feel Brey's arms under my knees and then behind my back as he lifts me. I stare into his eyes while he walks. The cool blue is soothing, even though his eyes seem too frantic to look at me.

At some point while he climbs the stairs, my eyelids close, but not in the same way they were earlier. It's not numbness on the other side, but exhaustion through the pain. They're too heavy to lift again, so I don't.

There aren't any dreams. No visions and no awareness. Just a distinct knowledge that I have a choice. I can come back, or I can be at peace.

I'm sick of choices.

Chapter Twenty-Nine

The noises beckon me forward before anything else. Voices surround me, but they aren't directed *at* me. Some are familiar, and others I've never heard. They don't sound distressed, which somehow seems wrong to me, though I'm not sure why.

One of them laughs, a boy, and his laughter seems to spark something in my soul, although I can tell that it isn't genuine. There's an undercurrent of something wrong to it.

The entire scenario is like a riddle, begging to be solved. The beeping next to me is something I've focused on before, so I let my mind count through the pulses for several minutes.

"Next," a girl's voice says over the chatter. Nobody stops their discussions in response, but I focus on her voice. "Lift your shirt." A groan of pain comes from whoever she's talking to. "This is much deeper than I thought. I should've had you closer in line. This will hurt, here take this."

Her voice brings another specific memory, this time with more clarity. But it was Ms. Williams then.

I want to force my eyes open to take in the damage that was done, but my heart aches at what I might find.

And then the shame comes, stronger than the pain from my injuries, though I suspect that's thanks to pain medication dulling the latter. My gut and heart seem to twist uncomfortably, wrenching inside me.

"She's awake," a voice says through the rest of the conversations. It pulls the attention of most everyone in the room, and everything else seems to die down.

Varick's ability can be wildly frustrating.

"And now she's mad I ratted her out," he says, a hint of a smirk to his tone.

"Stop," I mumble.

A warm hand picks up my own, and I open my eyes to see Brey standing beside my bed.

"Hey," he thinks silently to me, a sad smile tugging at his lips.

"Hey," I croak with a hoarse voice.

Looking beyond him, students are lined up to the door. Based on the distant chatter, I'd say they're all the way down the hall. Jaylee seems to be working on the person in the front. Every bed is full, most of the occupants awake, though Mr. Regis is next to my bed, his face smoothed in sleep.

"We lined everyone up based on need. Those seriously hurt were treated by Jaylee first. Now she's getting to everyone with less threatening injuries," Brey informs me.

"Oh," is all I can manage to get out. The guilt that everyone is in here because of me is too much at this moment, and I don't miss how he fails to mention Ms. Williams.

"Remember how you saved my ass?" Valor asks from the other side of my bed. The bruises from his face have become more pronounced, though it's obvious he's cleaned the cuts. "Not to be dramatic or anything, but I think I might be in love with you now."

A huff escapes me, and the movement hurts my stomach and chest. My fingers clamp over the spot, as if to stop the pain. My hand is wrapped in a brace, forcing me to remember JC's reaction to seeing what I did during our graduation.

Jaylee finishes up with a student before approaching my bed.

I get a better look at the line of those waiting to be treated, to see some dining hall workers, a handful of teachers and several other students.

"Broken ribs, broken wrist, a third-degree burn and a bullet wound," Jaylee says with her mouth in a thin line. "I was too weak to heal you all the way at the time, so most of your injuries are still bad, but my goal was to keep you alive, and it's lucky I succeeded with the shape you were in. I can give you something to sleep a bit more. It might be good for your recovery."

"No, that's okay," I say quickly. Suddenly, my stomach feels like it's turning, and I fear I might get sick.

"All right." She gives me a sad smile.

"Lucky," I murmur in a late response to her earlier statement. Varick shoots me a look, and I realize he must be feeling my guilt, knowing how badly it's trying to consume me. I wonder if his chest is tight like mine is.

"Jaylee can heal you more thoroughly later," Brey informs me.

Jaylee walks back to the line of people. Her eyes have dark rings, and I doubt she's gotten a bit of sleep since everything happened.

"How long…" I start to ask, but I don't know how to phrase what I want to say, or how I want to classify what happened.

"You've been passed out for about twenty-four hours," Brey answers, understanding my internal dilemma. "Everything happened yesterday. It's Sunday."

"What about everyone? Stealth, JC…" My voice trails off and I hate the hitch of fear that's notable at the end.

"Everybody who was still alive and fighting for the other side are now in Stealth's containment cells, along with anybody who was previously occupying them," Varick answers with a nod at his subtle explanation about Uncle Al.

"Stealth got away," Valor continues next to me. There's more hatred seeping out of his tone than I've ever heard from him. "He has no backbone. The second things started getting heated, he ran. He didn't even try to fight."

"We'll find him," Cynthia says from a bed across from me. She gives a sad smile, but the movement only fills half her face since the other half is bandaged.

My heart sinks at that information. Stealth being out in the world means I'm not safe yet.

There's another question on the tip of my tongue, but I don't know if I'm ready to hear the answer yet, so I swallow it down. I suppose in the coming days, I'll learn the answer when I find out who didn't survive the fight. In fact, our entire group is sitting around my bed, except for Lottie. Her absence is so pronounced that I'm certain of what it means. I watch Jaylee's work, and as her hands move like those of a ghost, my suspicion grows stronger.

If Jaylee's sister died, the biggest person to blame is me.

I catch eyes with Varick. He shakes his head in a small movement that nobody else notices. I know what he's trying to say. He doesn't blame me for that.

But I do.

A few of the students in line stand a little straighter, their eyes on someone approaching. Some of them even shift out of the way. I can feel those around me tense at whoever is about to come in and I don't like it. Weren't we supposed to be rid of fear now that we'd been through all this?

I recognize the woman immediately, not just from the dream, but also from our recent interaction. She's tall with bronzed skin and brown hair, and her movements are sure and calculated. She wears leather pants and a tight shirt, a stark difference to the pajamas I last saw her in, and she's flanked by men in similar outfits.

"Mercer Lewis," the woman says in a smoky voice, "I owe you our lives. You have my gratitude." Everyone exchanges confused looks since nobody else here knows about my graduation. She doesn't force an answer from me, so I don't offer one. "I'm Vera." She extends her hand for a firm shake.

Though I don't want to, I lift my arm, pulling the IV cord with it, and fight the grimace as she grips too firmly.

"You're hurting her," Varick mutters from behind the woman. "Stop."

Vera's eyes don't shift to him. Instead, they analyze me closely before she mutters a sound of disapproval and lets go. I fight the urge to rub my hand to alleviate the sting of her grip.

I can't fight the memory of Stealth's words to me about the leadership of Unnaturals.

Surely, nothing can be worse than Stealth's cruelty, right?

"When will she be discharged?" Vera asks Jaylee, as if I'm not even here.

"She should be fine in a few hours," Jaylee replies. I can tell from the sharpness in her eyes that she doesn't approve of this woman much either. "But she needs to continue resting for several days."

"Mother," Varick approaches the woman, "she can have more than a few hours."

Vera shifts her gaze away from Varick and looks at me, calculating and analyzing.

"Right, okay. Well, when you do get discharged, please find me. We'll have a meeting to regroup," she says through tight lips, which I now notice are painted in sharp red, though I don't understand how someone could worry about makeup with so many injured and dead around us.

Without another word, her group leaves. In their wake, the sense of tension seems to fall away.

"What—" I start to ask but then change my question. "When?"

"They showed up sometime after you were unconscious, though a few of them slipped in earlier. They came here soon after you got her out of the house," Varick supplies. His voice is nothing short of grateful and it bothers me for some reason. "We wouldn't have won without them. The numbers weren't in our favor."

I suppose I should feel something about that, something like awe or gratitude, but I can't fight the suspicion rising inside me.

The rest of our group decides they can go eat breakfast now that I've woken up. They tell me that with many of the workers injured or dead, whoever is healthy enough to find food and prepare it is being asked to lend a hand.

Cynthia and I get discharged together a few hours later. Her bandages are removed, and the scarring along the top of her head looks weeks old.

"Perks of being best friends with the healer of the Domain," she says grimly, and I can tell she doesn't actually view it as a perk. Her own guilt is clear in her eyes. "Although you couldn't pay me to trade places with her."

"She must be exhausted," I concede as we ride down the elevator.

"More than that," Cynthia muses. She's always been honest with me, even when I don't want to hear it. That is, except for when she was ordered to kill me. "In those first few hours she had to prioritize who she could work on. Her choices resulted in a lot of deaths. I can't imagine how she could justify who to save, who to prioritize. That's not going to be something she gets over quickly. Although I guess you could say it also resulted in a lot of life, but we tend to focus on the negative."

"Oh," I mutter, my heart wrenching, like it's wringing itself out.

Silence hangs between us, not uncomfortable, but sad, as I consider all the things I want to ask but don't want to hear the answer to.

I finally settle on the most important one.

"Lottie?" My voice is unsure but I need this answer.

Cynthia meets my questioning look; she bites her lip to keep it from quivering.

"It happened fast," she says through her own choked emotions. "She was dead before Jaylee even got to her. There was nothing that could be done."

I picture Lottie's body on the floor of the Pitch and the fervor Valor and I used to get to her.

Tears start to prickle in my eyes, but I swallow to force them back.

"Aren't you supposed to go see the new boss?" Cynthia asks as the elevator stops at the cafeteria while I press the button to the Eye. Stealth's warning rings in my ears at her classification of Vera.

"I'm too tired. I'm going to rest for a bit, then I will." She gives me a look, one that tells me she knows exactly what I'm doing. This is more than exhaustion. This is a power play, and one that I need to do to show Vera that she's not in charge of me the same way Stealth was.

"Right," she says. "If anybody asks, I'll tell them exactly where you are." A smile spreads on her lips and she waves goodbye before exiting to the dining hall.

The Eye isn't busy. I would imagine that most everyone is either helping in the dining hall or getting treated in the hospital.

Our dorm is empty, but something eerie hangs in the air. I don't know if the ginger twins survived, but I do know that at least two of the occupants of this room will never walk through that door again.

Lottie's bed is made up, nice and neat like it was every day.

Trinka's, however, looks like she might be under the mound of blankets. Her bed was her haven. It's where she went to escape the world here. Somehow, it feels almost disrespectful to leave it like this.

My body floats over to her bed, not realizing exactly what I'm doing.

I strip the blankets and start with the sheets, making sure the soft fabric is smoothed against my fingers until it lies flat without a single wrinkle.

Then I place her comforter with the same attention. The entire time I let the memory of her final moments soak back—the bullets, the amount of blood.

Did she die immediately, too?

Did she feel any of the pain?

My tears cascade and I let them come freely.

As I adjust her pillows, my fingers graze against something underneath.

Part of my heart skips as I realize that this must be something Trinka hid, a secret piece of her that she's going to let me see. The magnitude of my sorrow over her death feels like it's being spoken to in this moment.

I pull out a pen and folded piece of paper, only hesitating for a moment before opening it to find a partially written letter… to me. Panic chokes the back of my throat while I start to read. Perhaps I should respect her space and throw this note away, but I can't. I would do anything to hear from her again.

Dear Mercer,

If you're reading this, then I found a way out of this hell hole. And I can only hope that after you understand, maybe our paths will cross in the future and it won't be with anger, but with recognition and love. I haven't been able to find the right words to tell you how sorry I am, but after what I did to Brey and to your aunt, I know I have to try. This was never about my feelings for him or our failed relationship. In all my life, I never found love and acceptance in friends. I was either surrounded by people who feared me, or I was so afraid of being around people that the opportunity for love in relationships never presented itself.

You changed that. I don't think you will ever understand what your friendship meant to me. I'm sorry that the relationship with Brey clouded my vision when it came to you. I've never had a boyfriend, and that became a priority, when it was far less important than what I had in both of you.

I hope that you can understand that I just can't

The note just ends there, like she couldn't figure out the words to what she wanted me to understand, or like someone walked in and she stuffed it away in a hurry with plans to resume later. I wish she could have finished it. I want to know; I want to understand.

My tears come faster as I reread her first line. She had been planning on getting out, and now she's gone in a way that she never expected. She deserved better than this. And I should have given her the chance to voice that in person.

I'm not able to sleep, at least not peacefully. Stealth's voice keeps permeating my mind.

I can only pray that he's wrong.

Chapter Thirty

I can't hide in my dorm forever and my stomach turns with hunger, so I get up to grab lunch. During my walk to the cafeteria, I try to tie my hair back, only to be reminded that it isn't all there, at least not at the length I remember. Thanks to Nick's fireball, it falls just below my shoulders. I drop my arms with a huff of frustration.

The smells in the cafeteria are different, not like the normal scents that usually greet me.

"Everyone is doing their best, but you can tell they aren't professional cooks," Valor explains when he sees me. Sure enough, there aren't any labels describing what we're looking at, just a hodgepodge of offerings, some of them hardly looking edible.

Valor takes something and agrees to meet us at a table, while Varick follows me around the other warmers. He hasn't left my side since I emerged from the dorm.

"Are you going to tell me why you're feeling what you're feeling?" Varick voice is soft and concerned.

"What are you talking about?" I try not to sigh with my annoyance.

"This isn't your fault," he says to me in a low voice. I don't answer him.

Lottie is dead. Trinka is dead. Who knows where Stealth is? Everything has changed and I'm the reason.

"You okay?" Breyson leans down and whispers in my ear. I

hadn't noticed him in the cafeteria, but he must have seen us because he pulls out a chair across from Valor.

"Fine," I snap. They both do me the courtesy of avoiding my gaze and not pushing the issue.

Moments like these, I would have tried to find Lottie for company. She had a calmness about her without forcing conversation or dissection. Her absence makes the hole in my chest feel like it sucks the air from me when I breathe.

"Anybody know what's going to happen now?" Cynthia asks while pulling out her own chair. She looks between Varick and Valor.

"What do you mean?" I ask, not because I don't understand her question, but because I don't know how else to answer.

"Well, the new recruits come soon. Is anybody going to tell them to stay where they are?" I let the uncomfortable question hang in the air. For some reason, it seems like that type of decision is on me, or at least it's on me to disagree with how Vera proceeds.

"No idea," I finally say. Varick's attention shines on me like a beacon, but I ignore it.

I also tune out the rest of their conversations, eager to go find Jaylee and get whatever medication will allow me to sleep once my stomach is full. I don't want to be around people anymore.

"I'm here if you need to talk," Breyson thinks silently to me as I start to stand. I give him a sad smile.

"I'll see you all later." Everyone bids me farewell, Varick still giving me the too-knowing look.

Turns out, the medication Jaylee had in mind was exactly what I needed. It helps the physical pain in, but also the ache in my heart. I fall asleep clutching Trinka's half-written note in my hand.

By the time I wake, Cynthia is in Lottie's bed nearby while Jaylee snores lightly next to her. Cynthia's eyes light up at the sight of me but she puts a finger to her mouth and points at Jaylee's resting form.

"She was afraid to sleep by Lottie's bed alone," Cynthia whispers. I nod and leave the room as quietly as possible. For the hundredth time since waking up, the guilt over what happened to Lottie threatens to consume me. I wouldn't fault Jaylee for blaming me one bit.

I have no idea how long I slept, but I do know I'm still not ready to be around other people. The Eye is busier than it has been, buzzing with students who are trying to return to normalcy, though I have no idea how anything could ever feel normal again.

I want to be alone. Truly alone.

The only place I can imagine nobody will bother me is also the one place I'm not sure I want to revisit. But maybe that's why I should. Maybe I deserve to feel the pain that was inflicted there as part of my punishment for causing it.

My feet descend the stairwell, but it feels different than it has in the last months. It's as if the ghosts of those who died here are now haunting these walls, trying to tell their unfinished stories.

It's clear that nobody has bothered to fix this part of the Domain. The bodies have all been removed, but smears of blood and gore cover the surfaces. The smell is suffocating, but something about this room begs for the smell of blood, so it's not completely out of the ordinary.

There are burn marks on the walls of the Pitch, a clear path of Nick's vengeance. The other damage doesn't tell such specific stories, but it is obvious that the theme is destruction. My heart sinks at the constant reminders. The noise of the guard hitting that boy sounds in the back of my mind. I haven't seen the boy, but I also haven't asked if he's gone.

I don't know where Nick is. I don't know if he survived and is upstairs, or if his body was moved with the rest of the dead. I'm not sure which outcome I prefer.

It feels like my memories of what happened in here are blurred through the lens of adrenaline, but I find myself kneeling in front of the spot where Trinka took her last breaths. I sit on the floor, my fingers tracing the outline of where her body fell. The floor is coated with a mixture of blood from both of us. I pull out the note from my pocket, reading it once more.

The door opens and I expect to see Varick or Brey, though I have no idea how they would even know I'm awake. I turn to look at my company, and my heart skips a beat as Mr. Regis walks in. He's noticeably limping.

I run over, embracing him furiously and breathing in the smell of cloves, though tainted with the smell of something medical, to remind myself he's really here.

"I'm so sorry," I start, but the sobs make it impossible for me to continue.

"Shh, child, I'm okay," he says. His hand rubs the back of my head.

Finally ending our hug, I take a step back.

"What are you doing here?" The last I had seen, he was still passed out on a hospital bed.

"Looking for you," he responds simply. "Let's sit."

I follow him to the stairs and watch as he lowers himself, wincing on the way down.

"Are you okay?" Fear for his safety makes my voice sound more worried than I had intended.

"Fine," he says. "Better than fine, I'm alive." He smiles at me, a twinkle in the movement despite everything that's happened. "Mercer, I am so proud of you."

I try to think of a response, but I don't have anything to say. He's only proud because he doesn't know the entire story. He doesn't know that I should have said something months ago. Or that there was an alternative to this scenario where more people would survive. His faith in me is flawed.

"I can understand why you are feeling guilty for your fallen peers, but you owe them more than that," he says while fresh tears fill my eyes.

I know they deserved more. That's the entire problem, isn't it?

"You should remember them for what they did." He sounds so sure.

"But I could have stopped it," I say through a choked voice. The tears that have been threatening to spill from me are at the edge. Everything inside me is begging to be released.

"No," he says simply. "You could not have." I take a few shaky breaths. "The most honorable thing one can ever do is fight for what they believe in. All those people, they fought for what they believed in; they fought for you. They have lived the most honorable of lives."

I want his words to help me, but they don't. I didn't deserve that kind of devotion from them.

"Stealth was never a good leader of this place," Mr. Regis continues. "A leader doesn't take power because of fear. A leader is appointed, followed despite the fact that sometimes they don't find themselves worthy." He looks over and winks at me. It's strange to see when his face is swollen.

I hunch my shoulders over my arms so that the sobs don't tear through me.

"I have to offer an apology." He pushes his shoulders back

and looks at the far wall of the Pitch. "I've been avoiding you. I could have told you much more, but I didn't. For your own safety. They were watching me, and it would have put a target on your back sooner."

"I always had a target on my back." I huff, still unsure what exactly he's trying to tell me.

"Well, let's say I knew they would put a target on your back much sooner, because you weren't disclosing the information they wanted," he says through a chuckle. "I hoped to avoid that. I never wanted him to find out you had multiple abilities."

My mouth opens with a pop. I want to ask a question, but words don't come out.

"You see, I was a history teacher before the Censorship. Teaching was my passion. I was at a university for twenty years in what was known as 'Michigan.'" His smile lights up his face as he remembers. "Your father was passionate about it, as well."

"You knew my dad?" I blurt. My shock mutes the sadness that had been so overwhelming just moments ago.

"You are so very like him, Mercer." His looks at me and the wrinkles around his lips come out when he smiles. "He would be so proud of you."

Tears well up in my eyes and it's difficult to swallow.

"Your father told me about your abilities. Perhaps you were too young to remember, but the dreams came while he was still alive, well after your compulsion manifested. He wasn't sure if it was a dream ability or just a general psychic ability. But he definitely knew what your compulsion was." Mr. Regis laughs heartily, a sound that reaches deep inside his belly and forces a smile out of me in response. "Oh, he hated your compulsion. You would demand something, and he'd be forced to give it to you."

His laughter dies down and I feel like this information is

forming a balloon in my chest, waiting to be popped.

"He was worried about what would happen if anyone found out. We saw what the government was doing with these pods." He gestures to the space around us.

"You knew about this before it started?" I can't hide my stunned reaction.

"We did," he says with a frown. "We formed a group to fight back, the group Vera now leads. We called ourselves the 'Unblind.'" He laughs again but this time it doesn't contain humor or reach his wrinkles. "We thought we were the only ones who saw through their tricks."

"Oh," I mumble, and my voice breaks while I speak. I bite my cheek to control my emotions, but he sees through the action.

"Ironic, isn't it?" He looks at me. "We called ourselves the 'Unblind,' but none of us saw what was coming. We didn't know they would take me, didn't know about the attacks disguised as graduations, didn't know about you… I guess you could say that you're the only one who's actually been unblind from the start."

I digest his words as my fingers run through my short hair. It's true. I only acted differently because of my visions. I questioned this place because I was unblind to the facts.

"Knowing the future is a burden," he says seriously. "But knowing the future can give you the opportunity to change it. Blindly following someone can lead to destruction. We owe you a debt because you embraced the fact that you were unblind. You let your sight lead us out of the hell we were in, even though it was an uphill battle the entire time."

I try to let his words bring me something good, anything, but they don't. So instead, my eyes trace the hole in the black punching bag that Varick and I used our first day training together. There are singe marks around it, begging to tell the story of how the fight started.

"How did you end up here?" I finally manage, almost desperate to change the conversation so we aren't talking about me anymore.

"Stealth was in The Unblind, as well. I believe he and Vera both wanted to do their best by their Unnatural sons, but they disagreed about the right way to do it. Anyway, that's how he recruited me." Mr. Regis looks far off into the Pitch at the memory. "Thankfully, your parents weren't heavily involved, out of fear for your safety, so Stealth never realized I knew you or your father."

"So why…" my voice trails off. I don't know how to ask what I want without being rude.

"Why did I work for him?" Mr. Regis finishes my thought.

I nod.

"Well, he forced me, but I would have likely agreed even if he hadn't because it's easier to look out for you from the inside." The smile reaches his eyes at the comment. "And I believed I was the only living person who knew about how special you were after your parents passed. I knew it was only a matter of time before Stealth found you and learned of what you could do."

We sit this way for a long time, with my heart weighing heavily in my chest.

"So, what now?" My voice holds the strain that my emotions feel.

"Well, my dear," he responds, "I believe that you hold the power in answering that question."

I raise an eyebrow at him.

"As I said," he clarifies, "leaders do not demand power. They take it because it's forced on them. How do you want to move forward?"

I look at the wall of the Pitch and the hole in the black punching bag. I don't want that responsibility. I can't be trusted with something like that.

"You are," he says after I don't respond, "the only person unblind to the issues we might face." I know he's talking about my ability, but my mind jumps instead to Stealth's warning about Vera.

The door opens and Brey walks in, allowing me the courtesy of not answering Mr. Regis. The relief is obvious in Brey's smile at the sight of us.

"Breyson Jones," Mr. Regis greets him by his full name, making me smile.

"Mr. Regis," Brey responds. "Are you doing okay?"

"Oh, I'm doing wonderfully, I'll leave you two. I've been told the kitchen could use my help with dinner. I was once rather popular because of my knack to whip up a delicious meal." He winks at me before turning slowly and limping out. The words he said seem to simmer in the air above us, settling into my heart.

Brey sits down next to me, and I know he can feel the weight of my guilt because it covers us both like a blanket.

"Trinka deserved better," I say to him. It's been heavy on my heart, and I feel I have to clear her reputation since she's not here to do it herself.

"I'll always be grateful to her for saving you in the end." There's a bitter edge to his tone. "She did deserve better."

"Is Mr. Clayton," I begin to ask, but my throat tightens and I'm not able to finish.

"He's alive," Brey answers without requiring my full question. "He's upstairs. Though he's probably beating himself up more than you ever could."

I turn to stare into his blue eyes, wondering why he might

think that.

"He was her uncle," he says in almost a whisper. "I swore I'd keep it a secret, but it doesn't matter much anymore. Her mom is a terrible person. She used Trinka's ability against her. Clayton is her mom's brother."

My heart shatters. Trinka deserved better in so many ways.

"I had no idea," I mutter, a tear coming with the realization. Her note burns in my pocket. I want to pull it out and open it again, but I fight the urge in front of Brey. For some reason, the note feels private, like it's our last conversation and I want to be selfish and keep it just for myself.

We sit for several minutes, and he doesn't make a big deal of the silent tears that keep streaming down my face.

"You know…" he finally says with something different in his tone, "the day before we were taken, I was going to tell you how I really feel about you, but you were so upset about your uncle, that I didn't. Then the next day I worked up the courage, but you never showed up."

Images come back to my mind. I knew he had been keeping something from me that day.

"Oh," I say. I can't find any emotions to adequately respond to this situation right now.

"I wish we would have had that opportunity." He sighs.

"I wish a lot of things would have happened differently," I respond, avoiding the direction of this conversation.

We continue to sit in silence holding hands. I don't know how much time passes before the door opens again and Varick walks in.

I know that I should feel worried about what emotions Varick reads in the room, but I can't seem to care about that.

"You okay?" Varick asks me.

"Is anyone?" I answer, once more fighting the urge to allow the sobs out. My stomach turns as I force the emotions down.

He studies my face and then looks to Brey.

I expect him to say something, but he doesn't. Instead, he just takes a seat on the other side of me.

"What do we do now?" Varick asks.

My mind races. Stealth, however evil, still had a point with his warnings of Vera. I feel more certain of that than I did earlier. Could we be entering another period of being trapped? Are we unable to live freely because of the fear and suppression we've always suffered?

"I want to find Lizzy." It's the only thing I'm sure of. The issues with Stealth and Vera will always be here, always sit on our horizon. I still have to meet with Vera and see what she wants. I need to help everyone move on and learn about who else died, but my statement gives me strength. The decision gives me a sense of power, and I can feel the responsibility that Mr. Regis seems to think I have. Not to mention, there's a red folder that's pulling me to Texas, and I can't help but feel the contents of it will alleviate the pressure that's been suffocating me since learning of Aunt Pam's death.

Neither of my friends answer me, but perhaps they don't have suggestions outside of that. So, I continue to consider Mr. Regis' advice while we sit in silence.

For the first time in my life, maybe I can see my own future.

USA
n can be obtained
om
23
001B/4